EQUIVOCAL
DEATH

EQUIVOCAL DEATH

A NOVEL

AMY GUTMAN

LITTLE, BROWN AND COMPANY
BOSTON NEW YORK LONDON

First Edition

Quotations from *Practical Homicide Investigation: Tactics, Procedures, and Forensic Techniques, 3d ed.*, by Vernon J. Geberth, Retired Commander, Bronx Homicide, NYPD, © 1996 by CRC Press, Inc. Reprinted by permission.

Quotation from the Buddha from *A Heart As Wide As the World: Stories on the Path of Lovingkindness* by Sharon Salzberg © 1997. Reprinted by arrangement with Shambhala Publications, Inc., Boston.

Quotations from *Sexual Harassment of Working Women* by Catharine A. MacKinnon © 1979 by Yale University. Reprinted by permission of Yale University Press.

Lines from M'naghten's Case, as reprinted at pages 968–970 in *Criminal Law and Its Processes: Cases and Materials, 5th ed.*, © 1989 by Sanford H. Kadish and Stephen J. Schulhofer. Published by Little, Brown and Company. Reprinted by arrangement with Aspen Law and Business Panel Publishers.

The characters and events in this book are fictitious. Any similarity to real persons, living or dead, is coincidental and not intended by the author.

Library of Congress Cataloging-in-Publication Data

Gutman, Amy.
Equivocal death : a novel/Amy Gutman. — 1st ed.
p. cm.
ISBN 0-316-38195-0
1. Women lawyers — Fiction.
2. Law firms — Fiction.
3. New York (N.Y.) — Fiction. I. Title

PS3557.U885 E68 2001
813'.6 — dc21

00-028241

10 9 8 7 6 5 4 3 2 1

Q-FF

Printed in the United States of America

For my family

Equivocal death investigations are those inquiries that are open to interpretation. There may be two or more meanings and the case may present as either a homicide or a suicide depending upon the circumstances. . . . The deaths may resemble homicides or suicides; accidents or naturals. They are open to interpretation pending further information of the facts, the victimology, and the circumstances of the event.

— *Practical Homicide Investigation*, 3d ed.
Vernon J. Geberth

Those who are heedless, or unmindful, are as if dead already.

— The Buddha

EQUIVOCAL
DEATH

Wednesday, December 23

ICE cold. He pressed his hand to the window and watched the frost dissolve, felt the moisture collect on his palm. He'd switched off the lights, and the interior darkness mirrored the inky void outside. Standing immobile, he could almost imagine that he was alone in the world or better yet that he did not even exist, that he was simply a part of this floating emptiness, transported by waves of black snow.

But his lungs filled with air. He felt the rhythm of his breath, stark and fatal as an accusation.

He was alive.

And there was work to be done.

Moving away from the window, he switched on a Bestlite floor lamp, acquired from a British import company during his last year of school. He liked things to be well made. He surveyed the scene before him. The space where he stood was cavernous, at least thirty feet long and twenty feet wide. Part of a former warehouse, it was isolated enough to meet his needs. His desk faced a sweep of tall windows, while his clothes — Brooks Brothers suits, several shirts, a tux — hung neatly on a portable chrome garment rack. A Bose CD player sat on an antique table.

He was pleased with the space. Everything was just as he liked it. The barren surroundings only underscored the beauty and fineness of his few selected possessions. His eyes traced the narrow confines of his life.

Then, decisively, he made his entrance.

Moving to the CD player, he pushed Play. Instantly, the room filled with the opening chords of Cherubini's *Medea*. A 1959 recording. Remarkable music. Potent. Full of a terrible rage. He glanced down at the CD cover, at the diva Maria Callas. Arched nose. Raven hair. Hands splayed like claws. What was it he saw there? A passion for vengeance — for justice — that matched his own. The promise of its fulfillment. And with this, an unflagging sense of order, of timeliness, of fate. It was this he needed above all else. For even as the time for action grew closer, his confidence had started to ebb. Why had he waited so long? The plan that had seemed so brilliant when he first conceived it could at times seem almost absurd. Again, he tried to push back these thoughts. It was dangerous to think this way.

Sitting down at his desk, he turned on his laptop computer. The screen flashed bright. From here on, it was almost too easy. The most profitable law firm in the country. Thirty-seven partners who counted themselves among the most respected lawyers in the world. Power brokers and advisers, they counseled governments, corporations, and the rare private individual with sufficient wealth to pay their fees. And yet cracking their computer safeguards had been child's play.

Strange, the unerring detection of their clients' vulnerabilities and the utter disregard of their own. Samson's computer network had just been overhauled at huge expense. The mere fact of this investment had seemed to assuage their concerns. There was something touching in this naïveté, the almost childlike belief in money. Their computer network was top of the line. Nothing more need be said.

Besides, the elder statesmen of Samson disdained technology, the proliferation of desktop computers. They yearned for the days of dictation. Of pretty secretaries, heads bowed, recording their every word. But in the end, even Samson had been forced to submit. The firm's quaint refusal to communicate by e-mail, once seen as a charming relic of its patrician past, had begun to interfere with business. And Samson was, first and foremost, a business. Bowing to the inevitable, the firm edged its way into cyberspace, a territory as alien to its rulers as the planet Mars. E-mail. The Internet. Standard issue for more than a decade in the modern business world but still suspect intruders at Samson.

And so he found himself in the happy position of breaking and entering an unlocked house. The attorneys' "secret" passwords gave the illusion of privacy but none of its substance. Remarkable, really, the faith placed by these brilliant men and women in a technology they didn't understand. *Hubris*. The fatal flaw.

He typed in her user ID, MWATERS. Then came the password prompt. He grinned as he typed in the response: PASSWORD. That was it. The same word for everyone. Something easy to remember. She could have changed the defaults, of course. It would have taken only a minute. But she hadn't taken the time. Like the others, she couldn't be bothered.

A few more clicks, and he was scrolling through a list of her files. Luckily for him, she was one of the new breed, treating her hard drive like a filing cabinet. He'd dipped into these files in the past, not out of any real interest, but for the thrill he took in the fact that he could. Confidential memos outlining trial strategies for lawsuits worth tens of millions of dollars. Clinical dissections of the odds of success. Privileged information that, if leaked, would mean the loss of fortune and career. If blackmail were the goal, he'd have had it made.

But he had other things on his mind.

Exiting WordPerfect, he clicked on the Calendar icon. In an instant, it appeared before him, everything crystal clear. The perfect map. Madeleine Waters's anticipated movements for the next twelve months. He felt an adrenaline surge, stiff heat in his shoulders and neck. The room was growing colder as the night chill deepened, but he barely noticed. He had work to do, decisions to make.

He reviewed the recent additions. December 23. With Christmas approaching, the week had been slow: the usual assortment of professional engagements, lunches, meetings, the occasional benefit or awards banquet in support of a worthy cause.

And then a single entry struck his eye.

Dinner with Chuck Thorpe. At Ormond. January 5. He knew the restaurant. Had in fact eaten there when it opened last year, unable to absent himself discreetly from the Civil Rights Forum's annual dinner. Such occasions always left him aching with hatred for the world he'd been forced to inhabit. The smug corporate sponsors. The self-satisfied attorneys who came to be feted, confident that their brief forays into pro bono work conferred a sort of secular sainthood.

But this miserable dinner had finally proved a gift in disguise. He remembered the restaurant clearly, the low lights, the widely spaced tables. Yes, it was almost ideal, better than he could have hoped. A sense of euphoria swept through him.

Then, without warning, it was gone, and he was spinning, spinning down a cold black chute.

No. Make it stop.

He pressed his teeth together, already knowing what would come. Dizzy, he grasped the table's edge. A sour sweat leaked through his pores. The smell of fear. The smell of death.

I'm moving as fast as I can.

He tried to fight back, to win a reprieve. But it was no use. He was already tumbling back. Back to where it all began.

A dark room. And everywhere the scent of fear.

She's sprawled across the floor. He looks down at her from above. It feels strange to look down. He's always looked up at her face, her beautiful, smiling face.

It's so dark. For a long time, now. Why is she lying so still?

He sleeps.

And then it's light. She's still there, sprawled and broken in ways that he can't comprehend. She's floating in a sea of red.

He wants to get up, to go to her. But he can't stand up, can't seem to move at all.

He cries out, but there's something in his mouth.

At first, he thinks she's asleep. But not really. Really, he knows that she's dead.

He's hungry. He's thirsty.

And, even then, he knows that she's dead.

She's dead, and it's all his fault.

And then it was over. Slowly, the vision faded. Still trembling, he stared at the wall. He felt weak, depleted, as if he could sleep for days. But he couldn't give in to these feelings. Not with success so close. He had to think of the plan. *He had to think of the plan.* Soon, it would all be over.

And he was finally ready to begin.

Monday, January 4

MONDAY morning. 7:05 A.M. A gray fog hung over the ice-glazed spires of Manhattan. Pulling her red cashmere cape tight against the winter air, twenty-six-year-old Kate Paine walked purposefully across Fifth Avenue. The snow-dusted sidewalks were still sparsely populated. A good two hours remained until the explosion of rush hour, with its shrieking horns and screeching tires. In the relative quiet of the morning, lulled by the city's dull roar, Kate clutched her cape close and smiled.

The holidays were behind her. She was home.

Approaching the plate-glass doors of Samson & Mills, Kate felt a swell of excitement. After more than a year at Samson, she still could hardly believe that she'd been hired as an attorney at this legendary firm. That of all the thousands of law school graduates who poured into the workforce each year, she'd been one of the chosen few. Just out of Harvard Law, and she'd already worked on cases that most lawyers only dreamed about, cases that routinely figured on the front pages of the *Wall Street Journal* and the *New York Times*. Fascinating cases of first impression that stretched the limits of the law. And even more important, she had the chance to hone her skills with the nation's most formidable attorneys.

Kate passed through the revolving doors and into an enormous lobby. Tossing off greetings to the security guards, she slipped her card key through an electronic scanner. Then she moved toward the elevator, high heels clicking on the marble floor.

Four days into the new year, the lobby was already stripped of holiday decoration. The scarlet poinsettias, with their incongruous shock of color, had been whisked away. As had the majestic Douglas fir and the electric menorah. Once again, the stately entry stood sober and unadorned. Kate relaxed into the familiar space, felt its timeless weight enfold her.

Thank God, the holidays were over.

The elevator was already waiting. Kate stepped on, and the doors slid shut. Twenty. Thirty. The floors flashed by. As she'd hoped, Kate was the first person to arrive on fifty-one. Making her way down the deeply carpeted hall, past a row of identical doors, she flipped on lights as she passed. Her own closed door was the next to last. As she rummaged in her purse for the key, she studied a small brass plate. *Katharine T. Paine*. The *T* stood for Trace, her mother's maiden name. On impulse, she ran a finger across the engraving, the metal cold to her touch. Then she turned the key and pushed open the door.

Stepping into the office, Kate inhaled its familiar smells, furniture wax mingled with Chanel No. 19, a fragrance she sometimes wore. She cast an approving eye around her ordered domain, with its panoramic views of the Hudson River and beyond. Even in the morning haze, she could make out the Statue of Liberty in the distance, a tiny, brave figure engulfed in mist. The room was just as she'd left it. Neat stacks of paper lined her desk. Cartons of documents were stacked against the wall. The preholiday cleanup. She'd try to enjoy it while it lasted.

Kate pulled off her cape and hung it in her office closet. Before closing the door, she paused to take stock in a mirror affixed to its back. She looked healthy and rested, her skin lightly browned from a week of sun. She quickly ran a comb through her dark brown hair, cut in the jaw-length bob favored by Samson's female lawyers, then straightened her horn-rimmed glasses. The glasses were a recent addition, acquired when she started work. Studying her face in the mirror, Kate decided that she liked the effect. Professional. In control. A woman to be reckoned with.

How different she looked now from two years ago, when she'd roamed the Harvard campus in ratty jeans and a backpack. Yet one thing remained the same. Her reflected image inspired the same sense of dislocation that it had since she was a child. *Who is that woman? Me but not me.* She didn't dislike what she saw. To the contrary, she knew she was pretty. Clear skin, high cheekbones, a fine straight nose. Her eyes were a deep shade of blue. "Stormy," her mother used to call them. A full-length mirror would have gone on to show the strong but delicate form: shoulders broad enough that she always cut the pads out of her suit jackets, a sweep of breast not entirely concealed by her black-and-gray Tahari suit, narrow hips tapering to long, slim legs.

So why couldn't she see this person as *herself?*

It was an old question, one that she'd long tired of considering. She shut the closet door and turned toward her desk.

I'm proud of myself, Kate thought, surveying the well-appointed office. *I did this all on my own. I could have fallen apart. But I didn't. In the end, Michael did me a favor. . . .*

But Michael belonged to the past; he had nothing to do with her new life. Pushing the memories aside, Kate sat down and turned on her computer. The screen flashed on. Responding to computer prompts, Kate quickly typed in her user ID followed by the word PASSWORD. Then it was on to e-mail. Among the usual clutter of junk e-mails — a paralegal looking for a downtown sublet, a secretary with free kittens, an associate seeking a financial planner — she culled the few messages that demanded immediate attention. From Justin Daniels, her old friend and Harvard classmate: "Welcome back! We missed you and we *know* you missed us. Let's shoot for drinks later this week. Cheers. J. D." From Andrea Lee, her friend and comrade on countless late nights: "Can't wait to catch up. Call me ASAP." There was also a plaintive note from Jonathan Kurtz, a Harvard classmate who'd occupied the office two doors down until a few months back, when he'd been shipped off to Kansas for a trial. "I fully believe that I will be here in Wichita from now until the end of time. I will never perform any task other than the preparation of cross-examination books that will never be used at trial or anywhere else. I will never see any of my friends or family again. On the upside, I will never have to pay for another meal as long as I live."

Kate laughed. Again, she felt a glow of pleasure, happy to be precisely where she was. But the sense of satisfaction was short-lived. Soon, she sat staring at an e-mail from Peyton Winslow, a senior associate at the firm. "Greetings. I hope that you enjoyed your vacation. Please prepare for a meeting this morning at 10 A.M. with Carter Mills regarding a new matter. The Complaint (which we believe will be served on January 13) and related papers are in distribution. Please review and be ready to discuss."

Kate glanced at her watch. Already after eight. Quickly, she thumbed through the mountain of mail that had piled up during her vacation. "Will someone just shoot me?" she muttered. Still, beneath the anxiety, she felt a burgeoning excitement. A *new case*. And a matter significant enough to involve the illustrious Carter Mills. To get in on a case like this at the very start — what a coup! So many of Samson's massive cases had been gathering dust for decades. There would be nothing for years and then a brief flurry of activity when the current crop of Samson underlings would try to make sense of what their predecessors had done. The work often seemed more archaeological than legal. Now she'd be in on things from the start, positioned to watch the strategies unfold.

The phone rang, but Kate let voice mail pick up as she continued to search through the mail. She finally found what she was looking for. The complaint, stamped "Draft" across every page, was captioned for the Southern District of New York, the federal trial court of Manhattan. The plaintiff's attorneys must have sent over a draft in hopes of an early settlement. It was often done, the draft complaint serving as leverage, proof of the seriousness of plaintiffs' intent and the prima facie strength of their case.

The draft complaint was twenty-three pages. Kate quickly skimmed its contents, trying to get the gist of the claims.

And then paused to let it all sink in.

This was, in no uncertain terms, a sexual harassment suit charging Chuck Thorpe and WideWorld Media with violations of both state and federal law.

Chuck Thorpe.

WideWorld Media.

Kate grappled with the implications.

WideWorld was one of Samson's largest clients, a sprawling communications behemoth with a seemingly insatiable appetite for new acquisitions. Its recent purchase of *Catch* — a "relentlessly provocative" men's magazine edited by Thorpe — had sparked a firestorm of protest among stockholders. If they had been upset before, this would send them over the edge. While the controversy might be good for circulation — further enhancing Thorpe's status as publishing's reigning enfant terrible — it would not play well with the board of directors.

A tentative knock on the door broke into her thoughts.

"Come in!"

"Hi, Kate. Welcome back!" In the doorway stood Jennifer Torricelli, her unflappable nineteen-year-old secretary. Jennifer's dark fantasia of a hairstyle gave new meaning to the phrase "big hair," but there the stereotype ended. She typed ninety words a minute, kept flawless tabs on Kate's ever-changing calendar, and managed to be nice as well. In theory, Kate was supposed to share her services with a first-year associate named Terry Creighton. But for the past six months, Creighton had been in Nebraska, where he spent his days in an unheated warehouse, poring through corporate files. Kate could barely remember what he looked like.

"You must've had a good vacation," Jennifer said. "You look great!"

Kate gave her a distracted smile. "It was fine. Relaxing. But it's good to be back."

Jennifer looked at her, incredulous. "I don't believe you guys. The hours that you put in here. And then you don't even like vacations. Boy, if I ever went to the Caribbean, I don't think I'd ever come back."

Kate glanced anxiously back at the papers on her desk. "I'll tell you about it later. Right now, I have to get ready for a ten o'clock meeting with Carter Mills."

Jennifer's eyes widened at the mention of Samson's presiding partner. "Wow. Good luck. Listen, I just wanted to say that there's a message from Tara on your voice mail."

"Thanks," Kate said. She'd been right not to pick up the phone. Tara was her best friend and college roommate. It would have been hard to cut short the conversation.

"Let me know if you need anything," Jennifer said, closing the door behind her.

Returning to the complaint, Kate glanced back at the caption to find out the plaintiff's name. Stephanie Friedman. Briefly, Kate wondered what she looked like, this woman behind the lawsuit. But her thoughts quickly moved on. Where would things go from here? Of course, everyone knew that sexual harassment cases were notoriously easy to file and hard to get rid of, making them a frequent weapon of choice for disgruntled employees. In her year of legal practice, Kate had already seen more than a few such suits filed on tenuous facts in hope of a speedy and substantial settlement, a sort of legal blackmail. Who knew what had really happened? Still, it didn't take hours of research to know that Thorpe and WideWorld had a mess on their hands. There was nothing subtle about the allegations.

Thorpe routinely referred to women as bitches, cunts, whores.

He demanded that the women who worked for him wear short skirts and tight sweaters.

He interrogated female employees about their sex lives, demanding detailed descriptions and subjecting them to elaborate dissections of his own encounters.

He'd threatened to fire several women if they refused to sleep with his music producer pal Ron Fogarty.

It went on from there.

Kate tried to remember what she knew about Thorpe. With her eighty-hour work weeks, she had scant time to keep up with current events. But it would have been impossible to miss the media frenzy that broke out several months back when *Catch* weighed in on sexual harassment. The magazine's glossy cover featured a parody of *Hustler*'s famous meat grinder shot, a woman's legs thrust high in the air as her body disappeared in the utensil's gears. But on the *Catch* cover, the head disgorged by the grinder was that of feminist icon Anita Hill. Smaller photos inside paired head shots of prominent female activists with bodies from lasciviously positioned porno pix.

By all accounts, the credit for the uproar was entirely due to Thorpe, a flamboyant entrepreneur whose editorship of *Catch* had made him a household name. A North Carolina native, Thorpe had started *Catch* straight out of college with money raised from wealthy classmates. Kate recalled him from television interviews, a compact, powerful figure who pulsed with contained energy. He seemed to take a grim delight in baiting the talking heads who grilled him. "I respect women," he said repeatedly, in an exaggerated Southern drawl. "In fact, my mother was one. My sister, too."

Intriguing legal issues, celebrity scandal — what more could a young lawyer want?

She couldn't wait to begin.

Rounding the corner outside Carter Mills's office suite, Kate slammed into the portly figure of Bill McCarty, who was charging in the opposite direction. Her notebook and pens scattered to the floor.

"Excuse me," she gasped, bouncing back from the impact.

McCarty, red-faced and breathing hard, responded with a short grunt and continued full-speed down the hall, his short arms joggling at his sides. As she gazed after the stout, balding figure, Kate rubbed her shoulder and wondered what had him so upset. While she'd never worked with McCarty, she knew him by reputation as diffident and unassuming. McCarty was a workhorse, not a show horse. Rumor had it that his election to the Samson partnership stemmed from his willingness to endure crushing workloads without complaint. Fits of temper seemed entirely out of character.

Kneeling to pick up her things, Kate heard a clipped British accent behind her.

"No need to bow before entering. They did away with that *years* ago."

Kate looked up to see Peyton Winslow. Not that she'd had any doubt who was speaking. Despite three years at Yale Law School and six at Samson & Mills, Peyton's Oxford intonations only seemed to grow stronger with each passing year. Today, he sported a large pair of red-framed glasses. The glasses were Petyon's signature; he had a wardrobe of different styles, all slightly eccentric by office standards.

"Very funny," said Kate, clambering back to standing position and smoothing her gray wool skirt. "I was just cut off at the pass by Bill McCarty, and everything went flying. He seemed furious about something. Any idea what?"

Peyton gave her a skeptical look. "Interesting," he said. "I thought he was computer-generated. It never occurred to me that emotions were part of the package."

Kate grinned. She was always surprised by Peyton's bouts of irreverence. A rangy figure in his early thirties, Peyton often seemed younger than his years, all eager legs and feet. But appearances could be misleading. Everyone knew that Peyton was a rising star. He was, in the Samson vernacular, "highly regarded." Affectations aside, he was incisive, hardworking, and an excellent manager. He'd be up for partner in two years and was widely viewed as a shoo-in.

Together, they proceeded into Carter Mills's reception area. His secretary, Clara Hurley, was immersed in dictation, her fingers flying across the computer keyboard. She jumped when Peyton tapped her on the shoulder.

"You *scared* me," she said reprovingly, pulling the Dictaphone headset off her tight gray curls.

"Sorry 'bout that," said Peyton. Clara visibly softened. Peyton had clearly gotten on her good side. Smart move, Kate thought. When you were trying to get a brief out on time, a good relationship with the person typing it was at least as important as your legal skills.

"Have a seat, and I'll see if Mr. Mills is free," she said. Clara's use of Mills's last name sounded quaint to Kate's ears. Except for the most inveterate old-timers, everyone at Samson was on a first-name basis. But of course, Clara had been with Mills for decades.

Waiting outside the closed office door, Kate felt shy and very young. She could feel her heart beating faster. From the corner of her eye, she saw that Peyton was working. His features were locked in concentration as his pen flew across some junior associate's draft. Kate envied him his seeming calm.

For what felt like the fiftieth time, Kate turned back to her notes. If even a fraction of the allegations were true, Thorpe and WideWorld had a major problem. And even if they *weren't* true, the case had all the earmarks of a public relations nightmare. The timing — right on the heels of Thorpe's splashy attack on the very laws under which he was sued — couldn't have been worse.

"Come in, come in." Carter Mills was standing in the doorway. As she jumped to her feet, Kate felt a subtle change in the atmosphere, a sort of electric charge. Up close, Mills was even more imposing than she remembered. He was tall, well over six feet, with penetrating slate-blue eyes. Despite gray streaks in his thick dark hair, he gave an impression of youthful vigor. Everything about him — his voice, his bearing, the aristocratic cut of his features — seemed to exude authority. Mills's grandfather, Silas Mills, was one of the firm's two founding partners. Yet family connections were the least of Carter Mills's credentials. He was widely regarded as one of the nation's leading trial lawyers, the subject of countless feature stories and news reports and a perennial fixture on top-ten lists. Mills was, Kate thought, a rare blend — a scholar who could still woo a jury, a $600-an-hour mega-lawyer who could roll up the sleeves of his $300 shirts and speak directly to the people.

Mills gestured them into his office. Peyton slipped into a chair. Kate sat down beside him. As Mills returned to his desk, Kate took a quick look around. Several large abstract paintings. A black leather sofa. The decor took Kate by surprise. There were, to be sure, some traditional touches. Family photographs. Harvard diplomas. An impressive grandfather clock. But it was not what she would have expected. She was intrigued by the room's appearance, intrigued and also pleased. It seemed to affirm Mills's uniqueness.

"Madeleine Waters will be joining us shortly," Mills said, after buzzing Clara for water. "If you'll excuse me for a moment." He was already back at work.

The words pulled Kate back to the present. Another intriguing surprise. Madeleine Waters, the acknowledged beauty of the Samson fold. Madeleine wasn't the first female partner at Samson & Mills — there was Karen Henderson in the tax department and Michelle Turner in trusts and estates — but she still stood in a class by herself. The first female partner in the litigation department, a club within a club at Samson, she was a role model for younger women. She seemed to embody a bright new world, a place where power and femininity could coexist.

Kate briefly wondered if Madeleine could be working on this case and then rejected the thought out of hand. Madeleine Waters working with Carter Mills? No way. While Mills had once been Madeleine's mentor, they were now said to be barely on speaking terms. Something to do with a failed love affair, if firm gossip was to be believed.

A rustle at the door. Clara Hurley appeared with a crystal water pitcher and glasses. The perfect secretary of the old school. Carefully setting down the tray, Clara poured water for Mills, her stolid features suffused with a maternal glow.

Without looking up, Mills accepted the glass.

"Clara, could you see what's keeping Madeleine. Tell her we're ready to meet." Beneath the sonorous calm of his voice, Kate sensed an edge of irritation.

"Yes, Mr. Mills."

And then Madeleine was standing in the doorway, a slim figure in a jade silk dress.

"I'm sorry I'm late," she said. Her voice, slightly breathless, was lower than Kate had expected. Madeleine sat down on the black leather couch, a little apart from the group.

Peyton jumped up and motioned toward his empty chair. "Would you —"

"No. I'm just fine here. This is perfect." Catching Carter Mills's eye, Madeleine gave him a faint smile. "*Perfect.*"

The smile seemed familiar. Then Kate realized where she'd seen it before. On a sphinx at the Metropolitan Museum. The so-called archaic smile, mysterious and ever watchful. Again, Kate studied Madeleine's face. *She really is lovely*, Kate thought. Up close, she'd expected to discern flaws, a harshness of expression or tone. What she saw instead was an utterly harmonious play of feature: a tumble of dark hair tamed by a velvet band, high cheekbones, clear skin, wide-set eyes that seemed to match the vivid green of her dress. Madeleine must be in her late thirties by now. However, hers was the sort of beauty that lasts, defiant of the passage of time.

Carter Mills drew a pair of reading glasses from the pocket of his starched white shirt. After placing the glasses on his nose, he clasped his hands on his desk. "I assume you've all read the draft complaint. Based on the facts alleged, I don't see much chance of dismissal or summary judgment, though we'll certainly want to examine those options. Assuming the complaint's actually filed on the thirteenth, when is our answer due?"

"Under Rule 12, we have twenty days," Peyton said. It was the sort of critically important yet mundane fact that associates were charged with tracking. Failure to meet a deadline could result in dismissal of a case. "So if the complaint is actually served next Wednesday, the answer would be due on February second."

"Fine," Mills said, making a notation in a leather-bound appointment book. "In the meantime, we need to get straight on the facts and law. I've scheduled a meeting on Wednesday at one with Chuck Thorpe and Jed Holden. Please plan to be there. After that we'll be in a better position to devise a game plan."

Again, Kate felt a thrill of excitement. Jed Holden. WideWorld's CEO. One of the nation's most powerful businessmen. The closest most Samson associates would ever get to someone of Holden's stature was preparing an affidavit for his signature. For an associate, and a junior associate at that, to attend a meeting with Holden present — it was almost unthinkable.

"Are there any questions?" Mills said.

"I have a question, Carter." Madeleine's low voice seemed to linger in the office air. "Would you agree that we can't represent both WideWorld and Thorpe without a conflicts waiver from WideWorld's board?"

Mills looked at her, his face impassive. "No," he said. "I would not."

The two partners locked eyes. Sensing the tension, Kate found herself staring at her lap. There was something unsettling about the scene. She was curious, of course — who wouldn't be — but also strangely disturbed. It was almost like she was very young again, listening to her parents argue.

Seemingly oblivious to the younger lawyers, Madeleine pressed ahead, her tone deceptively light. "You can't ignore the fact that WideWorld has potential claims against Thorpe. When WideWorld agreed to buy Catch, Chuck Thorpe was fully aware of Ms. Friedman's sexual harassment claims. He'd already been informed that the EEOC would investigate. Yet he failed to disclose the potential liability — something the stock purchase agreement clearly obligated him to do. If there's an adverse judgment in this case, WideWorld may have to consider asserting claims against Thorpe. WideWorld's stockholders can't be expected to foot the bill for Thorpe's —"

"We'll talk about this later, Madeleine." There was a warning note to Mills's voice.

Madeleine shrugged, and settled back in her seat. The same faint smile Kate had noticed earlier again played on her lips.

Kate tried to make sense of the exchange. What Madeleine had said seemed logical, obvious even. Samson's duty was to its client, WideWorld. You didn't need to be a specialist in legal ethics to know the dangers of dual representation in a situation like this. But simply thinking this through felt somehow disloyal. After all, Kate chided herself, without actually *reading* the purchase agreement, it was impossible to know anything for sure. And even if Madeleine *did* have a point, why raise the issue like this — why pick a fight with Mills in front of two associates? Only one thing seemed clear: if Carter and Madeleine had ever been lovers, the affair had not ended well.

For a time, Mills seemed lost in thought. Then, he suddenly resumed command, as if the previous exchange simply hadn't occurred. "That's about it for today." He was speaking directly to the junior lawyers, as if Madeleine wasn't there. "Madeleine will be overseeing your work on this case. Of course, you're free to come to me with any questions."

Surprised, Kate glanced across the room. Her eyes met Madeleine's. There was an appraising glint in the other woman's eyes. For a confused moment, Kate wondered if Madeleine had been watching her. But before she could be sure, it was over. Madeleine was studying her folded hands, and Carter Mills was winding up the meeting. "I want a legal memo by the end of next week. I'd like Kate to start in on that. If there aren't any other questions, I'll see you all Wednesday afternoon."

⚜

AFTER the two associates left the room, Madeleine Waters remained seated on the leather couch. Still smiling, she studied Mills. But when she spoke her voice was cold.

"I can see that the magic hasn't faded."

He returned the gaze but said nothing.

"In any case, that was quite a demonstration. Make them feel like they're part of your world. The quickest path to loyalty and devotion. Not to mention endless billable hours. That's what you taught me, isn't it? Well, congratulate yourself. It worked like a charm. You could see it in their faces."

Mills had assumed an air of calm detachment. "You see what you want to see," he said. "You always have."

Madeleine paused, as if contemplating the next maneuver in some delicate game of chance. "How comforting to find that nothing has changed," she finally said. "It's been quite a while since we've worked together. *Closely*, that is. And you always wonder" — and here she pronounced the words with odd emphasis — "if — something — might — change. And then you realize that nothing ever does."

A smile flickered across Mills's face.

"It sounds like you've got it all figured out, Madeleine. Let's be clear about this. Neither of us is happy with this arrangement. Unfortunately, Thorpe has demanded that you work on this case. Obviously, we have no choice. *You* have no choice. I'm sure you understand that."

But Madeleine was barely listening. Her mind seemed to be somewhere else. "That associate. Kate Paine. You hired her, didn't you? It's because of you that she came to work here."

Mills's expression didn't change. "I have no idea what you're talking about."

And now it was Madeleine who was silent as her eyes roamed Carter Mills's face. Then, abruptly, she laughed. When she spoke her voice was heavy with scorn.

"You're so *obvious*, Carter. It would be fascinating if it weren't so pathetic. Are you wondering how I knew? *Just look at her.*"

Tuesday, January 5

9:22 A.M. The morning was not going well. Just out of the shower, Kate had spent a good five minutes rubbing hair conditioner into her sunburned legs before realizing her mistake. Swearing under her breath, she stuck her legs under the bathtub faucet and turned on the water full force. What was it with chic cosmetic lines? Why did all the little bottles have to look alike?

Toweling off her legs, Kate smeared moisturizer into her tanned skin — carefully checking the label first — and grabbed a new pack of stockings from her dresser drawer. She'd already snagged one pair. She skipped breakfast, planning to grab a bagel at the firm cafeteria. But by the time she got to her desk, the red light on her phone was already flashing. A message from Madeleine Waters, who wanted to see Kate right away.

Now, twenty minutes into the meeting, Kate was still unsure why she'd been summoned, and the rumbling in her stomach wasn't helping her concentration. After a good fifteen minutes of small talk, Madeleine had embarked on a series of questions about the memo Kate would be writing. But as Kate wracked her brain to respond, she had a strong feeling that Madeleine's thoughts were elsewhere. Madeleine's gaze seemed to wander from Kate to some point far in the distance. The older woman's face was pale against the neckline of her black raw silk suit and there were faint violet circles beneath her eyes.

"So I think that the key issue will be whether Stephanie Friedman welcomed — or at least consented to — Chuck Thorpe's advances," Kate concluded, trying to convey a confident enthusiasm that she was far from feeling. After all, she'd just gotten the assignment yesterday morning. What did Madeleine expect? But when Kate looked up, she saw that Madeleine was drawing on a small notepad. Kate sneaked a look at her watch. She'd scheduled dinner tonight with Tara, but every minute away from her desk was putting those plans in jeopardy. Then, feeling slightly guilty, Kate forced her mind back to the case. *Concentrate*, she told herself.

The phone rang. From the two short rings, Kate could tell it was a call from inside the firm. Madeleine glanced down at the LCD display and, with an audible sigh, picked up the receiver.

"Hello, Bill." Madeleine's voice was cool. Kate could hear muffled words from the other end. Bill. It must be Bill McCarty on the line.

As Madeleine shifted the telephone receiver beneath her chin, Kate noticed a thin gold band on the ring finger of her right hand. Not a wedding ring; that would be on her left hand. And besides, it was common knowledge that Madeleine was single. Had she ever regretted not marrying? But then, she must have had many chances.

"We went through this yesterday," Madeleine said, irritation suffusing her voice. "I'm sorry, but I just can't help you."

Another pause while Madeleine gazed stonily ahead. Once again, Kate could hear what sounded like impassioned pleading from the other end. What could have Bill McCarty so upset? Recalling his inflamed demeanor outside Carter Mills's office, Kate wondered if there was some connection.

"I really have nothing more to say about it," Madeleine said shortly. "You're going to have to handle this without me."

After Madeleine hung up, she looked reflectively at Kate. "So where were we?" she said.

Damn. Kate had been sure that the meeting was near an end. She blinked against the harsh winter light that poured through the plate-glass windows and tried to gather her thoughts. She hadn't slept well last night — postvacation fatigue coupled with Thorpe case adrenaline — and today she was feeling the effects.

"I was saying that the threshold question is whether the plaintiff welcomed Chuck Thorpe's advances. Obviously, that's a factual issue."

"Obviously." Madeleine's lips curved softly. Again, Kate thought of the smiling sphinx. A winged creature with the head of a woman.

Madeleine had stood up and was walking away from her desk, toward a floor-to-ceiling bookcase across the room. Kate turned to watch as she scanned the shelves briefly, then pulled out a large paperback. Heading back to her desk, Madeleine handed the volume to Kate.

"You might want to take a look at this," she said. "For background. Historical interest."

Kate glanced at the book. *Sexual Harassment of Working Women* by Catharine A. MacKinnon. She was momentarily dumbfounded. Catharine MacKinnon was probably the nation's most well known feminist legal scholar. She'd also been a prime mover in the antipornography movement, one of its earliest and most vigilant activists. Hardly inspirational reading for a lawyer defending Chuck Thorpe.

"I read some of MacKinnon's work in law school," Kate said, trying to muster an air of detachment while she figured out where this was leading. "It's interesting, but . . . doesn't she say that sexual relations between men and women are never consensual?"

"Something like that." Madeleine smiled. She did not seem inclined to continue.

In the silence that followed, Kate's eyes scanned the room. As a general rule, partners' suites were dense with signs of their private lives — family photos, mementos from past victories, children's artwork. However, this human detritus was notably absent from Madeleine's office. Hanging on the back wall was a single abstract oil — a vibrant composition of blues, greens, and orange. If they shared nothing else, Madeleine and Carter seemed to share a taste for the modern. Though since Madeleine was younger and a woman, Kate found her choices less surprising. Was it Madeleine who'd shaped Mills's taste?

Aside from the painting, the only other item on the ivory walls was a black-and-white photograph behind Madeleine's desk. A rugged coastline, waves cresting against huge rocks. Kate found herself staring at the image. She sensed Madeleine watching her.

"That's a wonderful picture," Kate said. She wasn't sure what to say next.

Madeleine's face softened as she turned to look at the picture. "A good friend of mine took that many years ago," she said. "I've always had it with me." Then she looked back at Kate.

"How long have you been at Samson & Mills?"

The question caught Kate off guard. "Just over a year, I guess."

Abruptly, Madeleine stood up. As if she'd reached some sort of decision. Circling her desk, she came up alongside Kate's chair. Leaning forward, she grasped her shoulder. "You need to be very careful." Her green eyes glittered. Her fingers dug into Kate's flesh. "There are things —"

Again, the phone rang. After a brief hesitation, Madeleine released Kate's shoulder and went back to her desk.

"Yes, Carter?" This time, Kate could hear nothing from the other end of the line. Madeleine's head was bowed. Kate couldn't make out her expression. She felt a sharp tingling sensation on her skin where Madeleine's hand had been.

Moments later, the call was over. Madeleine seemed once again preoccupied as she pulled open a drawer and began to rifle through its contents. When she spoke, she didn't look up. "There's something I need to take care of," she said. "We'll have to finish this later."

⤞⤝

1 P.M. It was time. He'd put it off as long as he could. Any further delay and he might not reach her. Of course, he'd logged on to Samson's computer network to check Madeleine's calendar. That was a daily practice. Click in. Click out. He knew she was in for the afternoon. Conference call on some boring Micro-Net matter at three. A new client prospect at four.

He picked up the phone, punched in her number.

Breathe in, breathe out. Everything will be fine.

"Madeleine Waters's office. How may I help you?" He recognized the voice of Carmen Rodriguez, Madeleine's secretary. *So far so good.*

"I'm calling from Chuck Thorpe's office. Mr. Thorpe has had a slight change of schedule. He'd appreciate it if Ms. Waters could meet him an hour earlier than planned. At seven instead of eight."

Good. Take control. Remind her that you're the client. You set the terms.

"Just one moment. Let me check with Ms. Waters." He heard the click of the hold button. And then the interminable wait.

Say yes, say yes, say yes.

Finally, another click. Carmen Rodriguez was back. "That will be fine. Ms. Waters will meet Mr. Thorpe at seven o'clock at Ormond."

"Thank you. Mr. Thorpe very much appreciates the accommodation."

"You're quite welcome."

Yes.

⤞⤝

KATE leaned against the doorway of Andrea Lee's office, waiting for her phone call to be over. Kate could barely make out the top of Andrea's sleek black hair, bobbing rhythmically behind the stacks of *Federal Reporters* and Westlaw printouts piled high on her desk. But her emphatic tones were unmistakable.

"This is outrageous," Andrea declaimed. "We're absolutely entitled to see the customer service files. If we don't have them by tomorrow, we're filing a motion to compel."

Kate grinned at the familiar scene. Born in Hong Kong and raised in New York, Andrea was a one-woman rebuttal to the myth of the retiring Asian woman. They'd met as summer associates and bonded during their first year of work when they both ended up on a nightmarish document review on one of Martin Drescher's cases. As the two most junior lawyers on the team, Kate and Andrea had put in more than their share of all-nighters, drinking gallons of coffee and sending out for endless amounts of sushi, pizza, and Chinese food. Both of them had billed upward of ninety hours a week during that insane six months. They'd also become fast friends.

Now, as if sensing Kate's presence, Andrea glanced up. Her eyes widened, and a broad smile broke across her face. Signaling to Kate to wait, she returned to her caller.

"I think we've said about all there is to say, Tim." Andrea's features once again reflected an icy intransigence. "We know your position. Now you know ours. I have a meeting."

As she slammed down the phone, and jumped up to hug Kate, the familiar grin reclaimed her face. Kate returned the smile, amused by her friend's seamless shifts from power lawyer to gal pal. She wondered if she did the same thing herself.

"You look great!" said Andrea, releasing Kate from a quick embrace. "Can't wait to hear about the Caribbean. Ready for lunch?"

"Yep." Kate glanced around the sunlit room. Except for the view — Andrea's windows faced directly west, looking over the Hudson River — their offices were identical. But while Kate's walls were bare except for her Harvard diploma, Andrea's were covered with colorful posters of the far-flung places that she loved to visit. Kate saw that a raging Chilean river now occupied the place of honor to the right of Andrea's desk.

"The Futaleufu," Andrea beamed. "Some of the best white water in the world. We're going in February. It'll be summer down there."

"We" referred to Andrea and her husband, Brent, an investment banker. While both held high-powered corporate jobs, they were perennially broke due to their endless appetite for wilderness adventure. Andrea made no secret of why she stayed at Samson: money pure and simple. Money to travel and pay off her law school loans.

"Better you than me," said Kate. "From the looks of things, I'd stay afloat three minutes tops."

"Foolish girl. You'd love it if you'd give it a try." Andrea grabbed her purse. "Shall we?"

The noise level in the cafeteria had already reached a steady din by the time Andrea and Kate, lunch trays in hand, headed toward a corner table. It was the usual scene. Tables of slick-haired young men, ties tossed over their shoulders. A few scattered clusters of women, mainly secretaries and other support staffers.

"Return to GQ Central," Kate whispered to Andrea, who responded with a short laugh.

"How *do* you explain the shortage of females at this firm?" Kate asked, after they had settled into their chairs. "There must be five men for every woman. What was the count for last summer's associate class? More than sixty guys and only eight of us, right?"

"Well, it's a little like this at any white-shoe firm," said Andrea. Her eyes narrowed as she studied a colorful concoction of rice noodles and bean sprouts that she'd spooned off the salad bar. Samson's latest foray into Asian cuisine. "*We* don't eat this cold — why would *you?*" she muttered. "Why do they even bother? Each dish is more preposterous than the last."

"Kitchen diversity. So you're practically the only Asian associate. At least the cooking can be pluralistic."

"Good point." Andrea shoved the salad aside and picked up her cheeseburger. "Who needs noodles anyway? You want to know what I really think?"

"About *noodles?*"

"No, about the woman thing. It's to keep costs down. Samson

offers great maternity benefits. Four months of paid leave. Looks great when the firm gets written up in *American Law*. Very progressive. Very PC. But what would happen if half the associates were actually *taking* it? Need I say more?"

"Hmm. Isn't that just a little bit cynical?"

Andrea raised her eyebrows in mock horror. "Oh my God, how can you *say* such things about me?" She popped a french fry into her mouth.

"Then again," Kate said, "you could have a point." She turned to her own cheeseburger, took a large bite, and chewed. "Did you get away at all over the holidays?"

"Nope. I'm saving up all my vacation for February. I've put in for three weeks," Andrea said absently. She was looking over Kate's shoulder. "When *is* that girl going to get married?"

"What are you talking about?"

"Behind you. Angela Taylor. She's showing off that ring again. It's her sole topic of conversation. That and *Ally McBeal*."

Kate craned her neck to look at Angela Taylor. She was wearing a sleek navy suit that set off her preppie good looks. Her left hand was extended for appraisal by another young lawyer of similar type and vintage. "I don't get it," Kate said. "She went to law school at Yale. Clerked in the Southern District. It's strange, isn't it?"

"Not really," said Andrea. "Just because you're smart doesn't mean you can't be superficial. Angela Taylor has it all. Hey, speaking of weddings, guess who else is getting hitched."

"Who?"

"Susan Deveraux."

Kate stared at Andrea. Susan Deveraux was a senior associate and one of a handful of Samson attorneys known to be openly gay. She was a fixture at on-campus recruitment events, where even the most competitive law students sometimes clung to vestiges of an early idealism, demanding that firms show diversity in their hiring practices.

"You mean she's . . . marrying a woman?" Kate asked.

"Nope. A guy. A lawyer for Dewhurst Securities."

Kate stared at Andrea uncomprehendingly.

"Hey, it's not so complicated, Kate. Susan's up for partner next year. Get it? The fiancé's just the latest stage of a transformation. Come on, you must have noticed. First she lost the short haircut. Then she went blond. The wedding was only a matter of time."

Kate sat back in her chair as the pieces fell into place. But Andrea was already moving on. "Hey, I got an e-mail from Collins yesterday." Craig Collins was a former colleague, an associate who'd left the firm a few months back to start a judicial clerkship.

"Does he still like clerking?" Kate asked.

"Loves it. Says that when you get rid of both the partners and the clients, it's amazing how much better the profession gets."

Kate giggled. "Makes sense to me."

Andrea picked up another french fry. "So how are things on the WideWorld watch? That's quite a case you've got."

Kate sneaked a hand toward Andrea's plate for a fry; she'd resolved to skip the added calories today but now regretted her decision. She chewed ruminatively, her eyes lingering on a large and indifferent painting on the opposite wall, a run-of-the-mill landscape that reflected both great diligence and an utter absence of native talent. There were canvases like this all over the building, prominently hung in out-of-the-way rooms and hallways, a concession of sorts to familial pressures. *Partner-wife art*, Andrea called it.

"Say, what do you know about Madeleine Waters?"

Andrea leaned the side of her head on a hand. "Not a lot," she said. "Just the rumors about her and Mills. I've been wondering about her myself."

"Why's that?"

"The last few days, I've been doing some work again for Drescher."

Kate's eyes widened. "Oh my God, Andrea. You poor thing."

Andrea shrugged her shoulders philosophically. "It's okay. I mean, it won't be forever. He's just short an associate, since Belknap left last month."

If left to his own devices, Kate thought, Martin Drescher could clear out the firm single-handedly. Drescher was what was known in Samson parlance as a "screamer" — a partner known for blowing up on the tiniest provocation and sometimes for no reason at all. For a moment, Kate pictured him in her mind's eye. The thin orangish hair, the damp, red face, the protuberant eyes. She recalled his habit of storming into a room and barking off orders. Orders that often contradicted what he'd said just an hour or two before. "Why doesn't he just line us up and say, 'Fuck you,' 'fuck you,' 'fuck you'?" Andrea had once remarked. "It would take a whole lot less time."

"Has he been managing to act marginally human?" Kate asked.

Andrea shrugged again. "He's been okay. I'm trying to cut him some slack. You know, he's not the typical Samson partner. He's really had a tough life. I was talking to Sheila about him last week, asking her how she's managed to be his secretary for as long as she has, and she sort of defended him. Said he had this alcoholic father who used to beat him up and stuff. His family was really poor. Anyway, after both his parents died, he supported a bunch of sisters along with working his way through law school."

"Interesting." Kate was reluctant to see any redeeming qualities in Martin Drescher. But there was no need to press the point.

"Anyway, I haven't even seen him today," Andrea continued. "We were supposed to have a meeting at nine this morning, but I don't think he's made it in yet. It's the second time this week he hasn't shown up for something."

"Do you think he's drinking again?" Kate asked. Drescher's history of alcoholism was a well-known secret. Though word was that he'd been on the wagon for the past few years, since a stint in an upstate rehab.

Andrea rubbed her chin. "It's certainly occurred to me," she admitted. "But please don't spread it around. It's not like I have any proof. And besides I . . . I sort of feel sorry for the guy."

"I can think of better people to feel sorry for. Like the lawyers who work for him. But fine, I'll shut up for now. How did we end up talking about Drescher anyway?"

"You asked about Madeleine. She's been around his office a lot. At first, I thought she might be working on the case, but I don't think that's it. Especially if she's working on that WideWorld thing with you. I can't really imagine Drescher and Mills sharing her."

Andrea was probably right. Mills and Drescher were leaders of opposing camps, with conflicts dating back more than a decade, to when Mills had defeated Drescher in a bitterly fought contest for managing partner. Now, recalling the unmistakable tension between Madeleine and Mills, Kate wondered if it might be linked to her newfound coziness with Drescher.

"What's Madeleine like to work with?" Andrea said.

"Fine, so far. I mean not much has happened yet. I did have sort of a weird meeting with her this morning, though. We were talking about the Thorpe case. Then, out of the blue, she comes over to me, grabs my shoulder — hard — and tells me that I should be *very careful*. Those were the words she used."

"Any idea what she meant?"

"None. She was about to say something more, but the phone rang. We never finished the conversation."

"Well, I wouldn't worry about it. It was probably no big deal. Something related to the case. You'll clear it up later."

"Yeah," Kate said. "That's what I've been thinking."

"So, what's it like working with Carter Mills?"

"We're just getting started. But so far so good. Actually, I'm really excited."

To her surprise, Kate found that she was blushing. Andrea looked at her curiously.

"Didn't Mills interview you at Harvard?"

"Yeah." Kate felt a quiver close to her heart as the memory flooded back. Samson & Mills. As legendary for the demands it placed on attorneys as for the unparalleled prestige of its name. No wonder the firm was often referred to by its initials, S&M. And yet, despite the horror stories, despite the tales of exigent partners, impossible deadlines, and endless rounds of all-nighters, Samson still had its pick of young lawyers.

Kate thought back to the scene at Pound Hall. Surrounded by giddily anxious classmates, waiting for their names to be called, she'd had to force herself to stay put. The simple act of putting on a suit and pumps had been almost more than she could take. All she'd wanted was to crawl back home. To curl up in bed and cry.

And then she'd met Carter Mills.

"Carter is probably the reason I came to Samson & Mills." Kate's voice was soft.

Andrea frowned. "How's that?"

"It's hard to explain. He was just so . . . charismatic, I guess. He made you feel like being a lawyer at Samson & Mills was the most wonderful thing in the world. I know, it probably sounds stupid, but it meant a lot to me. I still remember what he said. 'You've been number one all your life. Don't short-change yourself now.'"

"What becoming modesty," Andrea said dryly.

Kate ignored her. "It was great," she said earnestly. "My self-esteem was at an all-time low. And here was this amazing man actually taking an interest in me, telling me that I had a future. Which was something I hadn't felt for a while. Remember, Michael had just broken up with me. Before that, I'd just assumed that I'd be moving to Washington with him that fall, when he started his clerkship on the D.C. Circuit. And there I was suddenly without a boyfriend, with no idea what I was going to do next."

Andrea looked at her skeptically. "Come on, Kate. You were graduating from Harvard Law School. You had great grades. You knew you were going to practice law, right?"

"Well, sure. But it was tied up with the idea of being with Michael, too. All of the firms I'd looked at were in D.C. And I was mainly looking at 'lifestyle' firms — you know, where they actually don't expect you to spend the night on a regular basis. I wanted us really to have a life together."

Even as she described the scene, Kate felt a sharp pain in her chest. "Anyway," she said, anxious to complete the story, "I was wandering around campus feeling like a lost soul. I only signed up for a Samson interview because Justin made me. I definitely wasn't expecting much. And then — it's hard to explain — but when I met Carter Mills, everything seemed okay again. For the first time in weeks, I felt hopeful, like my life was going to work out."

Andrea looked at her frankly. "Kate, you know I adore you. But I have no idea what you're talking about."

"Well, it began like a normal interview. He asked me about Harvard — classes, journal work, that sort of thing. But then we got to talking about my family. I told him about my parents splitting up when I was a kid. And then we talked about what it was like when my mom died — that was during my last year in college. I . . . I even told him a little about breaking up with Michael."

"You talked to Carter Mills about that kind of stuff? In an *interview?* Were you out of your mind?"

"I know. It's strange, isn't it? I'm generally not so keen on discussing the past. I'm a big believer in forward momentum. But he seemed interested. Really interested. Like he cared."

"If you say so. But it sounds a little bizarre."

"It didn't feel bizarre at the time. It just felt . . . good." Kate felt herself blushing again. "You know, for weeks after that interview, I had this fantasy that Carter Mills was my father. That we'd go away for a trip to the country or the beach and that I could tell him everything — everything that was wrong with my life — and that he'd tell me how to fix it."

Andrea shook her head. "I'm not even going to touch that one," she said.

Kate was about to respond but stopped herself. Andrea's parents had recently celebrated their thirtieth wedding anniversary. How could Andrea, with her parents and husband and teenage kid brother, ever understand how it felt to be facing the world alone? As she herself had since her mother died. There was her father, of course, but she hadn't seen him for more than a decade, since he moved to California with his new wife and child. For several years, he'd sent birthday cards, and then even these had become sporadic. Those had been the most painful years, the occasional cards only serving to underscore his general lack of concern. It was better once the cards stopped coming.

Kate felt a hand on her shoulder.

"Hey there!"

"Justin!" Kate jumped up to give him a hug. As usual, Justin Daniels looked as though he'd just stepped away from a photo shoot for some men's fashion magazine. He was almost too handsome, with an athlete's graceful build and strong, chiseled features. They'd met over lunch at the Hark, as the law school commons was called. She'd immediately decided that no one that good-looking, and smart enough to be at Harvard, could be anything other than a jerk. But she'd been wrong. Four years later, he was one of her closest friends.

"It's great to see you!" Kate said. "Why don't you join us?"

Justin paused, then shook his head. "No thanks, it's going to be a working lunch. I'm taking a tray downstairs. But how about drinks after work?"

Kate brightened. "Perfect. I'm supposed to have dinner with Tara, so I'll meet you afterward. Say, nine-thirty at the Harvard Club?"

They finished making arrangements, and then Justin headed off toward the cafeteria line. Kate felt her spirits lift. If anyone could figure out what was up with Madeleine Waters, Justin could. He seemed to have a sort of sixth sense about what lay beneath Samson's surface, about the current pecking order among the firm's partners and the reasons for these distinctions. How he had accumulated this knowledge in the one year that they had both worked at the firm, Kate had no idea. But it definitely came in handy.

Andrea's voice interrupted her thoughts. "He's yummy," she said. "I still think you should think about changing the terms of your relationship."

"Changing the terms," Kate scoffed. "You make it sound like a contract."

"Seriously, Kate. Don't wait too long. Guys like Justin don't come along every day."

"Look, Justin and I are friends. And it's going to stay that way. I'd never risk screwing up our friendship. You know how it is. When sex gets involved, all bets are off."

"I don't know, Kate. Brent and I started out as friends, and now we're married. Very happily married, I might add. Some risks really are worth taking."

Kate shook her head. "It's different for you," she said. "If things hadn't worked out with Brent, you still would have had your family. Something to fall back on. But for me . . . I guess Justin's about the closest thing to family I have. You know the story. He practically saved my life after Michael and I split up. He even signed me up for job interviews when I just wanted to stay home in bed with the shades down. If it weren't for him, I wouldn't even have *interviewed* at Samson let alone come to work here."

"Like I was saying. Sounds like he'd make a great husband."

Kate rolled her eyes. "No wonder you became a litigator," she said. "You're relentless. Can we please just change the subject?"

"Okay, okay," Andrea said. She was playing with the remnants of her pan-Asian salad, building a little rice pyramid with her fork. "So how are things going with Josie?"

Kate gave a short laugh. One more thing to worry about. She briefly wondered what she'd been thinking when she agreed to take on this sixteen-year-old girl as part of Samson's pro bono effort. At the time, the idea of serving as a high school mentor had sounded like fun, and she'd liked the idea of giving back. She'd even hoped she might *make a difference*. But two months later, disillusion was setting in.

"I'm not sure what to do," Kate confessed. "We had a meeting scheduled right before I left on vacation, but Josie didn't show up at all. The week before that, she was half an hour late. I had this idea that we'd be talking about books — *To Kill a Mockingbird*, *Catcher in the Rye* — that sort of thing. I was looking forward to being a teacher. Instead I'm turning into a drill sergeant. Be on time. Do your work. Don't get me wrong — she's a terrific kid. She's smart, energetic, full of ideas. But she can't seem to focus. I can't seem to get through to her."

"That's par for the course," said Andrea. "I had the same experience with Vicky when I started to work with her. Just keep pounding away at the ground rules. Eventually, it'll sink in."

"I hope so." Kate glanced at her watch. "Damn, it's nearly one. I need to get back to work. Ready?"

As they carried their trays toward the kitchen conveyor belt, Kate's thoughts moved back to that morning. "So you really don't think I should worry? About what Madeleine said?"

"Worry? No way. You'll straighten it out the next time you see her. Just ask her to explain what she meant."

"You're right," said Kate. "That's exactly what I'll do."

⋙⋘

HE stood outside the windows, watching. A little past seven, and already the restaurant teemed with people. Set flat in the middle of a run-down industrial zone, Ormond still pulled in a random assortment of black-clad artist types — few actual artists could afford the price of a meal — and Wall Street apparatchiks who liked to let their hair down at the end of the day. Ormond, he mused, catered to a bourgeoisie in denial, to wealthy patrons with a yearning to be rich *and* hip; to live on the edge without giving up the status and perquisites of wealth.

It was cold, with temperatures hovering close to zero, but he barely noticed the chill. A thin crust of ice slicked the sidewalk. Carefully picking his way, he moved in for a closer look. His reflection wavered in the plate-glass expanse. Then, he forced his gaze back, beyond.

She was already there, seated at a back corner table. That was bound to make things more difficult. Still. He'd come prepared. The challenge only fueled his excitement. Since making the reservation, his emotions had alternated between elation and fear. Now that the time had come, he found himself trying to prolong it. It was tempting to extend the moment. To continue to wait and watch. To watch her grow restless. To watch as she glanced once again at the gold Cartier watch on her wrist.

Like a connoisseur, he savored the possibilities.

But it was time to move on.

As he stepped through the restaurant's glass doors, he felt a burst of warm air. He was greeted by the hum of conversation, the tinkle of cutlery on plates. Pushing forward through the human throng, he got within earshot of the pony-tailed maître d'. Translucent bored face. Vacant gaze. Probably thinking about where he'd like to be tonight if it weren't for this frigging job. From where he stood, he could hear the maître d' murmuring to a petulant couple in line. "The very next table, madam. Would you like to have a drink at the bar?" No she would *not* like, what she wanted right now was a table. The caustic tones drifted in his direction until, having no choice, the woman and her date moved to the crowded bar. He'd counted on this level of quiet chaos and disarray.

Now came the delicate part.

Quickly, he edged past the podium. Perfect. The maître d' would never remember him. Hadn't seemed to notice him at all. Slowly, deliberately, he made his way toward her table, an animal stalking its prey. He was seven or eight minutes late. Not enough to prompt suspicions. But it was definitely time to begin.

"Why, hello there, Madeleine," he said.

༄

"So, try the tempura. Fried vegetables, shrimp, tofu — even you can't complain about that. What's not to like?"

"Tofu. Yuck." Kate wrinkled her nose and continued to scan the menu.

"Well, what about the soy eggplant Parmesan? It really *does* taste like cheese."

Kate sighed. Her college roommate had always shown a suspect yen for healthful food — green salad and hold the dressing — but lately things were getting out of hand. If she hadn't been so frazzled at work, Kate would have vetoed this choice, the latest in the seemingly endless array of fluorescent-lit nonfat nondairy restaurants that Tara patronized these days. Kate wondered privately how any of them stayed in business. Tara's strange affinity for soy products and bitter greens could not be so widely shared.

"Okay," Kate mumbled, trying not to sound sulky. After all, she hadn't seen Tara in weeks. She could at least try to be polite. "The cabbage salad with carrot dressing and the, uh, shrimp tempura. No tofu, though."

"No tofu?" The waiter raised a pierced eyebrow. Kate could see that he'd sized her up for what she was: a meat eater who wouldn't recognize a vegan dumpling if it bit her.

"I'll take her tofu," Tara volunteered.

The waiter looked grateful. "And what would *you* like?" He turned to Tara, seemingly relieved to be done with Kate.

"I'll have the tempeh primavera, and the seaweed salad to start," Tara said.

"Cool." He headed toward the tiny open kitchen at the back of the cramped dining space. It was early, a little after six. Kate and Tara had the place almost to themselves.

Settling back in her seat, smoothing her tailored skirt, Kate was struck by how odd they must look together. She in her fitted suit and lawyerly horn-rimmed glasses, Tara in full bohemian regalia. Tonight, Tara was wearing a long batik skirt with a baggy moth-eaten sweater. Her red curls were lassoed back with a velvet band, while stray tendrils fell over her forehead and cheeks. Silver earrings hung just above her shoulders. It was hard to imagine that she and Tara had once traded clothing so often they'd sometimes lost track of an item's owner. College seemed very long ago.

"What's with the Woodstock refugee look?" Kate asked wryly.

"What's with the corporate clone look?"

Kate laughed. "Touché."

"If I showed up for an assignment dressed like you, people would fear for my sanity," Tara said. An aspiring novelist, Tara had spent two years in a low-level publishing job before opting for the free-lance life. She wrote for a baffling array of women's magazines on subjects ranging from fake eyelashes to sexual politics. Kate often stumbled on Tara's bylines while waiting to have her nails done.

"Seitan." Kate mused. "I always forget what that is."

Tara raised her eyebrows. "You just want me to describe it so you can tell me how repulsive it sounds. And really, it's delicious. Not to mention being packed with protein."

"Anything that looks and tastes that disgusting better be packed with something to justify its existence as a food product."

"How do you know how it looks and tastes if you don't even remember what it is?"

"Deductive logic. Based on my extensive observation of your dietary habits."

"Very funny."

Kate grinned. The familiar banter was a perfect antidote to the tensions of the past two days.

"I've missed you, Tara."

"Well, it's been a long time. You left town before Christmas, and I hadn't seen you for weeks before that. Not that I'm counting."

"It's not exactly like I have a choice, you know," Kate said. She felt a twinge of annoyance. Why did Tara always have to start in on her schedule? "That's just how Samson is. It's the same for everyone."

Tara was about to respond when the waiter appeared with their meals. As he set down the steaming plates, Kate noted with satisfaction that her meal bore a marked resemblance to genuine edible food. Tara, on the other hand, had her usual brown mess of indecipherable lumps and strips.

"Mine looks good," Kate said. "I won't say what yours looks like."

Tara beamed. "You don't know what you're missing."

They ate for several minutes in companionable silence. Conversation from a nearby table filtered past.

"My sister's, like, very linear about time?" The speaker's voice was softly indignant, her assertions concluding with a slight upswing. "It's like, really important to her that you're on time? She's like — *I'm on time, you should be on time.*"

"Wow, I don't even like watches, to wear them. Like I don't even like how they feel on my *arm*."

"I *have* to wear one." A dejected sigh. "I just don't have a body clock."

Oh, brother, Kate thought. *Get me out of here.*

Then Tara was talking again. "Why do you stay at that place?" Tara was chewing thoughtfully, watching Kate as she ate.

"What?" But of course she knew what Tara meant. For all her laid-back demeanor, Tara was nothing if not persistent.

"That law firm. Why do you stay there?"

Kate tried to stay calm. "Look, it's only been about a year. Anyway, it's not as bad as it sounds. It structures my time." Even as she spoke, it occurred to Kate that this did not sound like an especially strong defense of a job that consumed more hours per week than most people spent awake. But it was already too late.

"It structures your time?" Kate could hear the exasperation in Tara's voice. "Kate, I'm worried about you. *Slavery* structured people's time. I don't see that as a point in its favor."

"No quarrel here," Kate said lightly. She really wasn't in the mood for one of Tara's tirades. "Look," she temporized, "I'm not going to stay forever." But the words felt false in her mouth. Almost without exception, junior associates claimed to have no interest in partnership. Everyone planned to move on. After all, Samson associates were highly sought after by smaller firms, and only one or two members of a given class had any hope of making partner. But didn't most associates secretly wonder if they could beat the odds?

The conversation had ground to a halt. Kate hurried to fill the gap. "Look, I'm sure it won't always be this bad," she said, hearing and hating the defensiveness in her voice. "It's just that I'm starting out." Not true, of course. But maybe it would placate Tara.

"Glad to hear it." Tara's voice was noncommittal. There was a pause as she took another bite and chewed. "Hey, before I forget, I want to tell you about this guy I think you should meet. He's an architect. Does some sort of work with low-income housing. His name's Douglas. Douglas Macauley."

"Nice name," Kate said, hoping that her obvious lack of interest would forestall any further discussion. What was it with her friends today? First, Andrea, now Tara. Didn't they have better things to do than try to find her a mate?

"He's a friend of Tom's." Tara said. Tom was Tara's long-term boyfriend, a computer whiz with an artistic bent. "They met a few months ago when Doug worked on the renovation at Mundo Novo."

Kate briefly wondered, as she had before, about the name Tom and his partners had chosen for their Internet start-up. Mundo Novo sounded more like an eighties dance band than a serious business venture.

"Have you met him?"

"Yeah. We had dinner with him a couple of weeks ago. He's cute *and* smart. I really think that you two might hit it off. At least you would if you gave him a chance."

"If he's so great, why doesn't he already have a girlfriend?"

"I didn't ask."

"Well, maybe you should ask."

Tara rolled her eyes. "Kate, you're being —"

"What? What am I being?"

Childish. Kate knew the word was childish. But she didn't care. "I just don't think it's a good idea."

Silence. Kate returned to her meal. Much better than she'd expected. She dipped a shrimp in tamari sauce and raised it toward her open mouth.

"Look, it's been more than two years since —"

"I don't want to talk about it," Kate snapped. "How many times do I have to say that? It's my life." That was the problem with old friends. They knew you too well.

Tara was not dissuaded. "So what are you telling me? That you're never going to date again? That you're just going to bury yourself alive in that exploitive mausoleum you call a law firm?"

"I like my job."

"Great. I'm glad that you like your job. That doesn't mean you can't also have a life."

"I really just don't want to talk about it. Besides, I hardly even have time to see *you*. How would I make time for a boyfriend?"

"Fine. It's your decision. Forget I said anything."

Kate reached over and touched Tara's arm. "Look, maybe after this new case calms down, I'll have more time. Maybe I'll feel differently then."

Tara met her eyes. "Maybe. But you've been saying that for a long time."

"I know."

"Kate, I really think that you should consider talking to someone."

"I *am* talking to someone. I'm talking to you, aren't I?"

"You know what I mean. A therapist. Someone who can help you move through this. You're fixated. Everyone goes through relationships that don't work out. Remember that creep Eric? The guy I went out with before Tom? I was crazy about him. But it didn't work out. That's how life is. Sometimes, things just don't work out. And you have to move on."

"What makes you think that this is about Michael?" Kate said. It had been a long time since she'd spoken the name out loud. For a moment, his face floated up in her mind. The disarming quicksilver smile. The wavy light brown hair, always slightly in need of a trim. They'd met on the first day of law school, assigned to adjacent seats in Contracts, and had been inseparable for the next two years. As well as part of a third. Kate felt a tightening in her chest. "Maybe I'm just focused on my job," she said defiantly. "What's wrong with that?"

"I'm sure *Bill Gates* is focused on his job, and he still managed to get married."

"He's a man. It's different." Even to herself, Kate sounded ridiculous. She tried to recoup. "Look, I went out with Michael for almost three years. Through most of law school. We met on our first day of classes. It's natural that I'd have a hard time getting over him."

"Kate, he's engaged. He's getting married soon. You told me that yourself."

"Thanks for reminding me." Kate could hear the bitter edge to her voice. Time, the cushion on which she'd relied to soften the blows of memory, seemed to collapse beneath her.

"I'm sorry if I upset you," Tara said. "But I hate to see you suffer like this. I just don't think you have to suffer so much."

"I'm not suffering. I don't have *time* to suffer."

Tara raised her eyes skyward. Kate felt a wave of fatigue. "Look, I'll think about it, okay? The therapy thing."

"Really?"

"Maybe. Can we change the subject now?"

Tara sighed. "Be my guest."

⁜

HE gazed down at the seated figure. She was smaller than he remembered, her hair swept back in a twist. Her dress, a rich shade of midnight blue, had a square-cut neck and fitted sleeves. She held a glass of red wine. Even as his heart raced with anticipation, he took a moment to appreciate the play of color and form. How the somber hue of the fabric set off the whiteness of her skin. How the garment's tailored lines only emphasized her body's curves. An aesthetic of contrasts.

"How've you been?" he persisted.

Slowly, she lowered her glass. The faintest of flushes suffused her face. "I'm sorry, but you'll have to excuse me." Her voice was quiet but firm. "I'm meeting a client here."

Standing beside her in this public space, he felt a rush of power. His entire body — blood, muscle, heart, sinew — seemed to be humming at her nearness. He pulled out a chair and sat down. "Yes. Well. There's been a — how shall I put this? — change of plans."

She looked at him warily, a latent uneasiness emerging. She had no idea. Still, her instincts were good. She knew that something was wrong.

"I'm going to have to ask you to leave," she said, sitting up straight in her chair.

"But I don't want to leave, Madeleine." As he spoke, he slipped off his coat and placed it across his lap. He waited a moment, relishing her stunned confusion. Then, reaching under his coat, he went on. "Beneath this table, I am holding a loaded gun. A gun with a rather remarkable history. But I digress. The point is this: If you make the slightest move to suggest that everything is not, shall we say, as it should be, I won't hesitate to shoot. Given our respective positions, I'd guess that the bullet would probably strike you somewhere between the abdomen and lungs. Of course, you might survive. But there's sure to be a fair bit of damage. All and all, I'd say that it's quite a gamble."

Her pale skin seemed to grow even paler. But she didn't say anything at first. Her brilliant mind, so adept at sorting out logical inconsistencies, the weakness in an opponent's argument, must be rapidly reviewing the alternatives, reviewing and dismissing them at lightning speed. Then, strangely, she smiled. When she spoke her voice was playful.

"Look," she said lightly. "This is some sort of joke, right? Okay, you got me. *You really did.* Now, why don't you let me buy you a drink at the bar?"

He met her smile with his own. "This isn't a joke, Madeleine," he said. "You couldn't be further from the truth."

Slowly, her smile faded. "Let's look at this rationally," she said. "If you —"

He was suddenly impatient, impatient and not a little anxious about the steady passage of time. No point in pressing his luck.

"It's time for us to go," he said abruptly.

"For us —?"

"You're coming with me, Madeleine," he said.

She looked at him, incredulous. "You're crazy. I don't know what it is you're after, but you'll never get away with this."

He laughed out loud. "You may be right," he said. "Maybe I *am* crazy. But, frankly, Madeleine, if I were in your shoes, I don't think that would reassure me."

"Why are you doing this?" Madeleine whispered. Her green eyes shone. "Why are you doing this to me?"

He was pleased to hear the beginnings of fear in her voice, uneasiness evolving into something more. "You don't need to know that, Madeleine," he said. "Really, there'd be no point. And it would take too long. It's not really about you, anyway."

Signaling the waitress with his free hand, he kept his gaze pinned firmly on Madeleine's face. "I'm afraid my companion is feeling sick. If you could bring us the check right away. . . ." With sympathetic sounds, the waitress hurried to comply.

He looked at Madeleine intently. "Now listen carefully. There's not much time. You kept your coat with you. Good. When I get up, you'll stand up slowly and put it on. You'll notice that, as I stand, my coat will remain over my arm, concealing my right hand. In that hand, as I think I previously mentioned, I am holding a loaded gun. Keeping that in mind, you will walk, slightly ahead of me, out the door. I'll leave cash on the table to pay the bill. There's no reason to stop up front. Understood?"

As they stepped out into the cold, black night, he reached his left arm around Madeleine's waist; in his right hand, he held the pistol, firmly lodged against her side. Stars glimmered above them in a frosty sky. Their footsteps crunched through a shell of ice. Through the weight of her cashmere coat, he felt Madeleine stiffen at his touch. Streetlights sent off a dusty glow. The area shops were dark. Rounding the corner, he saw the rental car parked at the end of the block. A few more yards, and he was unlocking the door, roughly shoving Madeleine inside.

And then, just as he'd planned, there were no witnesses when he firmly pressed a chloroform-soaked cloth over the beautiful, startled face.

❧

IT was with a sense of relief that Kate quickly hugged Tara goodbye before hailing a cab and heading uptown. She was glad to have the excuse of her Harvard Club date with Justin to short-circuit the discussion of her personal life. After giving the driver directions — 27 West 44th between Fifth and Sixth — Kate leaned her head back against the seat and closed her eyes as the cab rocketed through the night, zipping in and out of traffic lanes like a ball in a pinball game.

As the cab careened uptown, Kate let her mind wander back to her meal with Tara. Now that she was free from her friend's probing questions, she felt a little guilty. She'd call Tara first thing tomorrow, apologize for being a jerk.

"Miss?"

The cab had come to a stop next to the club's crimson canopy. Kate fumbled in her purse for the fare and then scrambled onto the sidewalk. It had started to rain, an icy drizzle. Kate hurried through the door.

Once inside, Kate could feel herself relax. She smiled at the doorman before heading straight for the crackling fire, where she held out her hands to warm them.

Kate knew that her fondness for the Harvard Club was slightly perverse. With its fusty Old World demeanor, the club was almost a parody of itself. But that was part of what she liked about it: the pervasive if unconscious self-irony. Trophy animals gazed down from the walls, remnants of big-game hunts. Kate had a particular fondness for the green-tinged elephant, with its enormous extended trunk. ("Looks just like the elephant king Cornelius did after he ate the poisoned mushrooms," Kate had once observed, referring to a picture in the Babar book she'd loved as a child.) Some months back, one of the ancient specimens had crashed to the floor — the head of a wild boar or something equally preposterous. Kate had almost wished that someone had been hit if only to see what the tabloids did with the story. She'd come up with a few headlines herself: *Dead Head Strikes Talking Head. Head of the Beast Kills Head of the Class. Taxidermy Kills Tax Attorney.* The possibilities were endless.

Kate glanced at her watch. Almost nine-thirty. She was right on time. Pulling off her coat, Kate sank into a chair to wait for Justin's arrival. Her eyes wandered around the room. The club was a sea of crimson — crimson carpets and crimson walls — punctuated by portraits of old white men. Lately, there'd been some progress on the gender front, with money raised to bring in more pictures of women. Until the recent push, there'd been only two, the black contralto Marian Anderson — might as well get two minorities for the price of one — and Helen Keller — a role model, to be sure, but was it mere coincidence that the club had selected a female icon who was blind, deaf, and mute?

Kate was skimming the headlines of the *Wall Street Journal* when Justin bounded into sight.

"Am I late?" he said, sounding slightly out of breath. "I got tied up with some last-minute document work."

"Just on time," Kate assured him. "I was on the early side." She felt a glow of pleasure in his company. Justin wasn't just a close friend; he was also a touchstone, a reminder of how far she'd come. Again, she thought about that last year of school. It had been Justin who pulled her through. Not only had he given her a shoulder to cry on; he'd also offered advice. "Don't let a guy — any guy — screw up your life," he'd said. "Make this work *for* you. After you spend a couple of years at Samson & Mills, you'll be able to write your own ticket. You may not think that matters now, but you will later. Besides, what have you got to lose?" And he'd been right.

As Justin leaned down to kiss her on the cheek, Kate felt her face grow warm. *Sounds like he'd make a great husband.* Andrea's lunchtime pronouncement. Luckily, Justin didn't notice.

"Shall we dump our coats?" He was already heading toward the cloakroom.

"Sure." Following Justin down a narrow corridor, Kate saw that his hair was damp. He must have stopped by the gym. Crazy as things got at Samson, Justin never seemed to miss a day. Something she couldn't say for herself. Kate tried to remember the last time she'd taken advantage of her firm-subsidized membership in the Mercury Athletic Club. Mercury was one of the city's pricier and more exclusive gyms. It was ridiculous not to avail herself of this perk. She'd definitely make it over this week. *Really*.

The Grill Room was a sea of overstuffed leather sofas, chairs, and tables populated by the usual mix of old and young Harvard types. A table of four elderly men in suits, white-haired and distinguished, huddled over a vigorous game of backgammon with the same high seriousness that they must have once accorded their business deals. Several professional couples dined à deux. A cluster of twenty-something guys with slicked-back hair were trading jokes over drinks. They reminded Kate of puppies, high-spirited and not quite housebroken. The mood was quiet and restrained, with the club's strictly enforced "Gentlemen's Rules" barring any display of cash or business papers. Payment was discreetly effected by way of a member's signature.

"How about over there?" Kate gestured to a corner table to the right of the entrance. She wanted to be assured of privacy.

After settling in at their table and ordering drinks — white wine for Kate, vodka and tonic for Justin — Justin turned to Kate.

"So how was the cruise?" he asked.

"Terrific," said Kate. "Great." It wasn't quite the truth. While the weather had been beautiful, balmy and hot, she'd counted the hours till her return. What was so great about having time on your hands? Better to be busy and productive.

"You were by yourself?"

"I wouldn't put it that way." Kate could tell she sounded defensive, the residue from her dinner with Tara. "There were ten of us on the boat. I shared a cabin with another woman. A French translator. I had plenty of company."

She quickly changed the subject. "So how about you? How were the holidays?"

Justin rolled his eyes. "The usual pandemonium at home. But good. Delia's already planning for college, can you believe it? Only thirteen and she's got her heart set on Brown."

"I love your family." Kate had met Justin's parents and younger sister the week of their law school graduation. Justin's father was a history professor; his mother, a child psychologist. Kate, who had toyed with the idea of majoring in psych before settling on English lit, was fascinated by Sarah Daniels's stories about the children she counseled in southeast Washington D.C. "What's your mom up to these days?"

"Busy as usual. She just finished this book about adoption she's been writing for about a hundred years. So she's a little burned out. But happy."

"That's so cool. When will it be out?"

"Hmm, let's see. We're talking about an academic press here. Probably in about 2010."

Kate laughed. "You know, I really admire your mother. But I'd never have the patience for that sort of thing. What I like about law is, you write a brief and then, boom, you either win or lose. I mean it's not immediate, but you don't have to wait forever."

"Ah yes," Justin mused. "Yet another reason to love the law."

"Speaking of the law, what happened at S&M while I was gone?"

"It's been pretty slow. I've been more or less full time on the Haber-Tech antitrust case. The document production has been a nightmare. Last week I came in on Monday morning and didn't leave until eight o'clock Wednesday night. It got to be sort of surreal. The sun goes up. The sun goes down. The sun goes up. The sun goes down. The only sleep I got was a half hour Tuesday night, hidden under my desk. It's the only way to get those goddamn lights to go out. The least little flutter of detectible movement, and on they go."

Kate laughed. "You want to hear something funny?" she said. "When I first started work at Samson, I assumed that the lights went on when you entered your office because the lighting mechanism somehow sensed the weight of your body on the floor."

Justin hooted. "Now let me get this straight. The floors were precisely calibrated to reflect the weight of all the furniture, books, and other stuff in the office and could somehow *figure out* just when a certain hundred-and-ten-pound associate crossed the threshold?"

"I didn't exactly *think it through*," Kate said. "Anyway, sorry you've been stuck at work so much."

Justin shrugged, his shoulders moving easily beneath his dark suit jacket. "Hey, I've got no complaints. You want to work at a top firm, you've got to put in the hours."

He sipped his vodka and tonic. "So what's new with the Thorpe case?"

"I'm just putting together a research memo," Kate said. "Sexual harassment law is still so murky. You've got to be really careful. Cases decided last year are totally out of date. There is one thing I wanted to ask you, though —"

"Hold that thought," Justin said. "I've got to get something to eat." He gestured to the adjacent bar where a snack table was always set up. "Want something? Some chips?"

"No thanks," Kate said. "I'm still full from dinner."

"Back in a second."

Kate watched Justin cross the room. She had to admit that Andrea had a point. Guys like Justin *didn't* come along every day. And beyond that, she'd be hard-pressed to find someone more compatible. They shared the same values, liked the same books and movies, laughed at the same jokes. They also shared a history, not just the law school years but Samson & Mills as well. Still, she'd meant what she said at lunch. Justin was almost like a brother, the brother she'd never had. He'd seen her at her worst, red-eyed and tearful, lethargic and morose. He'd brought her food and magazines when she didn't want to leave her apartment and listened to her endless disquisitions on Michael's betrayal. Even if she *were* in the market for a boyfriend, she just couldn't picture Justin in that role. Didn't romance require an element of mystery?

And then Justin was back, balancing a plate heaped with chips, pretzels, and other snacks.

"Are you really going to eat all that?" Kate asked.

"No time for dinner," Justin said. He picked up a Ritz cracker, piled high with processed cheese spread, and stared at it appraisingly. "I really don't get the food here. Some of the other school clubs have really good spreads — fruit, water biscuits, Brie. This stuff looks like it was recycled from a fifties dorm party."

"Well, this *is* the Harvard Club," Kate said, taking a potato chip from Justin's plate. "Maybe it's a bow to tradition."

Justin raised a skeptical eyebrow. "The tradition of *Cheez Whiz?*" he asked.

Kate shrugged. "Hey, are you up for a game of chess?"

"Why not?"

Kate reached back behind her chair, where a velvet curtain concealed a set of built-in shelves. From the bottom shelf, she pulled out a plastic box of chess pieces.

"Black?" she asked, snapping off the lid to the box.

"Of course."

Justin pushed his plate to the table's corner so they could set up their pieces on the inlaid chessboard.

Playing chess at the Harvard Club was one of Kate's favorite ways to spend an evening. It was Justin who'd first suggested it during one of their early visits. At first, Kate demurred; she hadn't played since junior high. But after Justin persuaded her to try, she'd been surprised at how quickly the moves came back.

Justin had already made off with both of Kate's knights and one of her rooks by the time she remembered what she'd meant to ask.

"You've worked with Madeleine Waters, right?"

"Huh?" Justin was giving the chessboard his full attention.

"Madeleine Waters. Haven't you worked with her?"

"Sure," Justin didn't look up. "On the Titan Pharmaceuticals arbitration. Right after I started at the firm. It was Martin Drescher's case. She was the junior partner."

"Drescher," Kate said. She rolled her eyes.

Justin moved a pawn one square forward and looked up.

"He's not so bad. The way I look at it, it's the same thing with any partner. You just have to know how to handle them."

Incredible. That made *two* associates leaping to Drescher's defense. Andrea at lunch and now Justin. Were they drugging Samson's water supply, creating Stepford associates along with billable hours? But, brushing these thoughts aside, she forced herself to stay on track. "So, what did you think of Madeleine?"

"You know all the history, right? The whole blow-up over her partnership election?"

"Well . . . , I know the part about Carter Mills. That he was Madeleine's mentor. And that they had some sort of falling out."

"Right. But there's a lot more to it than that."

"Like what?"

Justin laughed. "Geez, Kate, where have you been?"

"At my desk," Kate said. "Working. That's why I keep you around. To be sure I stay informed."

"I'm hurt. And here I thought you loved me for *myself*. For my —"

"Come on, Justin. Just tell me what happened."

"Okay, okay. Sometime in the late eighties — after Mills beat out Drescher for managing partner — Drescher and his crowd started accusing Mills of taking advantage of his position. Mainly, Drescher was furious about WideWorld Media. When the Wide-World business first started coming in, Drescher and Mills worked on it together. But as time went on, more and more of it went directly to Mills. While he's never been able to prove it, Drescher's always believed that Mills edged him out."

Justin rattled off the history as if he were reading from a report.

"How do you *know* all this stuff?" Kate asked. "I mean, I knew about the basic conflict, but how do you know all those details?"

Justin grinned. "Just a little hobby of mine. I keep my ears open."

"I have to admit, I'm impressed. But what does this have to do with Madeleine?"

Justin twirled the remains of his drink. "It was Madeleine's part-nership election that brought things to a head. Everyone thought the dispute between Mills and Drescher had been pretty much smoothed over. But when Madeleine came up for partner, it blew wide open again. Drescher — who *hates* Mills — saw this as the perfect opportunity to screw him. Madeleine was Mills's protégé. He brought her to the firm and trained her. It would have been a huge humiliation for him if she hadn't made partner. So a rumor starts going around that Madeleine isn't really such a great lawyer. That she's only up for partner because she's fucking Mills. Drescher tried to keep his fingerprints off, but it was pretty clear that he was the source."

"D'you think they really had an affair? Madeleine and Carter, I mean."

"Sure. Probably. Have you seen that wife of his? She looks like a Valium addict."

Kate thought of Diane Mills, whom she'd seen at several firm functions. She was a pretty but fragile blond who always seemed slightly frightened. Had she always been that way? Or had it come with the passing years? Had Diane Mills known about Madeleine?

Madeleine Waters. That's who she wanted to talk about now.

"What about the other stuff?" Kate asked. "Is it true that Madeleine only made partner because of her relationship with Mills?"

"Hard to say."

"What do you mean?"

"The thing about Madeleine is that she had almost no trial ex-perience. She was Mills's senior associate on the United Telephone case. Everyone says she did a great job. She organized document productions all over the country, coordinated with local counsel on all the state cases. But in the end the case settled."

"Well, that's not her fault." Kate felt defensive, as if she and not Madeleine had been called to account.

"Of course it isn't. At the same time, it means that she was never really tried under fire. So everyone agrees she's a great facilitator, great at organizing things. But that's hardly the same thing as going to trial. I mean, a lot of people would say that someone who pays that kind of attention to detail is probably not going to be so good at the big picture."

"But that's ridiculous. I mean, it's like she's being penalized for doing well. If she'd screwed up, she wouldn't have had a shot at being partner. They would have said that if she can't even handle pretrial work, she'd never be able to function at trial. But when she does a good job, they turn that against her, too. It's like she couldn't win."

Justin shrugged. "I'm not saying that I agree. I'm just repeating what I've heard. Hey, why are you so upset?"

Kate looked down at her hands. "I'm not upset. It's just . . . I don't know. It just doesn't seem fair."

"Life *isn't* fair. You know that."

"Well, I don't have to like it."

Justin's eyes moved back to the chessboard. "Uh, Kate, are you going to make a move or what?"

"Oh. Yeah." Kate looked back at the game. After a few seconds, she moved her remaining rook across the board.

"Are you sure you want to do that?"

"Why?"

"Because then I'll be able to take your queen."

"Oh." Kate moved the rook back to its previous position and reconsidered the board. "It'd be good if this bishop were a knight," she said. "Then I could take *your* queen."

"You're right," Justin said. "But you don't have any knights. They're all gone."

"And whose fault is that?" After briefly surveying her options, Kate moved a pawn. "So what happened with the partnership vote?"

"The partnership vote? Oh, you mean, about Madeleine. Let's see . . . this big piece came out in *American Law*. Of course, Drescher planted it, but it totally backfired. Madeleine ended up being the centerpiece. The angle was something like 'brilliant,

beautiful woman sabotaged by evil patriarchy.' Made it look like
the old boys' network was alive and kicking at Samson & Mills.
Really bad PR. Carter grabbed the opportunity. Convinced the
middle-of-the-road-guys — McCarty, Stroesser, some others —
that Drescher was out of control. Basically forced Drescher's camp
to fold. And Madeleine was elected partner."

Kate was getting confused. "So given all that history, why's
Madeleine been working with Drescher?"

"Now that I don't know." Justin eyed her across the table. "Why
are you so interested in Madeleine anyway?"

"Didn't I tell you? She's going to be working on the Thorpe
case."

Now it was Justin's turn to be surprised. He stopped with his
hand in midair, a pretzel still clutched in his outstretched fingers.
"You've got to be kidding," he said.

"No, really. I thought I told you. Anyway, she was at this meeting yesterday in Carter's office. He said that Madeleine would be
overseeing the day-to-day stuff."

Justin whistled softly. "I'd sure like to know the story behind *that*
little arrangement."

"Me too." She'd hoped that Justin would have some answers.
But apparently there were limits even to his encyclopedic knowledge of firm politics. They went back to the game. As the minutes
ticked by, Kate realized she was growing tired.

"Checkmate." Justin grinned across the table.

"Hmmm." Kate stared at the board. "If this bishop were a rook,
then I'd be home free."

"But it's not a rook. I have both rooks right here." Justin gestured to a cluster of white pieces.

"You're gloating," Kate said. "I hate it when you gloat. Fine. Go
ahead and take my king."

"You don't *take* someone's king, Kate. Once it's checkmate
you —"

"Whatever," said Kate.

Justin smiled.

"I don't know why you're so pleased with yourself tonight," Kate said. "You always win. It's not any big surprise."

"Come on, Kate. I'm a junior associate at Samson & Mills. How many pleasures do I have left in life?"

"How about the pleasure of my company?"

The words hung in the air, sounding less flip than she'd intended. She was annoyed to find herself blushing again. What was going on? After all, it was just Justin. They'd spent dozens of evenings together over the years. It was all Andrea's fault, Andrea and her stupid matchmaking ideas. Before Justin could respond, Kate moved on.

"I hate to be a slug, but I'm still exhausted from traveling," she said, careful to keep her voice neutral. "Do you mind if we call it a night?"

"Sure. I've got a busy day tomorrow anyway." Justin took a final gulp of his drink and pushed back his chair. Kate followed suit, smoothing down her skirt as she stood up. Her feet were sore. She should have worn running shoes for that cross-town walk to meet Tara, but she never could get used to how they looked with a suit. That crazed yuppie race-walker thing.

"Hey, Justin, do you have a copy of that article you were talking about? The *American Law* piece?"

"Probably. Do you want me to try to dig it up?"

"Yeah, I'd sort of like to see it."

"No problem. I'm sure I've got it somewhere."

Together, they headed to the cloakroom and then out to the street. It was getting colder. Midtown was closing down. Across the street, Kate saw an entwined couple emerge from the Royalton Hotel and slip into a waiting car. A wave of sadness passed through her. Or maybe it was just fatigue.

"Let's get you a cab," Justin said.

Kate could smell the wool of Justin's coat, still damp from the early-evening sleet. It reminded her of something, some ancient memory that she couldn't quite place. For a moment, she wanted to bury her face in its roughness. Then she took hold of herself.

"Thanks. But I'm okay. I mean, I can get a cab myself."

Justin gave her a quizzical look. "Of course you can." But he was already flagging one down. It screeched to a stop by the curb.

"Well, thanks," Kate said. As she leaned forward to give Justin a peck on the cheek, she breathed in a musky scent, aftershave mingled with wool. Justin placed a hand on her shoulder. The familiar smells seemed to pull her toward him. For a moment, she was tempted to relax in his arms, just like in the old days, when he'd lent her a shoulder to cry on. But instead she quickly pulled away.

"'Night," she said, stepping into the cab. "That was fun."

Justin pushed the door closed behind her. "See you tomorrow," he said.

Wednesday, January 6

A COLD bright morning. Carter Mills leaned back in his chair and gazed out at the sparkling city. Everything seemed possible today. As usual, he'd arisen at six-thirty. After half an hour of calisthenics, he'd showered before retiring to the breakfast room, where Molly, the latest in a string of maids, served him his standard breakfast of raisin bran, coffee, and fresh orange juice. Diane was probably still sleeping. She rarely came downstairs until he'd left for the day. After reading the *Wall Street Journal* and skimming the *Times*, he'd gone to his study for an hour. He'd left home promptly at nine in his Mercedes S500, late enough to miss the morning rush hour. The drive from Greenwich to midtown had taken just forty-five minutes.

Glancing at the grandfather clock by the door, he saw that it was almost ten-thirty. Still plenty of time to prepare for this afternoon's meeting. Sipping his customary water and lemon, his eyes lingered on the clock's carved case. How his father would hate to find this heirloom installed at Samson & Mills. Which, of course, was why he'd brought it here. An exorcism of sorts. And yet it hadn't worked out that way. More than five years later, the clock was still redolent of his childhood in Boston, of those dreaded Sunday meetings in his father's study. It seemed to stand apart from the rest of the room, taking its measure, judging.

Just as his father had.

Again, Carter stared out the window. It was a long time since he'd thought about his childhood, those endless weekly talks. He'd been eight or so when the meetings began, small enough that he'd needed to place his feet on a stack of books to keep his legs from swinging. The movement annoyed his father. From his perch on a hard wood chair, he'd listen to his father's words. *I'm proud of you, son. But remember, each day is a new beginning. Never rest on your laurels.*

As a child, Carter had feared his father. As an adult, he'd come to scorn him. A complicated scorn, it was true, never entirely free of trepidation. Still, the contempt was there. Who was his father, after all? A historian. A scholar. A collector of Americana. Someone who'd spent his life comfortably wrapped in family wealth, with little to show for his years on earth but a couple of history books. Some years back, Carter had picked up an autobiography of Clarence Darrow. Flipping through the opening pages, a single phrase had caught his eye. "For my part, I seldom think about my ancestors; but I had them; plenty of them, of course. In fact, I could fill this book with their names if I knew them all, and deemed it of the least worth."

And deemed it of the least worth.

The words had stayed in his mind. He'd been enchanted by the tossed-off line, a cavalier dismissal of everything his father lived for.

It was now more than five years since James Mills's death. How he'd struggled to come up with a eulogy, a fitting farewell to this trivial man. It had been an arduous task. He'd been hard-pressed to fill the time. After all, his father had prided himself on never standing out, on never being the first. He liked to tell his children how their forebears hadn't rushed to this country on the *Mayflower*. Instead, they'd waited for reports to filter back. When they finally set sail some ten years later, the risks and rewards had been carefully weighed.

And even then, listening to the story from his father's lips, Carter Mills had thought to himself, *What a fool*.

He'd always known that it was better to be first.

And where better to be first than Manhattan? Even as a child, he'd been drawn to the city. To the noise, the competition, the scent of money. His own inheritance, while useful in its way, had nothing to do with his plans. He saw it as a simple convenience. Like being dealt a good hand at cards.

It was during his second year at Harvard Law that Carter had made the break, informing his father that he'd spend the summer at the law firm founded by Grandpa Si, as Silas Mills was known. James Mills had been nonplussed. He'd fled that world without looking back. The decision, Carter thought, had been a master stroke, playing off his father's reverence for family against his hatred for New York City. In the end, he'd given his blessing, as Carter had known that he would. For all his seeming reverence for tradition, James Mills was as mesmerized by money as the rest of them. The hypocrisy was astounding. Yet another reason to hate his father.

But all that was in the distant past. It was time to get down to work. Turning away from the window, Carter picked up a Mont Blanc pen.

First on the agenda was Bill McCarty. Carter paused for a moment, recalling McCarty's accusations during that astonishing encounter on Monday. McCarty, the dogged workhorse, always docile, always compliant. Who would have thought he had it in him? But the reflection was only fleeting. After all, McCarty didn't really interest him. The only thing that mattered was the source of his information.

Carter sat still for several moments, waiting for the answer to come clear. As he knew that it ultimately would. His mind was reliable that way, moving with the same smooth precision as his car. It was a sensitive issue, with no room for error. After considering several options, he finally settled on a plan. He'd start by confronting Martin Drescher. One-on-one and as soon as possible. A first step toward setting things straight. His mind made up, Mills jotted a note and moved on.

Next on the list: this afternoon's meeting with Holden and Thorpe. A much more enticing prospect. Already, he could feel the adrenaline high, the intimation of a battle to come. He loved that feeling, the sense of impending conflict. A conflict he was destined to win. Not simply because he was right — a relative term, after all — but because he was the best player. Litigation was a sport. And he was one of its champions.

Yes, everything was shaping up beautifully. He'd been worried about Madeleine, annoyed that Chuck Thorpe had insisted on her involvement. But he'd taken care of that now. So why this subtle pressure, something pushing at the back of his mind? It was so faint that he might have ignored it. But that would have been a mistake. His instincts were one of the reasons for his success. Over the years, he'd learned to listen.

So what was it? What issue was demanding attention? The question tossed in his mind. And then the answer emerged.

Kate Paine.

Madeleine's scornful words seemed to echo in his mind.

That associate. Kate. Kate Paine. You hired her, didn't you?

Are you wondering how I knew? Just look at her.

Mills frowned. He could still see Madeleine's face, that damned smile pasted on her mouth. He had no idea what she'd meant. Not that he'd let on at the time.

But now he wanted to know. He tried to picture Kate Paine. Dark hair. Fashionable attire. Pretty. But the image wouldn't come clear.

Just look at her.

What had Madeleine seen when she looked at the younger woman? Mills tapped his pen on the desk, his exasperation rapidly building. He didn't have a clue. Well, to hell with Madeleine.

What could it really matter? Besides, whatever she'd been thinking, she was wrong. He'd requested Kate Paine for this case for the obvious reasons. Because it involved claims of sexual harassment. And, quite simply, he'd needed a woman. Prospective female witnesses needed to see a woman on the team. A tacit reassurance that they were not alone, that they were not betraying their sisters.

And the selection of Kate Paine herself, why that, too, was easy to explain. He'd interviewed her on campus at Harvard, been struck by her energy and drive. It was only natural that he'd chosen to work with her. It all made perfect sense.

It all made perfect sense.

So what had Madeleine been getting at?

⤝⤞

CHUCK Thorpe slammed his hand against the conference table.

"Goddamn it," he said. "What the hell's going on? Don't we pay this law firm enough that she can at least manage to show up? First she stands me up for dinner, and now she can't even make it to a business meeting."

"Now, Chuck." Jed Holden placed a restraining hand on the younger man's arm. "I'm sure there's some good reason." He looked questioningly at Carter Mills.

"Let's give her five more minutes," Mills said calmly. His gray-blue eyes moved from Holden to Thorpe and back again. "This isn't like Madeleine at all. There must be some good explanation."

Kate looked at her watch. It was twenty minutes after one, and repeated calls to Madeleine's office had failed to elicit a response. Kate herself had placed a call ten minutes ago to be sure there wasn't a mix-up. Madeleine's secretary had assured her that the meeting was on her boss's schedule. "We talked about it right before she left for dinner last night," Carmen Rodriguez said.

An undercurrent of tension filled the room. Lowering her gaze to the yellow legal pad in front of her, Kate pretended to flip through notes as she furtively studied the scene. They were six altogether. She and Peyton were seated on Carter Mills's left. With his finely tuned sense of protocol, Peyton had left vacant the seat

immediately next to Mills, allowing for the Samson team to be
seated in descending order of seniority. As senior associate on the
case, he'd be seated next to Madeline, assuming she ever arrived,
with Kate bringing up the tail.

Across the table was the WideWorld contingent. The all-
powerful Jed Holden, WideWorld's CEO, sat directly to Mills's
right. On Holden's right was Chuck Thorpe, a thick fireplug of a
man with powerfully developed upper arms. Completing the party
was Richard Epstein, a thin, dark figure who was WideWorld's top
in-house lawyer.

Kate had been stunned by her first sight of Jed Holden. For all
his vast power, WideWorld's chief executive was nondescript. He
was slightly built, with jutting ears, pale skin, and wispy light
brown hair. Only his piercing gray eyes gave some hint at the un-
derlying strength of will that must have driven his career.

Thorpe, on the other hand, was almost exactly what she'd expected. The heavy body, the perpetual sneer that lingered at the
corners of his mouth — all this conformed to what she'd seen on
TV. He reminded her of a Jack Russell terrier, one of those quivering, densely packed dogs that weighed far more than you'd imagine. It was his eyes that seemed out of place. They gave the
impression of dead things, empty of all expression. Kate couldn't
be sure of their color. They seemed almost translucent, devoid of
any color at all.

With a start, Kate realized that Thorpe knew she'd been watching him. Briefly, their eyes met, and Kate saw his mouth stretch
wider. She quickly looked back at her notepad. Her face was hot.
Then Thorpe was speaking again, irritation suffusing his voice.

"So let's get on with things. We can't just sit here all day."

Kate saw a flicker of displeasure cross Carter Mills's face. She
was somehow reassured by the sight. Mills, she felt sure, did not
like Chuck Thorpe.

"Fine," said Mills. "Let's start with the facts."

"The *facts*," Thorpe exploded. "Who the hell cares about the
facts? The media is out to crucify me."

Mills looked down the table at Thorpe. "Chuck, I know where you're coming from. Believe me, we're with you one hundred percent. But I'm going to need to ask you some questions."

Mills's voice was gentle, soothing. He might have been speaking to a lover. Kate found herself admiring his diplomacy, his capacity to focus on the problem at hand. Michael had been like that, too, possessed of a scientist's capacity for abstraction. She stopped herself short, annoyed at the turn her thoughts had taken.

When Thorpe didn't answer, Mills went on.

"First of all, I'd like to ask you about the plaintiff — Stephanie Friedman." Mills's voice carried a hint of apology for the imposition. "I've got some of the basic information from Mr. Epstein here, but I'd like to get your perspective."

Thorpe exhaled audibly. "Whatever. Okay. What do you want to know?"

"I understand that Friedman was your secretary?" Kate was struck by Mills's offhand use of Stephanie Friedman's last name. It seemed to depersonalize her. Which, she supposed, was the idea. Stephanie Friedman was no longer just a former employee. Having threatened to file a complaint, she'd become the opposing party. As such, she'd given up all claims to sympathy, let alone respect.

"Yup. My assistant."

"How long did she work for you?"

"About five years."

"And she resigned ten months ago?"

"Yeah."

"Any contact with her since then?"

"Nope."

"Good. What sort of work did she do?"

"She did, you know, what assistants do. Typing, filing, phones. That sort of thing."

"Attractive?"

Thorpe snorted. "*She* thinks so."

"She claims" — Mills scanned his notes — "that you regularly demanded that she discuss her sex life with you, and that you re-counted your own . . . assignations."

"*Assignations.* Christ. What century is this? Look, Mr. Mills, I'm sure you're a very fine lawyer, but you don't have the slightest idea how to run my magazine. Did I ask Stephanie who she was fucking? Sure I did. Did I ask her what he did to her? What got her excited? Sure. And did that turn me on? Absolutely.

"But you know why I asked those questions, Mr. Mills? Because that's the sort of magazine I run. It's a sex magazine, Mr. Mills, in case you haven't noticed. Sure we write about politics, culture, all that shit — just because a guy likes to look at tits doesn't mean he's stupid. But the bottom line is sex. I go to my staff for ideas. Stephanie knew what she was getting into when she took the job. What'd she expect, *Good Housekeeping*?"

Kate struggled to keep her mind focused on the facts, to separate her visceral reaction to Chuck Thorpe from the argument he was making.

Mills smiled. If he shared Kate's distaste, it didn't show. "This is actually quite helpful, Chuck — and please, call me Carter. You see, without focusing too much on the law at this point, it's signif-icant that she didn't complain. To prevail in this suit, she'd have to convince a jury that your conduct was unwelcome. But from what you're telling me, she never told you — or anyone else you know of — that she had a problem with it."

"A problem? *Stephanie?* Don't make me laugh. She'd have had a better chance of offending me than I would have of offending her. Compared to Stephanie, I'm a puritan."

"So she had an active sex life?"

"You could say that."

"Do you remember any names?"

"Some guy named Bob, I think. She talked about him a lot. That's really all I remember specifically." There was a tray of past-ries in the middle of the conference table. Thorpe reached for a tiny cheese Danish and tossed it into his mouth.

"If you think of anything else, be sure to tell me," Carter Mills said. "Also — and I'm sure that Richard has gone over this with you — don't speak to anyone about this case. Anyone you talk to could become a witness."

"Got it."

Kate noted that Richard Epstein wasn't saying much. Relations between Samson and in-house attorneys could get thorny at times, with the corporate guys — they were almost always guys — resenting what they perceived as Samson's high-handedness in managing farmed-out cases. Often, the in-house lawyers seemed to see Samson's involvement as an implicit rebuke, an implication that they were not capable of handling complex legal matters on their own. But having dealt with Samson for over a decade, Epstein must have made his peace with the arrangement.

"Friedman claims that you required her to have sexual relations with Ron Fogarty as a condition to keeping her job," Carter Mills continued. "I understand that Fogarty's a friend of yours?"

"That's bullshit," Thorpe said, spitting out the words. "I could hardly keep Stephanie away from Ron. It got to be embarrassing. She was all over the guy every time he came to my office. I said, 'Stephanie, enough's enough. He knows you're interested. We *all* know you're interested. Now you gotta be cool. Let events take their course.' You ask me, that's probably why Stephanie's pulling this shit. To get back at Ron."

Kate tried to suppress her growing aversion, to listen without making judgments. She glanced sidewise at Peyton, whose eyes were on Thorpe, a sympathetic smile affixed to his mouth. No sign of inner conflict there. That's how she wanted to be. That's how she *would* be, purely focused and objective.

"I assume that Fogarty will back this up?" Carter Mills said. "That he rejected Friedman's advances?"

"Absolutely."

Carter Mills again referred to his notes. "Moving on, Friedman claims that you required her to wear sexually provocative outfits, and that you made sexually explicit comments about her appearance."

"I didn't *force* Stephanie to dress the way she dressed. That's just how she came to work. Hell, she would've had a problem if I'd made her dress like a normal secretary. I might have told her that she looked good or something. I really don't remember. Except I *know* that I didn't say what she says I said. She's flattering herself."

"Fine," Mills said. "The next allegations have to do with physical contact. She claims that you fondled her, kissed her."

"Hey, Stephie and I were *friends*, at least I thought that we were. It was just horseplay."

"Did she ever tell you that anything you did bothered her? Ask you to stop?"

"No way."

"I don't suppose the magazine has any formal sexual harassment policy?" Under ordinary circumstances, Kate thought, this would have been among the first questions asked. Here, however, the possibility was so farfetched that she could see why Mills had slipped it in obliquely. Starting out with questions about office policy would only have further alienated Thorpe. Again, she was impressed with Mills's finely calibrated attunement to the human equation. It was, she realized, the ultimate source of his power.

When Thorpe responded with an exasperated shake of his head, Mills moved on without comment.

"Who were her friends at the office?"

"Well, I don't know about *friends*. She had lunch sometimes with Linda Morris and Melissa Lyle."

"And they are?"

"Secretaries. Linda works for Brian Keck, the managing editor. Melissa works for Oliver Leary, the deputy editor. She does overflow work for me, too. Like when there was too much for Stephie to handle."

"Who's doing your secretarial work now?"

"Depends. Some days, I just work with Melissa and Linda. If there's a lot going on, I call in a temp."

Epstein looked alarmed. "Temps? I didn't know that, Chuck. We need to talk about that. We don't need any more potential witnesses than we already have. Especially third-party witnesses we don't control."

Thorpe rolled his eyes. "Sorry, folks. Just trying to run my magazine."

"Actually, Chuck, it's not your magazine," Epstein snapped. "It used to be, but you sold it. Remember? It belongs to WideWorld now. To WideWorld's stockholders."

Holden spun around in his chair, his gray eyes flashing. "Hey Richard, that's no way to talk to Chuck. We'll work this out."

Epstein seemed about to respond but instead returned to his notes.

Mills cut in. "I think the first order of business is to nail potential witnesses to their stories. No point in worrying about whether the accounts are going to change if we go to trial. We'll start by getting affidavits from Friedman's coworkers. From what you've said, Chuck, I assume that they'll be cooperative."

Thorpe nodded.

"In addition to getting witness statements," Mills continued, "we need to get any information that we can about Friedman's personal life. Lovers, drug use, any history or sign of mental illness — that's the sort of information we want. Anything that could show —"

"That she's a little nutty and a little slutty. Right?" Thorpe grinned.

Holden grinned back and winked at Thorpe. Epstein stared at the opposite wall, rhythmically tapping the floor with a black leather shoe.

Mills paused, his lips turned up slightly in a benign smile. "You're going to want to watch it with the wisecracks, Chuck," he said lightly. "You too, Jed."

Jed Holden looked chastened. "Sorry, Carter. You're absolutely right." Thorpe smirked and said nothing.

Epstein looked up. "Gentlemen, I'm sorry to raise an unpleasant issue, but I want to put myself on record.

"I believe that WideWorld and Mr. Thorpe have divergent in-

terests. I think the idea of joint representation under these circumstances is extremely ill-advised. Simply put, I just don't see
how Samson & Mills can effectively represent both Chuck Thorpe
and WideWorld Media."

Holden glared at Epstein. "Richard, we've already discussed
this," he said. The icy tone revealed a fixity of purpose at odds with
his low-key demeanor.

"Yes. And I'm afraid that we disagree." Epstein's voice was flat.

Kate glanced over at Mills, who showed no reaction. It was precisely the point that Madeleine had made on Monday. She waited
for Mills's response. But before he could speak, Thorpe broke in.

"What the hell's wrong with you, Epstein?" Thorpe's voice was
laced with fury. "Don't try to tell me this isn't personal. Every step
of the way, you've —"

"You can think whatever you like, Chuck," Epstein interrupted.
"That's entirely your concern. But I have ethical obligations to this
corporation. Ethical obligations. Not something you'd know a
whole lot about."

"There's not a goddamn thing wrong with that schedule,"
Thorpe shot back. "You didn't ask for a list of every single goddamn stupid threat that any idiot ever made against *Catch*. There
aren't enough trees in the world for *that* list. What you wanted —
and what you got — is a list of pending and foreseeable litigation
with a *material adverse effect* on my income statement. That's what
MAE stands for, in case you've forgotten. *Material adverse effect.* I
had no idea that Stephanie was going to pursue this thing like she
has. Surprised the hell out of me. Still does. To be honest, I
thought it was sort of a joke, just a way to get my attention."

"Well, I guess she got your attention," Epstein said dryly.

Mills intervened. "Jed and I've discussed this," he said, directing
his words to Epstein. "I understand your concerns, but I don't share
them."

So that's that, Kate thought. But why had Madeleine been so
convinced of the truth of what Epstein was saying?

Epstein opened his mouth as if he were about to speak, the clamped it shut. Mills turned to Thorpe.

"Of course, if you want to retain a personal lawyer, Chuck, you're certainly free to do that."

"Whatever." Thorpe yawned. He seemed to have lost interest in the conversation, and his eyes drifted across the table. Kate could feel his gaze slipping over her. Almost reflexively, she crossed her arms. Was she imagining it, or did a triumphant smile flash across Thorpe's face? Before she could be sure, his eyes moved on. The tension seemed to have left his body, as if his anger had played out.

"Now where, oh where, could Miss Madeleine be?" Chuck Thorpe asked the room at large.

꧁꧂

It was almost eleven that night by the time Kate got home. Flipping on an overhead light, she glanced around her apartment. In Manhattan, they called this a "luxury" one-bedroom, though just what the luxury consisted of remained unclear. White stucco ceilings, worn parquet floors, a windowless galley kitchen, and a tiny bathroom. Large sliding windows looked out on an adjacent building. Still, the apartment had its advantages. Simply put, it was clean and safe. After three years in ramshackle Cambridge apartments, Kate had opted for modern convenience over charm. The building had a doorman — pretty much a necessity, given her round-the-clock schedule — and it was less than two blocks from the subway. It was quiet, another New York anomaly. And it was only — *only* — $2,500 a month. Faced with a rental market tighter than at any time since the booming eighties, she'd snapped it up.

She still had some work to do. Dropping her coat and briefcase on the couch, Kate made her way toward the kitchen. Coffee. That was what she needed. She opened the freezer and pulled out some Gold Coast Blend — her favorite Starbucks mix — and dumped it in the Braun coffeemaker. Good thing those machines were built to last. Hers was certainly doing overtime. She was a little hungry, too. Opening the refrigerator door, she gazed inside. Slim pickings. Half a loaf of Zabar's semolina bread purchased God knows when. A hunk of cheddar cheese, its rind chalky with age. A few jars of jam. Pickles, chutney, Dijon mustard, organic peanut butter. She finally settled on peanut butter and saltines, one of her law school mainstays for late-night snacks. She did her best to spread the peanut butter, still stiff from the cold. Then, munching on the crackers, she wandered off to her bedroom for a change of clothes.

The rich smell of brewing coffee drifted in from the kitchen, and Kate felt her spirits lift. Sometimes it really didn't take much. She was rummaging through a dresser drawer, trying to locate her favorite ratty and ultrasoft Harvard Law School sweatshirt, when the telephone rang. *Tara,* she thought immediately. *Damn, I forgot to call her.* But when she picked up the receiver, the voice was male and unfamiliar.

"May I speak to Kate Paine?"

"Speaking." Holding the receiver under her chin, Kate pulled out a pair of tattered black leggings, acquired several years back at the Gap. Just the thing.

"This is Douglas Macauley," the voice said. "I'm a friend of Tara Wilkie's. I think she mentioned me to you. I —"

Kate sat down hard on her bed. "I know who you are," she said, the words sounding more abrupt than she'd intended. After all, it was hardly his fault. But she could *kill* Tara. Could she have made her feelings on the subject any clearer last night?

"I was wondering if you'd like to have dinner Friday night. Maybe go to a movie afterward."

"Listen, I appreciate your calling, but I —" *What? Don't go out on dates since my boyfriend dumped me two years ago?* She felt a renewed burst of annoyance at Tara for putting her in this spot.

"Tara told me that you're really busy," Douglas said. "If Friday isn't good for you, I'm pretty flexible."

"No, no . . . , it's just that —" *I don't go to the movies or eat dinner?*

I'm coming down with Lyme disease? I can already tell from your voice that you're not my type?

"So Friday's okay?" He sounded tentative, as if he didn't quite get what she was saying. Too late, Kate realized that she should have said that she *already had plans*. The fact that she almost never had plans had caused her to overlook this simple all-purpose excuse. And if she tried to wiggle out now, it would sound fake. She decided to cut her losses.

"I guess I could meet you for a movie," she said. "As long as it's after seven." A movie would be all right — three hours tops — hardly any time for conversation and then she'd beg off as soon as it was over — early day tomorrow, not much sleep last night. She'd hardly have to talk with him at all! She congratulated herself on this solution: she'd see a movie and get Tara off her back, all in one easy step.

"Great!" He sounded genuinely pleased. Kate wondered what Tara had told him. "You live on the Upper West Side, right?"

"Right." A jolt of annoyance. Why had Tara told him where she lived?

"Shall I pick you up?"

"Let's just meet at the theater," she said quickly. "Why don't you call me at the office on Friday morning, and we'll figure out the details."

"Fine. So . . . I'll talk to you then. I'm looking forward to it."

"Right. I'll speak to you Friday," Kate said.

After hanging up the phone, she finished getting dressed. The call had been disconcerting, but all in all she'd handled it well, she decided. Maybe this would even convince Tara that she was on the road to a normal social life.

Kate slid on a pair of worn shearling slippers and padded back to the kitchen for coffee, her mind already racing to the legal cases waiting on her desk. Before sitting down, she turned on the television for company. The cheery sit-com voices provided a soothing illusion of companionship. In a few minutes, the news would be on. Outside it had started to rain, a dull pounding against the windows. Sipping her coffee, Kate felt cozy and safe, as if she were a law student again, cramming for the big exam.

A stack of Westlaw cases beside her, she was absorbed in the Supreme Court's decision in *Meritor Savings Bank, FSB v. Vinson* when a familiar name caught her ear. "Madeleine Waters, a partner at the eminent law firm of Samson & Mills —" At first Kate thought she'd misheard. But as she turned her chair to face the twelve-inch television screen — a relic from her student days — she heard the name again. *Madeleine Waters*. An unprepossessing middle-aged man, windblown and impatient, spoke rapidly into a microphone held by a slender young woman in a short red coat, the two figures outlined against a desolate urban landscape. In the background Kate could make out water — the Hudson River, by the looks of it. The man was all business, clearly eager to have done with this frivolous intruder. "The body was identified earlier today," he said curtly, his voice raised to be heard over the din of traffic. "I'm not at liberty to say anything more at this time. We're keeping all our options open, and I'd rather not speculate on any specific possibilities."

"Thank you, Detective," the young woman said, her voice fighting with the wind and street noise. Standing up abruptly, Kate almost knocked over her coffee. She felt a sudden need to walk, to move. She started across her apartment and then turned back toward the television, forcing herself to listen. She tried to focus on the words that continued to flow from the cherry-red lips of the young reporter. "Brutal slaying . . . sure to spread shock waves through New York's legal community . . . one of the few female partners at what is often described as the city's most prominent law firm." The words seemed random, disconnected. *Concentrate*. Instead, Kate found herself incongruously noting that the shade of the reporter's lipstick exactly matched her coat.

As the report wound to a close, the screen filled with a photograph of Madeleine. The picture showed her smiling, triumphant in a royal blue jacket and white blouse. It must have been taken some time back, perhaps at the time of her partnership election. Her hair was straight and much shorter. She looked both older and younger than Kate remembered. While her demeanor was strictly professional, it also hinted at a sort of jaunty optimism entirely absent from the woman she'd briefly known.

The next story flashed on the screen.

Kate found herself rubbing her hands together, as if she were trying to keep warm. Shock, fear, anxiety — the feelings swarmed through her along with a deeper pain that she couldn't name. She had a sudden urge to speak with Justin. Justin. Just the thought of him seemed to bring her emotions down a notch. She picked up the phone with a trembling hand and punched in the familiar number. Justin picked up right away.

"H'llo?" His voice was hazy with sleep.

"Justin, it's me," she blurted. "Madeleine Waters was murdered. They just found the body. It was on TV. My God, I just can't —" Kate could hear the agitation in her voice as the words tumbled out hot and fast.

"Whad . . . Whad're you talking about?"

Struggling to stem the flow of words, Kate tried to recount the facts she'd just heard. A lawyer's recital. Everything she could recall. The mental discipline soothed her, and by the time she finished, her voice had steadied. She was very tired.

"Are . . . you sure?" Justin asked. He still sounded groggy, as if he didn't quite get what she was saying.

"Of course I'm sure, Justin," Kate snapped. "Do you think I'd make up something like this?"

"No, I know. I just . . . I was sleeping." He sounded dumbfounded, as if the act of speech were newly discovered.

"Look, I'm sorry to wake you like this," Kate said. "It's just that I'm so freaked out. And . . . and I thought you'd want to know."

"Madeleine . . . I mean, I worked with her." Justin said. Now there was a subtle change in his voice, as if her words were finally sinking in. "I don't see how this . . . Listen, Kate, can you hold on for a second?"

Kate heard some rustling, the snap of a light. Then Justin was back on the phone, this time sounding almost alert.

"D'you think they could have . . . gotten it *wrong* or something? On TV, I mean?"

She gave it a moment's thought. "I guess it's possible, but it doesn't seem very likely. Do you think they'd go with a story this big if they weren't sure? Besides, they had her picture."

"Oh." Kate could hear Justin's breathing. "How . . . how was she killed?"

"I don't know," Kate said. She felt deflated, as if she'd failed to complete some important assignment. "I'm not sure that they said. Does that seem right? That they wouldn't say anything about it?"

"Don't know. Did they say if there'd been an arrest? Do they know who did it?"

"No. I mean, not so far as I know. It didn't sound that way. The guy on the news — he was some sort of detective, I think — said they were keeping their options open." She shivered. "It sounds like something you'd tell an investment adviser."

There was a beep on Kate's line. Call waiting. "Justin — I've got another call. One second."

It was Peyton Winslow.

"Kate. Have you heard the news?"

"Yes, just a few minutes ago. It's horrible. Listen, Peyton. I'm on another call. Give me a second."

She returned to Justin. "I've got to go. I've got Peyton Winslow on the line."

"Just hang in there." Justin's voice was gentle. "I'll see you to-morrow."

As she clicked back to Peyton, Kate curled up on her couch.

"Kate? I just wanted to be sure you'd heard about Madeleine." In the background she could hear the muffled cadences of the television news mingled with strains of music. Something classical, slow and melodious.

"I can't believe it." The old cliché, but somehow it was all that came to mind.

"I know," Peyton said. His voice was soft, the clipped British intonations less noticeable than usual.

"That's why she wasn't at the meeting today," Kate said. "Why didn't we realize that something might be wrong? Why didn't we do something?"

"There's nothing we could have done, Kate," Peyton's voice remained calm. "She was already dead. It happened sometime last night."

Sometime last night. While she ate dinner with Tara, played chess with Justin. Sometime during those hours — while she was laughing, talking, arguing with her friends — Madeleine Waters had been murdered. Justin was right: it just didn't seem possible.

"How do you know?"

"What?"

"When it happened. How do you know when it happened?"

"It was on the TV news."

"Oh. I didn't hear that part." From the back of the couch, Kate pulled a blanket and wrapped it around her legs. On the one hand, it was a relief to know that there wasn't anything she could have done. There was no reason to feel guilty. On the other, it was appalling to know how powerless they all had been. She would have liked to think that, if they had known, if they had somehow guessed, then Madeleine could have been saved.

"There's no way we could have known," Peyton said, as if reading her thoughts. "This isn't the sort of thing that anyone thinks will happen."

"I . . . I know."

"The next few weeks are going to be rough. It's going to be important to stay focused."

"Focused?" Kate felt as if she must have missed something. Stay focused on what?

Over the phone, Kate could hear Peyton take a deep breath.

"Look, Kate. Until Madeleine's killer is apprehended, her death is going to be the major concern for everyone at the firm. It will be up to us to keep things on track with the Thorpe case. The firm's going to be counting on us. And I'm going to be counting on you."

At that moment, Kate caught on: *His partnership, that's what this was about.* Peyton's instinct for self-promotion took her breath away. No wonder he'd advanced so quickly. Beneath the dry wit, beneath the patrician veneer, was an ambition that never wavered.

"Right," Kate said, careful to keep her tone neutral. She liked Peyton, she really did, but she still found his attitude chilling. Was this what it took to make partner?

Peyton continued, oblivious to her thoughts. "Hard as this is, we have to think about what needs to get done. We can't bring Madeleine back. The greatest tribute we can pay to her memory is to keep doing the firm's work."

Peyton paused for a moment, as if waiting for Kate to respond. When she didn't answer, he moved on. "So . . . how's the memo?"

The memo? A partner had just been killed, and Peyton was asking her about a *memo?* The conversation seemed more and more surreal.

"It's . . . it's fine. I've already pulled most of the cases."

Five minutes later, when Kate finally hung up the phone, she sat for a moment unmoving. Through the windows, she could hear the rain. It was coming down harder now. The news had moved on to sports. Kate grabbed her remote from the coffee table and flipped through the other channels, searching for further word. But there was nothing. A few minutes later, she turned off the television. Then she got up and went to the kitchen, where she dumped out the dregs of her now-lukewarm coffee before rinsing out the mug. All that caffeine had made her jittery. She decided to make some herbal tea.

Standing at the stove, waiting for the water to boil, she tried to imagine Madeleine's final hours. But her mind was blank. Now that she'd begun to absorb the news, she realized how little she knew. How had Madeleine died? Was she shot? Strangled?

Stabbed? The reporter had used the term "brutal murder" — that tabloid journalist's cliché — but what did it mean? Who was responsible? And why? Was Madeleine killed by a stranger, a victim of random violence? Or had there been some personal motive?

As the kettle began to whistle, Kate automatically picked it up and poured the water into her mug, dropping in a mint-chamomile tea bag. A sense of anxiety engulfed her, heavy and inert. She carefully checked the gas. Off. Checked the front door. Locked. Checked the blinds. Down. There was nothing to worry about. She was safe, absolutely secure in this upscale building behind layer upon layer of doormen and locks. Still, she could feel her heart pounding.

Kate forced herself back to her chair, where she stared blankly at the stack of legal opinions on her desk. It felt like hours since she'd left off reading. In fact, it had been less than an hour. Her mind darted from thought to thought. *Andrea.* She should call Andrea to be sure that she knew. She picked up the receiver and dialed. The phone rang once, twice, three times, in Andrea's East Side apartment, before the answering machine engaged. Kate hung up without leaving a message. It was late; maybe Andrea was sleeping. She tried once more, hoping her friend would wake up, but again she got the machine.

If only she had someone to talk to.

She thought about calling Justin back. But what did she have to say? All she really wanted was the sound of a friendly voice, the feeling that she was not alone. She was overcome by a sense of desolation. Suddenly, she missed her parents, missed them with a desperate fervor. The mother she'd loved, the father she'd barely known. With a sigh, she went back to her chair and sat down. She looked at her watch: Ten minutes before midnight. The Supreme Court's *Meritor* case remained folded open, just as she'd left it on her desk.

Placing her mug on a ceramic coaster, Kate began to read.

It was raining, waves of crystal beads hammering against his windows. Inside, he felt safe, content.

He was glad to be alone. There was a lot to think about.

Finally, he could relax, glory in the knowledge of his first success.

Madeleine Waters was dead. Because of him.

He felt a renewed sense of power. For a time, he'd worried about overreaching. Worried that he was foolish to make changes when success was so very close. That was when mistakes were made.

But he was an artist. Artists worked with the materials at hand. Madeleine's appearance had been a stroke of fortune. He'd been right to make use of her. Contemplating his plan, he'd never thought anything was lacking. But he'd been wrong. Without Madeleine, his work would have been incomplete. And now, now it was perfect.

Yet something was nagging at him. In the restaurant last night, Madeleine had said that he was crazy.

Crazy.

A silly word. A child's word.

He'd tried to shrug it off. Just one small word, tossed off in the heat of battle. It was nothing, nothing at all. Silly to let this bother him, to prevent him from enjoying this moment. And even if it were true, what did it really matter? He was, after all, an artist. Artists were often mad. It was part of what made them great. Part of what distinguished them.

Still, the word grated on his mind.

A flash of lightning ripped the sky in two.

Twice, he paced the length of his apartment, trying to calm himself. Then he had a new idea. Crossing the room again, he slid open the door of a large storage closet filled with neatly stacked boxes. He rapidly reviewed the printed labels. The container he needed was second from the top. Standing on a chair, he reached up and pulled it down.

Back on the floor, he used a Swiss Army knife to slice open the sealed top. The box was filled with books. He removed them one by one until he found what he was looking for. *Criminal Law and Its Processes: Cases and Materials.*

He turned to the Index. Insanity. There were more than a dozen entries. But it was the classic definition that he was looking for — the seminal M'Naghten rule. The standard handed down by the House of Lords after the attempted murder of Sir Robert Peel. The genesis of the modern insanity defense.

Again he flipped through the book, until he found the famous case, then scanned it for the definition. There. He'd found it. Neatly underlined in red: "to establish a defence on the ground of insanity, it must be clearly proved that, at the time of the committing of the act, the party accused was labouring under such a defect of reason, from disease of the mind, as not to know the nature and quality of the act he was doing; or, if he did know it, that he did not know he was doing what was wrong."

The language was difficult to follow. He went over it several times, reading the words out loud. So. Had he known the *nature and quality of the act he was doing?*

Certainly.

He had murdered Madeleine Waters. In cold blood. For a purpose of his own.

Under that first definition, he was certainly not insane.

But the second part of the rule required further thought: Had he *known that he was doing wrong?*

He folded his legs beneath him and gazed out the window at the driving rain.

Doing wrong. It all depended on your point of view. Of course, he knew that murder was prohibited by law. But was it wrong? That was a different question. Madeleine's murder had been the crowning touch. A fitting prologue for the plan's unfolding.

No, he could not, did not, believe that it was wrong.

A wave of displeasure passed through him, as if he'd lost an important debate.

But he refused to give in. Impatiently he flipped ahead. There must be something else, an interpretation that would prove him right. Prove that he was no less sane than Madeleine herself had been.

State v. Crenshaw. This was it, the case he'd been looking for. As his eyes passed down the page, he began to smile. He read the words slowly, relishing what they said. It was interesting what had happened here. A man believed his new wife to be unfaithful. And so, during their honeymoon, he'd killed her. Stabbed her twenty-four times. Sitting back on his heels, he tried to imagine the scene. The terrified young wife, watching her husband change from lover to enemy. How much blood there must have been!

As much, perhaps, as when he killed Madeleine Waters. . . .

After a dreamy moment, his eyes moved back to the text. Now this Crenshaw fellow had tried to mount an insanity defense. Had argued that since God condoned the murder of an adulterous wife, he'd had no knowledge of a moral wrong. But the court had refused to accept this logic. Crenshaw had known that murder was barred by law. And that, the court said, was enough.

A much better rule. More in accord with reason, with common sense.

And under the *Crenshaw* rule, he, too, would be considered sane.

Slowly, he felt the tension ease from his neck and back, felt the vertebrae unclench. Of course, he had no intention of being charged, no intention of ever being caught. Still, it was comforting to know. It would be humiliating to be thought crazy. Humiliating and unfair.

Replacing the book in its carton, he stood up and stretched his legs. It was getting late, but he wasn't the least bit tired. Already, he was moving on. To the final act of the drama. The final step in his plan.

January 16. A Saturday. Just ten days from tonight.

For years now, he'd marked this day, created rituals to acknowledge its passing.

But now the time of waiting was over. His fantasies would become real. He was finally taking action.

And the circle would be complete.

Thursday, January 7

DARKNESS everywhere. At first, Kate didn't know where she was. The room was hot and dry. Beneath a weight of bedding, a layer of perspiration drenched her chest. Something was wrong, but what? Then, as she turned her head to one side, everything flooded back.

She was at home, in her New York apartment.

And Madeleine Waters was dead.

Kate lay still for a moment, letting the knowledge sink in. Then she kicked off the blankets and swung her legs to the floor. The fluorescent numbers on her bedside clock read 6:48 A.M. She'd slept about six hours. The alarm was set for 7:30. She turned it off, flipped on a lamp, and clambered out of bed.

The *Times* had already arrived, and Kate quickly scanned its contents. The brief news item about Madeleine was short and to the point. Nothing she didn't already know. She'd have to go to the newsstand. The tabloids would certainly have more.

Kate moved quickly around the apartment, eager to get out the door. No need to make coffee, she'd go by Starbucks after picking up the daily papers. She took a five-minute shower then slipped on a loose gray jersey dress and black tights. A long strand of cultured pearls, a black scarf, and black suede shoes completed the ensemble. It was an outfit she kept on reserve for days when she couldn't deal with the constrictions of a suit. Slightly funky but still suitable for office wear. She clipped her hair back with a black suede-covered barrette — she didn't have the time to wash and dry it — grabbed her red cape and black leather gloves and was out the front door of her apartment.

A bitterly cold day. No snow yet, but a leaden sky loomed overhead. The sidewalks glistened with ice, the residue of last night's downpour. Carefully picking her way, Kate headed for the nearest newsstand, one block over to Broadway and two blocks down to Seventy-ninth Street. The bold-faced headlines jumped out at her from a distance. BEAUTY AND THE BEAST: MEGA-LAWYER FOUND DEAD IN SEX SLAYING. She bought copies of the city's two tabloids and walked quickly toward the Starbucks at Eighty-first Street.

Once inside, she didn't bother to stand in line. Instead, she immediately grabbed a stool at the counter that ran along the store's plate-glass front and spread out the *Daily Press*. The front page featured the same studio portrait of Madeleine that was broadcast on TV. Flipping through the ink-smudged pages, Kate found what she was looking for. The dogged tabloid press had managed to dig up information to supplement the brief report on the late-night news. Had, in fact, managed to interview the unemployed mechanic who had found and reported the body. Madeleine's body. "Worst thing I ever seen in my life," he'd told a reporter. "I could barely tell it was a woman, there was so much blood all over. The lady was stripped naked, with some sort of object — looked like a candle — sticking out from her lower parts. Her face and chest was all cut up. Looked like someone took a cleaver to her."

Kate pressed a hand to her mouth as a wave of nausea passed

through her. Still, she kept reading. Investigators had refused all comment on the eyewitness account. But a criminal psychology expert had been more forthcoming. "From the description, this sounds like the work of a disorganized offender," he concluded. "The insertion of an object into the vaginal cavity, the extreme assault to the face — these are all hallmarks of disorganized killers. This type of less intelligent criminal is most often a young male between the ages of seventeen and twenty-five, an underachiever with no close friends. He's likely to be delusional."

Lifting her eyes, Kate gazed out the window at the well-heeled Manhattanites streaming toward the subway entrance, oblivious to the nightmare underside of city life. Two days ago, Madeleine had been just like them, rushing on to the next appointment, the next meal. And now she was dead. It was a terrifying reminder of what could happen when you started taking safety for granted. Thanks to the city's declining crime rate, Kate gave little thought to the dangers around her. But the fact that murder was rare didn't mean that it never happened. Thinking of her own tendency to jump on the subway regardless of the hour, Kate told herself she'd be more careful. There was no reason to take foolish risks. Yes, that was it, she'd take more taxis. Kate felt her muscles relax. There was something reassuring about the thought.

A practical step she could take to protect herself.

۞

CARTER Mills composed his features in an expression of weighty sorrow as he accepted condolences from Mike Glaser, one of two NYPD detectives now seated in his office. The other was a woman, Hispanic. Her name was Cathy Valencia. As Glaser spoke, Mills's eyes briefly, almost imperceptibly, flickered over Valencia, before shifting to the grandfather clock behind her. It seemed to be running slow. He made a mental note to look up that clock expert he'd read about in the *Times*. Clara would remember the name.

Glaser flipped open a notebook. He appeared to be in his early forties, with thinning brown hair and frank blue eyes. He had one of those disarmingly guileless faces that often hide a keen intelligence. Like a good trial lawyer, he'd use his appearance to effect. Mills knew better than to underestimate him.

"Mr. Mills, like I said before, we're gonna need to get into Ms. Waters's office. The longer you put us off, the harder it is for us to do our job."

Mills concealed his growing annoyance. "We're moving as quickly as possible, Detective. Once we've determined that confidential client information won't be at risk, you'll have full access."

"So when are we talking about?"

"Later today. Sometime this afternoon."

Glaser frowned. Mills could tell he wasn't happy with the delay. But short of going for a warrant, which in itself would take some time, there really wasn't much the detective could do.

"I assume you understand the importance of leaving everything just as it was." Glaser's voice was hard.

"Of course, Detective. You have my word."

"D'you think we could at least get a snapshot of the room? I've got a camera with me."

"I'll get back to you on that, Detective."

Glaser seemed poised for another push, but in the end he let the subject drop. "You got any idea at all who could have done this, Mr. Mills?"

Mills raised his hands for a moment before placing them flat on his desk. "Absolutely not," he said. "This came as a total shock. I can't imagine anyone less likely than Madeleine to be a murder victim. Especially this sort of thing. Horrible. I can only think that it was some terrible stroke of misfortune."

"You worked directly with Ms. Waters?"

"Yes."

"When was the last time you saw her?"

"That would have been Tuesday morning. The day she was killed. She came to my office to discuss a new case. It was a short meeting. Only about twenty minutes. We're both busy people. We pretty much stuck to business."

"Anything unusual about her? Did she seem worried, upset?"

"No, Detective. Believe me, I've thought about it. But there was absolutely no sign that anything was wrong."

"Anyone else at the meeting, or was it just the two of you?"

"We were alone."

Nodding, Glaser settled back in his chair. As if to say they were just getting started. In rapid-fire fashion, the questions resumed. "You got any idea what she did later that day? After she left your office."

"I know she had an eight o'clock dinner downtown. With a client. We had a meeting with him the next day. He complained that she hadn't shown up at the restaurant. That was the first indication that something was wrong. Though at the time, I just assumed that there'd been some sort of misunderstanding. That one of them had gotten the time wrong."

"The client's name?"

"Chuck Thorpe. He runs a magazine."

"I know who he is," Glaser said. "You got a number for him?"

"You can get that from my secretary," Mills said.

"Let's just take care of that now."

Mills hesitated a moment. Beneath the matter-of-fact exchange, a subtle power play was under way, a battle over who would control the flow of information. But this one wasn't worth fighting. Mills buzzed Clara.

After jotting down Thorpe's number, Glaser scanned his notes before moving on with his questions.

"Ms. Waters have a boyfriend that you know of?"

"I don't think there was anyone special. She'd been dating various people. And she'd been spending some time with Thorpe. I don't know where that stood. From time to time, I'd see her with a date at firm functions. The faces changed over the years. I don't recall ever seeing her with someone more than a couple times."

"Any other names come to mind?"

"I'm afraid not."

"What about enemies? Anyone have a grievance against her? We're looking for motive here."

"If you mean someone who would want her dead, I can't imagine. Of course, she'd had her share of run-ins with people over the years. Samson & Mills is an intense place. I'm sure there were associates who felt she worked them too hard or didn't treat them fairly. Predictably, there was some controversy when she was elected partner. There always is. But nothing that would lead to murder."

"Anyone especially upset by that?"

"Well, there's Martin Drescher. Another partner here. He was strongly opposed to Madeleine's election. But that wasn't about Madeleine. It was about me. Martin and I have a long history. He ran against me for managing partner. Madeleine was my protégée. He was trying to get back at me through her."

Glaser scribbled another note. "What about rivalries among Ms. Waters's peers? This place must be pretty competitive."

Mills gave a cool smile. "You could say that. This year, we'll hire over a hundred first-year associates from the best law schools in the country. Of those, only a few — four or five — will still be here in eight years, the point at which they'd be considered for partnership. One or two of them may actually be elected."

"So someone who hung around for that many years and didn't make partner might be pretty upset?"

"Our senior associates are all remarkable lawyers, Detective. Most can write their own tickets when they leave Samson & Mills. They go on to stellar careers."

"But perhaps not the careers they'd have chosen," Glaser said. Without waiting for Mills's response, he went on. "What about the year Ms. Waters became partner? Were some of her colleagues passed over?"

"Of course. Five or six that year, if I recall correctly. A larger than average group. Madeleine was the only one elected."

"I'd like to get those names. We'll also need a list of all the cases Ms. Waters was working on, along with the names of clients and anyone else she worked with."

"Fine." Mills glanced pointedly at his watch, but Glaser didn't take the hint. "Who kept track of Ms. Waters's schedule? She got a secretary?"

"Yes, of course. Carmen. Carmen Rodriguez. She's worked for Madeleine for years."

"We're gonna need to talk to her. We'll also wanna look at Ms. Waters's calendar, Palm Pilot, address books, that sort of thing. Anything that can help us trace her movements, figure out what she was doing, who she was with last night. The secretary in today?"

"I'll see." Mills buzzed Clara in the outside office. "Check and see if Carmen is in yet. Ask her to come to my office."

Mills turned back to Glaser. It was becoming a strain, this keeping up of pretenses. He wondered if his feelings showed. But what did it really matter? They could hardly consider him a suspect. And even if they did, his alibi was ironclad.

"What can you tell us about Ms. Waters's friends? Who would she have confided in if something was on her mind?"

Mills shook his head. "You know, I don't think Madeleine had close friends. Don't get me wrong. She was a marvelous woman. But she didn't really open up to people."

"So you wouldn't necessarily have known if something was bothering her?" Mills could tell Glaser was taking everything in. The woman, too. He'd already forgotten her name. Almost forgotten she was there. Now he sensed her watching him.

"Actually, I believe that I would have. Not that Madeleine would have told me outright. But, you see, I knew her very well. I would have sensed that something was wrong."

Mills waited for a follow-up question. *Listen to the question. Never volunteer information.* It was the first instruction he gave clients preparing for deposition or trial, a basic rule of engagement. But rules were made to be broken. The most important thing was to seem candid. As if he had nothing to hide.

Leaning forward slightly, Mills folded his hands. "I hired Madeleine out of Columbia Law School. That would be ten or twelve years ago now. There weren't many women here then. Not that we're doing as well as we'd like on that score, but it's far bet-ter than in the past."

That last comment was aimed at the woman detective, an effort to reel her in, and Mills shot a quick glance in her direction. But she was taking notes on a steno pad, and he couldn't gauge her re-action. He moved on without missing a beat.

"Anyway, I knew right away that she had what it took. It wasn't just her intelligence, though God knows she had that, it was some-thing more. Madeleine was someone who thrived on extremes. That's the kind of lawyer who does well here."

"And since then?" Glaser asked.

"We worked closely together for a number of years. I guess you'd say I was her mentor. In addition we had a . . . romantic relation-ship that ended some years ago. It ended quite amicably, by mutual consent. We remained friends. In fact, we'd recently started work on a case together."

"I see," said Glaser, his tone noncommittal. "That must have been a little touchy, working together like that. Would have been hard on me, I think. Though what do I know? I've been married going on twenty years."

Glaser's tone was bland, but Mills sensed something beneath the surface. But before he could be sure, Glaser was moving on. "Ms. Waters ever been married?" he asked.

"Yes, once. Years ago, when she first started work here. It didn't last long, though. Maybe a year or two."

"You know the guy's name?"

"I don't remember offhand. He's a photographer. Last I recall, he lived somewhere out on the Island. But that was years ago."

"Why'd they split up?"

Mills smiled. "The demands placed on young associates here are extraordinary," he said. "I'm afraid a lot of early marriages break up as a result. Madeleine didn't talk much about her ex-husband. But from what I understand it was the usual reasons. He wanted her to work less. They fought. Things went downhill from there."

"And you took up with Ms. Waters before or after her divorce?"

"It may have been before the actual divorce. But the marriage was already over."

"Did they stay in touch, Ms. Waters and her ex-husband?"

"No. At least not that I know of."

"You have any idea who Ms. Waters's beneficiaries are? Who stands to inherit?"

"Not offhand," Mills said. "But a copy of her will is probably on file with our Trusts and Estates Department. They generally handle that sort of thing for partners."

There was a buzz on Mills's phone. He punched on the speaker-phone.

"Carmen Rodriguez is here."

Mills gave Glaser an inquiring look.

"Great," Glaser said. "We're ready to talk to her now."

❧

9:03 A.M. Kate huddled over her second cup of sludgy Samson & Mills coffee — the East Coast's answer to Exxon Valdez — punching in Andrea's extension for what felt like the hundredth time. As the phone rang, Kate rested her chin in her hand, and closed her eyes. Andrea was an early riser, usually at her desk by eight. What could be keeping her? The voice mail recording had just engaged — "I'm sorry, the person that you're calling, Andrea Lee, is not available" — when Kate heard footsteps outside her office. The door flew open and Andrea herself appeared, still wrapped in her winter coat.

"Jesus Christ, Kate, did you hear?" Andrea asked breathlessly. Her usual poise was gone. She wore the same expression of disbelieving shock as every other Samson employee Kate had seen that morning.

"*Where have you been?*" Kate asked. She could hear the sharpness in her voice. "I've been trying to call you since last night."

Shaking her head, Andrea collapsed into one of two chairs facing Kate's desk and pulled off her coat. When she spoke, her voice was shaky. "I was feeling a little sick when I got home last night, like I was coming down with something, and I . . . I decided to turn in early. Brent's out of town on business. In Chicago. After I talked to him, I just unplugged the phone. I didn't know a thing until I turned on the radio this morning."

"Some night you picked to go AWOL." As the words emerged, Kate realized that she'd been scared. Scared that the same nameless, faceless menace that had so abruptly ended Madeleine's life had somehow caught up with Andrea, too.

"Has there been any statement from the firm yet?" Andrea asked, her voice subdued. "I haven't been to my office."

Kate picked up a single sheet of paper from her desk. "This was in my box when I got in this morning. A memo from Carter Mills. It doesn't say a whole lot. The firm regrets the tragic death of Madeleine Waters, extends its sympathy to her family. Refer any media inquiries to Carter Mills. Yada, yada, yada."

"Can I see?"

Kate passed her the sheet. Andrea skimmed the memo's two short paragraphs, then handed it back without comment.

"Do they know any of the details?" Andrea asked after a brief hesitation.

Kate looked up at her, surprised. "Didn't you see the morning papers?"

Andrea shook her head. Wordlessly, Kate reached for her briefcase. She pulled out the folded stack of papers and passed them across her desk. As Andrea read the headlines, her eyes widened. "My God," she said softly. "How awful." Moments later she roughly pushed the papers back toward Kate. "I've read enough for now," she said.

The two friends sat for a time in silence.

"I really can't take this in," Andrea said finally. "This just isn't the sort of thing that happens to a lawyer at Samson & Mills. I mean, I guess that sounds stupid. It's not like we have immunity or something. But, somehow, the randomness . . . I feel like I've been living in a dream world."

"How's that?"

"Well . . . ," Andrea seemed to be searching for words. "It's like any time disaster strikes a little too close for comfort — the World Trade Center bombing, someone shot on a subway line that I take all the time — I've always found some way to convince myself that it could never happen to me. I do it almost without thinking. I say to myself, 'Okay, so I take the R train, but I never take it *at that time of day*.' Or, 'So I interviewed with a law firm that has offices in the World Trade Center, but *I never really considered going there*.' See what I mean?"

Kate shrugged uneasily. *I'll just take more taxis. It could never happen to me.* "I think we all do that," she said. "It's sort of a survival mechanism. Who could function if they constantly focused on what could go wrong? It's like flying in planes. You just have to count on the law of averages."

"And you *hate* to fly," Andrea noted wryly.

"True. But I still do it. Maybe that's what separates the clinically paranoid from the rest of us. That we can choose to ignore stuff, to make decisions based on the odds. I guess that's what they call perspective. Or sanity."

"Maybe you're right. Still, something like this . . ." Again, Andrea's voice trailed off.

Kate found her thoughts returning to that final meeting with Madeleine. And then the terrible scene described in the morning's papers.

The phone rang. Kate looked down at the LCD screen, then back to Andrea. "Carter Mills's office," she whispered.

Andrea rose as Kate picked up the receiver. "Talk to you later," Andrea mouthed, gently closing the door behind her.

"Ms. Paine?" Kate recognized Clara Hurley's voice, calm and even, utterly impervious to the events of the past twelve hours. The perfect secretary.

"Speaking."

"Mr. Mills would like to see you."

Kate's heart skipped a beat. "Now?"

"Right away, please. He's waiting."

꧁꧂

CARTER Mills extended his long legs and leaned back in his chair. With one hand he held the phone to his ear. With the other he rubbed his forehead. The gentle rise and fall of his chest was barely detectible beneath his starched white shirt. His suit jacket hung on the back of his chair.

"I've already answered that." From the doorway, Kate could hear the fatigue in Mills's voice. "At this point, there are no suspects that we know of."

There was a pause as Mills listened to the voice at the other end of the receiver. For the first time, Kate noticed deep grooves running between his brows and along the sides of his mouth.

"The firm will be offering a substantial reward for any information leading to an arrest," Mills said. "My partners and I will be discussing the details this afternoon."

Another pause, longer this time.

"There's absolutely no reason to think so," Mills finally said. "If she'd received threats of any type, I'm certain she would have informed us."

After a final brief exchange, Mills hung up the phone and looked up at Kate. "Please," he said, waving her toward the same chair she'd occupied Monday morning. "I was just finishing up with the *Times*."

He didn't say Madeleine's name. He didn't have to.

"I'm so sorry," Kate said. It was hardly an original response, and she worried it might sound unfeeling. But Mills barely seemed to hear her words.

"We were very close," Mills said. His voice was slow and rhythmic, almost as if he were talking to himself. "I was her mentor, you know. I hired her."

"Yes," said Kate. "I know." As she spoke, Kate felt a tightness in her chest. It was a moment before she realized that she was jealous. Jealous of the young woman who had once so captivated Carter Mills. Madeleine Waters was dead. Yet, her strongest emotion was envy. What kind of person was she?

"It's such a waste," Mills said, his eyes meeting Kate's. "Such an incredible tragedy and waste. Madeleine Waters was one of the finest lawyers — and people — ever to enter this firm."

Again, the small stab of jealousy. A wave of shame overtook her. Her father's voice floated back from the distant past. *Everything's not about you, Kate. The world doesn't revolve around you.* She felt a sudden determination to talk back to that voice, to show that she was, after all, capable of sharing someone else's pain.

"I know how you must feel," she said. "I — when my mother died — it was the hardest thing in the world for me. And even then, I had time to prepare. It must be so difficult, everything happening so fast —" She broke off midsentence. Again, she worried that she'd said the wrong thing. Hadn't she hated it when people told her they knew how she felt? When secretly she'd been convinced that no one had ever felt as she did, that no one had ever been so alone? But Mills seemed touched.

"That's right," he said softly. "I remember talking to you about that when you interviewed with me at Harvard."

He continued to look at her, with the gently penetrating gaze that she recalled from their first meeting. He remembered. A slow warmth melted through her body, and she felt inexplicably lighter. *He remembered.*

Mills was nodding reflectively. "When a death happens so suddenly, you don't have time to . . . to say the things you would like to have said. The things that you ought to have said."

Kate had an odd sensation that he was pleading with her, asking for reassurance. "I — I'm sure Madeleine would have understood that," she said.

"Perhaps." For a moment, Mills looked almost wistful. He seemed younger than he had when she walked in. Younger and strangely vulnerable.

Kate felt herself leaning forward. Something in Mills's expression touched her, made her want to do something to prove her concern. "If there's anything that I can do," she began. And then stopped short. Ridiculous. After all, what could she possibly do?

But the words seemed to call Mills back to the present. "That's actually what I needed to speak with you about," he said. His face once again registered a calm authority. Kate could feel herself relax. The brief intimacy had been tantalizing but unsettling.

"I need your help in cataloguing the contents of Madeleine's office. We're under a lot of pressure from the police. This has to be done by tonight. I've dictated the protocol. You can get it from Clara. Talk to me if you have any questions."

Kate sat for a moment, stunned, her mind rapidly outlining the parameters of her task.

"Kate?" Mills's voice was peremptory. He was waiting for her response.

Kate quickly looked up. "I'll get started right away," she said.

In a world of open doors and soft voices, the door to Madeleine's office suite was shut tight, a tacit announcement that something unusual had occurred within. Not that this was likely to come as news to anyone passing by. Kate knocked three times, her knuckles dully reverberating against the solid wood.

She heard a rustling inside, and then Carmen Rodriguez cracked open the door. Kate could see that Madeleine's former secretary was not having an easy time. Carmen's dark eyes were red, and her vivid makeup had a slapdash look. Instead of her usual bright suit, Carmen wore blue jeans and a yellow shirt. Her dark brown hair was held back in a yellow scarf.

"Oh, hi," she said flatly, opening the door to let Kate pass.

Inside, Carmen had already begun packing up the contents of the built-in cabinets lining Madeleine's reception area. Several large cartons were piled full of folders. Nearby a stack of collapsed boxes stood ready to be constructed. The tinny sound of soft rock clattered from a radio somewhere.

"These are just old client files that I had in my drawers." Carmen sounded defensive, as if she expected to be challenged. "Carter told me to go ahead and pack them up. I'm keeping a list. I haven't touched anything in Madeleine's office."

Kate nodded, searching her mind for something to say. Not only had Carmen's boss been killed, but she would also have to be reassigned, which meant dealing with Samson's notoriously inept support staff bureaucracy, a division that often seemed to take sadistic pleasure in incompatible pairings.

"This must be really hard on you," Kate said. "How long had you worked for Madeleine?"

"Five years." Carmen looked down. Kate could tell that she was trying not to cry. Even the support staff at Samson knew that tears were a sign of weakness.

"Do you know where you'll go now?"

Carmen's eyes flashed. "I'm getting the hell out of this place," she said, her voice cracking with emotion. "Now that I've seen how they treat people . . . I never would have believed it. Everyone thinks that Samson & Mills is such a fine place. Well, they can *have* it. I've got a friend at Paul Weiss. She thinks she can get me a job there. And even if she can't, I'm not hanging around. I'll move in with my mother if I have to." Her tirade ended, Carmen turned back to the boxes. The look of weary defeat returned to her face. "It doesn't matter anymore," she said. "I gave notice first thing this morning."

Kate watched Carmen pack, her movements sharp and birdlike. The reception area was quickly assuming the impersonal air of places that no longer belong to anyone in particular. In the background, Kate was vaguely aware of the radio, of the Supremes singing about how you can't hurry love. But she was still focused on Carmen's words.

"I don't understand," Kate said finally. "What are you talking about?"

"Chuck Thorpe," Carmen said.

Kate looked at her, surprised. "What about Chuck Thorpe?" she asked.

Carmen placed her hands on her hips. Her eyes, almost black in the harsh office light, seemed to send off sparks. "They used her," Carmen said. "She couldn't stand the man. But he wouldn't take no for an answer. Not that anyone cared. All *they* cared about was money. Using her to keep him happy. Made her have dinner with him and God knows what else. Disgusting. Finally, she stood up for herself. And look what happened."

"You think Thorpe had something to do with the murder?"

Before Kate could think, the words were out. Carmen's head snapped back to the file in her hand, her face gone blank as a plate. Kate knew at once she'd moved too fast. The question had reminded Carmen of what was at stake if she spoke her mind. Samson employee or not, she could hardly take on WideWorld Media.

"I'm not saying *anything*." Carmen's voice had turned sullen. "Look, if you have any questions about the files, I'll be back in about an hour. I've got some errands to run. Just be sure that no one else gets into Madeleine's office, okay?"

Kate chewed on a thumbnail and looked around. Madeleine's office was perfectly still, illumined by a clear winter light. The polished top of her desk was almost empty. Just a phone, a small lamp, and a recent issue of *American Law*. Her leather chair was pushed back slightly, as if she'd just left the room. Kate found herself thinking of a painting she'd studied in a college art history class. *Still Life with Lemon Peel*. A bright yellow fruit nestled in a clutter of silver and crystal, its peeled skin scrolling off the table's edge. You had a sense of something interrupted, as if a diner had been called away. Her professor had called this painting a *vanitas*, a reflection on the transience of life.

From Madeleine's desk, Kate's eyes drifted to the wall behind it, to the photograph she'd noticed Tuesday morning. A seascape. She could see why Madeleine loved this picture. There was something mesmerizing, transporting about it. The surf slamming hard against the shoreline. The impervious rocky coast. The photo seemed to suggest a contest of wills, a contest with a far-from-certain outcome. Madeleine had said the picture was taken by a friend. Was it a place from her past, somewhere she'd once spent time? Or was she, like Kate, simply drawn to the image itself?

Pulling her gaze from the picture, Kate walked over to Madeleine's desk. After a moment of hesitation, she sat down. Madeleine's chair was larger than her own, larger and softer, with a buttery leather cushion. The simple act of sitting there filled Kate with a vague unease. She felt strangely exposed, as if she were taking some sort of unwarranted risk. As if at any moment Madeleine might appear, demanding an explanation.

What are you doing in my office?

But time was flying by. Kate tried to forget about Madeleine's murder, about the facts that had brought her here. Gingerly, she reached for the handle on the top drawer of Madeleine's desk. An irrational anxiety coursed through her, as if she were an actress in some B-grade movie, in search of a terrible secret. But there was just the usual assortment of paper clips, pens, and rubber bands, all neatly arranged in a plastic tray.

What Carter Mills wanted was pretty straightforward: a list and description of office contents. Jennifer could type up her notes at the end of the day, and the list would be on Carter's desk by morning. Kate closed the top drawer and moved on to a much larger drawer on the desk's left-hand side. As she'd expected, it was stuffed with folders. Gathering up the first bunch — fifteen or twenty files — Kate heaved them off the hanging metal rods and placed them on top of the desk. On a yellow legal pad, she began to jot down captions from the labels. The first few folders contained general firm materials: interoffice memoranda, time sheets, general correspondence. Then came a file labeled Investments. Madeleine's personal records. Kate felt a twinge of curiosity. Nothing to do with the murder. Still, she couldn't seem to stop herself. *It's really none of your business.* But she'd already opened the file.

The top page was a summary from a brokerage house statement. Kate's eyes scanned the sheet, looking for the bottom line. Three million dollars. And that was just in this account. Kate wasn't really surprised by the amount. It went without saying that Samson partners were wealthy. And three million dollars was hardly what it used to be, not in an era when young investment bankers were bringing home more than a million bucks a year. But there was something arresting about seeing the figure in black and white. Three million dollars was still a lot of money.

Staring at the figure, Kate felt a wave of desolation. All that effort, all that stockpiling, and for what?

Vanitas, vanitas . . .

What had Madeleine planned to do with her savings? From the firm directory, Kate recalled Madeleine's Park Avenue address. She must already own an apartment. Had she perhaps planned to retire early? To collect art or antiques? To engage in some sort of philanthropy? Or maybe it was simply a nest egg, put aside for a future she had yet to plan. For a future she'd never have.

Chewing at her thumbnail, Kate felt a glint of pain. Looking down, she saw that the nail was ragged, bitten down to the quick. She stared at it in surprise and then examined her other fingers. Without even realizing it, she'd gone back to biting her nails. She hadn't done that for years, not since that last year in law school. When had she started again?

Kate's eyes lingered on her right hand. On her forefinger, below the bitten nail, she wore a small ruby-and-pearl ring set in gold. A gift from her mother on her sixteenth birthday. Her mother. That must be part of what had her so distraught. Strange she hadn't made the connection until now. Of course, it was different, death from natural causes versus murder. But at the time, she hadn't seen it that way. The cancer had seemed to her a murderer of sorts, every bit as evil, as bent on destruction, as any human killer could be.

It was more than five years since her mother's death, but Kate knew she hadn't come to terms with it yet. It had happened in July, the summer before her senior year at Barnard. At the time, she'd just tried to keep busy. Funeral arrangements. Then selling the house. Once that was over, she was back in college. It was then she'd decided on law school. Next came Harvard and Michael and Samson & Mills. Plenty to keep her occupied.

Kate's eyes returned to Madeleine's brokerage statement. The orderly records seemed an implicit rebuke. Kate thought of her own haphazard files, a clutter of unopened correspondence. Once a month, she received statements from the investment firm that handled her mother's estate. Once a month, she dumped them, unopened, in a drawer. She couldn't face them just yet, these monthly reminders of her mother's death.

Kate closed the file and pushed it aside. She reached for another folder, then stopped, dropping her hand back to her lap. While she couldn't quite articulate the reasons, something about her position here was making her uncomfortable. What was she doing in Madeleine's office, rifling through her papers? Madeleine had never consented to her presence. And yet, here she was, privy to the most intimate details of the dead woman's affairs.

The more she thought about it, the stranger it seemed. What had Carter Mills been thinking when he delegated this task to her? He obviously thought she could be trusted, and she was grateful for this confidence. Still, there was a nagging uneasiness. Was she really the proper person for this role? And beyond that, what about the murder investigation? Should anyone be here before the police had taken stock? Carter had told her to leave everything as she found it. And the office wasn't the crime scene. It was just where Madeleine had worked. Still . . .

Glancing at her watch, Kate saw that it was already eleven-thirty. As she turned to gauge her progress, her eyes encountered a small, flat object lying at the bottom of the drawer, in the space from which she'd taken the files. She peered closer to see what it was, then picked it up. An unlabeled cassette tape. It must have fallen from one of the folders that she'd removed. *Damn.* She needed to be more careful. Maybe if she listened to the tape, she'd be able to figure out where it belonged. She stuffed the cassette into her purse, along with Madeleine's black leather Filofax. These smaller items she could take back to her office for review. No point in hanging out in Madeleine's office any longer than she had to.

Kate was moving on to the next file when the door swung open. Her head snapped up and she was face to face with Martin Drescher.

Drescher stared at her incredulously, his eyes bulging froglike from beneath bushy brows. "What are you doing here?"

Kate tried to stay calm. After all, she had every right to be here. She was simply following instructions.

"Carter Mills asked me to prepare a summary of Madeleine's files," she said, gratified to find that her voice held steady.

Drescher's face had taken on the same orange-redness as his hair. Even from across the room, Kate could smell stale tobacco mingled with a fetid sweetness. Breath mints, perhaps?

"Let me make myself clear, Ms. Paine. I want you to get the hell out of this office."

Kate hesitated. She'd worked for Drescher, knew how quickly his anger could escalate. But Mills was counting on her to get this job done.

"Maybe I should at least call Carter," she said, glancing toward the phone on Madeleine's desk.

"Ms. Paine, I *said* I'd take care of it," Drescher bellowed. "Have I —"

"Yes, of course," Kate said quickly. She picked up her purse and legal pad from Madeleine's desk. "I'm sorry if I've done something wrong," she said, in a last-ditch attempt to salvage what remained of the encounter.

Drescher gazed stonily ahead. If he heard Kate, he did not let on.

As Kate headed toward the door, she heard a rustle of papers. Glancing back, she saw that Martin Drescher was already absorbed, flipping rapidly through the files on Madeleine Waters's desk.

❧

BACK in her office, Kate immediately picked up the phone and called Carter Mills. Clara picked up. "He's not in, Kate. Is there anything I can do?"

"I . . . if you can just tell him I called. Do you know when he'll be back?"

"He didn't say. I'd guess within the hour, though. I don't see anything on his calendar."

Kate hung up. Where should she go from here? When in doubt, make a list. Reaching in her purse for a pen, her fingers closed on an unfamiliar object. She pulled it out, to see what it was.

The cassette tape from Madeleine's desk.

And with it, Madeleine's date book.

Kate bit her lip. In her haste to get out of Madeleine's office, she'd forgotten about the objects she'd pocketed for later review. *It is critical to the investigation that you leave everything just as you found it.* That's what Mills's protocol said. She considered returning the objects now, before they could be missed. But that wouldn't work. Drescher was probably still there. She'd have to wait. If she was lucky, she could get Carmen to slip the items back into Madeleine's desk before anyone knew they were gone. Until then, she might as well see what she had. If Mills countered Martin Drescher's directive, she'd have to make up for the lost time.

Kate opened the cover of Madeleine's Filofax. The first section of the book contained a calendar of the week-at-a-glance variety. Three days on one page, four on the adjacent leaf, with Saturday and Sunday squished into a single tiny block. Madeleine had already swapped out last year's pages. The calendar seemed to be devoted to private matters. Madeleine must have used this book as a personal reminder, a supplement to some more comprehensive calendar that she probably kept on her office PC.

Kate scanned the few entries before Madeleine's death, noted in a small, precise hand. A haircut at Louis Licari. An alumni event at Columbia. An appointment with a personal trainer from the Madison Square Club. Then she came to January 5, the day Madeleine was killed. A single penciled notation. Dinner with Chuck Thorpe. Ormond. 8 P.M. Kate stared at the entry as Thorpe's face rose up in her mind. She recalled the smile he'd flashed her across the conference table, rife with animal cunning. She thought of Carmen Rodriguez's bitter words. *Made her have dinner with him and God knows what else.* Was it just a coincidence that Madeleine had dinner plans with Thorpe on the same night that she was killed? On Wednesday, Thorpe had seemed truly angry, furious that he'd been stood up. But could the whole thing have been an act?

Kate examined another few pages. Appointments that Madeleine would never keep. She found herself thinking about a childhood friend. Julia, that was her name, had come up with the concept of a death day. "Just like each year you have a birthday. Each year, there's the day that someday you'll die. You just don't know what that day is." That was back in the fifth grade. But the idea had exerted a morbid fascination, and Kate had never forgotten it.

The notations for the days after Madeleine's death were few and far between. On January 24, she'd planned to have dinner with SH. Kate paused for a moment, but the initials didn't strike a bell. On the following Thursday, she'd scheduled dinner with MD. Martin Drescher? Turning back, Kate glanced at the days preceding Madeleine's death. Two dinners with MD, within a few days of each other.

A sharp knock on the half-open office door. Before Kate could respond, Carmen Rodriguez stormed into the room. From her rapid breathing, Kate could tell that Carmen was upset.

"Martin Drescher was in Madeleine's office when I got back." Carmen glared at Kate.

Kate raised her hands, in a show of helplessness. "Look, I'm really sorry, but he just kicked me out. There wasn't anything I could do. When I talk to Carter, I'll tell him it wasn't your fault."

Carmen's features relaxed slightly. "When he left, he took a file," she said, her voice calmer than at first. "I tried to stop him. I told him that Carter wanted everything accounted for. Everything left like it was. But he ignored me. He wouldn't even tell me what he took."

"Oh, great." Kate rubbed her forehead. She could really use a massage. Then, looking back at Carmen, she tried to muster a smile. "Thanks for telling me. I'll definitely let Carter know."

"Okay, then." Carmen left the room.

Kate looked back at the book on her desk. She quickly flipped through the address portion of the date book — entirely free of entries — and then the memo and budget sections. Again, nothing. Her review complete, Kate snapped closed the leather flap and stowed the book in the top right-hand drawer of her desk.

Next came the cassette. Because the tape was unlabeled, she couldn't tell which side was first. Kate turned to a portable tape player on the window ledge behind her desk. She opened the cassette compartment, flipped out a Cranberries tape, and snapped in Madeleine's tape. Then she pressed Play.

She'd just begun an ineffectual search for the case belonging to the Cranberries cassette — why were those little plastic boxes so hard to keep track of? — when a male voice broke the room's silence. Turning up the sound she could just make out the muffled end of a sentence, "— good time." Then a woman's voice, still fainter and hard to understand. Kate caught the words "end of my rope" and "can't make me" — the last phrase uttered in a defiant tone. And then the male voice again: "You think Ron can't get any girl he wants? You should be flattered."

With a start, Kate realized that the male voice belonged to Chuck Thorpe. She lowered her ear closer to the cassette player. The woman's response was incomprehensible, though there was no mistaking her agitation. The next words that Kate could make out were Thorpe's. "I'm counting on you, baby. If you get my drift." This pronouncement was followed by footsteps and the sound of a slamming door. A moment later, Kate heard a muffled click. Then she was left with dead air.

She listened for a few moments more before fast forwarding to see if the recording resumed. There didn't seem to be anything more. Kate turned off the recorder. What she seemed to have stumbled on was a recording of Chuck Thorpe putting the screws on someone. Could it be Madeleine? But even with the fuzziness of the recording, she'd detected a nasal twang to the woman's voice, nothing like Madeleine's uninflected speech. Besides, Kate simply couldn't imagine Madeleine subjecting herself to this sort of abuse.

No, it must be someone vulnerable to Thorpe, someone over whom he exercised power.

Kate rewound the tape and played it back. *You think Ron can't get any girl he wants? You should be flattered.* Ron. She recognized the name from the draft complaint. Ron Fogarty. The music executive who had figured in Friedman's allegations. Essentially, she'd claimed that Thorpe had acted as Fogarty's pimp, coercing female employees to have sex with him. Could the woman on the tape be Stephanie Friedman? Or one of the other women?

It seemed to fit.

Revulsion flooded over Kate, and she had to struggle to stay clearheaded. "You're a lawyer," she told herself. "*Lawyers defend their clients.*" Besides, she didn't know anything for sure yet.

Only one thing was clear: if the recording was what it sounded like, it could be disastrous to Thorpe's defense. Within weeks, Stephanie Friedman's lawyers would be starting discovery. If this cassette fell within the scope of their requests — as it undoubtedly would — the Federal Rules of Civil Procedure would require that Samson hand it over. No one would relish the prospect of trial with this sort of ammunition in an opponent's hands.

Where in the hell was Carter Mills?

As if on cue, the telephone rang. Kate grabbed the receiver but instead of Mills's sonorous tones, she heard a woman's unfamiliar voice.

"Ms. Paine? I'm Cathy Valencia, a detective with the New York Police Department. I'm calling about our investigation of Madeleine Waters's death. I understand that you were working with Ms. Waters at the time she died."

"I . . . I'd just started."

"Right. I have a few questions for you. Would now be a convenient time?"

Kate froze. She'd expected this moment to come, but she'd assumed she'd have time to prepare. To plan what she wanted to say.

"Ms. Paine?"

"Yes." Kate was thinking quickly. "I'm not sure that now is such a good time. I'm in the middle of —"

"It won't take long," Valencia said smoothly.

"Well . . . , okay." Kate didn't know what else to say.

"Thank you, Ms. Paine. I'll be right on up."

Kate ejected the cassette and stuck it in her desk along with Madeleine's Filofax. Closing the drawer, she heard a knock. "Come in," she called. The door swung open.

Looking up, Kate saw two people. One, an athletically built Hispanic woman, she assumed to be Detective Valencia. The other was Dave Bosch, one of Samson's newest litigation partners. Bosch, a wiry figure in his mid-thirties, had done a two-year stint in the U.S. Attorney's office before returning to Samson & Mills.

"I don't think we've been formally introduced," Bosch said, extending a thin, dry hand. "I'm Dave Bosch. And this" — he gestured to the woman beside him — "is Cathy Valencia. Detective Valencia is with the police department. She'd like to ask you a few questions about Madeleine Waters."

"Of course," Kate said. As Valencia reached out her hand, Kate glimpsed the policewoman's neat manicure, nails filed square and coated in a clear polish. Kate felt a twinge of embarrassment at her own bitten nails and quickly released the handshake.

Valencia was simply dressed in a navy blue pants suit with brass buttons. She had an attractive face, with clear olive skin, wide-set brown eyes, and a generous mouth. Her thick dark hair was pulled back with a clip. She had an air of confident directness.

"Shall we sit down?" Bosch said.

Kate returned to her desk, while Bosch and Valencia settled into the two chairs facing her. While Bosch's presence had caught Kate off guard, it wasn't hard to figure out why he was here. The last thing the firm's partners wanted was to have employees privately venting grievances and crackpot theories to the NYPD. And while ultimately no one could stop them, a partner's presence could be a strong deterrent, reminding them who signed their paychecks.

"I won't take too much of your time," Valencia said. She pulled a steno pad from the outside compartment of a brown leather purse and quickly elicited the basics — Kate's address, phone numbers, length of employment — before moving on to the subject of Madeleine.

"I understand that you had a meeting with Ms. Waters the day she was killed. Can you describe that meeting for me?"

Kate paused, wondering how forthcoming she should be. She thought of the cassette tape and date book now stashed in her desk. She was in an awkward position, having removed these items despite Mills's instructions to leave everything just as it was. Besides, did Valencia even know that she'd been asked to catalogue Madeleine's office? Did she know about Madeleine's aborted date with Chuck Thorpe? And if not, was she the one to raise these points? In the end, Kate decided to answer only the questions that were asked. She could always elaborate later.

"The meeting concerned a case I'd just been assigned to," Kate began. "Madeleine wanted to talk to me about a research project. Basically, I just updated her on how it was going. She . . . she gave me a book to read, something to do with the case. We didn't meet very long. She had to cut it short. The managing partner called and needed to see her."

"That would be Carter Mills?"

"Yes."

Valencia jotted a note. "Did anything strike you as unusual? Did Ms. Waters seem upset or out of sorts at all?"

Memories flowed through Kate's mind: Madeleine and Carter's sharp words the previous day over the conflict-of-interest issue.

And then on Tuesday, Madeleine's glittering eyes, the strange warning spoken just before her death. *You need to be very careful.* But she needed to keep her feet on the ground, to be ruled by reason not emotion. Unsettling as these exchanges were, she had no logical reason to think they were linked to Madeleine's murder.

"She seemed fine," Kate said carefully. "I mean, I'd never met with her before, so I can't make any comparisons. But from what I could tell, everything was fine."

"Did she seem at all anxious, upset?"

"Not that I noticed. Maybe a little tired, but that's all I remember."

"Is there anything that you've seen or heard that you think could be related to Ms. Waters's murder? Anything that might give us some insight into who might have wanted her dead?"

Fleetingly, Kate thought of the hours she'd just spent in Madeleine's office. Of the calendar entry showing Madeleine's planned dinner with Chuck Thorpe. Of Drescher's impassioned search of Madeleine's desk. She could feel David Bosch watching her.

"No," Kate said. "Nothing at all."

"Is there anything you think I should know? Anything I haven't touched on that you think might be important?"

Kate shook her head, careful not to betray her uneasiness. Was she wrong not to mention the issues on her mind? Right now, she couldn't be sure.

"Is it necessarily someone she knew?" Kate said. "I'd been assuming it must have been random."

Valencia sidestepped the question. "We have to consider all the possibilities," she said.

Then the policewoman was closing her notebook and stuffing it back into her purse. When she stood up Kate noticed that her navy pants were free of wrinkles. Reaching across Kate's desk, Valencia handed her a card. "Here's where you can reach me," she said. "In case you think of anything else."

⁂

PICKING up her fork, Cathy Valencia surveyed her large salad: iceberg lettuce, hard wedges of pale pink tomato, a few strips of green pepper. A squeeze of lemon in place of dressing. Across the table, Mike Glaser was wolfing down a platter of spaghetti and meatballs.

"That the family size?" Valencia asked. They were seated in a booth at the bustling Friendly Diner. Just two blocks from Samson & Mills, it felt like a different world.

Glaser gave his bark of a laugh. "Hey, nobody's making you starve yourself. Get yourself a real lunch. How you gonna get through the afternoon on that rabbit food?"

He had a point. The morning had been hectic, and the rest of the day was shaping up to be at least as crazy. But that couldn't stop Glaser from enjoying his lunch. This was a man who liked food. Not that it showed. Glaser could eat anything in sight without gaining an ounce. His moonlike face was deceptive; from the neck down he had the body of a twenty-five-year-old. Valencia bet he didn't weigh a pound more than he had some twenty years back, when he got out of the Police Academy. She, however, had only to look at a piece of pastry in order to gain five pounds. Come to think of it, she'd probably put on at least that much just watching Glaser eat today.

Valencia's eyes followed Glaser's movements as he spooled up another forkful of pasta. A veteran detective with the Manhattan South Homicide Task Force, Glaser was the best investigator she'd encountered in her two-plus years as a homicide detective in the thirteenth precinct. They'd worked together once before on a contract killing. At first, Glaser had struck Valencia as a traditional guy, someone who'd question whether women should be cops at all, let alone homicide detectives. But she'd been wrong. With five daughters and an outspoken working wife, Glaser was more of a feminist than she was. She'd been amazed at how well their styles meshed. When she'd been assigned to the Waters case, Valencia had immediately called Manhattan South to ask for Glaser's assistance.

Glaser looked up from his plate. "So where do we stand?" he asked.

"Pretty much where we did when we split up this morning."

Early in the day, there'd been a brief surge of exhilaration. From Waters's secretary — who, Valencia wryly thought, was the only other dark-skinned person she'd seen all day — they'd learned about a male caller who'd rescheduled Waters's date with Chuck Thorpe. It had been a huge break, evidence that the murder had been planned by someone with access to Waters's schedule. But from there the trail had cooled. The call had come from a stolen cell phone whose owner, one Mr. Philip Schneider, came complete with an alibi. Except for what he'd seen on the news, he'd never heard of Madeleine Waters. Of course, they'd follow up on the lead. But Valencia wasn't holding her breath.

So far, what they knew was this: Waters had been picked up by her car service at six-thirty sharp. About twenty-five minutes later, she'd been deposited at Ormond. Valencia had spoken to the restaurant's maître d', who recognized Madeleine from a snapshot. "Great-looking woman," he said. "Was she some sort of a model?" Yet hard as Valencia pressed, he couldn't add anything more. He didn't remember if Waters had been alone or if there'd been some-one waiting to meet her. He did confirm that there were two separate reservations in the name of Thorpe, the first for a C. Thorpe at seven, the second for a Chuck Thorpe at eight. Both reservations were for two.

The waitress who'd handled the seven o'clock table was equally vague in her responses. "It was real busy that night, you know?" She did remember a couple who'd left around seven, shortly after arriving. The woman had been sick, she thought. But that was all she could offer. Looking at a snapshot of Madeleine, she wasn't even sure that this was the woman she'd seen. And she could give no description at all of the man. "Could this be the guy?" Valencia asked, showing her a picture of Chuck Thorpe. The waitress had stared at it, undecided. "Maybe," she said. "He does look familiar.

But I really couldn't be sure." Valencia had put in calls to other diners who'd been seated in the vicinity that night, but she wasn't too optimistic. In her experience, fashionable New Yorkers had little interest in anyone of noncelebrity status. Other than themselves, that is.

While she'd been busy at Ormond, Glaser had met up with Thorpe. Valencia had half-hoped that Thorpe might prove to be a viable suspect. She'd had a preexisting dislike for the man, based on what she'd heard on the news. But Thorpe had been at a staff meeting until quarter of eight, throwing a screaming fit. That didn't rule him out, of course. He could have hired someone to do the job. Still, her instincts told her that they hadn't yet found the culprit.

"So what next?" Valencia said.

"That's not really up to us, is it?" There was an edge to Glaser's voice. He was ticked off that they hadn't gotten access to the victim's office yet.

"We'll get in tomorrow," Valencia said. "Mills said they need to go through her papers. They have to think about clients and all." It was a pattern they'd fallen into, one of them assuming a low-key posture when the other was blowing off steam.

"Yeah, well maybe they should think about the fact that a woman is dead. Maybe they should give that some thought."

"It's not worth the hassle, getting a warrant." Valencia pushed away her half-eaten salad. She'd have a candy bar this afternoon for sure. "Why get them all riled up? Besides, whatever they want to do to that office, they've already had time to do it."

"Yeah, I guess you're right," Glaser said.

"We told them to leave everything in place, just as she left it. That's really all we can do."

"Yeah," Glaser said again. He glanced wistfully at his empty plate as if looking for another meatball.

"I didn't get much from that associate I talked to after you left," Valencia said. "She was one of the last people at the firm to see the vic. But she said it was all just business. Nothing unusual."

"They still got that Bosch jerk following you around?"

"What do you think?"

Glaser shook his head. "Piece of work, that guy. Think he works at being a prick or was he born like that?"

Valencia ignored the comment. "I gave her my card. In case she wants to talk to me alone."

"Yeah, I'm sure she'll be burning up the phone lines." Glaser's voice was heavily sarcastic. "Still nothing from the lab?"

"I checked back with Bartlett this afternoon," Valencia said. "They just don't have much to work with. No semen at the scene. No blood except for the vic's. No saliva. Nothing useful from the swabs and smears. Whoever he was, he cleaned up good."

"So we're still pretty much at ground zero."

"I've got more interviews lined up for this afternoon. Some of the other lawyers she worked with. How about you? Any word on the ex-husband?"

"Tracked him down this morning. His name's Sam Howell. Lives in Sag Harbor. He was having dinner with friends in Bridge-hampton the night she was killed."

"The alibi checks out?" Valencia asked.

"For what that's worth."

"How did he describe the relationship?"

"Says Mills broke up the marriage. After that he and Madeleine didn't talk for years. But they'd recently gotten back in touch. She wrote him a letter last month. He's sending us a copy by overnight mail. Claims it shows she was scared of Mills."

"Scared? Of Mills?" Valencia was suddenly alert.

Glaser shook his head. "It just doesn't sit right with me. The job was too messy for someone like Mills. And think about it. Howell was jilted. Mills stole the woman he loved. How rational d'you expect him to be?"

"But we're getting the letter?"

"We're getting the letter." Glaser stretched back, arching his arms overhead and then sat up again. "You ask me, I think we should focus on the law firm. Clients, partners, anyone she worked with. Hell, they're the only ones who saw her enough to get pissed off. You saw her apartment. It was like a hotel suite. Immaculate. Nothing in the refrigerator."

Valencia rubbed her upper lip. She noticed the beginnings of a hangnail and made a mental note to trim it once she got home. She found herself thinking about the sleek young woman she'd interviewed right before lunch. Kate Paine, that was her name. Elegant clothes, luxurious office, and yet Valencia had sensed a certain sadness.

"I feel sort of sorry for the lawyers over there. The young ones, I mean," Valencia said.

Glaser shot her a strange look. "Sorry for them? What are you talking about? I'll bet those kids make double what we do. Maybe more. And right after they leave school. They get to a place like that, they've got it made. No one's forcing them to work there. You want the big bucks, you gotta put in the hours. That's the trade-off."

Valencia picked up a fork and toyed with the remains of her salad. Somewhere behind her, in the kitchen perhaps, a glass shattered on the floor.

"She has the same name as me," Valencia said.

"Huh?"

"The lawyer I talked to before lunch. Her name's Kate. That's short for Catherine. She spells it with a 'K,' though."

"Um." Glaser made no effort to conceal his lack of interest. He wiped his mouth with a napkin and stood up. "You 'bout ready, Cath?" he said.

◈

It was almost one. Kate was waiting for Mills to call her back. With Carmen's help she'd managed to restore Madeleine's Filofax to its proper place, but she hadn't mentioned the cassette. It remained stashed in her desk, waiting for Mills's review.

Jennifer popped her head in the door. "Want anything from upstairs?"

Kate realized she'd forgotten lunch. She was about to ask Jennifer to get her some food when the phone began to ring. From the LCD display she saw it was Mills.

"No thanks," Kate said hastily.

Jennifer left the room.

"Hi, Carter," Kate said. Just two short words but already she sounded anxious. "I found something in Madeleine's office that I think you should know about. It's a cassette tape. A recording of Chuck Thorpe laying into some woman. Maybe Stephanie Friedman. I think you should hear it."

There was a rustling sound and then a click, as Mills turned off the speakerphone and picked up the receiver. "What is it, exactly?"

Kate glanced at her notes. "The recording's fuzzy. It's hard to make out all the words. But at one point, Thorpe says, 'You think Ron can't get any girl he wants? You should be flattered.' It sounds like he's talking about Ron Fogarty. In the complaint it's alleged that —"

"Right," Mills said, cutting off the explanation. "What else?"

"Well . . . , at the end, Thorpe says, 'I'm counting on you, baby. If you get my drift.'" The words felt peculiar in her mouth.

"Anything else?"

"That's pretty much it," Kate said. "The rest of the tape's blank."

"I see," Mills said. He sounded thoughtful, disinterested. "Well, it's hard to know what it means. This was in Madeleine's desk?"

"Right. In a file drawer."

There was a long pause. "I wouldn't worry too much about this," Mills said finally. "From what you're telling me, there's not a whole lot there. But you're right. I should hear it. Ask Clara to set up a time."

"Okay," Kate said, making an effort to conceal her surprise. *Not a whole lot there.* What did Mills hear, or fail to hear? What was she missing?

"There's one more thing. I was just getting started in Madeleine's office when Martin Drescher showed up and told me to stop. He seemed . . . really upset for some reason."

Mills exhaled audibly. "I just got off the phone with Martin," he said. "Listen, why don't you hold off for now? Martin seems to want a partner to handle the job. Personally, I don't see the point. But it's not worth a fight. I'll see if we can bring in Dave Bosch."

"Dave Bosch. He was just in my office," Kate said. "A detective wanted to ask me a few questions about Madeleine. He sat in on the interview."

"Right, right," Mills said. "I meant to tell you they'd be by. The investigators are talking to everyone who had recent dealings with Madeleine. It all went smoothly?"

"I was happy to help. Not that I could really . . ." Kate let the sentence trail off.

"We do appreciate it. Anything else?" Mills's voice was once again distant. Kate could tell he was eager to end the conversation.

"No, that's all," she said hurriedly.

"Good," Mills said. "Oh, Kate, there is one more thing. I'll need you at WideWorld tomorrow for a witness interview. A woman by the name of Morris."

"She was a friend of Steph — of Friedman's?"

"Right. Arrange for a car. The meeting is set for two. Thanks so much."

Before Kate could respond, she heard a click. Carter Mills had hung up the phone.

The phone rang just before four. Josie was on time today. Waiting for the girl to make it upstairs, Kate rehearsed in her mind what she'd say. She had to appear sympathetic; that was the important thing. Already, she felt slightly uncomfortable with the role she'd agreed to take on. The beneficent white adviser to a young black girl who faced challenges she couldn't imagine. Her own privileges seemed almost ludicrous, embarrassing in their profusion. What did she know about Josie's life? Why should Josie listen to her? Still, she wanted to help. And to do that, she needed some answers.

A timid knock on the door. "Come in," Kate called.

The door opened, but Josie stayed put. In her black North Face parka and baggy jeans, she hovered at the threshold as if hoping to be dismissed. Her eyes shifted to Kate's for a short moment and then returned to the floor.

"Josie!" Kate's voice was artificially cheerful. "Come on in, have a seat." Josie edged into the office and looked around briefly before dropping into a chair.

"How about a chocolate chip cookie?" Kate asked.

Josie shrugged. "Okay."

Kate handed Josie a large cellophane-wrapped cookie acquired earlier in the day at the firm cafeteria. "Something to drink?"

"I guess . . . maybe a Diet Coke."

As Kate headed down the hallway, she thought about the contrast between the Josie who faced her today and the Josie of just a few months back. When they'd first started meeting, Josie could barely contain her excitement at being at Samson & Mills. It was, she'd confided to Kate, like something on TV, and she'd made breathless inquiries about every aspect of the place. Where Kate ate lunch. Who made the coffee. Where the secretaries had gone to school.

"You could work somewhere like this," Kate had told her. "And not as a secretary, either. In ten years, you could be doing what I'm doing. Although I should warn you, it's not as glamorous as it looks."

Josie had given her a skeptical look, as if doubtful that Kate's life could be less than perfect, doubtful that she could ever dream of holding Kate's job. Kate hoped that both ideas would grow on her with time.

Back from the vending machine, Kate handed Josie her drink and sat down next to her. It seemed less formal than speaking from behind a desk.

"How were your holidays?" Kate asked.

"Okay." Josie's eyes focused on her cookie.

Kate bit her lip. "Josie, I can tell that something's wrong," she said. "What is it?"

"Nothing's wrong." Josie didn't look up.

Kate tried another tactic. "You missed our last meeting before the holidays," she said, making her voice as gentle as possible. "Were you sick?"

"No," said Josie. Her voice was low.

Kate looked at her questioningly. "Were you —"

"It was my mom," Josie interrupted. "My mom's been a little sick so I've been helping out with the other kids. That's all." Kate knew that Josie had two much younger siblings, eight-year-old Freddy and five-year-old Shari. She'd never mentioned her father, and Kate hadn't asked.

"I'm really sorry to hear that," Kate said. "Is she all right now?"

"She's . . . she's better. She's going to be okay," Josie said.

"I'm glad that she's better," Kate said. "But what about you? You look really *tired*."

"A little," Josie said grudgingly. "Freddy had bad dreams last night, and he kept waking me up. The kids are just at that age."

"I know you've got a lot going on," Kate said. "But I don't want you to shortchange yourself. You have so much potential. Your PSAT scores were really strong. I know that you can get into a good college. I can help you get there. There are scholarships, grants — all sorts of things. But I can't help you if you're not here. I know that your family's important, but you're important, too. Do you understand what I'm saying?"

For a moment, Kate thought she detected a spark in Josie's eyes. Then Josie looked down again, kicking her feet against the bottom rung of her chair. "I guess so," she mumbled. She didn't sound convinced.

"I want you to promise me that you'll do everything you can to make our meetings," Kate said. She took a deep breath. "Something really bad happened last night. I found out that one of the partners I work for here was killed, murdered. But I still wanted to meet with you today, because I know it's important."

"Someone that works here was *murdered?*" Josie said. The rhythmic back-and-forth movement of her feet stopped, and she stared at Kate wide-eyed.

"Yes. A lawyer. Her name was Madeleine Waters."

"Man, I just can't picture someone who works here being killed," Josie said, her voice softly awestruck.

Andrea had made the same point, in the same disbelieving tone. That both Andrea and Josie could share this point of view was a stark reminder of life's unfairness. Josie lived in one of the city's public housing projects. Kate suspected that by age sixteen Josie had seen more violent death than she or Andrea would see in their lifetimes. Still, Josie shared their astonishment that Samson & Mills could be touched in this way. She seemed to accept without question the fact that life accorded some people — Kate, for example — protections that she herself had been denied at birth. Or perhaps it was something else. Perhaps Josie's response stemmed from a basic human yearning. Perhaps everyone needed to believe that there existed, somewhere, a place that was absolutely safe and secure. Inviolate. To Josie, Samson & Mills had represented that place.

As it had to Kate herself, until last night.

"I'll try to make it," Josie said. "Sometimes it's hard, though . . ." Josie's voice faded off.

Kate still felt uneasy, as if she'd failed to reach Josie in some basic way. But she'd pushed enough for one day.

Kate smiled. "I guess that's all I can ask," she said. "That you try as hard as you can."

It was already after ten, and the firm had fallen silent. Kate looked up from the legal opinion that had absorbed her attention for the past half hour and wondered why she had no recollection at all of what she'd read. It wasn't uncommon for Samson & Mills to be in full gear at this hour, with paralegals, secretaries, and attorneys in a frenzy to meet some early-morning deadline. But not tonight. From the sound of things, she was alone.

Kate leaned back in her chair, trying to decide whether to stick around for another hour or to finish her reading at home. Home was more comfortable but also more risky, with the seductions of sleep looming all too accessibly in the foreground. Still, what was the point? No one was around to appreciate her late-night industry.

She'd just decided to call it quits when a thought shot through her mind. In all the excitement over the Thorpe cassette, she'd entirely forgotten about her talk with Carmen. She hadn't said a word to Mills about the file Drescher had taken from Madeleine's office. *Damn.*

Of course it was too late now. Partners did not make a habit of burning the midnight oil. Kate made a quick note in her desk calendar in capital letters — TALK TO CM ABOUT FILE — and then sat back in her chair. For some reason, she was feeling guilty. As if she should have stopped Martin Drescher. Though, really, what could she have done? Drescher was a partner. She was a junior associate. Still, Mills had trusted her to see that everything was left as it was. Irrational though it was, she felt as though she'd let him down.

For some time, the feeling bore down on her, a weight pressed against her heart. Then she had a sudden idea. Drescher, like Mills, was undoubtedly gone for the day. Why couldn't she just slip into his office, take a quick look around? It would take a few minutes at most. Unless Drescher had taken the file with him, there was a pretty good chance she'd find it on his desk. That way she'd at least know what he'd taken and could pass on the information to Mills. She wouldn't really be doing anything wrong. Even if someone saw her, a cleaning woman perhaps, she could simply explain that she was looking for a document she needed. She wouldn't even have to lie. She just wouldn't tell all of the truth.

Minutes later, Kate stepped out of the elevator onto the fifty-seventh floor. Just as she'd expected, she'd yet to see another person. The corridor was tomblike, office doors closed and locked. Kate stopped at the door to Drescher's corner suite, and quickly surveyed the scene. Still no one. She turned back to the door. The knob turned easily in her grasp.

She stepped into Drescher's reception area, closing the door behind her. The corner suites were all laid out according to the same plan, and Kate knew that Drescher's private office was behind the closed door she was facing. It was probably locked tight, in which case she'd just go back downstairs. But when she turned the knob, the door swung open.

Quickly, she proceeded to Drescher's desk. But except for a blotter, a telephone, and a paperweight, its polished wood surface was empty. She'd planned to leave at this point, if the file wasn't in plain view. But now that she was here, something pushed her on. She tried the top two desk drawers. Locked. The bottom two were locked as well. She plopped into Drescher's leather chair and considered where to look next. Against the far wall, her eyes lit on a bookcase with cupboards at the bottom, and she was instantly on her feet again.

Back across the room, Kate opened the right cupboard door and there, on top of a stack of papers, she saw a file folder labeled in the neat printing she recognized from Madeleine's date book: Billing Records. Kate pulled out the contents of the file and rifled through the slim stack of papers. Then she stopped, puzzled. What the file seemed to contain was a collection of duplicate WideWorld bills signed by Carter Mills. This sort of information was readily accessible from Accounting. So why had Drescher been so hot to get it from Madeleine's files? And what was it doing in Madeleine's desk in the first place?

Kate was just mulling over these questions when she heard the sound of muffled voices from the reception area. Not the lilting Spanish and Italian accents of the female cleaning crew, but low men's voices. One of which sounded like Drescher's.

Kate felt her blood go cold. The possibility that Drescher himself might return at this hour was something she hadn't even considered.

In a flurry of activity, Kate closed the cupboard door, turned off the light — thank God partners' offices were spared the automatic lighting system — and raced across the room. Pushing back the chair, Kate squeezed herself into the cubbyhole space under Drescher's desk. She'd just pulled the desk chair back behind her when she heard the door swing open. A wedge of light fell across the room. Then a click and the whole room was bright as day.

"Have a seat." She'd been right; the voice really was Martin Drescher's.

Kate heard the faint sound of bodies settling into upholstered seats. As her brain sought to organize the information she'd received, Kate realized that she'd made a terrible choice. After all, she might have been able to explain her simple presence in Drescher's office. Say, a file needing immediate attention that someone in the managing clerk's office had thought Drescher might have. But how could she possibly explain her presence beneath his desk? Her situation was ridiculous, absurd. If she'd seen it in a movie, she would have rolled her eyes. Things like this didn't happen in real life. Certainly not in hers.

And yet, here she was.

Curled in a fetal position, her head smashed against the top of the desk, her legs crushed against her chest, Kate desperately tried to come up with a story. Then she felt a renewed burst of hopelessness.

Clutched in her right hand was Madeleine's file.

"What the hell were you thinking, Martin? Why the hell did you tell McCarty?" To her astonishment, Kate recognized that this second voice, brusque and commanding, belonged to Carter Mills.

"I've told you." Drescher's voice was tense. "It didn't come from me. What would I have to gain?"

"Jesus, Martin. Who else could it have been? We're the only litigators involved. You're not suggesting that the leak came from one of the corporate guys?"

"I'm just saying that it wasn't me," Drescher said. "If you ask me, this thing has your fingerprints all over it. You know what I think? That you set this up to discredit me."

Carter Mills snorted. "I won't even respond to that. There's no question that the e-mail came from you. I had computer services check it out. From you to Bill McCarty."

Kate shifted slightly, careful not to make any noise. All of her senses seemed heightened. The outline of her hand against her knee seemed oddly distinct. The smell of dust and wood was over-powering. For one terrifying moment, she thought she might sneeze, but she managed to hold it back.

"Let's cut to the chase," said Drescher. "What are we going to do now?"

"There's not a hell of a lot we *can* do," Carter Mills said curtly. "I took a poll this morning. Without Madeleine, we're two votes short. If we'd been able to handle this quietly *as we agreed*, we still could've pulled it off. But McCarty's on the warpath now, and he's rounding up support. As it stands, the rank and file have enough votes to keep the lockstep draw in place for the foreseeable future. And you can kiss Stroesser and the rest of his M&A gang good-bye. They'll be out the door by the end of the year. Do you have any idea what that means for this firm? Mergers and Acquisitions brought in more than $40 million last year."

Even in her panicked state, Kate found herself mesmerized by the exchange. Fragments of conversation, so inscrutable only moments before, now fell into place. *They were planning to do away with lockstep compensation.* Lockstep, as everyone knew, was a relic of Samson's patrician past. While associates received fixed salaries, partners were paid from firm profits. Under the lockstep system, partnership profits had always been based strictly on seniority, with rainmakers getting no special treatment. While most New York firms had discarded such systems in recent years, adopting "eat what you kill" payment structures, Samson had shown no signs of budging. The lockstep system had always been viewed as sacro-sanct, a safeguard against unseemly squabbling.

Until now.

Kate's mind raced ahead as she pictured the storm that would ensue if the lockstep system were ditched. Millions of dollars would be up for grabs. There would be big winners, such as Mills and Drescher, and big losers, such as McCarty and other team players who could never compete with the rainmaking kings. Bruce Stroesser, the high-flying chief of M&A, must be threatening to jump ship. No wonder Mills was upset. Losing Stroesser and his clients to another firm would mean phenomenal losses for everyone, not to mention the publicity.

Suddenly things fell into place.

Bill McCarty's stormy exit from Carter Mills's office the day he'd practically knocked her down.

McCarty's insistent phone call to Madeleine Waters's office.

Bill McCarty was in a fight for his professional life.

"For now, we're going to sit tight," said Mills. "The last thing we need on top of Madeleine's murder is some media explosion tied to firm politics."

"It'll blow over," said Drescher. "We're not the first prominent firm to have a partner murdered. Think of Cravath, with that partner killed in a sleazy motel by some black kid he'd hooked up with for sex. That's much worse than what we're facing here. Remember the publicity? That big article in the *New Yorker* a few years back. People talked about it for weeks. But Cravath came out of it all just fine."

"There *is* one critical difference," said Mills. "At Cravath, they knew from the start who the killer was. And they knew it had nothing to do with the law firm."

"What are you saying?" Drescher said. A note of uncertainty had entered his voice.

A pause. When Mills spoke, his voice was low and deliberate. "The night Madeleine was killed, she was supposed to have dinner with Chuck Thorpe at Ormond. Earlier that day, someone claiming to be from Thorpe's office called to reschedule for seven, an hour earlier than they'd planned to meet."

"So you're saying she was set up?" Drescher sounded incredulous.

"I don't really think it's a coincidence, do you, Martin? Madeleine shows up at the restaurant — we've checked the reservations, and she did make it there — and a few hours later she's dead."

"What about Thorpe?"

"He got there at eight, waited half an hour or so, and then took off."

"He has an alibi?"

"Yes, Martin. He has an alibi. We spoke with the driver." Mills's voice was cold.

"So, what's your point?"

"That whoever killed Madeleine knew about her meeting with Thorpe. And used it to ambush her."

"My God." Drescher was clearly stunned. "So you're saying that it could be someone here at the firm, someone with access to her schedule."

"We don't know that, Martin." Impatience was evident in Mills's voice. "We have no way of knowing who Madeleine told about that meeting. Or who Thorpe told, for that matter. We don't have enough information to speculate."

"But . . . it wasn't random."

An exasperated sigh from Mills. "No. I don't think that it was random. Do you?"

"Was it Thorpe? Is he the bastard who killed her?"

"Don't be ridiculous. Thorpe has enough trouble on his hands."

"But he'd be capable of it, the son of a bitch."

"I didn't say that, Martin."

"Thorpe was after Madeleine, you know that as well as I do. He'd been trying to get into her pants for months."

"If that were a motive for murder, Madeleine would have been dead a long time ago. And Chuck Thorpe wouldn't be the only suspect."

The two men continued to talk, but Kate had stopped following their words. All her thoughts were centered on the astounding thing she'd just heard. Madeleine's killer wasn't some random psychopath. He was someone who'd known her plans, someone who'd tracked her movements.

By the time Kate regained her focus, Carter Mills was speaking again. "— and on top of everything, we're facing this mess with McCarty. As I see it, Martin, that's your baby. You got us into it, and you can bloody well find a way out."

"Don't threaten me," Drescher said sharply. "How many times do I have to tell you. I had nothing to do with that leak."

Kate heard the abrupt sound of a body rising. "This meeting's over," said Mills. The words were followed by the thud of a closing door. Then the room went silent.

In the dim light, Kate checked out her watch. Just after midnight. She strained her ears for sounds inside the office. Had they both left? Then she heard a heavy sigh, and her heart skipped a beat.

She was alone with Martin Drescher.

As this realization hit, she heard the slow movement of footsteps edging closer to the desk. *Don't let him find me, don't let him find me.* Hands clenched, her head bowed against her knees, she waited for Drescher's shadow to fall across her hiding place, for the exclamation that would signal her discovery. But then the footsteps stopped. To her left, Kate heard the soft squeak of a cabinet opening, followed by the pop of a bottle being uncorked. The splash of liquid tumbling against glass. Martin Drescher was pouring a drink. Seltzer? Somehow, she didn't think so. After another few moments, she heard the clink of glasses being restored, the closing of the cabinet door.

And then, hardly daring to believe her ears, she heard what sounded like preparations for departure. The rustle of fabric and upholstery. The metallic snap of a briefcase latch. The click of a light going off. Once again, the office door opened and closed. Kate waited in quivering silence, listening. Seconds later, she felt the faint reverberation of the outer door. And then, again, silence.

Absolute silence. Kate eased her head out from under the desk and scanned the darkened room, now bathed in the eerie glow of lights from surrounding buildings. Empty. The office was empty. The relief that flooded over her was so intense that she thought she might collapse. She grabbed hold of the desk to steady herself, painfully straightening her legs. Both feet were asleep, and she thumped them against the carpeted floor, trying to stop the tingling.

Think. Crossing the office, she checked to be sure the door was locked. Good. Still, she needed to move fast. Who knew what could happen next? A tape-recorded message that used to play in the city's taxis floated absurdly through her mind, a purring Catwoman's warning: *Cats have nine lives, but you have only one. So buckle up!*

The file she had clutched in her hand for the past hour was damp from perspiration. She was about to put it back in Drescher's cabinet when she hesitated. The file obviously had some significance that she'd yet to discern, a significance that must somehow be related to the ongoing power struggle between Drescher and Mills. Their relationship was certainly more complex than she'd thought. But there was no mistaking the animosity that suffused their dealings regardless of any temporary alliance. Of course, she couldn't just take the file. But what if she kept a copy?

Heart pounding, Kate pressed her ear to the office door. When she failed to detect any sound, she cracked open the door and peered into the reception area. The coast was clear. She rapidly crossed the room before halting at the door to the corridor. Again, she paused before slowly opening the door and looking out. The corridor was deserted. After several long moments, she slipped into the hallway and walked quickly to the photocopy machine located in the same position as the copiers on each of the other office floors.

Checking the settings on the copy machine, she could feel her pulse slowing down. She was out of immediate danger. Should anyone see her, they would just assume she had work to do. She decided not to risk the automatic feed. The added speed was not worth the risk of a copy malfunction that could leave pages crumpled and ragged. The file was slim — under thirty pages — and she was done in less than five minutes.

Heading back to Drescher's office, Kate took a deep breath. The last thing she wanted to do was to return to the scene of her narrow escape. But she had no choice. Back inside Drescher's office, she carefully replaced the file before taking a final look at the room to be sure that she'd left no trace. As her eyes passed over the office furnishings, Kate's eye was drawn to a shiny spot where Drescher had splashed his drink. Curious, she crossed the room, touched a finger to the spot and licked. Scotch.

No doubt about it now. Martin Drescher was drinking again.

Friday, January 8

ANOTHER gray morning, fiercely cold, with the threat of snow hanging in the air like the shadow of an upraised hand. But as she joined the other commuters filing down the narrow stairway to the Seventy-ninth Street subway platform, Kate was oblivious to her surroundings. Her body, flooded with adrenaline last night, seemed suspended in a dreamlike calm.

As commuters swarmed around her, Kate unfolded the *Daily Press* and reread a short follow-up report on Madeleine's murder. No new leads, just something to fill up space, to feed an audience hungry for detail. The centerpiece of the brief article was further speculation by a criminology expert, who warned that this killing could be the first in a series. "The high level of violence to the body suggests that this is someone who will kill again," he told the reporter. There was no suggestion that Madeleine's death was anything other than the work of a psychopathic stranger. No suggestion that she'd known her attacker. The omission further added to

Kate's sense of dislocation, as if what she'd overheard last night had been some sort of hallucination.

When the train finally screeched into the station, Kate had to cram herself into the packed subway car. Stuck next to the door, she tried to sink into herself. Carter had intimated that someone at the firm could be connected to Madeleine's death. Who else more likely to know her plans? Though, to be fair, any number of people might have known about her date with Thorpe. A psycho cab driver who'd listened in on a cell-phone call. A doorman obsessed with a beautiful tenant. Improbable as they might sound, such things could happen. Kate thought of the unsuspecting women who ran into serial killer Ted Bundy, never imagining that they would be that one-in-a-million victim.

Yes, the more she thought about it, the harder it was to believe that someone at Samson & Mills had caused Madeleine's death. The brutally savaged body, sexually assaulted and dumped — it just wasn't a Samson & Mills kind of murder. Not that there *was* a Samson & Mills kind of murder, but if there was, this definitely wouldn't be it. Whoever had killed Madeleine had been crazy, out of his mind. A *disorganized killer*, that's how the newspaper's expert had described him. Likely to be delusional, an underachiever. Not the description that came to mind when you thought of Samson & Mills.

Immersed in her thoughts, Kate almost missed her stop. Lunging for the door, she just made it out. She headed down a concrete tunnel toward the exit.

By the time Kate reached her office, Jennifer was already at her station, reading a paperback novel. At the sound of Kate's arrival, Jennifer looked up, her glossy curls cascading down her shoulders.

"'Morning," Jennifer said brightly. "You here late last night?"

"You could say that," Kate said dryly.

Jennifer put a marker in her book and followed Kate into her office. "I put your mail on your chair," she said, gesturing to a neatly arranged stack. "You got anything else for me to do?"

While the pace at Samson could be ferocious, work was never

consistent. Though Jennifer often had her hands full, the past few months had been slow.

"Not yet," Kate said. "I'm doing a lot of research. But stay tuned, it won't be long."

Jennifer lingered in the doorway. "It's really awful about Madeleine Waters."

"Horrible," Kate agreed. "You know, I'd just started working for her."

"I know," said Jennifer, wrinkling her pretty forehead. "This must be terrible for you."

Jennifer was about to leave when Kate had a sudden thought. While associates were out of the partnership loop, secretaries at Samson & Mills had their own networks. Working intimately with the partners, they had access to many of their secrets. Of course, Jennifer herself didn't work for any partners. But she certainly had friends who did.

"So, tell me, what have you heard?" Kate asked.

"You mean, about the murder?"

"Yeah, I was so tied up yesterday, that I didn't hear much. Is anyone talking about suspects?"

Jennifer looked uneasy. She stepped back into Kate's office and closed the door. "You mean, like Carter Mills?" she whispered.

Kate tried to appear nonchalant. "What about Carter Mills?"

Jennifer bit her lip. "Oh, it's just talk, you know how things are . . ."

"What are people saying?"

"Well, there's a rumor — I mean it's obviously totally ridiculous — but some people are saying that Carter Mills might have . . . might have had something to do with it. Because . . . you know . . . she broke up with him. I mean, I don't believe it for a second. But Carm —" Jennifer bit her lip. In identifying Carmen as her source, she'd obviously said more than she intended.

The notion that Carter Mills could be involved with Madeleine's death was so ludicrous that Kate almost smiled. Still it didn't really surprise her that Carmen considered him a suspect.

From their conversation yesterday, Kate already knew that Carmen blamed the firm for Madeleine's death. And who more embodied the firm than Carter Mills? But she was struck by something else Jennifer had said. *She broke up with him.* Of course, there was no way of knowing whether this was true either. Still, it was a tantalizing hint, the closest she'd ever come to specifics about the partners' rumored affair.

"Was Carter Mills even with Madeleine that night?" Kate asked. Ridiculous as the rumor was, she had an urge to clear his name.

"No," Jennifer admitted. "He was at some dinner with clients uptown. At least, that's what Clara said, and I guess she'd know. He doesn't make a move without telling her. It's just stupid gossip. I shouldn't even have mentioned it."

"People can be really crazy, can't they?" Kate tried to keep her voice light.

Jennifer seemed to relax a little. "I'll say."

"By the way, do you have any idea how Madeleine got along with the other partners she worked with?" Kate didn't want to target Martin Drescher directly. Though that was certainly where her thoughts were heading.

"I haven't heard anything, but I could ask around." Kate could tell that Jennifer liked the idea of being on a quest for information. Jennifer was energetic, a go-getter. Schlocky novels were a poor substitute for real-life intrigue.

"If you feel like it," Kate said casually. "I sort of wonder what her life was like."

Being with Carter Mills was a little like dating a movie star. Standing beside him, waiting for the elevator door to open, Kate noticed a scrawny first-year associate eyeing her enviously, his narrow lips pressed together. Kate tried to derive some pleasure from her prize position. Instead, she felt only a mild queasiness somewhere deep in her stomach.

Outside, they proceeded to a black Lincoln Town Car. As they crossed the sidewalk, Kate glanced sideways at Mills, whose sculpted features were focused in thought. She felt a rush of admiration. Even in silence, he was somehow more vibrant than other people. There was something timeless about him. Ignore the modern dress, and he could have commanded armies in ancient Greece, steered a frigate toward a New World. Kate felt his presence as a sort of weight, anchoring her to reality in a way that her own body could not.

When they reached the car, Mills seemed to come back to himself. "What a lovely cape," he said, flashing Kate a smile as she slid across the car's leather-upholstered seats.

"Oh . . . , thank you," Kate said. The comment had caught her off guard. It was almost becoming a pattern with Mills, the sudden interjection of the personal followed by an equally sudden return to the status quo. She wasn't sure how to respond. Should she answer in kind, prolong the moment, or was it better to let it pass? But Mills made the decision for her.

"You won't need to do much today besides take notes." The car was swinging west across town, in the direction of WideWorld's headquarters. "I'll be interviewing Linda Morris. She should be a strong witness for us. She was Friedman's closest friend at the magazine. Ate lunch with her several times a week. They had similar jobs. Friedman was Chuck Thorpe's secretary. Morris was secretary to the managing editor, a guy named Brian Keck. They were constantly in and out of each other's offices. And yet Morris says she never once heard Friedman complain about Chuck Thorpe. Not once."

Kate could hear the relish in Mills's voice. "That sounds great," said Kate. "If Stephanie Friedman didn't even complain to her best friend, what jury's going to believe that she confronted Thorpe to his face? She'll never be able to show that Thorpe's behavior was unwelcome. And if she can't do that, there goes her sexual harassment claim."

Mills smiled. "Exactly."

"What about other employees?" Kate asked.

"Everyone else is on board. Morris was our one wild card."

The car was pulling up outside the WideWorld complex, a massive limestone edifice that towered over the surrounding buildings. "Why are we doing the interview at WideWorld instead of at Samson?" Kate asked curiously. "Is that customary?"

Carter Mills tapped his chin with an index finger. "Customary," he mused. "I suppose you could say that. With the added advantage of reminding Ms. Morris just who pays her salary. She's not just dealing with Chuck Thorpe anymore. This is a whole new ball game. "

Carter Mills had commandeered the general counsel's office for this interview, but Richard Epstein was nowhere to be found. Mills had assumed Epstein's desk, an off-white French Provincial reproduction. Kate sat to Mills's left on a small pink-and-gold loveseat, while Linda Morris sat facing them. The delicate furnishings seemed strangely at odds with both Epstein's ascetic demeanor and the work to be done today.

"Thank you so much for coming," said Mills, gracing Linda Morris with a friendly smile. The appreciation in his voice seemed real, as if she were doing them a favor. As if she'd really had a choice.

"Ms. Paine" — Mills gestured toward Kate while keeping his eyes trained on Morris — "is an associate with my firm and will be taking a few notes during our meeting today. As long as you don't mind, of course."

Linda Morris shrugged. She was a thin, pale figure, heavily made up, with jutting conical breasts and long black hair. She wore an aqua blouse of some shiny synthetic material, and the hands that emerged from its sleeves were capped with blood-red nails. Around her neck dangled a slender gold chain and tiny cross, an improbable accent to the outfit.

Mills began the meeting. "Ms. Morris, I assume you're aware of the general nature of Ms. Friedman's claims."

Linda Morris nodded, licking her crimson lips. The kohl liner around her deep-set eyes gave her a scraggly, nearsighted look. She seemed nervous. It occurred to Kate that the seating arrangement — she and Mills seated opposite Morris, two against one — was reminiscent of a police interrogation. But perhaps that was the point.

Mills leaned back in his chair. He seemed expectant, as if he had all the time in the world. "As you know, Ms. Friedman is claiming that Chuck Thorpe sexually harassed her. Now, it's important to understand one thing. Under the law, sexual harassment occurs only when behavior is unwelcome, when the person claiming harassment has made it clear that she wanted the behavior to stop. Do you follow me?"

"Uh huh."

Mills studied Linda Morris before moving on, as if giving her time to absorb his point. "Now, from what I've heard, Ms. Friedman never once told Mr. Thorpe that she felt he was doing anything wrong. She never once told him that she objected to anything that he was doing. Do you have any reason to doubt that?"

Linda Morris licked her lips again. Then she reached into her purse and pulled out a tub of cherry lip balm, which she thoughtfully uncapped before rubbing a glob onto her lips.

"Well," she said, "I guess not. No." Her voice, light and breathy, seemed to come from high in her throat.

Mills gave an emphatic nod, as if approving what Morris had said. He seemed to be enjoying himself. "Thank you, Ms. Morris. Now, from what I understand, Ms. Friedman and Mr. Thorpe had a warm and friendly personal relationship. There was a lot of horseplay, that sort of thing. But all of it was in good fun. Ms. Friedman gave as good as she got. Isn't that right?"

"Okay." Linda Morris was staring at her lap. With her right hand she fiddled with her necklace.

"Ms. Morris." Mills's voice was edged with reproach. "What do you mean, '*okay?*'"

Linda Morris looked up. For a moment Kate thought she saw a glimmer of hostility in the woman's eyes, but it quickly faded.

"I mean that they got along good — Stephanie and Chuck," she said in the same childlike voice. "I mean that they didn't have conflicts or anything."

"Thank you, Ms. Morris." Carter Mills was once again the convivial master of ceremonies. "Now, Ms. Morris, I want to show you a complaint prepared for this case. That's the document in which Ms. Friedman sets forth her allegations. I want you to read it through, then tell me if there's any truth to Ms. Friedman's claims. We've marked the important parts in yellow."

Linda Morris took hold of the draft complaint with a limp white hand. Bowing her head, she began to read. When she turned the last page, she looked up.

"No," she said. "None of it's true, so far as I know."

"So Stephanie Friedman never told you about any of the things that she's claiming in there?" Mills said.

"No." Linda Morris again fingered the cross around her neck. Her voice was low; her eyes again focused on her lap.

"And you're sure of that? You've taken time to read the complaint?"

"Yes." Linda Morris studied her knees.

Something's not right, Kate thought. *She definitely knows more than what she's saying. And the complaint, could she really have read it so quickly?*

"And if this sort of activity *had* been occurring, would you have expected Ms. Friedman to confide in you about it?" Mills pressed.

"Oh, yes," Linda Morris said. "We told each other everything. About boyfriends, problems at the office — when we felt too much stuff was getting dumped on us instead of the other girls. She definitely would have told me."

The words emerged in a quick staccato, as if Morris were reading from a script.

Troubled, Kate glanced toward Mills, trying to catch his eye. But, turning to the next page of his notes, he was already moving on.

❧

THE movie theater was a mob scene by the time Kate arrived. The crowd was typical of New York these days, especially the once-funky West Side, where gleaming new high-rises seemed to pop up overnight and designer baby carriages complete with designer moms and babies blocked the narrow aisles of neighborhood stores. With its soaring ceilings and vast open spaces, the Sony Imax theater felt more like an elaborate hotel than somewhere to see a movie.

Kate glanced at her watch: 6:55. She was five minutes early. Already, she regretted her decision to come. If the idea of a date — any date — wasn't bad enough, this was a *blind date*, the very worst. Two complete strangers trying to make small talk while deciding if they might want to have sex. She thought longingly of law school, when she and Michael used to spend long evenings on the couch, rubbing each other's feet and reading.

But Michael was marrying someone else.

Pushing these thoughts from her mind, Kate elbowed her way through the crowd to the foot of the box office line, where she'd agreed to meet Douglas Macauley. She had only the vaguest idea of what he looked like. Brown hair, brown eyes, medium height. Tara claimed he was cute, but he sounded totally nondescript. She'd told him to look for her cape — bright red; you can't miss it.

"The 7:45 showing of *Cold Justice* is sold out," a female voice announced over the multiplex's loudspeaker system. "Tickets remain for 9:45, 11, and 11:40."

Damn. That was the movie they'd planned to see. Kate had picked it earlier that day as the most innocuous of the selections. A legal thriller with a PG rating. High on explosions, low on sex. She was weighing the remaining options when she felt a tap on her shoulder.

"Kate?" She spun around to face a pleasant-looking guy in a brown leather jacket and jeans. He smiled at her and Kate found herself smiling back. While there was nothing remarkable about Douglas Macauley, he was definitely appealing, with warm eyes and a bemused smile.

He touched her elbow. "You can get out of line. I got the tickets."

Kate slipped under the velvet cords that roped off the ticket holders' line. "It's a good thing you got them," she said. "The 7:45 show's sold out."

"Oh, I didn't get tickets for 7:45," Douglas said. "That's been sold out for hours. They're for 9:45."

As quickly as she'd warmed to him, the glimmer faded. How could Douglas simply *assume* that she'd go along with this change of plans? "I thought that we —"

"Oh, don't worry," Douglas said airily. "We're not *going* to the 9:45. We're going to the 7:45."

"What —"

"Don't worry, I've *never* been kept out of a movie. *Never.*"

"But —"

"Come."

Douglas steered Kate through the crowd to the soaring escalator bank. Once they'd reached the second floor, Douglas moved easily through the crowd, his hand still at Kate's elbow. There was something pleasant about letting someone else be in charge for a change, and she let herself drift along beside him.

Moments later, Douglas was handing over the tickets to a freckled young woman standing guard. She glanced at the tickets briefly before looking up again.

"These tickets are for the 9:45 show," she said. "We're not seating for that show yet."

Douglas was a picture of polite confusion. "But —" he looked at the tickets as if he'd never seen them before. "That's not right. We're going to the 7:45 show."

"The 7:45 show is sold out," the woman patiently responded.

"But I got these tickets *much* earlier today."

The woman looked at the tickets. "It says here that you bought them at 6:30."

Kate focused on the floor, trying not to laugh. She quickly edged away from the entrance, with Douglas trailing in her wake. "This has *never* happened to me before," he said in plaintive tones. "It's an *outrage.*"

To her surprise, Kate was enjoying herself. After the high seriousness of her day at Samson, there was something appealing about playing cloak-and-dagger games over movie tickets. She was amused by Douglas's good-humored bravado. With a pang, she remembered that life, small things in life, could be fun. Suddenly the prospect of spending a few hours with Douglas didn't seem all that bad.

"We could just get something to eat," she ventured.

"Absolutely not." Douglas's face was set in mock-determination. "We are *going* to that movie."

Back on the main floor, Douglas returned to the ticket line. His eyes scanned the illuminated timetable posted above the ticket counter. On reaching the ticket sales desk, he proffered the once-spurned *Cold Justice* tickets.

"These tickets are for 9:45, but we can't stay that late. We need to exchange them for two 8:30 tickets for *Gunslinger.*"

Kate frowned. "But I don't want to see —"

"Don't worry." Douglas pocketed the new tickets and grabbed her hand. She tensed at his touch and then relaxed as he pulled her back toward the escalator. He was probably just in a hurry.

Upstairs again, they handed over the tickets and easily made it through. Now they were standing on the edge of a vast concession area that led to the individual theaters. "We made it," Douglas said gleefully. But as he scanned the marquee lights above the various theater doors, his smile began to fade.

"I don't get it," he muttered. "Something is wrong. Something is very wrong." He approached an usher. "*Cold Justice?*" he asked in hopeful tones.

"Downstairs. Lower level."

Douglas and Kate exchanged blank stares. Then Kate started to laugh.

"She told us that they weren't *seating* for the 7:45. What she didn't tell us is that it's *downstairs*."

They were back on the run. "This is what we'll do," said Douglas, as they again descended the escalator. "We'll tell the guy downstairs that we need to go catch some friends who are going to *Cold Justice*. That it's an emergency."

"Right. A *movie emergency*. That'll work. Why don't you just tell him that the popcorn popper is broken upstairs? Or that they've run out of your favorite snack treat. Or that you just want to *see what it looks like* downstairs."

Douglas looked reflective. "The popcorn thing isn't bad . . ."

Reaching the main floor, they raced to the escalator leading to the lower level. Kate hung back as Douglas pled their case. "It will only take a minute. We'll be *right back*," he assured the blank-faced kid who stood guard.

"No."

"*No?*" Douglas's eyes widened. "But can't we just — we just need to —"

The line was getting longer, but Douglas stayed put. For a moment the attendant seemed confused. "Well . . . , okay. Just as long as you'll be right back. "

Unbelievable, Kate thought. Douglas gave her a surreptitious thumbs-up sign.

7:35. They took the steps on the downward escalator two at a time from the main floor to the lower level. The *Cold Justice* marquee was straight ahead. They slipped into the packed theater just as an action-film preview began. The few empty seats were scattered singles.

"We'll have to split up," Douglas whispered. "I'll meet you after the show. Why don't you take that seat up to the left? That looks like the best one."

A brief flicker of compunction passed over Kate. What if the rightful owners of these seats arrived and found no place to sit? At the same time, there was something fun about this minor transgression, so alien to her by-the-book life. Kate headed for the empty seat.

"Hey, Kate —" Douglas called softly. She turned, made out the engaging grin, the warm brown eyes.

"What did I tell you? I've *never* been kept out of a movie."

✧

IT was Friday night, just before midnight. He was seated alone in the brightly lit pastry shop. Around him couples chattered over dessert and coffee. He tried to ignore them, to block out their grating laughter.

On his plate was the flaky confection known as sfogliatella. He picked it up and bit down. The crisp top layers gave way, and he tasted the sweet cheese inside. He chewed slowly, with concentration, focusing on the texture, the flavor. And then he waited. It was one of his few good memories, this thing that he used to love. She'd brought them to him as a special treat. When he was a good boy. It had flashed into his mind last night, a picture of her watching him eat, her face suffused with love. She had been, was still in his mind, the most beautiful woman in the world.

He was sitting in front of a window. Outside, he saw people rushing past, hurrying toward light and warmth. And beyond them, across the street, was the place where it all began. He studied the square brick structure. Only four stories tall. That always surprised him. It seemed so much larger in his mind. His eyes wandered toward the top floor, to three dark windows on the right. He wondered who lived there now. Did they know what had happened there? Or were they utterly oblivious, concerned only with their own small lives?

"D'you mind if we sit here?" A woman was pointing to two empty chairs. She was fat as a pig, with curly bronze hair. Her date stood behind her, a pimply geek with a ridiculously large hooked nose. Both of them were disgusting. But the shop was filling up. He didn't really have a choice. Grunting an assent, he tried to edge closer toward the wall. Then his eyes returned to the building.

"And then, when I was ten, we moved to Scarsdale." The fat girl was nattering on. "I had this imaginary friend named Lulu. I was sure that we'd left her behind. I was driving my mother crazy. Finally, she drove me back into the city one day. She parked outside the building where we used to live, and went inside. When she came out, she said Lulu was with her. And you know what? I believed her. After that everything was okay."

It was a stupid story, he thought. Still, when he heard things like that, he was amazed at what others remembered. Childhood games. The names of teachers. The type of sandwich they'd eaten for lunch. While for him, whole years were blank. For the first decade of his life, he had only a handful of memories. The pastry he was eating now. The scene of her death. His old friend Ricky, holding out a small flask. *It's cool, man. But you gotta drink it fast.*

But that was all in the past. Before he'd come up with the plan. He laughed to himself about the Ph.D.'s who claimed to understand what he'd been through. *Trauma. Dissociation.* The fact was, they didn't know shit. Still, he'd let them believe that they'd helped him. What did he care after all? The only thing that mattered was the plan. That was the beauty of it. Every action could be put to one test: did it help or hinder the plan?

He'd come here tonight to reassure himself, to seek strength for his coming ordeal. He'd thought that being here would bring her closer. But it wasn't working out that way. Still, he had no doubt that he was on the right track. She'd sent signs telling him so. If he had any doubts at all, he just had to think of Kate. Only the glasses were wrong. It still annoyed him, to see her like that. But perhaps it was better this way. Better that others couldn't see what he saw. Kate was there, waiting. That was the important thing.

Then, without warning, he felt her presence. *The most beautiful woman in the world.* He felt her all around him, loving and urging him on. She was the one who'd brought him Kate, to remind him

he was not alone. He could feel her confidence in him, feel it fuel-
ing his resolve. Doubts fell away, dissolved into space, until they'd
never existed at all.

Everything was just as it should be.

Nothing could stop him now.

Saturday, January 9

THE phone rang. Barely awake, Kate rolled over and picked it up.

"Hi!" It was Tara, sounding energetic and alert, as if she'd been up for hours.

"What time is it?" Kate asked groggily.

"A little after ten," Tara said. "You weren't asleep, were you?"

After ten. Kate couldn't remember the last time she'd slept this late.

"No, no." Propping herself up on an elbow, Kate tried to focus on Tara's words.

"You *were* asleep. Go back to bed. I'll call you later."

"No, really, I'm up now."

"I just wanted to know how things went last night."

Kate found herself smiling, though she'd never in a million years tell Tara. "Fine," she said coolly. "Things went fine."

"Did you like Douglas?"

"I liked him fine."

"Liked him fine," Tara repeated. "Well, coming from you that's pretty close to a declaration of love."

"Don't sound so smug," Kate said. "It was just a movie." No reason to tell Tara about the lingering conversation over coffee that followed, about Douglas's fascinating tales of his recent trip to the Himalayas, about his promise to be in touch. She didn't want to get Tara's hopes up. Besides, she wasn't sure how she felt. She'd had a much better time than expected. Even the crazy ordeal with tickets had somehow added to Douglas's appeal. Still, he wasn't her usual type. She'd just have to wait and see.

"So what are you up to today?" Tara asked, letting the subject drop.

"Haircut, housecleaning — the usual Saturday entertainment."

"And tonight?"

"I'll probably order in sushi and watch a video. The perfect Saturday night."

"Hmm," Tara said. "I can see that I have my work cut out for me."

⚜

"Is Hercules your real name?"

"What?"

"Is that what your parents named you?"

Kate heard an exasperated sigh behind her. She felt a quick tug on her scalp followed by the sound of scissors. Wings of dark brown hair fluttered into her sheet-draped lap.

"Kate, you know I can't talk when I work." Hercules's voice was aggrieved. "How would you like it if someone tried to talk to you while you were writing a brief?"

"Sorry."

Kate surveyed the room, a shabby loft on the Lower East Side. She'd spent the morning racing through weekend errands, and the calm of Hercules's studio was a welcome break. She could do without the gloom, though. Only the palest haze of light made its way through the tall, dirt-encrusted windows.

Kate tried to keep her head steady as Hercules circled her chair, his eyes on the lookout for stray locks of hair. He was somewhere in his late thirties, with a mane of graying dark curls and a hawk-like nose. He called himself a sculptor. His recent efforts, from what Kate could see, involved the mutilation of retro toys. Everywhere you looked, there they were: an elaborately built Lincoln Log cabin sawed in two and splashed with red paint; a brunette Barbie doll, her hourglass figure skewered on half a dozen knitting needles; a shattered plastic Sno-Kone machine pieced together with electrical tape. If this was Hercules's calling, Kate thought, it was good that he'd kept his day job.

Still, whatever his credentials as an artist, Hercules was a genius with hair. Soon after she started work, Kate had noticed the Samson bob. After a summer spent studying for the bar exam, her hair had fallen well below her shoulders. She'd toyed with the idea of keeping it long but quickly changed her mind. Long hair, she concluded, was less professional. Besides, why stand out when the alternative was so appealing?

It didn't take long to get the name behind Samson's signature look, and after her first cut Kate was sold. Hercules was expensive, upward of $100 for a trim, but he was worth it. Easy maintenance — fifteen minutes with a brush and blow dryer — and even after twelve-hour days, her hair still kept its swing. How Hercules had come to be Samson's stylist of choice, Kate had no idea. She'd always meant to ask, but Hercules's strictly enforced no-talking policy was a strong deterrent to conversation.

As Hercules studied her head and clipped, Kate's thoughts wandered back to Douglas Macauley. *Stop,* she told herself sternly. *Just think about today.* If only she could flip through a magazine, that would keep her occupied. But reading was out of the question. Hercules claimed that the movement of eyes across a page interrupted the stillness he required. "What about breathing?" Kate had asked, the day of her very first cut. Hercules had ignored the question. She'd never tried to joke again.

"There." Hercules's voice was pleased. He whipped off the white sheet that had shielded Kate's clothing and handed her a mirror. Kate tossed her head from side to side, watching the graceful swish against her cheeks. "Hair with an attitude," Andrea called it.

"Stunning as always," Kate said. She hopped down from the chair and dug around in her purse for money. Hercules worked on a cash-only basis.

Kate was pulling on her black parka when she thought of her question again.

"Hey, Hercules?"

"Yeah?" He'd moved over to the loft's kitchen area, where he was stirring a large pot on a gas-fueled range.

"How'd you end up cutting hair for a bunch of lawyers? It doesn't really seem like your style."

Hercules snorted. "No, but it's more my style than what I was doing before."

"Which was?"

Hercules turned to face Kate, his upper lip curled back from his teeth. "I was a paralegal at Samson & Mills."

Kate took an involuntary step back. "You're joking."

"Nope. Did it for a couple of years during the eighties. To pay the rent."

"That's incredible. So how'd you go from that to this?"

"I used to cut my sisters' hair when I was growing up. When I moved to the city, sometimes I'd cut friends' hair. I'm an artist, you know. I keep my eyes open. I always sort of had a knack for it. While I was working at Samson, there was this woman lawyer I was sort of . . . friendly with. We used to joke around and shit. She was cool. Anyway, she was working on this big case and hadn't had a haircut for months. I was hassling her about it. She claimed she didn't have time. I offered to do it right then and there. It was really late, probably after midnight. I ran out to an all-night drugstore and picked up some scissors. Came back and gave her a cut. She loved it. Everyone did. Before I knew it, I had more clients than I could handle with a full-time job. Besides, I'd saved some money. And I hated that fucking place. So I quit and started doing hair instead."

"That's a great story. Who was it that got you started?"

"What?" Hercules seemed disconcerted.

"The lawyer whose hair you cut that first time. Is she still at the firm?"

"No, no. Well, she was until . . ." A wary expression had come into Hercules's eyes.

"It was Madeleine. Madeleine Waters." Crossing his arms, he looked squarely at Kate, as if daring her to react.

"*Really,*" Kate said, then stopped. Suddenly, for no particular reason, she felt a terrible uneasiness. Quickly, she began to talk, trying to hide her discomfort behind a barrage of words. "It's so awful about what happened to her, isn't it? I'd never worked with her until recently, but I'd always heard that she was a great lawyer. And beautiful, of course. But . . . I would never have guessed that you cut her hair. It was so wavy and tousled looking."

You're babbling, she told herself, and was relieved when Hercules stepped in.

"I hadn't cut Madeleine's hair for a long time," he said. "She got this perm thing going a few years back. Said she wanted a change."

As he spoke, Kate thought of the photo of Madeleine broadcast on the TV news. Of course. Her hair had been cut short in that picture, short and smooth. Just like her own hair now.

Hercules seemed to have regained his bearings. "Man, it's really awful about her being killed. I read about it in the papers. She was a nice lady. Really nice. Not like those other freaks. I don't know what she was doing there."

As Hercules talked, Kate's eyes had settled on the Barbie doll she'd noticed earlier. She stared at it in horrible fascination. The doll's wild dark hair spread out from her head like a storm cloud about to burst. Her staring eyes took no notice of the knitting needles plunged deep in her body. And then another image rose up in Kate's mind. Madeleine Waters's body, multiple stab wounds, a tide of black hair that must have framed her head just as . . .

With a start, Kate realized that Hercules was watching her, waiting for her to speak.

"I guess I should be going," Kate said, her voice artificially bright. She handed Hercules his fee and then fumbled in a pocket for her gloves.

"So, thanks a lot. I guess I'll see you next month."

Halfway down the six flights of stairs, something — perhaps a flicker of shadow on the concrete steps — caused Kate to glance up. There, from the top of the stairwell, Hercules was looking down. She tried to catch his eye, to wave, but he seemed not to notice the gesture. Pulling her parka more tightly around her, Kate continued, more quickly, down the stairs.

At home that night, miles from the bombed-out space that Hercules called home, Kate decided to take a bath. She felt jumpy, agitated. She'd always viewed Hercules as a colorful but benign eccentric. But that was before Madeleine's murder. Before she'd known that they'd worked together. Now, she wasn't sure what to think. Again, she thought of the ravaged doll, a plastic correlate to Madeleine's real-life death.

The tub was filling with water. Kate dumped in a capful of bubble bath, then added a second dose. Tonight she was going to relax. She flipped on the radio — always set for NPR — and let the restful strains of classical music filter through her rooms. Then she headed for her bedroom bookshelf in search of something to read. What would it be tonight? Jane Austen? Stephen King? Marissa Piesman? Glancing across a row of books, her eyes fell on an unfamiliar volume. *Sexual Harassment of Working Women*. The book Madeleine had given her just before she was killed. She'd brought it home that night to look over. But in the chaos following Madeleine's death, it had completely slipped from her mind.

Sitting down on the side of her bed, Kate folded back the book's red-and-black cover. Flipping through the first few pages, she noticed frequent pencil underlinings. *Sexual harassment, most broadly defined, refers to the unwanted imposition of sexual requirements in the context of a relationship of unequal power.* A pretty standard definition by now. And then, a few pages later: *The legal argument advanced by this book is that sexual harassment of women at work is sex discrimination in employment.*

Turning back to the front of the book, Kate checked the publication date: 1979. A generation ago in legal terms, written before the Supreme Court recognized sexual harassment as a cause of action. If she recalled correctly, this was a seminal work, outlining much of the doctrine later accepted as law. Curious, she flipped through the text. *Being at the mercy of male superiors adds direct economic clout to male sexual demands. . . . As work becomes degraded by mechanization and routinization, it becomes defined as "women's work." . . .*

The words seemed abstract, endlessly remote from her own life. Sure, a lot of her work was dull and routine — that was the nature of the large pieces of litigation in which Samson specialized. Thousands of documents to be reviewed and catalogued. Dozens of deposition outlines and routine motions. But did female associates get stuck with any more of the grunt work than their male colleagues did? Not from what she could see. In her year-plus at Samson & Mills, she couldn't think of one time when she'd been singled out because of her sex. Of course, she belonged to a privileged breed. For the vast majority of women, stuck in word processing or secretarial pools, the situation could be very different.

Kate was about to close the book when another underlined section caught her eye. *Not being attractive enough does have an economic effect. You know you can't get really well-paying jobs. If you ever go to the top floor of an office building, you know the women look a certain way.*

The women look a certain way.

Kate smoothed her newly trimmed hair. Hair carefully cut and styled like that of most of her female colleagues.

But, again, so what?

The tendentious writing was beginning to annoy her.

The point is that it is the very qualities which men find sexually attractive in the women they harass that are the real qualifications for the jobs for which they hire them. . . .

Sudden allegations of job incompetence and poor attitude commonly follow rejection of sexual advances and are used to support employment consequences. . . .

Men believe that whenever women are advanced on the job, an exchange of sexual favors must have occurred. . . .

Kate could hear the bathtub filling. Still carrying the book, she went to turn off the tap. While it didn't do much for her, she had to wonder what this book had meant to Madeleine. Had it perhaps called to mind her own career? Kate thought about what Justin had told her at the Harvard Club, how Drescher had argued that Madeleine had slept her way to the top. Kate hadn't really given the attacks much thought. Now she wondered if they'd contained a grain of truth. Of course, Madeleine was a very good lawyer. But had she really been so outstanding that partnership was a foregone conclusion? Had it been her abilities that set Madeleine apart from her less successful peers? Or was it her sexual relationship with Mills?

As the thoughts circled in her mind, Kate peeled off her clothes. She could feel the steam floating up from the tub, smell the bubbles' flowery fragrance. Suddenly, she was tired of thinking about Madeleine. Couldn't she just relax for one night? Still naked, she walked back to the bedroom, where she returned the book to its place. What she needed tonight was something soothing. She pulled out a dog-eared copy of *Sense and Sensibility* and headed back to the bathroom. She'd read and reread each of Jane Austen's six novels, and this was her favorite. An elegantly orchestrated moral fable that preached the eighteenth-century virtues of balance in life and love. Book in hand, she slipped gratefully into the tub. She closed her eyes and let herself drift, let the water's blissful warmth enfold her. The strains of a violin floated in from the living room.

This really was a perfect evening.

Sunday, January 10

KATE tried to stifle a cough. She'd awakened that morning with the beginnings of a cold, and the drafty church sanctuary wasn't helping. Furtively, she shifted in her seat, trying to find a more comfortable position on the hard wood pew. Her throat was raw, and her head felt as if it were stuffed with cotton. Pulling her cape more closely around her shoulders, she wondered if she might have strep.

It seemed as though the service would never end. Arthur Dawson had begun to speak. Dawson, who'd long since retired, was well over eighty by now. As his reedy voice droned on, Kate's eyes roamed through rows of black-clad figures until settling on Carter Mills. Mills had been one of the first speakers, delivering a careful and detailed account of Madeleine's career. Her arrival at Samson & Mills as a newly minted attorney, her rapid ascent in the Samson hierarchy, her election to partnership. As the words flowed out, mellifluous and measured, Mills referred obliquely to challenges faced, to obstacles surmounted. Kate had eagerly awaited Mills's turn at the podium, but once he'd started to speak, she'd found herself fast losing interest. The day after Madeleine's death, she'd seen real emotion in his face. By contrast, today's offering seemed artificial, prepared for public consumption.

Mills sat toward the front of the church, surrounded by other partners. As she studied the somber group, Kate realized that this was the first time she'd seen the thirty-seven partners all in one place. To an unknowing observer, they would hardly seem a remarkable bunch. A collection of middle-aged white guys — the few women seemed beside the point — barely distinguishable one from the other. The occasional bald head or goatee did little to alter the effect. Samson's partners were like tract houses, where occasional unique "features" only underscored a basic sameness. Tara was constantly getting them confused. Even the names, she claimed, sounded alike.

And yet, these ordinary figures were the stuff of legend. Mythic heros of an oral epic passed down through associate generations. There, behind Mills, was Colin Barfield, a litigator known for his single-minded vision. Barfield had once dragged an associate to the airport with him because she hadn't yet finished explaining a memo. When departure time came, and she still wasn't through, he'd taken her with him to Japan. With his tortoiseshell glasses and bow tie, Barfield looked like a gentleman lawyer. Who would guess that this courtly man made associates pack his clothes? Everything — underwear, shoes, shirts, and suits — had to be neatly stowed in his suitcase before checkout time arrived.

Next to Barfield was David Kirkpatrick, a man with strange habits of his own. Kirkpatrick insisted that associates telephone restaurants in advance to ask that any vegetable he ordered be served in its pureed form. Kirkpatrick couldn't be bothered with making the request himself. Nor did he want his associates distracted while they ate, interrupting the flow of his instructions. ("Ever try eating escargots and taking notes at the same time?" one of Kirkpatrick's associates had once asked a group of his peers. "It's *tough*.") A favorite Samson story was The Time That Kirkpatrick

Ordered the Artichoke, the agonized deliberations among associates on his team as to whether artichoke puree was in order. It went without saying that they couldn't ask. They were simply expected to *know*.

And on the other side of Kirkpatrick was . . . Martin Drescher. With a shiver, Kate snapped her head back toward Dawson, still rambling on up front. The time she'd spent under Drescher's desk still made her dizzy with remembered fear. But after taking a moment to collect herself, Kate shot another glance across the aisle. She'd hoped that something in Drescher's face would give insight into his emotions. But try as she might, she could discern no clue from his politely expressionless features. After a time she gave up; she looked back to the front of the room.

But while her eyes now focused on Dawson, Kate's mind continued to wander. As she picked at a hangnail, it occurred to her that it was strange to be here on a Sunday. This was a church, after all. Didn't they have services? Maybe someone had pulled some strings. It was a beautiful space, though.

A prism-like flicker danced on the floor. Kate tilted her head to the right, trying to locate its source. When she saw what it was, she rolled her eyes: Angela Taylor's ring. Angela was seated just across the aisle with several other third-years. Julie Whiting, Margo Price, Irene O'Shaunnessy. Out of Angela's conversational orbit, Kate could appreciate how pretty she was. Shiny blond bob, high cheekbones, a finely turned nose. And she wasn't the only one. The women clustered around her shared the same patrician good looks. Clear skin. Elegant profiles. Straight, gleaming hair.

If you ever go to the top floor of an office building, you know the women look a certain way. There was, perhaps, something to this observation. They were definitely a good-looking group, the female lawyers of Samson & Mills. Good-looking in a certain way. For the first time it occurred to Kate that Catharine MacKinnon might just be right. Not that women were hired based on looks alone. Of that, she was very sure. But was beauty perhaps a sort of threshold test? A way to limit the pool? What about a smart woman who wasn't much to look at? Would she still be in the running at Samson & Mills? Kate realized that she didn't know.

A brief shuffling up front and Dawson relinquished his post. Kate saw that the minister, a stocky man with a neatly trimmed beard, was again assuming the helm. A good sign. And then she heard the words she'd been waiting for. "And now, in closing, please join together in our final hymn." The song was Cat Stevens's "Morning Has Broken." Kate had to stifle a laugh — she couldn't imagine a song less in keeping with Madeleine's persona than this classic sixties anthem. Still, as the voices surged around her, Kate felt a lump in her throat. Andrea, seeming to sense her distress, gently squeezed her shoulder.

And then the service was over. Gathering up coats, the mourners began to file out. On the other side of the church, Bill McCarty hurried toward the door, dodging clusters of people who'd stopped to talk en route. Peyton Winslow huddled with Chuck Thorpe and a woman in a fur-trimmed suit. Kate couldn't suppress a wry smile. Even at Madeleine's funeral, Peyton was in networking mode. And Chuck Thorpe, what would he be thinking? Again, Kate wondered about the chain of events. Chuck Thorpe claimed that Madeleine had stood him up. But had it really happened that way?

"How're you doing?" Justin asked, curling an arm around Kate's shoulders.

"I'm all right," Kate said. She was a little embarrassed by the wave of sadness that had hit her as the service ended. "I think I'm coming down with a cold. You know how it is when you're feeling sick. Everything gets to you more than usual."

"Right." Kate was glad that Justin didn't loosen his grip.

"Do you guys want to grab something to eat?" Kate asked.

Justin consulted his watch. "Wish I could," he said. "But believe it or not, I have to get back to the office."

"Hey," Andrea whispered, grabbing Kate's elbow. "Look — coming down the aisle — Madeleine's family."

Kate turned as a nondescript threesome made its way toward the door. They were nothing like she would have imagined. Madeleine's mother — it must be her mother — was slack-faced and maternal. Beneath a stiff arrangement of gray-blue hair, her features were a baffled blur. She was propelled forward by a tall, thin man — Madeleine's father? — who grimly forged through the crowd. Both wore the shell-shocked look of unwitting tourists. Trailing after them was a harried-looking woman in her mid-forties tottering in black high heels. Behind the younger woman's pancake makeup, Kate made out a fleeting resemblance to Madeleine. She must be Madeleine's sister.

"Listen, I've got to split," Justin said, pulling on his coat. "I'll call you later on, Kate. See you, Andrea."

As Justin disappeared in the crowd, Kate caught sight of a dark-haired man who seemed to be watching her. But before she could try to place him, he'd already looked away. Briefly, she wondered if he was someone she knew. He didn't really look familiar. Still, she'd met so many people since moving to New York. It was hard to remember them all.

"Hungry?" Andrea asked.

"A little," Kate said. Her nose was starting to run, and she reached into her purse for a tissue. "You know what I'd really like? Some kind of chicken soup."

❧

OUTSIDE the church, Sam Howell walked quickly down Seventy-sixth Street, heading for the Seventh Avenue subway. He couldn't wait to get away. Couldn't wait to get out of the city, to be back at home in Sag Harbor. He thought about the work he'd set out for tonight. Film to be developed from his India trip. A stack of business correspondence to answer. He'd planned it all out yesterday, knowing that he'd need to keep busy, that he'd need to keep the memories at bay.

His mind went back to what he'd just seen. The girl. Her appearance had left him breathless. He'd stared at her mesmerized, unable to sort through his feelings. The cap of dark hair, the heart-shaped face. Only the glasses were wrong. Then she'd turned toward him and he'd looked away. Not wanting it to seem like he was staring. Furtively, he'd scanned the room. Could he really be the only one who saw it?

The wind pushed against Howell's face, but he barely felt the blast. His thoughts were still focused on the past two hours. He hadn't wanted to be there today, hadn't wanted to be there at all. At the same time, he'd had to come. He'd known it would be difficult. He'd tried to brace himself for the encounter. Still nothing had prepared him for the visceral rage that he'd felt on seeing Carter Mills. He'd clenched the edge of his pew. It was all he could do to stay seated. He'd wanted to leap into the aisle and take hold of Mills, to shake him until his teeth chattered. But of course, he'd managed to restrain himself. That showdown would have to wait.

Again, he thought of the girl. Her haunting beauty. Her youth. Was it just a coincidence that she'd been there today? Somehow, he didn't think so.

⁂

"My head feels like it's about to explode," said Kate, after she and Andrea had placed their orders. "I need to pick up some Tylenol."

They were sitting in a booth at Fine & Schapiro, just a few blocks down from the church. Fine & Schapiro was one of the few old-style delis to survive the rampant commercialization of the Upper West Side. A welcoming beacon amid the Gaps, Starbucks, and other chain stores that had turned this once-quirky neighborhood into a makeshift mall.

"I'm glad *that's* over," Andrea said, spreading cream cheese on an onion bagel. A chastened expression quickly followed. "Did that sound harsh? It's just been such a strain on everyone since . . . since it happened. Maybe now we can at least move on."

Kate raised a spoonful of broth to her lips. "Don't count on it," she said. "It's not like they even know who did it yet. There's still an investigation going on."

Andrea glumly studied her snack. "Three weeks until Brent and I leave on vacation, and I can't *wait*," she said. "The way things are going here, I may never come back."

"From the looks of that white water, you'll be lucky to *get* back," said Kate, recalling the roiling Chilean rapids in the travel poster on Andrea's office wall.

Andrea grinned. "Coward."

After a few more spoonfuls of soup, Kate began to revive. She looked across the table at Andrea. "Do you think it's strange that the women at Samson are so attractive?"

"Excuse me?" Andrea had no idea what she meant.

"I was just thinking that we're all definitely . . . above average in the looks department. I mean, why is that? Isn't there a single top female law grad who's ugly or fat?"

Andrea shrugged. "I never really thought about it. And I'm not even sure it's true. What about Kara Ouelette and . . . well, I'd have to think about it, but I'm sure there are others."

Kara Ouelette was a pallid, overweight sixth-year associate who seemed forever stuck in the library with the first-years.

"Okay, that makes one," said Kate. "But think about it. As a group, the women really are much better looking than the men. Objectively speaking. You'd have to agree with that."

Andrea smirked. "What about Justin?"

"The exception that proves the rule."

"I don't know, Kate. I guess you could be right. But so what? No one ever said the world was fair."

"No, but —" But what? At least its unfairness should be gender neutral? Kate was having trouble sorting through her thoughts. "You know, something sort of weird happened yesterday. I was getting a haircut, and —"

"It looks great, by the way," Andrea interjected.

"Thanks. Anyway, I was talking to Hercules, and —"

"Talking to Hercules?" Andrea raised her eyebrows. "Isn't that strictly forbidden?"

"We talked *after* he cut my hair. Anyway, while we were talking, Hercules told me that he used to be a paralegal at Samson & Mills."

"Really?" Andrea looked amused. "I'm glad that was before my time. Can you imagine persuading Hercules that he needed to hurry up with the copying? I can't quite see it."

"But wait, it gets stranger. Hercules said that it was Madeleine who got him started cutting hair. He began by cutting *her* hair, and then it sort of caught on."

Andrea's eyes opened wide. "I never would have guessed," she said.

Kate toyed with her soupspoon, trying to decide where to go from here. She didn't want to seem paranoid. Still, someone had murdered Madeleine. She decided to press ahead.

"The thing is, Madeleine stopped going to Hercules a while back," Kate continued. "He didn't tell me why. Actually, the whole time we were talking about Madeleine, he seemed sort of uncomfortable. And then, I noticed this one really disturbing piece of his. A Barbie doll with a bunch of knitting needles stuck through her body. So I'm looking at this creepy doll, and all of a sudden I'm thinking how much she looks like Madeleine."

"Kate." Andrea looked at her severely. "You're not saying that you suspect *Hercules* of killing Madeleine?"

"Not suspect, exactly." Kate was determined to hold her ground.

"And what's the motive? Hair stylist desertion? If that were enough to push someone over the brink, this city would be a bloodbath."

"Just because I don't *know* the motive doesn't mean there couldn't *be* one," Kate said. "I just think that I should talk to the investigators. And then there was that meeting I had with Madeleine. Right before she died. When she told me that I should be careful."

Andrea met Kate's eyes. "Listen, if it would make you feel better to talk to the cops about Hercules, go ahead. But I really don't think you should mention the meeting. That thing about being careful. It'll just make you seem neurotic."

"But you don't know how she sounded." Kate could hear the defensiveness in her voice.

"Fine. I believe you. But think about how *you* sound. And what would you really accomplish? What she said to you, it's just too little to go on."

Kate looked down at her plate. "I don't know," she said. "I guess I'll sleep on it."

"Just remember, Kate, we're junior associates, peons. We really have to watch our step."

&

LATER in the day, Kate lay curled up in bed, sipping hot tea and reading *Sense and Sensibility*. "Elinor saw, with concern, the excess of her sister's sensibility; but by Mrs. Dashwood it was valued and cherished. . . . " Only a little after five, but outside it was already dark. A gust of wind made the window shudder. Reaching for the wall unit next to her bed, Kate turned up the heat.

After saying good-bye to Andrea, Kate had returned home to messages from Douglas and Tara. At the sound of Douglas's voice, she'd felt herself growing tense. *I really enjoyed meeting you Friday. Call me when you have a chance.*

Now, tucked inside a warm bed, she just wanted to be alone. Madeleine's funeral seemed to have taken place days ago, rather than that same afternoon. Kate thought about Madeleine's parents, wondered what they were doing now. Were they consumed with rage at their daughter's killer? Or still numb and disbelieving?

As a child, Kate had found herself pondering questions of time and space. How could time go on forever? Didn't everything have an end? But how could time *not* go on forever? The same thing with space. How could it not be endless? But then, how could it possibly be? She'd been a wakeful child, lying wide-eyed for long hours after being kissed good night. There, in her small, dark room, she'd examine these puzzles again and again, awash in a dizzy confusion.

How could it be?

And how could it not be?

It was the same thing with Madeleine's murder. Someone was responsible for Madeleine's death. Some living, breathing person had taken up tools and done unspeakable things to her body. It seemed impossible that this person existed at all. At the same time, Kate found herself suspecting everyone. It was part of the paradox: if no one could have committed the crime, then anyone could have done it.

Again, Kate's thoughts returned to Hercules. Maybe she should call Valencia after all. Even Andrea had seemed to think that would be okay. Pushing back the covers, Kate climbed down from her bed and went into the living room. She found Valencia's card in her purse, stuffed in a billfold compartment. Kate stared at it a minute and then picked up the phone. She was still thinking what to say when Valencia's voice mail engaged.

"This is Kate Paine," she began hesitantly. "I'm an associate at Samson & Mills. We spoke on Thursday. There was just . . . something I wanted to mention to you. I'll be in the office tomorrow. So . . . thanks."

Hanging up the phone, Kate felt a slight sense of relief. It was good to have done something — anything — aimed at finding Madeleine's killer.

Monday, January 11

ANOTHER cold, bleak morning. A little before nine. Kate was approaching the doors of Samson & Mills when she changed her mind and turned a corner. She passed a row of dilapidated brownstones, then proceeded on to the Mug, a storefront coffeehouse with excellent lattés. Probably not the smartest move for someone fending off a cold. But in the life of a Samson associate, efficiency always trumped health.

The woman behind the counter was about Kate's age, but there the resemblance ended. She had multiple piercings and platinum braids. Rebecca of Sunnybrook Farm gone punk.

"Here you go," she said.

Holding her cup, Kate made her way to a couch by the window.

Her cough had gotten worse last night, and she'd downed two doses of NyQuil before finally dropping off to sleep. By morning, the cough had eased up, but she still felt hazy and tired, haunted by the remnants of dreams. Something about an airplane flight. An urgent meeting of sorts. She was flying to India, that was it, on her way to meet Madeleine Waters. Then the plane had begun to go down . . .

Engrossed in her thoughts, Kate didn't notice the man who'd come in behind her. He ordered a coffee and then, cup in hand, headed over to where she was sitting.

"D'you mind if I have a seat?"

Kate started at the sound of his voice. "Oh! Sure." She scootched to one side of the lumpy couch to let the stranger sit down.

"Didn't mean to scare you," he said. He was tall, with curly dark hair that tumbled over his forehead. He was wearing a black leather jacket and jeans. He seemed slightly familiar, though she wasn't sure why.

"Do I know you from somewhere?" she asked.

He studied her face, then shook his head. "I don't really think so," he said. Then, with a smile, he turned away.

Sipping her coffee, Kate stared outside at the midtown office brigade. On days she was in good spirits, rush hour could seem almost festive. Today it seemed meaningless. She looked at her coffee mug, at the milky brown liquid inside. She was trying to ignore the man beside her, but she couldn't seem to blot him out. It was distracting to have someone so close. It wasn't like there weren't a bunch of free seats. Would she be rude to get up and move?

"Hey, which of these do you like best?" The voice seemed to explode in her ear.

"Sorry, I scared you again." His teeth were very white, his eyes a smoky green. He was holding two photographs.

It wasn't like she really had a choice. Kate leaned forward and looked. Both of the 8 x 10 prints showed the same exotic scene. A massive ancient building on a river. Kate examined the pictures for a long moment, surprised at what she saw.

"Did you take these?"

"Yeah."

"They're good."

"Thanks," he said. He really had a very nice smile.

Kate turned her eyes back to the prints. She'd toyed with photography herself for a time, taken several courses back in college. Even fantasized about making it her profession. But looking at work of this caliber, she knew she'd made the right decision. She could never have been this good.

"Umm, this one, I think," Kate said, pointing to the picture on the right. She looked over at her neighbor with a new respect. "Where were these taken?"

"In India. Varanasi. The Hindu holy city."

"India." Kate had an image of a plane, wings dipping low in the sky. "Isn't that strange. I dreamed about India last night."

"Ever been there?" he asked.

"No," Kate said. She felt an unaccountable wave of regret. Now what was *that* about? "How long were you there?"

"Three weeks. On assignment."

"Really!" Kate no longer felt tempted to leave. She noticed an open box of prints. "Are those all yours?"

He nodded.

"May I look?"

One by one, Kate examined the prints. Most of them looked like India — temples, markets, camels — but at the end came several seascapes.

"These last two, they're different."

"Those were taken closer to home. I live in Sag Harbor. On Long Island."

"Beautiful." Kate looked at her watch. Almost 9:30. "I really need to get to work." Reluctantly, she handed back the photographs.

"You work around here?"

"Yes, I'm a . . . a lawyer," Kate said. She felt suddenly self-conscious, as if she should explain herself. She waited for the inevitable lawyer joke, but this time it didn't come.

"What kind of law?" Howell asked.

"I work for a firm, in litigation."

"Which firm?"

"It's called Samson & Mills." Braced for a barrage of questions, Kate was relieved when Howell let it drop. Of course, he lived out on Long Island. Maybe he hadn't heard.

Putting on her cape, she lingered a moment, thinking about the pictures. "So do you ever show your work around here?"

"As a matter of fact, I have an exhibit now. In Sag Harbor. At the Cavanaugh Gallery." He casually extended his hand. "I'm Sam, by the way. Sam Howell."

"Kate Paine." His hand was large and warm. "Do you ever have shows in the city?"

"Nothing planned right now. But Sag Harbor's an easy day trip. It's nice this time of year. The tourists have all gone home. You should think about coming out."

Half an hour later, Kate was editing her memo when the ringing phone made her jump. Still reading, she reached for the receiver.

"Ms. Paine?"

"Speaking."

"This is Detective Valencia." A pause. "I'm returning the message you left me."

"Oh! Right. I called you last night." Kate took a moment to shift modes. It was a little dizzying, this moving back and forth between the worlds of corporate law and urban violence.

"What can I do for you?"

"It's probably nothing," Kate said. "But I was getting my hair trimmed this weekend by this guy who cuts hair for a lot of the women associates here. He's sort of a strange character. Anyway, he told me that Madeleine —"

"I'm sorry, Ms. Paine, I don't mean to interrupt, but are you talking about Hercules Spivak?"

Spivak. Kate realized that she'd never known Hercules's last name. "How did you —"

"Let's say his name has come up a few times." Valencia's voice was dry. "We spoke to him. At his loft." She paused. Kate tried to imagine Valencia's reaction to Hercules's artistic oeuvre. Had she noticed the Barbie doll?

"Then this probably isn't anything new. It's just that he used to be a paralegal at Samson. I didn't know that before. He worked with Madeleine. He also cut her hair. She was actually his first Samson client."

"I see." said Valencia. Her tone was neutral. Kate couldn't tell if she was surprised. "Aside from his prior acquaintance with Ms. Waters, is there anything else about this man that seems significant to you?"

"Well, if you were down at his loft, you probably noticed his . . . artwork."

"Yes." Again, the same dispassionate tone.

"There was this one piece that caught my eye," Kate said. "A Barbie doll that sort of reminded me of Madeleine. It was partly the coloring, I guess — pale skin and dark hair. Also, the way that the hair was arranged, sort of rippling out from her head. Anyway, he'd done this really brutal thing to the doll, stabbing her again and again with knitting needles. There must have been six or seven of them, sticking out from the body. And it made me think . . ." Kate's voice trailed off.

"I did see the doll," Valencia said. Her voice had softened a bit. "Ms. Paine, do you have any reason to think that Hercules had any recent dealings with Ms. Waters?"

"No. Like I said, it's probably nothing."

"Is there anything else that comes to mind, anything that worries you?"

Kate paused for a moment, recalling Hercules's looming form as he watched her descend the stairs. "No," she said finally. "I don't think so."

"Well, please don't hesitate to call back if you think of anything else. We need all the help we can get. Oh, and Ms. Paine? I wouldn't want you to worry too much about Mr. Spivak. He was out of town the night that Ms. Waters was killed."

As she hung up the phone, Kate was feeling sheepish. Andrea was right: she needed to get a grip. She returned her attention to the memo, erasing all other thoughts.

She'd been working intently for some time when she was startled by a knock on the door.

"Greetings," said Peyton. "Hope I didn't frighten you."

Already, Kate felt at a slight disadvantage. Peyton had a way of doing that. Today, he was wearing a dark suit and bow tie, along with a pair of tiny glasses with hexagonal steel-rimmed frames. The glasses were a calculated risk, an ironic twist to the starched propriety of his clothing. Against all odds, it seemed to work.

"So let's see what you have." Peyton settled into a chair and folded his hands before him. Kate recognized the gesture immediately: vintage Carter Mills.

"I've summarized the relevant law on sexual harassment," Kate said, handing him her current draft. "I'm still finishing up one section — the standard by which a claim is evaluated. Basically, the conduct at issue has to be both subjectively and objectively outrageous. In other words, it's not enough that a given plaintiff was outraged by what happened if a so-called reasonable woman would not also have been. And vice versa. If a reasonable woman would have been outraged, but this particular plaintiff would not have been — again, there's no cause of action."

"So, if we could show that Friedman was less sensitive than most women to sexually aggressive conduct, that should help us, right?"

"Exactly."

"And what about the state law claims?"

"I'm still looking into them."

"What can you tell me so far?"

Kate glanced at her notes. "In the first section, I've considered the various grounds on which we could move for pretrial dismissal of the sexual harassment claims."

"And?"

"I don't think we have any really strong arguments. The action is timely. Well within the statute of limitations. And Friedman properly filed with the EEOC before moving to federal court."

"So where does that leave us?"

"As I see it, we have two main avenues of defense. First, we'll want to show that Friedman had no problem with Thorpe's behavior. That she was a willing participant in whatever went on. That in itself should dispose of her claim. Second, as I was just saying, we'll argue that Thorpe's conduct wasn't outrageous. And that, even if it might have been seen that way by some women, it wouldn't have been seen that way by Friedman. Based on what Carter says — and on our meeting yesterday with Linda Morris — I think we'll have strong arguments on all of these points. Still, they're all factual issues, and that means we can't get a pretrial dismissal."

"What's this about the First Amendment?" Peyton was pointing to a footnote.

"It's a thought I had," Kate said. She felt a surge of intellectual pleasure in Peyton's quick grasp of the issues. He'd rapidly zeroed in on the one innovative section of what was, for the most part, a pedestrian summary of current law.

"It's like this," Kate said. "To prevail on her sexual harassment claim, Friedman has to show that Thorpe's advances were unwelcome. My point is that this kind of factual showing should be a lot more difficult here than it would be in other workplace situations. Everyone knows that *Catch* is basically a sex magazine. When Friedman took a job at *Catch*, she had to assume that the workplace atmosphere would be sexualized. How do you put out that kind of magazine if you're prohibited from discussing the subjects it contains? It's like Thorpe said — what did she expect, *Good Housekeeping?*"

Peyton looked reflective. "Isn't that basically arguing that she assumed the risk of sexual harassment? That's a common-law doctrine. It sounds like you're trying to import common law into a federal statutory regime."

Kate paused to consider. Under the Supremacy Clause of the U.S. Constitution, federal law always trumped state law. The rule of preemption. Peyton was right in stating that assumption of risk — a doctrine aimed at barring suits by plaintiffs who had knowingly entered high-risk situations — was a principle derived from state common law, principles enunciated in the binding decisions of state judges. But that hardly ended the debate.

"I don't think so," said Kate. "It might *also* constitute assumption of risk — and then you're right, we'd have preemption problems — but what we're really considering here is whether the conduct was unwelcome. That's the standard set forth under *federal* law. Look at it this way. If you came into my office and started demanding lurid details of my sex life, you should expect me to be outraged. We're lawyers. That sort of information obviously has no possible bearing on our work together."

Peyton's face was impassive. Hard to say if she was making any headway. But she was in her element here, confident of where the argument was heading. She plunged ahead.

"Now compare that with Friedman's case. When Thorpe asks her about sexual stuff, there's arguably a legitimate business purpose. In other words, there's a *legitimate nondiscriminatory* reason for the discussion."

"I'll have to think about it," Peyton said. "But you still haven't explained how the First Amendment fits in."

"It's a supporting argument. The First Amendment protects the media's right to free speech. My point is that if you prevent Chuck Thorpe — or anyone else, for that matter — from engaging in essential editorial activities, you inhibit their constitutionally protected right to speak."

"The First Amendment doesn't protect obscenity," Peyton observed.

Peyton was right. In the so-called marketplace of ideas, obscenity was the outcast, deprived of the most basic First Amendment protections. Never mind that no one seemed quite sure just where to draw the line. But she was ready for the objection.

"*Catch* isn't obscene," Kate said. "Just because there are some racy pictures doesn't mean you can write it off as pornography."

"Like feeding Anita Hill through a meat grinder?"

Kate held her ground. "You're just making my point. *Catch* contains political speech — the sort of speech that's at the heart of the First Amendment. The sort of speech the founding fathers were most concerned with protecting. The sexual harassment story should be our Exhibit A. It's a spirited discussion of controversial political issues. Exactly the sort of speech the First Amendment was designed to protect. That story should help us, not hurt us. That's the beauty of it. We'd be taking their own evidence and using it against them."

Kate felt herself warming to the argument, trying to win Peyton over. It was her favorite part of law, figuring out novel ways around seemingly intractable roadblocks. There weren't so many opportunities for it as a young associate; too much grunt work to get through. But that would change as the years went by.

Peyton seemed intrigued, though undecided.

"I'll have to think about it," he said again. "We'll talk when I've read the cases."

That was one of the good things about Peyton. It was standard procedure for senior associates to steal ideas from more junior attorneys, presenting them as their own. Peyton didn't play those games. He was good, and the partners knew it. He could afford to share the credit.

Kate looked at Peyton curiously. From the neck up, he looked like a promoter for an alternative band. Below that, the conservative dark suit gave him away. Still, you had to admire him for pressing the boundaries, for pushing convention without posing a threat. Flair without subversion. Where had that impulse come from? Funny how you could work with someone every day and still know very little about him.

"What did you study in college?" Kate asked.

"Pardon?"

"I know it's a non sequitur. I was just . . . wondering."

Peyton gave her a pleasant smile. "I studied classics," he said.

"Classics?" Kate could hear the surprise in her voice. "I would have guessed economics or maybe even philosophy. But classics? It's so . . . literary."

"Well, yes," Peyton said dryly. "Anything else that you'd like to know?"

"Yeah," Kate grinned. "Have you always had a thing for funky glasses?"

The corners of Peyton's mouth edged slightly upward. Almost as if he was enjoying himself. "Now that's a fairly recent innovation. My sister has a friend who's a designer. She gives me the men's samples. Like them?" So Peyton had a sister. She never would have guessed.

"They're quite . . . striking," Kate said. "Can you see without them?"

"Not a thing. Blind as a bat."

"Your eyes can't possibly be as bad as mine," Kate said. "I can't even see the big *E* on that eye exam chart."

"That's nothing," said Peyton. "I can't even see the *chart*."

"Come on, you're just trying to one-up me," Kate said. "Here, trade. Let me put on your glasses."

Peyton rolled his eyes but complied, though he declined Kate's proffer of her own frames.

As Kate raised Peyton's glasses to her eyes, the room flew into focus.

"This is amazing," Kate said. "It's like we have exactly the same prescription. Or maybe I need my eyes examined. I think your prescription's better than my own."

Peyton reached out his hand. "Well, Kate, this is all quite interesting, but I've got some work to do." Placing his glasses back on his nose, he pushed back his chair and stood up. "Why don't you finish the research this evening. I'll take a look at what you've written so far."

After Peyton left, Kate looked out the window, at the Hudson

River sunk in fog. The meeting had gone pretty well, she decided. Better than she would have thought. She congratulated herself on how she'd handled Peyton, even getting him to loosen up a bit. Then, still staring out the window, she had a disturbing thought. Throughout the duration of the meeting, Madeleine's name hadn't come up once.

Madeleine had been killed on Tuesday. Less than a week ago.

And already it could almost seem as if she'd never existed at all.

By the time Kate finished up work in the firm library, it was after ten. Still, she wanted to get her thoughts on paper before going home for the night. She'd learned from experience that, like dreams, her legal theories often slipped from her mind if she didn't capture them right away. Hoisting a stack of *Federal Reporters*, she waved good night to Justin, who was still scribbling away in a cubicle by the window. Seeing him there, his handsome features consumed in thought, gave her a settled, peaceful feeling. It was as if they were back at Harvard. Just another late night at Langdell.

Back on the fifty-first floor, Kate swung by Andrea's office for a quick chat, but the door was closed and locked. She turned back and headed for her own office. The firm seemed to have shut down early tonight. She didn't see a single person. Nearing her office, she saw the door was shut. The cleaning crew must have closed up. Kate felt a flash of annoyance. Maybe it was silly, but she wanted colleagues to know that she was working late. The brightly lit office was a badge of honor, a sign that you were pulling your weight. Shifting her books to one hip, Kate fumbled in her purse for keys.

As she stepped into her dark office, Kate instantly knew something was wrong. Before any further thought could form, she spun around, back toward the door.

But it was already too late.

A powerful arm clamped around her neck, while a hand smashed over her mouth. Her body went rigid, arching out reflexively like a fish on the end of a hook. Her load of books dropped to the ground. She tried to scream but no sound came out. She could hear someone breathing behind her.

"*Just keep quiet.*" The commanding voice was familiar, but Kate was too disoriented to make a connection. "*I don't want to hurt you.*"

Her attacker exuded a pungent odor, frightening and unfamiliar. Heat radiated from his body in waves. Before Kate knew what was happening, a large hand forced open her mouth, shoving a wad of something soft inside it. Then she felt a band of cloth being wrapped tightly once, twice, three times around her jaw. Having completed this task, her assailant pinned her arms to her sides and pushed her toward the back of the office. His arms pressed against her like a vise. She bucked forward, trying to break free, but the grip only tightened.

"*You keep doing this, and these hands are going to be around your neck,*" the voice whispered matter-of-factly.

Kate let her limbs go slack.

Then he was hurling her into the corner at the rear of her office, his heavy body crushing her back into the place where the two walls met. Kate could feel herself trembling uncontrollably. She could barely breathe. If only she could see, she'd be able to get her bearings. The office was dark, so dark. It was then that she realized what had alerted her to danger in the first place. The lack of light. Always, when she entered her office, the lights flashed on. But that hadn't happened this time.

"*This will all be over before you know it,*" the voice continued. "*Just relax and try to enjoy it.*"

Try to enjoy it. The hand resting on her right shoulder began to move slowly downward, stopping when it reached her breast. Then, rhythmically, the hand began to squeeze, softly at first and then harder.

"*You like that, don't you,*" the voice crooned. "*Don't worry, we're just getting started.*"

Kate's muscles recoiled from the contact. But trapped against the wall, there was no place to go. She tried to think, to come up with a plan, but her mind seemed to be short-circuiting. The hand that had been squeezing her breast began to travel farther down her body. She felt a rough tug at her skirt followed by the sound of fabric ripping. The garment dropped to her ankles, and a hand was clawing at her stockings, pulling them down along with her beige bikini panties. She felt fingers against her, fumbling. Then, with a sharp flash of pain, he was inside her, fingers ramming up her body. Back and forth the fingers went, deeper and deeper, tearing at the dry interior tissue.

"*Come on, baby, relax.*" She could feel her assailant's heavy breath against her cheek, its pace increasing as his hand moved more quickly. While tears gathered in her eyes, another part of her remained the objective observer. Thoughts floated through, but they seemed to come from outside her. *He's going to rape you,* the thoughts said. *And then he's going to kill you. And there's nothing you can do about it.*

As the thrusting inside her grew harder, she saw the outlines of a bobbing head pressed hard against her breast. Her eyes were adjusting to the dark.

"*Come on, now, come on.*"

That voice, so familiar. But where . . . Then, in a blinding moment, she knew exactly who it was.

Chuck Thorpe.

The shock of the realization was so great that she almost stopped breathing. At the same instant, almost as if he could read her mind, Thorpe stopped. He roughly pulled his hand from her body, wiping it on her black suit jacket. Stepping back, he held her firmly in place, his hands pressing into her shoulders.

"*I guess that's enough for tonight.*" Kate could make out a sneering smile. "*You really should learn to relax, Ms. Paine.*"

Kate stared across the room, her mind still struggling to comprehend what had just happened. From the corner of her eye, she watched Thorpe brush off his clothes. Still watching her, he picked up the jacket he'd dropped on the built-in bookshelf and put it on.

Then he opened the office door and sauntered out. Kate was vaguely aware of minutes passing. Still, she continued to gaze straight ahead, leaning against the wall where he'd left her.

It was some time before she thought to move.

During the ride home, Kate sat silently in the backseat of the taxi she'd flagged down outside the building. On a normal night, she would have called for a car from one of the fleets retained by the firm to transport its late-working minions. But this was no normal night. The familiar sights of Broadway flashed by. She tried to focus on her surroundings, anything to stop herself from thinking. The deli where she sometimes grabbed a tuna fish sandwich. A burned-out fast-food joint, charred and vacant. All she wanted was to be home, alone, safe behind her own locked door.

An interminable fifteen minutes later, she was closing and bolting her apartment door. She scanned the familiar room. The well-worn sofa still cluttered with remnants of this morning's *Times*. The desk piled high with papers and unopened mail. The tall bookcases against the right wall. Everything was just as she'd left it. And yet, instead of calming her, the effect was one of further dislocation. Objects she'd left that morning — a half-full coffee mug on the pine coffee table, a blue glass vase full of dried flowers — seemed alien, sinister in their blank indifference. This apartment belonged to the woman she'd been before, to a person who no longer existed.

Slowly, as if she were a visitor in her own home, Kate walked to the small hall closet and hung up her cape. Then, in a burst of motion, she headed for the bathroom. Stripping off her crumpled clothing, she turned on the shower full blast and stepped inside. The water was scalding, but she didn't try to adjust it. She almost welcomed the pain, as if it could somehow erase what had happened.

For some time, Kate stood immobile under the stinging jets of water, letting them pound into her skin. Then she picked up a bar of soap and a loofah sponge and began to scrub, first gently and then harder. She could feel her skin smarting beneath the rough strokes, but she didn't care. All that mattered was getting rid of any traces of Chuck Thorpe. She brought her whole concentration to bear, moving over her body piece by piece, inch by inch, washing herself from head to toe. Still, she didn't feel clean enough. She could feel Chuck Thorpe's heavy weight pressing against her chest, his hands, damp and insistent, roaming over her body. As torrents of water pounded against her, Kate retraced the path again, paying special attention to the places that Thorpe had touched. Her shoulders. Her breasts. Between her legs. Finally done with this task, she squeezed a glob of shampoo into her palm and started in on her hair.

It was half an hour before Kate emerged from the bathroom, her head wrapped in a towel, her body encased in a full-length robe. After the dull roar of the shower, the empty silence of her apartment filled her with a vague unease. As she pulled the terry-cloth length of her robe more tightly around her body, Kate could feel a pulse beating in her head. Then, without warning, she was hit by a blinding rage. The emotion seemed to come from somewhere outside her, storming the fragile battlements of her self-control. It all came back to her, the scent of Thorpe's sweat, the sound of his breathing, the sensation of his hands on her breast, between her legs. Anger surged through her like an electric current. There was nothing rational about this feeling, nothing reasoned or considered. Thinking of Thorpe, she wanted, quite simply, to destroy him.

Then, just as quickly, the rage receded, leaving her desolate and alone.

What was she going to do?

The obvious next step was to call the police. And yet, what would that really accomplish? People would arrive; phones would ring; events would be set in motion. She saw herself in a hospital, interrogated by uniformed officers, klieg lights shining down on her body. Instead of the independent woman she'd struggled to become, she'd now be known as a victim. Someone to be questioned, pitied, and examined. Someone who, unable to protect herself, had been forced to seek help from strangers.

This was not who she wanted to be.

Leaning against the wall, Kate pressed her hand to her face. If she could just calm down, think more clearly. If she could just shut down her emotions and let her mind work, her cool, analytic mind. Then she could figure out what to do.

A drink. Maybe that would help. Somewhere in the kitchen she had a bottle of red wine, a Christmas gift from a legal transcription company. She located the dusty bottle in a cabinet behind a stash of seldom-used pots and pans. *Chateau Whyte Legal Services.* She'd kept it as a sort of joke, the ultimate bottle of bad Long Island wine. But tonight she'd hardly know the difference. Kate's hands trembled as she jammed a corkscrew into the bottle, and it took a few yanks before she finally pulled out the cork. She took a wineglass out of a cabinet and filled it almost to the brim. Still standing at the counter, she took two long gulps. Then, carrying the glass along with the bottle, she moved to the living room.

For a moment, she thought of calling someone. Tara or Andrea. Or maybe Justin. Someone who could help her decide what to do next. But she already knew what they'd say: they would tell her to call the police. And she couldn't do that. At least not yet.

And it wasn't just the immediate repercussions. There was also the question of her career.

Even if the charges stuck, her career at Samson & Mills would be effectively over. WideWorld Media was one of Samson's most valued clients, an account worth millions of dollars a year. If she accused Chuck Thorpe of sexual assault, she'd be launching an attack on WideWorld as well. Samson could never continue to represent Chuck Thorpe in a sexual harassment case when one of its own lawyers had accused him of sexual assault. LAWYER ATTACKED BY SEX MAG MAGNATE. She could see the tabloid headlines now.

And then there was the issue of Samson's reputation. If the fight over Madeleine's partnership election had drawn news coverage, just think what would happen now. One female partner murdered. Another attacked by a client. Samson would be caught in a media feeding frenzy. And it would all be her fault. Or so it would seem. So what if Chuck Thorpe was a psychopath? She would still be the one to pay the price. Nothing — not her Harvard degree, not the countless hours she'd put in at the firm — would be able to salvage her career. She could already imagine how events would unfold. She would be questioned gently, respectfully. She would be granted a paid leave to recuperate and rest. Everything would be done to show that the firm had her best interests at heart. The partners would act as though they were on her side, as though things would go on as before.

But everything would have changed.

Instead of a valued member of the Samson team, she would have become an outsider, a quantity to be contained and controlled. And when the furor had died down, she'd be urged to seek other employment. All for her own good, of course. They would do anything they could to help her. But they wouldn't want her around. Her presence would be inextricably linked to a scandal they hoped to forget. Even if they believed her, they still wouldn't want her around.

She'd have to start over. Again. The thought filled her with despair. It was as if she'd been starting over her whole life. Her parents' divorce. Her mother's death. Michael's betrayal. An endless succession of things breaking down. At Samson, she'd thought she finally would be able to rest. That in exchange for all her hard work, she'd be allowed to take root in one place. But now . . .

Taking another long sip of wine, Kate let her head fall back on the sofa. As if from a great distance, she looked back on the evening's events. Her late-night return to a darkened office. The surprise attack. The moment she'd first seen Thorpe's profile.

Again, a burst of anger shot through her. *Chuck Thorpe.* Who was he to place her in this position? To force her to give up everything she'd worked so hard to achieve? But there was something muted about the anger. Mingling with rage, she sensed another emotion, subtle but growing stronger.

Doubt.

It nagged at the edges of her mind, crowding out other thoughts. Had she really done all she could to fight back? Or was this whole thing partly her fault? *Why didn't you struggle? He didn't have a weapon, at least none you could see. Why didn't you try to get away?*

Kate drank down what was left in her glass and poured another. She drank patiently, industriously, waiting for relief. Slowly, almost imperceptibly, a heavy warmth settled in her stomach, like a cat curling up for a nap. Minutes passed. Kate drank some more and felt the glow build.

I should do this more often, she thought. *How wonderful not to feel.*

Maybe she should just try to forget about this, pretend that it hadn't happened. . . . But that was ridiculous. You couldn't just let it go, not something like this . . . or could you? Worse things, much worse things, happened on the streets of New York every day. Madeleine Waters's murder, for one. Here she was, safe at home, drinking a bottle of wine. Anyone who saw her now would see a woman to be envied. She still had her health, her job, her home. Nothing external had changed. Was it really so terrible what had happened to her? Or was she overreacting? Even if they believed her, would the New York police really care? She was still sentient. Still in one piece. She hadn't even been raped.

Or had she?

With an involuntary shudder, she remembered the brutal thrust of Thorpe's hand, his fingers groping around inside her. Penetration, yes, just not with the usual object. It was like an issue-spotter question on a law school exam, where they tried to trick you by switching the facts. Penetration, yes; penis, no. What result? She could feel laughter welling up inside her, but what came out was a strangled bark.

Kate took another long drink of wine. Through a deepening haze, she tried to remember what she'd learned in school. But it was so long ago, those Crim Law lectures in Pound Hall, and

they'd barely touched on rape. Never discussed the physical requirements at all that she recalled. She could summon up only bits
and pieces, odd fragments of information that had astonished or
interested her. Like the fact that rape prosecutions had once required the testimony of a corroborating witness, an effective bar to
all but the rarest of cases since even the clumsiest of rapists generally works alone. Or the largely discarded requirement that women
fight off their rapists, no matter that they fear for their lives. No re-
sistance, no rape.

Placing her wineglass on the coffee table, Kate abruptly stood
up. The room spun for a moment, and she steadied herself by leaning against the wall. Walking toward the full-length mirror on her
bedroom door, she stepped out of her robe, careful not to trip on
the sagging hem. Standing unsteadily before the mirror, she studied her unclothed form. Leaning forward, she looked closely at her
face. Then, craning her neck, she turned around, examining the
backs of her arms and legs. Except for the wild flush that stained
her cheeks, her skin was a translucent white. The eyes that met
hers gleamed feverishly, the glittering eyes of a stranger.

Done with the examination, Kate put her robe back on and returned to the couch. She picked up her wineglass and drained it.
Then she poured another glass. No marks. No signs. No evidence.
Just her word against Chuck Thorpe's. She herself could almost begin to doubt whether the thing she remembered had happened.

Leaning back into the sofa cushions, Kate studied the wine bottle on the coffee table. Almost empty.

Time to drink up.

Kate tipped the last of the crimson liquid into her glass. Crimson. The color of Harvard. The color of blood. Her mind went to
Madeleine Waters, her body lying splayed and brutalized near the
riverbank. Then, with a start, she sat upright, her heart beating
hard in her chest. Why hadn't she thought of it before? *You have to
be very careful.* It all came together. *Madeleine had been warning her
about Chuck Thorpe.* She thought of Carmen Rodriguez's words,
the day after Madeleine's body was found: *They used her to keep*

Thorpe happy. Finally she stood up for herself and look what happened. . . .

And look what happened.

As the words echoed in her brain, a wave of dizziness descended. Kate looked at the bottle of wine. Empty. It occurred to her that she was very, very drunk. She could feel her mind growing dimmer, as if someone had pulled a plug. The point that had struck her with such urgency had utterly slipped from her mind. What was it again? Something about Madeleine . . . Madeleine and Chuck Thorpe . . .

It was no use. Tomorrow. She'd come back to it all tomorrow. For now she just needed to sleep.

Lifting herself off the couch, Kate staggered through her bedroom doorway. She peeled off her bathrobe, and pulled out a nightgown from a dresser drawer. The flannel garment was freshly washed, smelling of laundry detergent. A gift from her mother many years ago. Tears sprang to Kate's eyes. And then the emotion faded, giving way to a blissful void. Collapsing onto her bed, Kate lay still for a moment in the dark. Then, she pulled back the covers and slipped between the sheets.

Within minutes, her mind went blank.

Tuesday, January 12

KATE woke up five hours later with a pounding headache and a mouth that tasted as if a small rodent had curled up inside. It was still dark out as she stumbled to the bathroom. Without bothering to flip on the light, she turned on the tap. She drank deeply, scooping up long gulps of water with her hands, letting the cold liquid course down her throat.

Leaving the bathroom, Kate tripped over something, a towel perhaps, and bent over to pick it up. Then she stopped cold. There, in a pathetic pile, were the crumpled, torn remains of the black suit she'd worn yesterday. With its fitted jacket and kick-pleat skirt, this outfit had been one of her favorites. Now, she stared at it in revulsion. Her first impulse was to bundle up the whole pile and toss it down the building's trash chute. But the lawyer in her protested. If any evidence remained of Thorpe's attack, it was probably on this clothing. And while she didn't plan to press charges, there was nothing to be gained from discarding whatever proof she had. Stomach heaving, she went to the kitchen and pulled out a garbage bag from under the sink. Returning to the bathroom, she knelt on the floor. Gingerly, with thumb and forefinger, she picked up first the skirt, then the jacket, and dropped them into the black plastic bag. Then, cinching the yellow drawstring tight, she tossed the whole thing into a hall closet and firmly shut the door.

An hour and three glasses of orange juice later, Kate decided to call in sick. It was a little after eight. She left a voice mail message for Jennifer, pleading the flu and saying that she could be reached at home if needed. Then she toddled back to the kitchen for more fluids.

Now, in the light of day, she was relieved that she hadn't called the police. It was definitely the right decision. Far better to proceed quietly. Tomorrow morning she'd go to Carter Mills and together they'd decide what to do. She'd describe the situation calmly, making clear that she was loyal to the firm, that she had no intention of creating trouble. Her recital would be slow and measured, devoid of emotional overtones. She would behave, in a word, like a Samson attorney.

Back on the living room sofa, Kate picked up the remote control and snapped on the television. In a strange way, she was glad to feel hungover. The physical discomfort provided a focus, something to keep her from thinking about last night. After all, there was nothing to be done today. She'd spend the morning watching television, something she hadn't done since childhood.

Kate was halfway through a rerun of *I Love Lucy* when the phone rang. Eyes still riveted to the flickering images, she waited for her machine to pick up. The recording clicked on, bright and alert. *"I can't take your call right now, but if you'll leave a message, I'll get back to you as soon as I can."* Could that really be her voice?

"Hey, Kate. Come on, I know you're there. Pick up the phone."

Breaking loose from her TV-induced trance, Kate grabbed the receiver. "Hey, Justin."

"What's up? Jen said you were out sick today." Justin's voice was brisk and hearty, as if he'd just returned from the gym. In fact, he probably had.

"Oh, you know . . . , I was coming down with something on Sunday. I thought I'd got it kicked, but . . ." She felt uncomfortable lying to Justin, but the prospect of disclosing the truth was even more disturbing.

"You don't sound so good," Justin said.

"I was just dozing off. I didn't sleep so well last night." Kate forced a cough, as if to underscore the point.

"Hey, I'm going to try to cut out of here early tonight for a change," Justin said. "How about if I stop over and bring you some dinner?"

Kate felt a rush of gratitude. As usual, her refrigerator was almost bare. And maybe some company would be good, prepare her for the day to come. "That's so nice of you," Kate said. "Are you sure you don't mind?"

"Mind? Of course not. Hey, it'll be like old times. Like we're back in school. "

Kate knew he'd meant it as a joke, but she felt a pang. Old times. Justin bringing her soup while she wept over Michael.

"That would be great, Justin," Kate said. "I can't thank you enough."

She'd just settled back into the couch when the phone rang again. Thinking it was Justin calling back, Kate picked up without waiting for the machine to kick in. But it was Tara.

"They said at work you were sick." *They.* Jennifer had been Kate's secretary for more than a year, yet Tara could never seem to remember her name. Just one of the subtle ways Tara showed her antipathy to Samson & Mills.

"Well, *they* were right," Kate said. "I've got the flu."

"I can't remember the last time you were sick," Tara said. She seemed uncertain how to continue. "It must really be bad to keep you home."

"I'll be fine," Kate said. "It's just something going around. I'll probably be better tomorrow."

"Well . . . , don't force yourself to go back to work if you aren't ready. D'you need anything?"

"No, no. I'm all set. Justin's going to bring over dinner."

"You're sure you don't want me to come by?" For a moment, Kate was tempted, lulled by the thought of a friendly presence. But she just couldn't risk it yet. Tara knew her too well. She'd know that something was wrong. "No," Kate said firmly. "Really, I'm fine. Besides, I should probably get some sleep."

When she hung up with Tara, it was just after ten. She still had the whole day to fill. Her mind moved briefly to the night before but she managed to stop herself. She didn't want to think about that. She didn't want to think about *anything*.

Turning back to the TV screen, Kate watched the last few minutes of *I Love Lucy*, then picked up the newspaper schedule to see what came next. *Roseanne*, *Grace Under Fire*, and then *Rikki Lake*. After that she could choose between *The Newlywed Game* — now that was a blast from the past — and *Jenny Jones*. Surveying her choices for the afternoon, Kate felt a sense of abundance. Show after show all day. She'd spend the rest of the morning and all afternoon immobile and entertained.

She wouldn't have to think at all.

"If you've gotta be sick, it's better to make it a Monday," said Kate, peeking into a fragrant cardboard carton. "What have we got here?"

"Hot-and-sour soup," said Justin, reaching into a bag. "From that Vietnamese place around the corner."

Kate dipped a plastic spoon into the take-out container. "Mmmm. I didn't realize how hungry I was."

"So why Monday?" said Justin. "What difference does it make?"

"Better TV," said Kate. "All of my favorite shows."

Justin rolled his eyes. "Glad to see that you've got your priorities in order." He lifted out another soup container. "So how are you feeling, anyway?"

"Better," said Kate. "Really a lot better." And, strangely enough, she was. She'd spent most of the day sleeping and watching TV. Old sitcoms with hokey plots and canned laugh tracks. The events of last night had no place in that well-meaning world. And having no place there, they'd ceased to exist. Now, sitting on the couch with Justin, Kate was struck by a giddy sense of power, as if by pretending that nothing had happened, she could actually make it so.

"So what's going on at work?" Kate asked between spoonfuls of spicy soup. She felt an urge to reconnect with the Samson & Mills she knew, a fast-paced, rational world that hummed like a well-oiled machine. A world where everything was clearly linked by cause and effect. A world where violence never occurred.

"Let's see." Justin leaned back into the couch. "The big news today is that Drescher threw a stapler at a paralegal."

Kate leaned forward. "He *what?*"

"It was Erik Parks, a new kid. Just graduated from Amherst. Anyway, Drescher had him stamping some huge document production. Parks had never done it before. He went back to ask Drescher some question, and Drescher just started screaming at him. Parks tried to back off, but I guess he wasn't fast enough."

Kate shook her head. Stories like this were the stuff of Samson legend, usually evoking an incredulous amusement. And yet, tonight Kate couldn't quite see the humor. The story just seemed bizarre. Bizarre and a little frightening.

"Did the stapler hit him?" she asked softly.

"No. He was plenty scared, though." Justin bit into a spring roll and chewed for a moment, reflective. Then he wiped his mouth with a napkin. "I talked to him at lunch. I mean, he was trying to laugh it off, but you could tell that it had freaked him out."

"Well, of course. God." Kate's thoughts returned to her own recent confrontations with Drescher. The repressed rage in his face when he'd expelled her from Madeleine's office. Her narrow escape later that evening, when she'd hidden under his desk. She'd really gotten off easy. Nothing at all like last night. . . . In an instant, she was back in her unlit office. She could feel Chuck Thorpe's hands.

No. Don't think about that.

"Kate?" Justin was looking at her strangely.

"Sorry, I just lost my train of thought for a second. What were you saying?"

"Just that I've got another one, another colorful story from the annals of S&M."

Justin was clearly relishing the opportunity to play raconteur, and Kate made an effort to seem responsive. "Okay, shoot."

"So do you know Daniel Weisbach?"

The name sounded vaguely familiar, but Kate didn't feel up to sorting through the possibilities. "Yeah, I think so," she hedged.

"He's a third-year. Went to law school at NYU."

"Okay."

"So he's this really hard worker. But, because of the Sabbath, he has to leave work early on Fridays and can't work on Saturdays at all. So he's sort of been trying to make up for it by pulling these constant all-nighters during the rest of the week."

"And?"

"He was interviewing some guy from Harvard today for a summer associate job. All of a sudden Weisbach starts feeling a little *queasy.* He excuses himself, and steps out into the hall. His secretary instantly sees that something is wrong. Then Weisbach just keels over. They call in the medics and cart him off to the hospital. It turns out that he has walking pneumonia and a hundred-and-three-degree fever. Not to mention that he's seriously dehydrated. He said he'd been too busy to notice."

Again, Kate shook her head. She tried to summon up a smile, but it died on her lips. In the past, she'd reveled in the gallows humor that accompanied the telling of these tales: the guy who committed suicide after working two 125-hour weeks in a row; the female associate who fell silent in the middle of a late-night conference call only to be discovered later at her desk, phone still in hand, and very, very dead, the victim of a sudden heart attack. The stories had always seemed unreal, like incidents from a movie. Kate had even laughed. But tonight the reality hit her. These were real people, real people who had died. What had she found to laugh at? There was nothing funny about death.

"You know, in Japan there's a word to describe people who drop dead from overwork," Kate said. "*Karoshi.* I read about it in the paper."

"Actually," said Justin, "there are two words. There's another word — I don't remember what it is — but it's for cases of work-related *suicide.* As opposed to, well, whatever you call the other kind. Spontaneous. Anyway, there've been a bunch of lawsuits, where Japanese families are suing for compensation."

"I wonder how you prove causation," Kate said dryly.

"Got me."

Kate was suddenly aghast at her train of thought. Was this what being a lawyer did to you? Instead of responding as a human being, you thought about how to prove a case?

"I don't really see what the difference is," she said gloomily.

"The difference with what?"

"Between *karoshi* and the other one, suicide from overwork. I mean, it boils down to the same thing. What's the difference between forcing yourself to work so hard that you die and shooting yourself in the head? One's just faster, that's all."

"Interesting," said Justin. "So I guess you'd say that all of us S&M minions are engaged in some sort of group self-destruction. We're in the process of killing ourselves, we're just not there yet. Just bring on the Kool-Aid."

"Kool-Aid?"

"Just a joke. You know. Jonestown. Where they drank the poisoned Kool-Aid."

"Oh. Yeah." Kate was feeling increasingly depressed. It was as though the room had suddenly grown smaller, darker. She sensed Chuck Thorpe at its edges.

Justin sighed. "Come on, Kate. Lighten up. Have some more soup."

"Okay." Obediently, Kate spooned up another mouthful. As she swallowed the warm liquid, her thoughts moved to Madeleine Waters.

"Is there any new word on Madeleine?" she asked.

"Just a couple of rumors," Justin said. "The usual paranoid stuff that she was done in by the partnership. Mills or Drescher. Or maybe both of them working together. Along with the Pope, the Trilateral Commission, and the IRS."

Kate tried to laugh, but none of it seemed very funny. Again, the memories pressed in on her. Chuck Thorpe's hands on her body, his breath on her face. The more she thought about it, the more likely it seemed that Thorpe was Madeleine's killer. Her mind went back to the events of the past few days. Madeleine's grip on her shoulder, her urgent words: *You have to be very careful.* Carmen Rodriguez's fury. *They made her have dinner with him, and God knows what else.* And then Thorpe's brutal attack. Yes, she'd been very drunk last night, but that didn't mean that she'd been wrong. She was sober now and could think it through. And the pieces of the puzzle still fit, just as they had last night.

Justin didn't seem to notice her distraction. He'd walked over to the TV and was studying the weekly broadcast schedule.

"Wanna watch a stupid movie?"

"If you do," Kate said.

Justin flipped on the television and returned to the couch. The movie had already started. Two sisters — one rich, one poor — were fighting over their mother's estate, but really what they wanted was each other's love. Giving Justin a sideways glance, Kate felt a surge of gratitude that he was here tonight. He'd always been there when she needed him, and tonight was no exception. The only difference was that tonight he had no idea, no idea at all what she was going through.

A commercial flashed on the screen. Justin turned toward Kate. "So what's up with that guy Douglas you've been seeing?" he asked.

Kate had barely thought of Douglas since their Friday night date. It felt like another lifetime.

"I'm hardly seeing him," Kate said, trying to cut short the exchange. "I've just been out with him once."

But Justin persevered, his voice warm. "I'm just really glad to see you moving on. That thing with Michael — he wasn't worth it then, and he's certainly not worth it now. It's important to have someone in your life."

"Can we just not talk about this now?" Kate asked. Still preoccupied with thoughts of Chuck Thorpe, she was only half focused on what Justin was saying. "Besides, you're hardly in a position to talk. When was the last time that you had a date?"

Justin opened his mouth, as if he was about to speak. But then, looking at Kate, he closed it again. There was something odd in his expression, an emotion that she couldn't place.

"What?" Kate asked. "Why are you looking at me like that?"

Justin shook his head and then laughed, a sheepish, boyish sound. He stood up and walked to the window. Then he turned back toward Kate. "This is ridiculous. I don't know why I feel uncomfortable telling you this. I mean, we're friends, right?"

"Right." She had a growing sense of trepidation.

"Well, the thing is . . ." Justin was briefly tongue-tied. Then he blurted it out. "I've started going out with someone. A woman, I mean." He ran a hand across his forehead and smiled, the familiar slightly lopsided grin that she knew so well. "Whew. I guess that wasn't so hard."

Kate's lips returned Justin's smile, but her face felt frozen in place. She felt disoriented, unable to situate herself in time and space. Almost as if she were drowning. Still, she managed to keep up the smile.

"So don't keep me in suspense. Who is she?" Kate's voice was unnaturally bright. Like Lucy Ricardo trying to keep something secret from husband Ricky.

"Well, not surprisingly, she's a lawyer," Justin began. "Since I'd have little chance of meeting anyone else." He took a deep breath.

"Her name's Laura Lacy. She works at Wilmot Dickerson. I met her last month when we did a joint document review with them. You'd like her, Kate. She went to Penn. Does a lot of pro bono work."

Now that the shock had begun to ebb, Kate was more confused than upset. Her reaction didn't make any sense. After all, Justin wasn't her boyfriend. He had every right to date anyone he wanted.

"That's wonderful," Kate said, trying to bring a warmth to her voice that she was far from feeling. "So, how long has this romance been going on?"

"Oh, not long," Justin said quickly.

Something in his voice made Kate want to know more. "So how long is that?"

Justin sat down on the couch, crossing one long leg over the other. "Oh, a few weeks, I guess. Maybe about a month."

A *month*. Kate felt as if she'd been slapped. She'd always assumed that Justin confided in her about the important things in his life. Before she could stop herself, the words were out. "Why didn't you tell me?"

"I *am* telling you, Kate. I'm telling you right now." Justin sounded awkward, as if he wasn't sure what to say.

Kate slumped down against Justin's side, her head turned away so he wouldn't see the tears in her eyes. She tried to sort through her thoughts. Was she jealous? She tried the thought on for size, then dismissed it. She didn't want Justin for a lover; she wanted him for a friend.

"Kate?" Justin's voice was soft. Kate shrank lower on the couch, keeping her head turned away. Maybe this wasn't about Justin at all. Maybe it was just a delayed reaction to what had happened last night. Her emotions were raw today, magnifying the impact of everything that happened. She wished she could explain this to Justin. But for now she had to keep it to herself.

Kate rolled her head back to look up at Justin. "I'm sorry," she said earnestly. "I don't know why I'm being like this. I'm happy for you. *Really*. Maybe I'm just afraid that if you get a girlfriend, you won't have as much time to hang out with me."

Justin grinned. "In that case, I guess I should be flattered," he said.

"So tell me her name again."

"Laura Lacy."

Even the name was impossible, Kate thought. Like something from a romance novel. Or *Melrose Place*.

"What's she look like?" *Is she prettier than I am?* Now where did that thought come from? Why should she even care?

"She's pretty," Justin said, the corners of his lips edging up ever so slightly. "Sort of an all-American type, blond hair, blue eyes."

"Your basic nightmare," Kate muttered. She meant it to be funny, but it didn't come out that way. She quickly moved on. "I can't wait to meet her," she said. "I'm sure we'll get along fine."

Wednesday, January 13

TAKING a deep breath, Kate flung open her office door. Heart pounding, she scanned the familiar space. Her body was on red alert, ready to bolt from the room at the first sign of danger. But there was nothing. Morning sun streamed through the window. Her desk, cluttered with computer printouts and reference books, looked as if she'd just taken a break. The corner where Chuck Thorpe had held her pinned against the wall was just that, a corner, an empty space by the window. The books she'd dropped were now stacked on her desk. And the office lights . . . whatever Chuck Thorpe had done to interfere with their functioning had already been repaired.

Kate unwrapped her cape and hung it in the office closet. Here, too, things were just as she'd left them. A couple of sweaters. Spare shoes. Not bothering to look in the closet mirror, she closed the door and went to her desk. She wasn't quite sure how she felt. On the one hand, it was a relief that her office had escaped contamination. On the other, it was a little disturbing. Shouldn't there be some sign?

Taking a seat at her desk, Kate tried to think about the day ahead. First thing on her agenda was a phone call to Carter Mills. But after picking up the receiver, Kate paused for a moment, uncertain. What exactly did she plan to say? After all, WideWorld was not just one of Samson's largest clients, it was also Carter Mills's personal crown jewel. However much he might like her, Mills would have a vested interest in rejecting her account, in finding some way to dismiss it.

There were other problems, too. Such as the lack of physical proof. While there might be some trace evidence on the black suit she'd stuffed away — hairs, fibers, something like that — what would it really show? Just that she'd had some contact with Thorpe. How could she prove that the contact was sexual in nature? Or that it had been without her consent? Then there was the fact that she'd waited so long. She hadn't reported Thorpe's attack at the time it occurred or even the following day.

Kate slowly put down the phone receiver as her mind continued to work. So many points that she hadn't considered. For one thing, there was Chuck Thorpe himself. It would be her word against his. Thorpe would have his own story, and it wasn't hard to imagine how that story might go. He'd claim she'd made the whole thing up. Or maybe that she'd led him on, that she'd invited him to her office for a private talk and tried to seduce him there. In that case, her failure to report the attack would add credence to Thorpe's story. As would the very recklessness of his actions. The whole scenario just seemed so far-fetched. Why would Thorpe risk attacking her in her office, a place where anyone might appear? Of course, she knew the answer: Chuck Thorpe was a psychopath. But why should Carter Mills believe her?

Jennifer appeared in the doorway, carrying a huge stack of mail. She looked at Kate, then did a double take.

"Are you okay?" she asked.

"Sure," said Kate. "I'm fine."

Jennifer put the mail in Kate's in-box. "D'you want me to get you something? Aspirin maybe, or coffee?"

"No, really," said Kate. "I'm okay. I'm just feeling a little tired."

Jennifer eyed her doubtfully. "Let me know if you change your mind." She was heading back to her station when she turned to look back at Kate. "There was something wrong with your office lights. I called downstairs. They fixed them right before you got here."

"Thanks," Kate said. "Thanks for taking care of that."

Jennifer closed the door behind her.

Kate sat unmoving, staring blankly ahead. Her thoughts continued to churn. Her mind returned to Carmen Rodriguez's words the day after Madeleine's death. "*All they cared about was the money. They forced her to work with him. And look what happened.*" If Madeleine had been pressured to work with Thorpe, that pressure must have come from Carter Mills. But she shouldn't make too much of this. There was still no reason to think that Mills knew about Thorpe's violent streak.

Violent.

The word seemed so neat and contained compared to the reality of what she'd been through. Again, Kate felt Thorpe's hands on her body, his wet, heavy breath. She picked up the receiver. Without pausing to think, she dialed Mills's extension.

"He's not in yet, Kate," Clara said. Kate could hear the sound of typing in the background. "Would you like to leave a message?"

"Could you just tell him I need to see him? And that . . . it's important."

After hanging up, Kate felt depleted. She'd finally gotten up the nerve to speak with Mills, and he wasn't even there. But at least she'd left the message. That was the important thing. Now she just had to wait.

She turned to the mountain of mail that Jennifer had left for her. Hard to believe that this much had piled up during just one day away from the office. Lethargically, she sorted through the first few envelopes. A mass mailing about CLE courses. A solicitation for Legal Services.

A few minutes later, Kate picked up the phone again, this time to call Andrea. After a few rings, she heard a click as the call went into voice mail. She listened to the first few words of Andrea's message, then hung up the receiver. She was feeling a little hurt. While Andrea obviously didn't know what had happened, she must know Kate had been out sick. Why hadn't she called to check in?

A rap on the door interrupted Kate's thoughts. Before she could answer, Peyton Winslow stuck his head through the doorway, his pale eyes distracted behind red-rimmed glasses. He looked like a fashion-crazed owl. "The Thorpe complaint is supposed to be served today. When will you have the rest of that memo?"

Today. The irony took her breath away. "I'll have it to you by tomorrow." Kate didn't mention her one-day absence, a tacit bow to the Samson equation of physical illness with a failure of will.

"The sooner the better," Peyton said. He was already edging out the door. "We've got a meeting tomorrow afternoon with Holden and Thorpe." The words trailed behind him as he strode down the hall.

A meeting with Holden and Thorpe. Just last week, the prospect would have filled her with elation, a sense that she had arrived. But today, just the sound of Thorpe's name made her feel physically ill.

Kate's hand was trembling when she reached for the next piece of mail. It slipped out of her grasp and fell to the floor. As she leaned over to pick it up, she noticed a glint of metal on the carpet underneath her desk. A lost earring, perhaps? Kate knelt down on her hands and knees and picked up the small gold object. A flat disk with crenellated edges surrounding an ornate monogram. Kate stared at it blankly for several seconds before realizing that it was a cuff link. A man's cuff link. Looking more closely, she made out an ornate letter *T*, then a *C*.

Chuck Thorpe.

Kate dropped the cuff link to her desk as if she'd been burned. It must have fallen off Monday night while they struggled. Evidence, concrete evidence, that Chuck Thorpe had been in her office. It wasn't much, but it was something. She tried to think what to do. Grabbing a white office envelope, she stuck the cuff link inside. After sealing the envelope's flap, she stashed it in her top left drawer. There was a small key in the drawer's pencil tray. She locked the drawer and put the key in the change compartment of her billfold. Then, still trembling, she returned her attention to the mail.

An hour or so later, she was almost halfway through when she came upon a large white envelope. Aside from her name, typed on a blank white label, there were no markings at all. Turning over the packet, Kate saw that the flap was secured with a red wax seal bearing the impress of the letter M. Curious, she studied the seal for several seconds, her previous concerns forgotten. Then, careful not to break the seal, she ran a letter opener under the flap and reached into the envelope. From inside she pulled out two 8½ by 11 pieces of plain white cardboard. Between them was a black-and-white photograph. A picture of a lovely dark-haired woman somewhere in her early twenties. Kate stared at the photograph, mesmerized. It was a picture of Madeleine Waters.

She was standing on the stairs of a low brick building, maybe a walk-up apartment. She was dressed in bell bottoms and platform shoes, smiling flirtatiously. With one hand, she pushed back a stray strand of hair. With the other, she reached toward the camera. The gesture was ambiguous, both welcoming and remote. Again, Kate looked at the envelope, searching for some explanation. There was no postage stamp, no postmark. It must have come from inside the firm. She turned back to the picture, searching the image for clues.

The longer Kate examined the print, the more her confusion deepened. As she studied the figure more closely, she saw her initial mistake. While this woman resembled Madeleine, there were obvious differences, too. The face was broader, flatter. The eyes were more widely set. And the clothing was early seventies, well before Madeleine's time. Madeleine would have been quite young back then, probably still in grade school.

And yet . . . what of the red letter M?

The ring of her phone interrupted these thoughts. Carter Mills would see her now.

Quickly, Kate tried to shift gears. Gathering up a notepad and pen, she rehearsed what she'd planned to say. *I was returning to my office, a little after ten on Monday night . . .*

She was almost out of her office when she turned to look back at her desk. She stared at the photograph for a second or two, then walked over and picked it up. She held it in her hand for another few seconds, uncertain about what to do. Then, with sudden decision, she put it back in the red-sealed envelope and added the packet to the pile in her arms. Once outside her office, Kate stopped by Jennifer's station. "If anyone calls, I'll be in Carter Mills's office." Then she turned and headed for the stairs.

Light sifted in through venetian blinds, patterning Carter Mills's face. He held the envelope in one hand, studying the red wax seal. Then he looked back at Kate.

"When did you receive this?" he asked.

"Either yesterday or early today," Kate said. "I'm really not quite sure."

"I see."

"The photograph is inside." Kate was anxious to wind this up, to move on to the subject of Thorpe.

"It's a picture of a woman," Kate said. "Someone who looks a lot like Madeleine Waters. I have no idea why it was left with me. But I thought you should probably see it."

Carefully, like a scientist handling a specimen, Mills reached into the envelope and pulled out the cardboard liners. With two fingers, he removed the top piece and placed it off to the side. From the slick photographic paper, the dark-haired woman smiled up at him, her strangely expressive hand reaching outward. Welcoming. Pushing away.

Mills looked back at Kate, his eyebrows raised. "You really think that this woman looks like Madeleine Waters?" he said.

Kate wasn't sure what to say. The resemblance was so striking. She hadn't considered that Mills might not see it. "I . . . yes, yes I do," she said. But the question opened a wedge of doubt. Could the pressure of the past few days be affecting her judgment? She'd made the connection so quickly: between the picture and the letter M seal, she'd immediately jumped to conclusions. But of course the letter M stood for many things other than Madeleine.

Mills, for example.

Or McCarty.

Or what about Martin, as in Martin Drescher? She felt giddy, lightheaded, as the names piled up.

Linda Morris.

Douglas Macauley.

Or even Michael . . .

Her head was swimming, but she couldn't seem to stop herself.

Mills was studying the picture. "I just don't see it," he finally said. "The mouth maybe, but aside from that . . ." He raised a dismissive hand.

"Well . . .," Kate didn't know what to say.

"Do you have any idea where it came from?"

"No. None."

Mills's eyes returned to the picture. Again, Kate noticed the bars of light that flickered across his face. The venetian blinds almost made it appear as if he were inside a cell.

Hands folded, Mills leaned forward. "You know, Kate, there's a lot of gossip flying around now. It's not helpful. Not helpful to the police investigation, not helpful to the firm. Have you talked to anyone else about this photograph, about the resemblance you see to Madeleine?"

"No." Kate felt a flutter of relief, as though she'd finally done something right. Then, without warning, relief gave way to resentment. All she'd thought about for the last two days was protecting the firm and her place there. What about protecting herself? The rush of feeling took her by surprise. She'd had no idea it had been there waiting, just beneath the surface of her thoughts.

But Mills was talking again. "Please keep it that way," he said. "I'm sure you understand the importance of keeping rumors to a minimum. There's only so much we can do to keep people from speculating. But we need to do what we can."

We. Even now, Kate felt the seductive lure of inclusion. *We.* The attorneys of Samson & Mills. She could feel the resentment ebb.

"Of course," Kate said. "I won't say a word."

"If anything else unusual happens, please come to me immediately."

Kate looked at Mills, confused. "But if the photo doesn't even look like Madeleine —"

Mills interrupted, impatient. "No, Kate, *I* don't see a resemblance. But obviously you do. And that concerns me. In a situation like this, it's impossible to be too careful."

There was an unaccustomed edge to Mills's voice. Still Kate found herself pressing ahead. "Do you think I should talk to the police then?"

"Absolutely not," Mills said. "I'll handle all communications with the NYPD."

His displeasure seemed almost tangible. Kate felt heat rise up through her face. "Of course," she said. It was an effort to keep her voice level.

"I'm sorry, Kate," Mills said, his voice softening ever so slightly. "I don't mean to be harsh. But it's imperative that we keep a tight rein over all outside communications."

"I understand," Kate said. She took a deep breath. This was hardly the atmosphere in which she wanted to discuss Chuck Thorpe, but she didn't have any choice. She'd already waited too long. Heart lurching against her ribcage, she tentatively embarked on the speech she'd prepared. "There's something else I need to discuss with you. It's about Chuck Thorpe. On Monday night —"

"I'm sorry, Kate, but this will have to wait. I have something important to take care of."

Kate stared at him, disbelieving. Her script didn't allow for this response. "But this is really urgent," she stammered. "It will only take a few minutes, and I need —"

"I'll speak with you as soon as I can," Mills said. His voice was pleasant but firm. "Check with Clara. She knows my schedule. I should have some time later today."

⁂

CARTER Mills stared out the window. His skin felt hot, as though he'd been struck with a sudden fever. He couldn't seem to order his thoughts. Words came together, then drifted apart. Mainly, they were questions, the stunned beginning of questions that he didn't want to consider.

Behind him was the photograph. It lay on his desk, waiting. Slowly, he turned back to face it. Just a single flimsy piece of paper, slightly worn at the edges. There was nothing remarkable about the image. Just an ordinary candid shot. A pretty woman on a summer day. Perfectly ordinary. Perfectly generic.

Yet not to him.

He hadn't thought of this scene for years. But now, with the picture before him, it came back like it was yesterday. Downtown Manhattan. Late August. A sultry summer evening. He'd left work early, having just finished drafting a brief. Rounding a corner, he'd caught sight of her, standing there on the doorstep. He'd called out to her amid the neighborhood clamor, and she'd quickly spun round to face him. Her face showed a blend of emotions, pleasure mingled with chagrin. He was early that day, and she hadn't had time to prepare.

Still, she'd been happy when he snapped her picture. Happy, he knew, because she'd seen it as a sign of love. A sign that even during their brief separations, he wanted her close at hand. Yet, somehow, he hadn't felt guilty. Merely amused by the irony: what she saw as a sign of devotion was really his first step away. Soon she'd belong to the past.

It had all come clear that afternoon. Though perhaps, at some level, he'd known from the start. Decades had passed since that day. But the memories were clear as glass.

"Very good." William P. Sloan raised his leonine head and looked at Mills appraisingly. "Very, very good."

"Thank you, Mr. Sloan." Mills felt a satisfying twist in his gut, like the sprockets of a gear engaging, like a plane lifting into the sky. He ran over the words in his mind. The great William P. Sloan liked his brief. Life was suddenly good. The future was his for the taking.

With casual grace, Sloan folded his hands. Mills filed the gesture away, knowing he'd adopt it as his own. "Your grandfather was one of this firm's founders. You show every sign of being a worthy heir. I certainly hope that you'll return to us after graduation."

Again, the surge of triumph. Formal offers of employment were not generally issued until summer's end. And yet, here he was, being personally wooed by the firm's presiding partner. But he was careful to keep his voice level, as if simply accepting his due.

"That's exactly what I'm hoping," he said.

Mills gazed at Sloan, so powerful, so complete. So different from his hidebound father, the keeper of books, of records, of family trees. Nothing compared to the vital figure before him, a man of action who lived for the day.

The sort of man he, Carter Mills, would become.

By the time he'd left work that day, his mind was already made up. Childhood was over. He was an adult. And she had no place in his life.

He'd purchased the camera and film on his way downtown. He'd meant to buy color film, had been annoyed on discovering his mistake. But the irritation quickly faded as she came into view. Focusing on the slender form, he'd felt a rush of power. As if the secret knowledge that he would hurt her somehow confirmed his strength.

And, really, she'd had no idea. She'd been giddy that evening, euphoric. They'd split a bottle of wine. He'd even smiled as she'd babbled about the future. A future that would never be. *She loved*

the theater, but she loved him more. She loved him more than any-
thing. . . .

As, for a time, he'd loved her.

Loved her with a reckless passion that he hadn't felt before or
since.

Mills shifted in his chair, remembering. It had begun as a chance
meeting, an instantaneous spark. He'd been on his way to a movie
when he'd seen her through the window of a small cafe. In an instant, he'd changed his plans. He went in and sat at a table, the
marble top cold to his touch. By the time he left two hours later,
her number was in his book.

But slowly that memory faded, and he was left with the picture
on his desk. He could feel the paranoia setting in, the sense of im-
potent rage. It had to be someone who'd known her. A family
member or friend. Someone who knew what he'd done. But even
with the resources at his command, how could he find out who?
Secretaries, paralegals, word processors, librarians — any one of
them could be the culprit.

If only he could figure out the motive, that would be some kind
of start. But he still didn't have a clue. If blackmail were the goal,
why not approach him directly? Why leave the picture on an associate's desk, not even knowing that it would reach him?

Mills felt a sort of buzzing, a vibration beneath his skin. Of all
the human feelings, powerlessness was the one he hated most.
Well, if he didn't yet have the answer, he could at least take care of
one thing.

From a table behind him, Mills picked up a granite ashtray. He
set it down on his desk. Then he took a pair of scissors from a
drawer. Neatly, methodically, he cut the photograph into long,
thin strips. Next, he stacked the strips together and cut them cross-
wise again and again. Now, there were dozens of tiny squares.
Holding the ashtray alongside his desk, he swept the paper bits
into its hold. When he was finished, he returned the ashtray to his
desk. He pulled out a dark red book of matches with the logo of

Café des Artistes. A match scraped across the igniter strip, and a yellow flame leapt up.

Mills stared at the flame for an instant, then dropped it down on the pile. But the match just lay there, smoldering, before silently going out. Annoyed, he lit another match, held it to a shiny fragment. Again the tiny flare, followed by a puff of smoke. In quick succession, he lit three more matches, tossed them into the ashtray. One by one they hit the paper; in seconds all went dark.

It must be something in the photographic paper, some chemical that wouldn't light. Staring at the picture's remains, he was conscious of a growing rage. As if these pathetic scraps had intentionally thwarted his will. He wanted to pick up the ashtray, to hurl it across the room. He could almost hear the sound, the crash of stone and wood. The ashtray gave up an acrid smell. He shoved it across the desk. Then slowly, the anger subsided, and he was able to think again. He found an envelope in his desk, and placed the paper bits inside. Nothing to get upset about. He'd dispose of them another way. Envelope in hand, he got up from his desk, on his way to the restroom down the hall. Already, he was feeling better.

Everything would be just fine.

⚜

"I'm sorry, Ms. Paine. Mr. Mills has a full schedule today. I don't know what he was thinking. But you know —" Clara raised one blue-veined hand in a gesture of philosophical acceptance.

"Are you *sure?*" Kate was on the verge of tears.

Clara studied Kate's face for several seconds, then let out a resigned sigh. "Look, why don't you tell me what it is? I'll try to run it by him."

Kate shook her head helplessly. "It's sort of confidential," she said. "But could you tell him it's really important?"

Back in her office, Kate again tried to reach Andrea. Andrea's secretary picked up the phone.

"She's out today," said Suzanne. Kate could hear stifled laughter in the background.

"All day?"

"Yeah, she's got the flu or something."

Kate was surprised. Except for vacations, Andrea had never missed a day of work. But then, except for yesterday, neither had she.

"She was out yesterday, too," said Suzanne, as if just remembering this fact.

Kate felt her spirits lift. No wonder Andrea hadn't called her. Here she'd been feeling bad that Andrea hadn't checked in, while Andrea was home sick, too. And probably wondering why Kate wasn't calling *her*.

"So she's at home?"

"Yeah. I guess." Suzanne sounded as if she couldn't care less.

"I'll try her there, then. Thanks, Suzanne."

But Andrea wasn't at home. Or maybe she was just asleep. In any case, she didn't pick up. Disappointed, Kate left a message, then turned back to her desk. It wasn't as though she'd planned to tell Andrea about Thorpe's attack. At least not until she'd spoken to Mills. But just the sound of Andrea's voice would have cheered her up, made her feel less alone.

So what now?

She could feel the tension in her body, running from her legs through her neck. She scrunched up her shoulders and let them drop, willing the stiffness to vanish. Then she had an idea. Why not go to the gym? She'd been vowing to go for days, since that night at the Harvard Club. Forty-five minutes of exercise would do wonders for her mood. Just the thought of it cheered her up. In minutes, she was out the door.

The locker room was sparsely populated with a motley assortment of female body types. A massive woman in flowered cotton underpants leaned over to brush wet hair, folds of flesh bulging around her waist, pendulous brown-nippled breasts swinging back and forth with the movements of her arm. A girl with well-toned biceps rubbed cream into her legs before examining her body in a mirror. Turning from side to side, she frowned, as if deciding whether to make a purchase.

Kate dumped her gym bag on a bench and fiddled with her combination lock. 26-16-24. It was easy to remember. Her age now. Her age 10 years ago. Her age the year Michael left her. She peeled off her office clothes, careful not to snag her stockings, and hung them on a hook inside a locker. Then she pulled on black spandex leggings and a blue-and-white Samson T-shirt. She closed the locker, grabbed her Sony Walkman, and headed for the workout floor.

The Mercury Athletic Club was colorful and brightly lit, the adult version of a day care center. The whir of machinery blended with a backdrop of seventies rock. Kate located a vacant Stairmaster and climbed on. After punching in her weight — 110 last time she checked — she set the timer for thirty minutes, adjusted the earphones on her Walkman, and started the climb to nowhere.

The club walls were covered with mirrors. Gazing at her reflection, Kate was amazed by her body's discretion. How calm and self-possessed she looked! Just another young professional opting for fitness over food.

Nothing at all like she felt.

Still looking into the mirror, she scanned the room behind her. In the sea of faces, she saw several colleagues: Jim Beller, a gangly corporate associate, red-faced and sweating on a stationary bike. A first-year female associate whose name she didn't know, struggling with a set of free weights. What would they say, these lunchtime athletes, if they knew what she'd just been through?

She still couldn't believe that Carter Mills had cut her off. She should have waited to discuss the photograph until after she'd dealt with Thorpe. Funny how the things you worried about were never the things that went wrong. She'd been worried that Mills might not believe her. She'd been worried about staying composed. Not once had she worried that Mills wouldn't hear her out.

But she'd come here to clear her mind. Glancing down at the monitor, Kate punched up the speed a few notches and tried to concentrate on the rhythmic movements of her legs.

Madonna's voice pulsed through Kate's earphones. The song was "Material Girl." It was a classic eighties anthem, a song she'd first heard as a kid. But now, listening to the words, Kate was surprised by a sharp jolt of envy. There was a picture of Madonna on the cassette jacket, all garters, black fishnets, and danger. Kate felt a sudden urge to be like that: tough, sexual, and well-defended. Someone who could take care of herself. Someone who would have stopped Chuck Thorpe.

Before she knew it, her mind flashed back to that first moment in her office. There had been a window of opportunity there. A moment when she could have torn loose. If she'd been stronger, if she'd been someone else, she would have instantly moved into action. But instead, she'd frozen. And then it had been too late.

As the scene ran through her mind, Kate felt a sickly churning in her stomach. Once, when she was very young, she'd gotten hold of a box of laundry detergent. She'd decided to make a snowstorm, to cover her room with white flakes. It had been a challenging task for a tiny child, tilting the heavy box at just the right angle. And then her father had appeared. She'd looked up at him, surprised and proud. But the eyes that looked back were cold. In that instant she'd felt the same confusion, the same roiling sense of isolation, that she felt right now.

Kate tried to focus on the music, on the steady rhythmic beat. But just as her thoughts were receding, she caught sight of someone she knew. Scraggly black hair. Jutting breasts. There on a treadmill was Linda Morris. Hit by a wave of dizziness, Kate quickly dropped her eyes. She'd come here in an effort to escape Chuck Thorpe, at least for an hour or so. Now she felt as if she'd been followed.

Kate looked hard at her legs, willing herself to stay calm. Then she glanced back at the mirror, studying Linda Morris's reflected form. Except for the workout attire, she looked much as she had before. The same heavy makeup, the same dark nails, the same gold cross on a chain. Even from the distance, Kate detected mascara bleeding down her cheeks. She felt a rush of distaste. The smeared makeup seemed to go to some deeper issue, to everything wrong with Linda Morris. Her abstraction. Her slovenliness. Her flagrant efforts to seduce. Kate pictured her in Epstein's office, paging through the draft complaint. The provocative clothing. The little-girl voice. It all seemed to go together.

Moving her legs in time with the music, Kate tried to think of other things. *But what was Morris doing here? WideWorld was way across town.* Of course, it could just be a coincidence. Mercury was, after all, a popular gym. And the fact that Morris was here midday? That, too, could be explained. She might be taking a vacation. Or some well-deserved comp time.

Another furtive glance at Morris; another surge of disgust. Puzzled, Kate tried to figure out why she reacted to Morris so strongly. It wasn't just Morris's ties to Thorpe, though certainly that played a role. Was it just that she was a control freak? That she wanted everyone to be like her? Or maybe it was some unconscious conflict, a collision of opposites. Kate thought about an article Tara had written about the concept of the human shadow. About how people react most strongly to traits they reject in themselves. She gave that idea a few seconds of thought before pushing it out of her mind. She was nothing like Linda Morris.

Really, nothing at all.

Kate returned to her office balancing a cardboard tray. Her phone was ringing. Jennifer was nowhere in sight. Lunging forward, Kate grabbed the receiver.

"Kate? It's Douglas. Douglas Macauley."

"Oh . . . , hi!" Kate felt instantly guilty. The day of Madeleine's funeral, Douglas had left a message. She'd never returned his call.

Happily, Douglas didn't bring this up. As she unwrapped her

tuna sandwich, he chatted amiably. He'd just finished a story about some work project when the words abruptly stopped. "I'm going on and on," he said. "I always do that when I'm nervous. Anyway, I've been thinking of you. How are you holding up?"

Kate opened her mouth, but no words came out. What could she really say? *I was sort of raped two nights ago by a client, and I still haven't decided what to do. Some unknown person left a strange photo on my desk that may be connected to a murder. My best friend from law school has a new girlfriend, and I can't seem to deal with it at all.*

"Kate?"

"Oh . . . the usual," she said lamely.

An awkward pause. Of course, Douglas knew about Madeleine's death. He knew Kate was shutting him out.

"So," he finally said. "I was wondering if you'd like to get together this weekend. Maybe we could —"

"I'm afraid I'm tied up." Before Kate could think, the words were out.

"That's too bad. Well, maybe sometime early next week we could —"

"It's hard to say. Things are really hectic right now. Why don't I give you a call?"

"Okay. Sure."

Kate could hear the doubt in his voice. She moved quickly to end the conversation. "Listen, I have to take another call. But I'll talk to you soon." *Liar.* "Take care."

Kate hung up the telephone receiver. She was suddenly starved. She ripped the rest of the plastic off her sandwich and took a large bite. As she chewed, she stared out the window. She hadn't planned to turn down Douglas's invitation, hadn't planned what to say when he called. But now that it was done, she felt relieved. As if she'd crossed something off a to-do list.

Kate made quick work of her sandwich, then turned her attention to work. To the memo she still owed Peyton. The law of sexual harassment.

Are you really going to keep on doing this? Defending a murderer?

The man who practically raped you? For a moment, emotions welled up inside, but she quickly reined them in. After all, this was her job. The memo still had to get done. She wasn't doing this for Thorpe. She was doing it for Samson & Mills. She was doing it for *herself,* to protect her own career. She'd lost so much already; she couldn't lose this as well. Without her work, who would she be? There was Thorpe the client, and Thorpe the man. She had to keep the two things separate.

Pulling open her top right-hand drawer, Kate reached for a pen. She was shutting the drawer when it struck her that something was wrong. *The cassette tape from Madeleine's office.* She was sure that she'd put it here. But now it was nowhere in sight. Kate yanked the drawer open wide and quickly searched its contents. Then, defeated, she closed the drawer and slumped down in her chair.

How could she have lost the tape? It just wasn't possible. She'd put the tape there; she knew it. But could she possibly be confused? Perhaps she'd put the tape in her left-hand drawer, along with Thorpe's engraved cuff link. She dug the key from her purse and quickly unlocked the drawer. The cuff link was still there, safe in the envelope where she'd left it. But there was no sign of the cassette.

Biting her lip, Kate closed and locked the drawer. It made no sense. How could something as solid as a cassette tape just vanish into thin air? And how would she explain its disappearance to Mills? Her job could be on the line.

For long moments, she sat immobile, her thoughts churning hopelessly. Then, with a jerk, she sat up straight. She knew exactly where the tape had gone.

Chuck Thorpe.

⌘

Only three days to go.

Nervously, like a caged animal, he paced the loft's confines. Then he forced himself back to his desk, sat down. He'd been over the plan hundreds of times just in the past week alone. And now he'd begin again. Step by step. Point by point. Preparation was everything.

His desk was clear except for the gun. The same gun he'd used to kill Madeleine. The gun he'd use Saturday night. He picked it up, felt its weight in his hand. A lovely object, a piece of art. Silver-plated, with an ivory grip. He'd gone to great trouble to get it back. Subjected himself to great risk. But in the end, it had all been worth it. The gun was part of the plan.

January 16.

The same day that *she* had died.

While his plan had shifted over the years, the date had never changed. It fell on a Saturday this year. At first, that had seemed a tremendous problem, an obstacle he might not surmount. Then, in a stroke of fortune, Samson had come to his aid. The firm's annual cocktail party had been rescheduled. Thanks to Madeleine's death.

Funny, how things had worked out.

Thursday, January 14

10:05 A.M. Kate had just arrived at work. As soon as she reached her desk, she picked up the phone and dialed. Andrea picked up right away.

"Where were you yesterday?" Kate demanded.

"Out sick. Flu."

"I tried to reach you all day."

"I had the phone unplugged. So I could sleep." Andrea sounded distracted.

"Are things okay?" Kate said. "You're feeling better and all?"

"Oh, yeah. It was just a twenty-four-hour bug." Andrea had put her on speakerphone. Kate could hear the rustling of papers. "Listen, I really have to get going. I had a bunch of documents dumped on me this morning. They have to go out by five."

"How about a quick break for lunch?"

"Sorry. Not with these boxes staring me in the face."

"Well . . . , call me when you come up for air. I really want to talk to you about a couple of things."

"Yeah, sure."

Before Kate could reply, the phone went dead. For a moment, she stared at the receiver, too surprised to do anything else. Work-related crises were a way of life at Samson & Mills, hardly an excuse for freezing out friends. It was almost as if Andrea was angry. But how could that be? They'd hardly seen each other since Madeleine's memorial service, when everything had been just fine. Briefly, Kate thought about calling back but decided to put it off. Andrea was busy now. She'd wait until the end of the day.

Kate turned to the papers on her desk. Luckily for her, the Thorpe complaint still hadn't come in. If it had, Peyton would be screaming for the memo. Now, she'd have time for one more pass.

She was just typing in a few last edits when the phone rang. Jennifer picked up the call. Seconds later, Kate's intercom buzzed.

"It's Peyton," Jennifer whispered, as if he might somehow overhear. "Do you want to take it?"

"Perfect timing," Kate said. Finally something was going right. "Go ahead and put him through."

"I've got the memo for you," she said, before Peyton could start in. "How many copies do you need?"

"One to me and one to files," Peyton said. "But I need mine right away."

"I'll have Jennifer bring it up."

"The meeting's at two," Peyton continued, "in Carter's conference room."

Kate felt her stomach lurch. *Just relax and try to enjoy it.* Picturing Chuck Thorpe across a conference table, she felt physically sick. No, she just couldn't do it, not before she'd talked to Mills. "I . . . I'm not going to be able to make it."

"Come again?" Peyton sounded nonplussed.

"I have a doctor's appointment that . . . that I'd forgotten about."

"I see." Peyton was clearly astonished. Nothing but an act of God would have caused him to miss this meeting.

"Is it something you could reschedule?" His voice was inscrutably polite. "It's rather an important meeting. You know, Holden and all."

"No, I . . . I can't," Kate said miserably. Three words that a Samson associate must never utter. However arduous the task, however unreasonable the deadline, you were supposed to accept it and smile.

"Let's see, then." Peyton's voice was solicitous, the sort of tone one might use in addressing someone very old or sick. *Not* the sort of tone generally used with subordinates at Samson & Mills. Maybe he thought she was dying.

"D'you think you could get me the memo before you leave? That would be a big help."

"Sure. I'll send it right up."

After hanging up the phone, Kate page-checked a copy of the memo before buzzing Jennifer. "Could you come in here for a second? I need you to make two copies of a memo and take them to Peyton Winslow." *I need you to.* A locution common among senior associates, one that Kate had always despised. It so clearly defined the other person as a means to your ends. And here she was using it herself.

But Jennifer didn't seem to notice. "There's something I need to tell you," she said. There was a note of conspiracy in her voice.

"Okay, but first get two copies of this to Peyton," Kate said, passing Jennifer the memo. "He needs them right away."

Jennifer disappeared through the door.

Kate looked at her watch. It was almost noon. It occurred to her that if Mills hadn't reached her yet, he probably wouldn't be calling until after the WideWorld meeting. She felt a growing frustration, a sense of helplessness. She hadn't even had a chance to tell Mills about the assault, let alone about Thorpe's theft of the cassette. And now she had a new set of worries. Would Thorpe use her absence from today's meeting to launch a preemptive strike? Or perhaps he'd already spoken to Mills, already moved to discredit her.

Then, for the first time, a chilling thought crossed her mind.

How had Thorpe known about the tape? Could Thorpe have stumbled on the drawer by chance? A lucky coincidence? No, it was too far-fetched. There was only one explanation that made sense. The information must have come from Mills.

Kate put a hand to her mouth. Her mind throbbed, as if on emergency alert. Then, gradually, her pulse rate slowed as rational thought resumed. Mills was a zealous lawyer, but he was also an honest one. He'd never collude with Thorpe, not on something like this. Just because Mills had told Thorpe about the tape didn't mean he was in on Thorpe's scheme. Thorpe was, after all, the client. Why shouldn't Mills tell him about the tape? To the contrary, it would have been strange had he *not* brought it up.

Jennifer appeared in the doorway.

"Did you get the memo to Peyton?"

"Did I?" Jennifer laughed. "He practically tore it out of my hand. You'd have thought it was *Playboy* or something."

Or *Catch,* Kate thought.

"So do you have a second?" Jennifer asked.

"Um, sure," Kate said, trying not to let her reluctance show. "What's up?"

Jennifer stepped inside and shut the door. Her eyes were bright.

"I've got some information for you," she said proudly. "About Martin Drescher, I mean."

Kate looked at her, confused. She wasn't sure what Jennifer meant.

"You know," Jennifer prodded. "About Drescher and Madeleine Waters."

"Oh, right!" It seemed ages since she'd encouraged Jennifer to engage in this girl detective act. Chuck Thorpe's attack had pretty much wiped out other concerns. But Jennifer seemed so excited, so eager to relate her findings.

"So what did you learn?" Kate asked, trying to look like she cared.

"You won't believe this," Jennifer said. "But people are saying that Madeleine Waters and Drescher had an *affair*."

Madeleine Waters and Martin Drescher? Kate looked at Jennifer, dumbstruck. "I don't believe it. You're kidding."

"Nope. It ended about six months ago. When Madeleine found out that Drescher was on the sauce again. Madeleine told him that she'd had it, that she didn't want anything more to do with him."

So, Kate thought, she wasn't the only one who'd noticed. Drescher's drinking must be common knowledge by now. "And how did Drescher react?" Kate asked.

Jennifer shrugged. "There wasn't really anything he could do," she said. "Madeleine wouldn't back down."

Madeleine Waters and Martin Drescher. Kate could hardly believe it. What had Madeleine been thinking? Drescher must have been beside himself, stunned by his strange good fortune.

"Where did you hear this?" Kate asked, trying to keep her tone light. For Jennifer, this was all still a game, like something in a dime-store novel.

Jennifer smiled coyly. "I just asked around," she said. "People overhear things."

"You're some investigator." Kate said, standing up to get her cape. "Listen, I've got to run to the doctor's. If anyone calls, tell them I'll be back around three."

After leaving the office, Kate took a taxi home. She spent an hour or so dawdling over a peanut butter sandwich, flipping through a newspaper as she ate. She ignored the news, focusing instead on the ads. Tiffany's. Bergdorf-Goodman. Bendel's.

When she got back to the office, a little after three, Kate went straight to the phone to check her messages. She stared at the dark message light. Nothing. Not a single call. She couldn't remember the last time this had occurred. It gave her an uneasy feeling, as if she'd slipped into some sort of netherworld, a no-man's-land of reduced expectations. She'd seen it happen before, to associates who weren't making the grade. First, they stopped getting assignments. At the start, this came as a welcome respite, a rare chance to leave work before dark. But after a few days, a few key meetings to which they weren't invited, the truth started seeping in. Most associates took the hint and began the search for new positions. Those who clung to their jobs, or stayed willfully obtuse, were eventually approached more directly.

Could that be happening to her?

The only thing on her calendar today was her four o'clock meeting with Josie. Eyeing the phone, Kate considered canceling, pleading a work-related crisis. But, really, what would that solve? Besides, she needed to set an example. As Josie's mentor, she'd tried to teach her the importance of keeping commitments. And the appointment would at least keep her occupied, keep her mind off what was going on.

By five, Kate's mood had only darkened. Still no word from Mills. And still no sign of Josie. Kate could feel the tension building inside her. She chewed at a fingernail. Maybe she should have gone to the meeting, if only to defend herself. And where in the hell was Josie? *Irresponsible. Immature. Selfish.* Here she was, rearranging her schedule for a girl who couldn't even show up. Now here was one place she *could* take some action. Turning to her Rolodex, Kate flipped through the cards until she reached Josie's number.

⚬❧⚬

JOSIE slapped the child — hard — across the face. For an instant, there was silence. The little girl's eyes got bigger. Then, she let out a howl. Josie reached out and grabbed her sister. Hugging her tight, she rocked the tiny figure back and forth. "I'm sorry, baby. I'm sorry."

As she rubbed four-year-old Shari's back, Josie stared at the chipped kitchen cabinets, now smeared with half a dozen raw eggs. She'd left Shari alone just five minutes — *five minutes!* — telling her to stay put at the kitchen table while she got the laundry out of the dryer. But by the time she'd gotten back upstairs, Shari had smashed every egg in the house. Yellow yoke slithered down the painted wood, mixed with the snotlike white. Josie wanted to burst into tears. Those eggs were supposed to be their dinner.

Shari's cries had grown softer, and Josie plunked her down on a kitchen chair. She'd promised herself that she'd never hit either of the kids. They took enough abuse from their mother without a big sister joining in. What was wrong with her today?

Closing her eyes, Josie leaned her arms against the kitchen counter. She wished she were a million miles away. She wished she'd been born into a totally different family. And most of all, she wished that Mama would come home like she'd promised. Or at least before the kids went to bed. But, she thought bitterly, what were the chances of that?

Josie flung open the refrigerator door. The bulb had burned out a long time ago, and she had to squint to see what was there. Nothing that would do for dinner. They did have some milk, though. And a box of cereal. Well, that's what they'd have to eat. And if Shari and Freddy didn't like it, that was just too bad.

Josie heard the front door open and close. Then Freddy was in the kitchen, an eight-year-old bundle of denim and attitude.

"Freddy!" Shari's small face grew bright. She was wild about her older brother, though the feeling wasn't mutual these days. Freddy grunted and slumped down in a chair.

"What'd you do at school today?" Josie said, pulling three bowls off a shelf.

"Nuthin'."

"What d'you mean nothing?" Josie turned to face Freddy, who was staring morosely at the egg-covered kitchen cabinets. He didn't bother to ask what had happened. "You're in school eight hours a day, you gotta do *something*."

"Not really. Hey. What we havin' for supper?"

Josie dumped cereal into the three bowls. "Cap'n Crunch."

"For *supper?*" He gave her a disbelieving look.

"Yup." Josie didn't feel like explaining. She put bowls down in front of the kids, then went back for her own. She poured milk on

Shari's cereal, then pushed the carton over to Freddy, who looked at it in disgust. Wasn't he going to eat? She was too tired to care. She picked up the milk and poured it over her own cereal. Everything was quiet. Which was fine with her.

But as she chewed, Josie found herself getting more upset. It was so unfair! Everything was so good until this fall. Mama had gotten so much better. She was even talking about looking for work or going to school. And then, after Grandma died, everything had fallen apart. That was when Josie had found the drug stuff, wrapped in a towel in the closet. Crack vials, a pipe, needles. She'd thrown the whole mess out, and Mama had never said a thing. But both of them knew the score.

The phone rang.

"I'll get it." Freddy was already out of his chair, bounding to the living room. Then, he was back, sullen and remote again. "'S for you," he mumbled and thrust the receiver at Josie.

Josie stared at the phone, her heart dropping in her chest. She didn't have to ask who it was. She could see Kate there in her office, perfect as a movie star. Compared to Kate, she felt so low. If only she could explain! But she just couldn't take that risk. Once she told someone what was going on, the BCW people would get involved. They'd take the kids away, split up the family. She knew all about it from her friend Tamika. Once you were in the System, you never knew what would happen. Tamika's little sister had been put in a foster family who later adopted her. They changed her name to theirs. Tamika couldn't even see her anymore. It was terrible, but that's how things were. And she wasn't going to let that happen with Shari and Freddy. No matter what.

"Josie, this is Kate Paine. At Samson & Mills."

"I was gonna call you, but . . ." Josie didn't finish the sentence.

At the sound of Josie's voice, Kate felt her anger collapse, and she just felt utterly sad. At the same time, she knew that she'd come to the right decision. She just didn't have the energy that Josie required. Not with everything else going on. Better for both of them to move on. When she spoke, she made an effort to be kind.

"Josie, this is the third session you've missed without calling. It doesn't make sense to go on this way."

"You mean . . . I can't come anymore?" Josie's voice was low, as if she was about to cry.

"You're not coming anyway, so I don't see what difference it will make." The words came out more sharply than Kate intended. Further proof of how on edge she was.

"But I . . . I . . ." Josie sounded dazed, and then the words poured out in a rush. "You gotta let me come back, Kate. *Please*. I'll do better. I won't skip anymore. Really. I promise."

Please. Kate paused, startled by the urgency in Josie's voice. Almost against her will, she felt a twinge of sympathy. Still raw from the morning's encounter with Peyton, she knew what it was like to be dismissed.

Kate sighed. "Okay. But this is it. One more no-show and we're through. Understood?"

"Yeah, yeah." Josie was fairly bubbling. "I'll be there next week. You'll see."

When Kate hung up the phone, she sat a few moments with her chin pressed in her hand. Her sense of isolation was so strong that it threatened to immobilize her. She checked her e-mail again. Nothing. She'd decided to wait another ten minutes, then give Peyton a call. In the meantime, she'd try to catch Andrea, who should have finished up by now.

She punched in Andrea's number. Suzanne picked up.

"Andrea's gone for the day."

The words almost didn't register. "But she . . . she said she had to get some documents out by five."

"Yeah, well, she finished up early. Want me to leave her a message that you called?"

"No, that's okay. I'll get her at home tonight."

Kate put down the receiver. *What was going on?* For more than a year, Samson & Mills had been a second home. More than a home, really. The one place where she'd felt secure. And now, within days, everything had changed. A partner was dead. She'd been attacked by a client. A close friend had cut her off. *You know what,* she said to the room at large. *I'm going home for the day. You want to reach me, you can get me there.*

❧

THE suspense was almost unbearable. He picked up the gun, as if to reassure himself. It was comforting to hold the revolver, to run his fingers along its ivory grip, to feel its cold weight in his hands. It was a promise of sorts. An intimation. Proof that the day he'd dreamed of would actually come to pass.

He thought back to when he was thirteen, when the plan had first come to mind. Just a bare outline of what was to come, only the very beginning. But he'd known he was onto something big. He could still feel the excitement.

A desperately hot summer day. He'd been grounded yet again, forbidden to leave the group home. He couldn't remember what he'd done. Stealing, perhaps. Or smoking pot. He'd been punished so many times. He was in Ms. Llewellyn's office. *Screw-ellen,* he called her in his mind. She was talking to him, all watchful and concerned. Screw-ellen wanted him to think about the future. He was intelligent, she told him. The tests that he'd taken proved it. He could do anything he set his mind to, if he'd only decide to try. She said that she wanted to help, that she wanted to make a difference. *Yeah, right.* He gave her about a year. There was a ring on her left hand. Soon, there'd be a baby and then she'd be gone. That's how it always ended.

He'd been staring out the window, ignoring her, when one sentence filtered through. *You only have one life,* she'd said. *You need to think about your goals.* Goals. It was something about that word. He'd never thought much about the future. Never really seen the point. Raise hell and die, that's pretty much what he'd planned. But maybe he'd been wrong. It was true what Screw-ellen was saying. He did only have one life. He'd thought about that for a while.

And the plan began to take shape.

Friday, January 15

"WHAT's it called again?"

"Ballet Slipper Pink."

"I *really* like it."

Kate picked at a tossed salad and tried to ignore the girl talk. She rarely ate in the firm cafeteria, and she was beginning to remember why. She'd chosen this table because Peyton was here, and she'd hoped they'd be able to talk. But so far, he'd been occupied. Instead, she'd been stuck with Angela Taylor, now waving a manicured hand. A basis for comparing the virtues of pink and mauve? Or just another chance to show off that ring? Kate chewed a piece of green pepper and contemplated a means of escape.

"So what are you wearing tomorrow?" Having exhausted the subject of fingernails, Angela was moving on to clothes. The firm's annual cocktail party, to be precise. But what was the point of her question? Everyone always wore black. Kate edged her seat to the left, hoping to find a new conversation.

"So my wife's standing in the elevator with Ryan beside her." Patrick Rittenhouse was talking about his toddler son. "Before she even notices that he's moved, he's tapping this guy on the knee. The guy looks down and my kid goes, 'Will you be my daddy?'"

Guffaws broke out. Someone pounded the table. Only Kate failed to crack a smile. A little boy missed his overworked father so much that he set out on his own to replace him. Why was that a funny story? With murmured excuses, she picked up her tray and headed back to her office. She'd thought that it would cheer her up, to share a meal with other people. But during the half hour she'd spent upstairs, her depression had only deepened.

Back at her desk, Kate checked for messages. Still no word from Carter Mills. Outside, an icy drizzle leaked from the sky. Everything seemed cold and bleak.

At a loss for what to do next, Kate picked up a stack of mail. Languidly, she began to thumb through it. A heavy square envelope caught her eye, and she pulled it out from the pile. A Sag Harbor return address. With a sense of anticipation, Kate ripped through the flap and pulled out a flat white card. *Sam Howell: New Work. Opening Reception December 10.* Below the printed text was a scribbled note in a strong, sloping hand. "Enjoyed our talk. You've missed the opening, but the work's still there. I'd love to give you the tour." At the bottom of the card, he'd scrawled his name and number.

As she read the words, Kate's spirits lifted. The world seemed suddenly larger. Over the past few years, she'd all but forgotten many things she'd once cared about. Photography was one of her hobbies, still listed on her résumé. Yet when had she last shot a roll of film? When had she last seen a show?

Still holding the note in her hand, Kate turned to stare out the window. The night before she'd met Sam Howell, she'd dreamed about India. And then he'd shown up with those pictures. Varanasi, the holy city. She wasn't superstitious, of course. All the same, it struck her as strange. In her mind's eye, she saw the photographs. They were really quite wonderful. A wave of yearning swept over her, a desire to escape her life. She'd planned to work tomorrow, but there was nothing that couldn't wait. She could go to Sag Harbor tomorrow morning and be back for the party that night. Without pausing to reconsider, she picked up the phone and dialed.

"H'llo!" The voice that answered the phone was sharp. She must have caught him at a bad time; she began a rushed introduction.

"This is Kate Paine. We met at the Mug. I —"

"Of course!" In an instant, his tone changed. "Good to hear from you. How've you been?"

"Fine, I —"

"Did you get my invitation?"

"Actually, I did. I just opened it. And I was thinking . . . , I know this is sudden, but I was thinking of coming out tomorrow."

"Terrific." He sounded surprised but pleased.

"I'd have to catch a morning bus. I need to be back in the city by early evening."

"That shouldn't be a problem. Why don't you check the schedule and get back to me? I'll meet you at the other end."

⁓

SAM Howell gently hung up the phone and returned to the cluttered table. Through a wall of windows, he could see the bay, sunk in a winter haze. But his eyes were focused on the table's surface. Boxes and boxes of photographs. Different images. Different years. But the model was always the same.

Carefully, he slid an 8 x 10 print out of its plastic casing. He studied the image critically. It was, he thought, very good. Clearly articulated whites. Richly modulated blacks. Then he felt a surge of disgust. How could he focus on the form itself, forget what he was looking at? There was something monstrous about it, this ability to detach. Especially now. It raised questions he didn't want to face. Such as whether he'd really loved her. Such as whether he could love at all.

Now he forced himself to look at the image, to actually see her

there. It was years since he'd looked at this picture. Yet he still remembered the day. A Saturday morning. Early fall. He'd gotten up
to make coffee, then gone back to the bedroom to get dressed.
She'd been lying there, still asleep. She'd looked like a goddess at
rest.

And now she was dead. *Now she was dead.* It was this fact he
couldn't get over. He'd always believed that he'd see her again.
And now that would never happen. Time spread before him endlessly. It was too much to contemplate. Then, with sudden hopefulness, he thought of Kate. How young she was, how young and
unsuspecting. A surge of protectiveness rushed through him.
There were, after all, still reasons to live. His work, for one. And
Kate. She'd be here tomorrow, just hours from now.

It was almost like a second chance.

⤜∾

KATE knew without checking that there wasn't any food in the
kitchen, at least nothing that would do for dinner. She decided to
head for French Roast, a popular neighborhood bistro. Looking for
something to read while she waited, her eyes lit on Madeleine's
book. *Sexual Harassment of Working Women.* After a moment's
pause, she tossed it into her bag.

At the restaurant, Kate put her name on the waiting list. Then
she snagged a seat at the bar and ordered a glass of merlot. Next to
her, a couple was drinking frothy blue drinks out of oversized tulip
glasses. The man's arm was draped casually across the woman's
chair. Kate could almost feel the weight of the arm, the slight intimacy with a promise of more to come. *Michael and I used to sit like
that.* . . .

Looking away, Kate pulled out her book.

She was just starting to read when a clean-cut guy in his twenties edged up alongside her. She watched as he strained to catch
her book's title. Probably trying to come up with a pickup line. But
as she glanced over in his direction, his head jerked up. His eyes
met hers. "A little light reading, huh?" The smile was cold, the

words unmistakably hostile. Without waiting for a response, he flagged down the bartender. "Hey! Two Stoli martinis straight up."

Kate flushed. For an instant she saw herself through his eyes: a woman with a chip on her shoulder. Someone who spent Friday nights drinking alone at a bar, devouring feminist dogma. A woman who had "issues" with men. Then, just as quickly, embarassment gave way to anger. Who was he to judge her, to make her feel this way? She gave him a cold stare before turning back to the book.

But somehow she couldn't concentrate. Gazing at the black-and-white words, she kept thinking of other things. Images floated through her mind's eye, remembered moments from the past few days. Carter Mills's desolate expression the day after Madeleine died. Madeleine's hand on her shoulder, her glittering green-eyed gaze. The way Chuck Thorpe had smiled at her when —

Chuck Thorpe.

There, he was back again. She'd managed to forget about Thorpe for an hour or so, but now he was back full force. Anxiously, Kate glanced around the room, as if assuring herself that he wasn't nearby. It was almost as if she credited Thorpe with supernatural properties, the ability to appear at will. She tried to be rational. There was no way Thorpe knew where she was tonight. And even if he *had* somehow managed to follow her here, she'd be safe in this room full of people.

Again, she tried to read, but still the words wouldn't sink in. Now that her thoughts had moved to Thorpe, she felt powerless to wrench them away. *You must be very careful.* It seemed so obvious now. The book. The veiled warning. Everything fit together. Thorpe had certainly known Madeleine's schedule. And what better way to ward off suspicion than to claim that you'd been stood up? Even if Thorpe had an alibi, that didn't rule out his involvement. He could always have hired someone to do the job. In fact, she would have expected that.

Staring blankly at Madeleine's book, Kate chewed over this thought. Then she forced her attention back to the text, to a heavily underlined passage. *The decisively nontolerating woman must suddenly be eliminated. Her mere presence becomes offensive; to be reminded of her existence, unbearable.*

The decisively nontolerating woman. An interesting phrase, though she wasn't quite sure what it meant. Kate's eyes retraced the words. And stopped at the end of the line.

Must suddenly be eliminated.

The words seemed eerily portentous. As if Madeleine had predicted her own demise. But that had to be a coincidence. If Madeleine had known she was in danger, wouldn't she have done something? Kate tried to put herself in Madeleine's place. It was difficult, since she knew so little about Madeleine's life and next to nothing about her dealings with Thorpe. But maybe the threat had been much less clear than it appeared after the fact. Perhaps Madeleine had sensed Thorpe's violent streak without ever imagining its reach.

"Miss? You okay?"

Kate raised her head. It was the bartender, a freckle-faced guy who didn't look more than eighteen.

"I'm fine," Kate said. "Just thinking."

Kate's eyes moved back to the book, lighting on another marked passage. *Plainly, the wooden dichotomy between "real love," which is supposed to be a matter of free choice, and coercion, which implies some form of the gun at the head, is revealed as inadequate to explain the social construction of women's sexuality. . . .*

Gun at the head.

The phrase leaped out from the page. Pictures flashed through Kate's mind. Madeleine's mutilated body. Madeleine shot through the head. It was the gunshot wound that had killed her, that's what the newspapers said. The rest of it had come later. What had Madeleine been thinking when she read these words? Why had she underlined them?

Kate's eyes slid to the next sentence and the next. She flipped ahead twenty, then thirty, pages before again coming to a stop. *Abuses of the person, such as rape and murder, are not condoned by public policy although they may "satisfy a personal urge" of the perpe-trator. Not all urges are given free rein in society, heedless of their impact on others. . . .*

"Kate Paine. Kate Paine." Over the hum of voices, someone was calling her name. Startled, Kate raised her head.

The hostess was waving her forward; her table was ready now.

Saturday, January 16

THE trip to Sag Harbor passed peacefully. During the summer months, the Hampton Jitney was packed to capacity with jazzed-up weekenders on cell phones. Today, it was almost empty. Kate grabbed two seats for herself and promptly fell asleep. She dozed for the next couple of hours, waking as the bus reached town. Through the window, she saw a snowy village street lined with small shops and restaurants. Stepping down from the bus, Kate was glad that she'd come.

"Kate!" Sam Howell was moving toward her, flashing an easy smile. Dressed in a navy parka and jeans, he was taller than she remembered, taller and better-looking. They shook hands, then stood for an awkward moment. Howell gestured across the street. "I thought we'd grab a bite to eat and then stop by the gallery."

"Good. Fine." Face to face with Howell, Kate felt a little shy.

The restaurant had leather booths and a black-and-white

checked floor. It smelled of sausage and roast potatoes and was doing a steady business.

"The Paradise," Howell said, as they slipped into a booth. "My favorite local place."

Kate took a deep, satisfied breath then turned her attention to the menu. She finally settled on bacon and blueberry pancakes. And orange juice and coffee, too.

"I've never been out here," Kate said, after they'd placed their orders. "It seems almost magical, like something from another time."

Howell smiled. "I love it," he said. "I moved out from the city a number of years back, and I've never regretted it. Small-town life suits me."

"You do photography full time?"

"Yeah, I've been lucky. I haven't worked at a day job since my early twenties. That's how I managed to live out here. I still have to be in the city a lot, but I can pretty much set my own schedule."

Kate nodded politely. She couldn't imagine planning her own time. Not just a day here and there but weeks and weeks at a stretch. She was about to say something to that effect, but Howell was talking again.

"That firm where you work, Samson & Mills. Isn't that the place a woman was killed?"

The question caught Kate off guard. "Well, she wasn't killed at the firm. But yes, one of the partners was murdered."

"Did you know her?" Howell asked.

"Not well," Kate said.

Howell seemed to be studying her. Then, after a pause, he went on. "So what's life like at those big city firms? Do you work for one person at a time?"

At least it was a harmless inquiry, one she didn't much mind answering. The mechanics of Samson & Mills she could deal with. "That's usually how it works for associates," she said. "Lawyers who aren't partners yet. Sometimes people split their time between two

people. It all depends on the firm's needs." She sounded like a re-
cruiting manual.

"I used to know someone who worked at Samson & Mills.
I can't remember his name, though. Who do you work for there?"

"His name's Carter Mills. He's the managing partner." Her earlier discomfort forgotten, Kate experienced a thrill of pride. Even
with all that had happened, she still felt the mystique of her position. "Who was the person you knew?"

"Oh, I forget his name. It was a long time ago now." He seemed
suddenly preoccupied.

"Are you okay?" Kate asked.

Howell quickly looked up, the smile returned to his face.
"Sorry," he said. "I was thinking about something else. Something
I have to do tonight."

After polishing off her food, Kate followed Howell a short way
down Main Street to a small gallery. A slim, blond woman stood up
from a small desk to greet them. Her smile widened when she saw
Howell.

"Sam. Good to see you!"

Howell turned to Kate. "I'd like you to meet Virginia Cavanaugh, the owner of this wonderful place. Ginny, this is Kate
Paine. She came out from the city today."

Kate smiled and extended her hand. Cavanaugh was elegantly but
simply dressed in black pants and a white silk shirt. There were a few
faint lines around her eyes. Still, she didn't look much over thirty.

The gallery was airy and bright, with polished light wood floors.
There appeared to be several rooms. "Have you been here long?"
Kate asked.

"A couple of years. I paid my dues in Manhattan. I was with a
gallery on Fifty-seventh for about five years. But I always planned
to move out here when I could."

Howell touched Kate's shoulder. "Let's get started," he said.

The first photograph that they came to was a black-and-white shot of an empty beach. The image seemed ordinary at first. But as Kate's eyes focused on the scene, she sensed an opening, a sort of expansion. She thought of 3-D postcards, the kind that offer up holographic images when you stare at them long enough. Only here, it wasn't so much a visual shift as something that happened at a physical level. As if the picture was taking root inside her.

Kate turned to Howell. "You're really good," she said.

"Don't sound so surprised."

Kate blushed. "It's not that. I just . . ." She let her voice trail off as she turned to the next framed image. A rocky coastline and an angry sea. Kate furrowed her brow. Hadn't she seen this somewhere before?

"That picture, where was it taken?"

"Maine. Up around Penobscot Bay."

She wasn't sure why it looked familiar. After a puzzled moment, she moved on.

All in all, there were several dozen prints, some black and white, some color, all showing ocean scenes. While the settings were different, Kate could clearly see they were the work of a single artist. In each picture, the elements were assembled against a backdrop of sky. There was a bleakness to the scenes, but a bleakness that hinted at secret riches. Something to be revealed. You stood before the pictures waiting.

"Thanks so much for inviting me," Kate said, as they stepped from the gallery back onto Main Street. It was still early, a little before three, but daylight was fading fast. The air had grown windy and colder. The town seemed to be folding in on itself, hunkering down for night.

"What time's your bus?" Howell asked. Kate could see the icy haze of his breath, rising in the air like frozen smoke.

"Around five," Kate said. "But I'm fine. I'll get a cup of coffee and read."

Howell frowned. "Listen, there's no point in you hanging around by yourself. I live right down the street. How about I make us some coffee and then run you back up here in time for your bus?"

Kate struggled to frame a reply. "Oh, thanks, anyway," she demurred. "But I don't want to cause you any trouble."

"It's no trouble," he insisted. "I have to go out again anyway."

Howell's hands thrust deep in his parka pockets. Dark hair curled across his forehead. Heathcliff meets L. L. Bean. Kate felt her resolution waver. After all, this wasn't New York City. And Howell was hardly a random stranger. Still, something held her back. For days she'd been nervous, on edge. The residue of Chuck Thorpe. Just the thought of his name made her mouth go dry. Her body seemed to shrink inward. Then from nowhere, she was hit by a blast of rage that overpowered every other thought. Who was Chuck Thorpe to dictate her actions, to force her to live in fear? With sudden defiance, she raised her chin. "I'd love to stop by your house," she said. "If you're sure you really don't mind."

Sam Howell's home turned out to be a restored fisherman's cottage; at least that's what it felt like to Kate. It was small and snug, with a row of windows facing the bay. The main room was simply and sparely furnished. A sofa. Two chairs. A handsome round table in some dark wood. The space had a settled aspect, as if everything had been there for years. After pointing Kate toward an armchair, Howell headed back down the hall.

"It must be beautiful here in the summer," Kate said, raising her voice to be heard.

"It is," he called back. "But fall and spring are best. Before the tourists descend."

Kate could hear the hollow sound of water pouring into a kettle. Her eyes took in the room. The walls, painted a soft terra-cotta, showed no signs of Sam Howell's work. There were several paintings, though. Kate's eyes lingered on one of them, a faded folk-art depiction of a young girl holding an apple.

The sound of footsteps on the smooth wood floor, and then Howell was back with two mugs.

"I already added milk. I hope you don't mind."

"That's just how I like it," Kate said, accepting one of the mugs. "No sugar, though."

Howell raised his eyebrows. "In a good cup of coffee? Never." He flopped into the armchair across from hers, his legs stretched out on a rug.

Sipping her coffee, Kate was struck by the quality of silence here. While her own apartment was fairly quiet, there was always some background noise. The muted bass of a neighbor's stereo. A distant car alarm. Footsteps in an upstairs apartment.

"You must sleep really well here."

Howell smiled. "Yes, I suppose that I do."

"Why no photographs on the wall?"

"Everyone asks me that. I'm not sure I have an answer. Maybe it's just that I need a break. To look at photographs while I'm eating or having coffee . . . it would be like I was working all the time."

"Which would make you like me," Kate said wryly.

"Long hours?"

Kate nodded. "I mean, I'm not complaining. Law firms get a bad rap, but I actually like what I do. It's just that, sometimes . . ." She ended the sentence with a shake of her head. "I'm not sure what I'm trying to say."

Howell watched her across the rim of his mug. "It must be stressful working in a place where someone was recently killed."

I don't want to talk about that. "So how long have you lived in Sag Harbor?"

"Close to ten years." If Howell noticed the change of subject, he didn't let it show.

"That must have been a big adjustment, moving out here from Manhattan. Why did you make the leap?"

Howell didn't respond right away. His eyes, more green than gray now, seemed to be searching her face.

"Kate, I haven't been entirely honest with you."

She returned his gaze, the words not quite sinking in. "What do you mean?"

"I didn't just bump into you by chance. I followed you the other day."

Kate put down her mug hard. Hot coffee splashed on her knees. The silence that had seemed so soothing was all too sinister now. For an interminable second or two, Kate didn't move. Then, heart racing, she sprang to her feet.

"Kate, please. I can explain." He held out his hands, entreating.

As she moved toward the door, Howell blocked her escape. Kate stood there facing him, her breath emerging in short bursts.

"Look, I just want to leave now. Will you just let me leave?" She could hear the trembling in her voice.

Howell reached out to grasp her shoulders. Even through her sweater, she could feel the strength of his hands. "I'm not sure what you're thinking, but you've got it wrong. I'm not —"

But Kate barely heard the words. She wasn't sure she could make it. Still, she was going to try. With a surge of energy, she whirled around, yanking herself from Howell's grip. He stumbled back against the wall. She could hear him struggling to regain his balance as she raced toward the front door. Grabbing the knob, she braced for an attack, but miraculously nothing happened. And then she was free, in the open air, running as fast as she could.

Back in town, Main Street sparkled in the early dusk. Kate stood on the sidewalk, panting, trying to sort out what went wrong. Everything had happened so fast. One moment, she was sitting in a warm, bright house, engaged in relaxed conversation. The next, she was fleeing down a windblown street, running in fear for her life.

Now that she was standing still, Kate realized she'd forgotten her coat. Her skin, damp from exertion, felt clammy and icy cold. She needed to find some shelter. Luckily, she *had* grabbed her leather backpack, which she'd carried in lieu of a purse. After some searching, she found a coffee shop open for business. She walked inside, ordered a cup of hot chocolate, and took a seat at a high round table.

Waiting for her drink to cool, Kate tried to make sense of what had happened. Howell had said that he'd been following her, that's what had set her off. She'd been right to get out when she did. It had been the only smart thing to do. Run first, think later. Still, reviewing the day, she wasn't sure she'd been in any danger. She went back over Howell's behavior, from the time she'd arrived that morning. They'd been seen together in public, first at the restaurant and then at the gallery. Howell had introduced her to Virginia Cavanaugh. In the end, he'd let her go. These facts didn't jibe with a picture of someone who'd meant to hurt her.

But if Howell hadn't meant to hurt her, what *had* he wanted from her? Why had he bothered to track her down, to invite her out to Sag Harbor? It could just be that he found her attractive, but that didn't make much sense. Howell was a handsome, successful man. There were millions of women in New York. As fear continued to ebb, curiosity settled in. But the more Kate thought about all that had gone on, the more baffled she became. Why had Howell wanted to talk to her? What had he wanted to say? Kate's eyes drifted to a phone on the counter. Should she give him a chance to explain?

Kate was still pondering this option when Howell walked through the door. Their eyes locked. For several seconds, neither spoke. Then Howell took a couple of tentative steps. Kate saw he carried her coat.

"I've been looking for you everywhere," Howell said, still keeping a careful distance. "Here. You forgot something."

"Thanks." Taking the coat from his extended hand, Kate felt a little absurd. Howell looked so calm, so *normal*. Instead of demanding an explanation, she found herself offering one. "I'm sorry for running out like that. But when you said you'd been following me, it really freaked me out."

Howell put out a hand to stop her. "It's my fault," he said. "I shouldn't have started like that. I don't blame you for being afraid."

He was still standing several feet away. After a moment of hesitation, Kate gestured at an empty stool. "You can sit down if you want," she said.

"Thanks." He slid onto the seat, still watching her face. "Listen, I have to explain. It's important. It . . . it has something to do with Madeleine's death."

Kate stared at him, confused. "Madeleine Waters?"

Howell bit his lip. "I should have told you right off. Madeleine was my wife. My ex-wife, I should say."

"Your ex-wife?" It was all Kate could do to repeat the words. They simply wouldn't sink in.

Now Howell was racing ahead, the words pouring out in a rush. "I saw you at Madeleine's funeral. I asked who you were. I knew that I needed to meet you."

"Madeleine was your *ex-wife?*" She'd never even heard that Madeleine had been married. Could Howell's words possibly be true?

Then it came back, the photograph in Madeleine's office. The crashing waves against the rocks. *Of course.* No wonder Howell's work had seemed familiar.

"Look," Howell said, "maybe I should start at the beginning."

Kate met his eyes and nodded.

Sitting there on his stool, Howell seemed tired but determined. "Madeleine and I went to college together in Chicago. We got married right after graduation and moved to New York. Madeleine was at Columbia, in law school. I was doing photography, trying to start a career. Doing odd jobs to make money. Things were fine the first couple of years. Then, after her second year of law school, Madeleine took a summer job at Samson & Mills. She loved it from the start, said she'd really found her niche. That fall, she stayed on part-time. The hours were crazy, but I accepted that. I was pretty busy myself.

"The following spring she finished school. That's when she told me she'd be moving out. I was completely astonished. I'd thought we were doing fine. I didn't hassle her about her hours. Was even proud she was doing so well. Anyway, I demanded an explanation. Demanded and later begged. But I never got much of an answer. Just vague words about growing apart. The next thing I knew, she was gone. We spoke only a few times after that. The divorce went through a year later.

"Flash forward to last month. Out of nowhere, I get this letter. It came in the regular mail. Addressed by hand. I recognized her writing immediately. You can't imagine how I felt, all the feelings that came up. I didn't open it right away. I took a long walk instead, trying to sort things out. I was afraid, I guess. Afraid of what the letter might say. Afraid of what might be left out. Confused, too. Did I want her to say it was all a mistake, that she wanted to try again? Not really. I couldn't imagine that. What I wanted, I finally figured out, was something I could never have. I didn't want Madeleine back. I wanted her not to have left."

Kate stared down at her mug, tracing the rim with a finger. *I wanted her not to have left.* He's got it exactly right, she thought. That's exactly the way that you feel.

After a time, Kate looked up. "So why was she writing you now?"

"She wanted to apologize. She said she'd been thinking about the past. And thought she owed me an explanation. That's when I found out about Mills. That they'd been having an affair. I knew the name, of course. She'd talked about him all the time. Carter this, Carter that. I'd tuned out most of it. You'd think I might have had some suspicion. But, really, I had no idea."

Hearing the pain in his voice, Kate felt a wave of empathy. And with it, a jolt of apprehension. Was this what her own future held? Ten years from now, would she still be thinking about Michael? She tried to push the thought away.

"What did she want?"

"I don't know exactly," Howell said. "I never had a chance to find out. We were supposed to have dinner, had actually set a date. But she was killed before we could meet. All I know for sure is that she was scared. She felt very isolated, very alone. She needed someone to trust."

Kate leaned toward Howell, electrified by what he'd just said. "Did she mention anyone by name?"

Howell looked her squarely in the eye. "She was scared of Carter Mills," he said. "Of what Mills might do to her."

"Of Carter Mills?" Kate eyed Howell doubtfully.

"I think she knew something about him. Something that would hurt his career."

Kate stared at Howell, disbelieving. She must have misunderstood. "You don't think that Carter killed her?"

"He wouldn't have done it himself."

"But you think he's the one who arranged it?"

"Yes."

"I'm sorry," Kate said, shaking her head, "but it just doesn't make any sense. I mean, I *know* Carter Mills. I work for him. He'd never —" Kate broke off midsentence, conscious of Howell's stony gaze. "Look, what did she say exactly? To make you think that about Carter Mills?"

"I don't remember precisely." Howell's voice had a sharper edge now.

"But . . . you talked to the police about it?"

"Of course. They have a copy of the letter."

"Well, then . . ." Kate looked at her watch. Saved by the bell. "Wow, I've really got to get going. I've only got about ten minutes."

Standing up from her chair, she pulled on her coat and extended a hand. "So . . . thanks."

Howell gave her an ironic look.

"No, really," Kate insisted. "It was great seeing your work."

She was almost out the door when a sudden thought made her turn back. "There's one thing I still don't get. That day you saw me at the church. What made you want to talk to me?"

Howell studied her face. "Take off your glasses," he said.

Kate had no idea what he was getting at. Still, she did as he'd asked. Without her glasses, the room was a blur, an interplay of light and dark. She couldn't make out Howell's features, though she sensed him watching her. Then, from across the table, she heard his disembodied voice. "Didn't you ever notice how much you look like her?"

Kate gazed out the window, watching the outskirts of town give way to endless winter fields. Traffic was light. Cold air seeped through the window. She tried to think about the evening ahead, the upcoming cocktail party. But she couldn't seem to shake Howell's voice.

Didn't you ever notice how much you look like her?

Head still turned toward one side, Kate reached into her backpack and pulled out a plastic compact. She held the round container in her hands a moment. Then she snapped it open and looked. First with glasses. Then without. Blue eyes stared back from the mirror. Madeleine's eyes were green.

And then, suddenly, she saw it.

Me but not me . . .

She stared at the image, as if hypnotized, wondering how she could have missed it. But then, she sometimes didn't recognize her own reflection. No surprise she hadn't picked this out. Besides, the resemblance wasn't so much to the Madeleine she'd known, but to the woman on the TV news. A Madeleine whose sleek dark bob had grazed her cheek. Just as her own hair did now.

For several minutes, Kate studied the image, in horrified fascination. Now that she'd seen this, what did she do? And what could it possibly mean?

Strains of a string quartet greeted Kate as she arrived at the cocktail party. The cafeteria had been transformed. The lights were low. Candles flickered. Tables were piled high with food. The men looked much as they did during the week; the women wore simple black dresses. Kate tossed off greetings as she edged through the crowd, scanning the room for Carter Mills.

She'd just picked up a white wine spritzer when she heard some-one call her name.

"Kate. Over here." It was Justin. He was standing with two col-leagues. One was Victor Lawson. She didn't know the other guy. "Come rescue me!" Justin called. "I'm trapped in the conversation from hell. We're deep in discussion of the subway system."

"Litigators," Kate said, approaching the group. "Is there any-thing they can't debate?" Returning Justin's smile, she felt a pang of sadness, sudden as it was unexpected. *Laura Lacy.* Of course, Justin had gone out on dates before, but there'd never been anyone serious. Somehow, she knew this was different.

"You know Victor Lawson," Justin said. Kate nodded. "And this is Mark Postino."

"Hi, Mark."

"Hi. Nice to meet you." With his strong Bronx accent and mus-cled build, Postino looked more like a wrestler than a white-shoe lawyer.

"What year are you?" she asked.

"Third. But I just started here last month. I used to be at Cra-vath."

"If you don't mind," Victor Lawson said, raising an eyebrow. "I was just making a *very important* transportation point."

The mock argument resumed. Kate took a seat on a window ledge. Outside it had started to snow. Wet flakes hurtled through the building's light before vanishing below. Turning back to the room, Kate again scanned the crowd. The partnership was out in full force. Bruce Stroesser huddled with Martin Drescher. Bill Mc-Carty and Karen Henderson talked nearby. One by one, Kate picked out another half dozen familiar faces. Colin Barfield. Dave Bosch. Warren Leverett. But still no sign of Carter Mills. Could she somehow have missed his arrival? She decided to check around.

"I'm going to get some food," Kate said, hopping down from her perch.

Justin put down his drink. "I'll go with you. I could use some-thing to eat."

Together they approached the buffet table. It was an impressive sight, filled with an array of complex hors d'oeuvres. Tuna sashimi on tiny potato crisps. Endive leaves filled with chevre and caviar. Mushroom caps stuffed with green-flecked puree. "*Big food*," Andrea called these ornate creations. It occurred to Kate that Andrea was someone else she hadn't seen yet tonight.

"Quite a spread, huh?" Justin was methodically filling a plate. "Definitely beats the Harvard Club. Although, come to think of it, these broiled oysters would taste great with a big glob of Cheez Whiz."

"Maybe you should suggest it," Kate said, still looking over the room. The conversational buzz was growing louder, all but drowning out the string quartet. "Justin, have you seen Carter tonight?"

"I don't know. I don't think so. But I haven't been looking for him. Hey, want to go back to Lawson and Postino?"

Kate managed a smile. "No thanks. I think I'm going to do a little mingling."

꧁꧂

THE ticking of the grandfather clock seemed louder than usual tonight. Mills saw it was almost eight. He was long overdue upstairs. But picturing the strained festivities — the pathetically elaborate hors d'oeuvres, the anxious young lawyers, desperate to make an impression — he just couldn't face it yet. Besides, he had other things on his mind, issues far more pressing than a cocktail party.

Mills sank back into his chair and folded his hands. Gazing out the window at the city's anonymous depths, he found himself wishing he could disappear. He was tired, terribly tired. What he really yearned for was sleep. A deep, dreamless slumber that would banish all thought. But sleep really wasn't an option. It was laughable, almost, how his luck had turned. Luck had been with him for so many years, he'd almost forgotten its presence. But now he sensed cracks in his life's foundation. So far, the movement was insubstantial. Nothing that couldn't be dealt with. But he was too much of a realist to think that it would end here.

Behind him, a gold hinged frame held studio portraits of two boys. Turning away from the window, Mills briefly studied the pictures. A pair of blond children with indiscriminate smiles. Looking at them, he felt nothing. Except perhaps irritation. After all, what did his sons — young men now — know of the pressures he faced? The boys had always reminded him of their mother, a resemblance that had grown more striking with the passing years. Diane accused him of being heartless, of caring no more for his sons than for her. He never responded to these accusations. For what was there to say? He looked at the boys and saw nothing of himself. Nothing to take hold of, to mold, to shape. Quite simply, he'd lost interest.

Then he was thinking of another picture. The one he'd destroyed last week. He could still see her face in his mind's eye. The sweep of dark hair, the broad forehead, the brilliant, wide-set eyes. If only he could have destroyed his memories along with her photograph. Instead, they were growing stronger. Ever since he'd cut up the picture, he'd been obsessed by the past. As if by reliving events in his mind, he could somehow alter their course.

If only they'd never met.

It was this thought that haunted him most. After all, what were the odds? They were different people from different worlds. Their paths need never have crossed. So many chances for avoidance! If only he'd picked a different movie. If only he'd gone to a later show. If only she hadn't worked that night. His mind had run on like this for days. He couldn't work, couldn't sleep. The mental discipline that was his stock-in-trade seemed to have deserted him entirely. He could almost imagine she was watching him. Staring through a keyhole, gloating.

Then, without warning, he heard a voice. *Each day is a new beginning. You must never rest on your laurels.* His father's words reverberated in Carter's mind, filling him with a trembling rage. Give up now? And prove his father right? *Never.* Not while he still had a choice. He was a litigator, one of the best. He'd built a career on beating the odds. He could certainly do it again.

The burst of anger seemed to have energized him. He could feel his self-confidence returning. The situation that had seemed so bleak now seemed entirely manageable. Why already he'd taken steps. Removed Kate Paine from the Thorpe case, started to resume control. Thorpe was a problem, of course. Mills thought of the horrendous cassette. Madeleine's secret weapon. That must have been how she'd seen it. Briefly, he wondered where it had come from — from Friedman's lawyer? from one of her friends? — but none of that mattered now. The only thing that mattered was the future. He'd raised the issue of the tape with Thorpe, hoping for some explanation. But all he'd gotten was blanket denials and improbable speculations. Thorpe knew that Jed Holden would back him. And, unfortunately, Thorpe was right. Jed Holden saw Thorpe as a surrogate son. It was Samson's job to protect him. And, most especially, it was Carter Mills's job, thanks to their private "arrangement."

Mills put his head in his hands. *How had he ended up here?* He'd never seen himself as a man who took risks. But lately, he'd begun to wonder. Why had he selected Kate Paine to go through Madeleine's office? If he'd thought about it even an instant, he'd have seen he was tempting fate. And then further back, when he'd started those side deals with Holden. It wasn't that he'd needed the money. Even before his father died, he'd had more than enough to pay the bills. And further back still, Maria.

Why hadn't he noticed it before, this pattern of seeking out danger? Perhaps because the events were so widely spaced in time. It wasn't a daily occurrence. Or even a yearly one. Still, these were not the actions of a rational man, of the man that he'd thought he was. His actions seemed to reflect a sort of death wish. A strange urge to self-destruct.

Once again, he thought of the photograph. Left as a calling card. He was not a superstitious man. Still, he had a growing conviction that his troubles all stemmed from her. And what of that strange resemblance to Kate Paine. No, *not* Kate Paine, Madeleine.

Not Kate Paine . . .

That associate, Kate Paine. You hired her, didn't you? Just look at her . . .

For a moment, they swam through his mind, these three women: Kate, Madeleine, and Maria. Their faces mingled and merged, a sea of lustrous hair and bright eyes. A thought was trying to break through, but he couldn't quite seem to grasp it.

And then there was a knock on the door.

~

KATE was heading to the bar for another spritzer when she felt a tap on her shoulder. Dave Bosch, the young partner who'd chaperoned her talk with Cathy Valencia. He looked crisp and well polished in his good dark suit; genetically designed to inspire trust in clients and fear in opposing counsel.

"Nice to see you, Kate. How've you been?"

"Just fine, thanks." *Yeah, right.* "And you?"

"Terrific." Bosch's voice was as starched as his shirt. "Listen, I'm really looking forward to having you on the team. We'll set up a meeting next week to get you up to speed on the Danbury case."

Kate gave him a baffled look. "What do you mean?"

Bosch seemed taken aback. "I . . . Carter must have spoken to you about this by now."

Kate continued to stare. Bosch pushed ahead. "I'm sorry. I thought you knew. You're being transferred to my team."

"Why?" The question was out before she could stop herself. *Ours is not to reason why. . . .*

"It's simply a staffing decision," Bosch said. "Nothing to do with your work. We decided the Thorpe case was overstaffed. That's all."

"I see." A dull pounding was beginning in her ears. Kate knew that she should ask about the Danbury case, to display some interest, but she just couldn't bring herself to care.

"The Danbury case is cutting-edge stuff, Kate." Bosch's voice held an edge of reproach. "It'll give you great experience. Much broader training than you'd get with Carter. Sexual harassment law may be hot, but it's not where the bulk of our work is. Anti-trust, on the other hand —"

Antitrust. Not only was she being bumped from Carter Mills to Dave Bosch — from the firm's most powerful partner to one of its most junior — but they were going to bury her in some endless commercial regulatory dispute. Endless mountains of documents to be reviewed in windowless conference rooms. Endless pages of in-terrogatories. And why? What was behind it all? There was only one thing Kate knew for sure: this was no simple staffing shift.

"— is at the heart of our practice. Samson & Mills has the largest —"

"Excuse me," Kate said, cutting off Bosch in midsentence. "But I need to catch up with someone." She barely noticed Bosch's as-tonished expression as she made a beeline toward Peyton Winslow. Peyton was standing in line at the buffet. His cool smile gave no sign that he knew what had happened. But of course that could just be an act. She didn't trust anyone now.

"Hello, Kate. Feeling better?"

"Excuse me?"

"Are you feeling better? You had that doctor's appointment."

"Oh. Yeah. I'm fine." Kate rushed ahead, urgency overriding cir-cumspection. "Listen, have you seen Carter? I really need to talk to him."

Peyton eyed her warily. He could tell that something was up. "He's probably still down in his office. I know he had some work to get through."

⚜

BEFORE Carter Mills could respond, the office door swung open to reveal a single visitor.

"May I help you?" Mills said.

"I need to speak with you, Carter." The voice was surprisingly assured.

Mills raised a dismissive hand. "You'll need to make an appoint-ment. I'm afraid that I'm busy now."

"But I'm not, Carter," the intruder said, turning to close and lock the office door. "I'm not busy at all. In fact, I've been waiting a long time for this conversation."

Mills stared at the intruder. With a sudden movement, he reached for the phone.

"Sorry, but I can't let you do that." And Carter watched, with rising disbelief, as the intruder drew from his pocket a silver-plated gun with an ivory grip. Stunned, Mills stared at the revolver. *It couldn't be the same one, it couldn't.*

It was then that he saw the gloves.

Quickly Mills rose to his feet, but the intruder was even faster. He was there by Mills's side, the gun aimed straight at Mills's head.

"Carter, I sure would appreciate it if you'd take a seat. Makes me a little nervous to see you fidgeting like that."

Mills sat.

"Now then, Carter, we'll have to take one more precaution." With the gun still pointing at Mills's head, the intruder edged a few steps back. "What I can assure you," the intruder continued, "is that this won't hurt a bit."

Mills gagged as something soft was thrust in his mouth, then twisted several times around his head. He tried to rise out of the chair, but the intruder jacked back an arm, forcing him down in his seat. Before Mills knew what was happening, his hands were bound tightly behind him.

"Not bad at all," the intruder said. Once again, he stood facing Mills. "For someone with not much experience. I'd say we're ready to have our little talk."

Mills's eyes darted furiously around the room, as if seeking a means of escape.

The intruder, however, was calm. "Of course, you're at something of a disadvantage, as far as conversation goes. But that's okay, Carter. That's okay. Because I have enough to say for both of us."

❧

ALONE in the brightly lit corridor, Kate walked toward Carter Mills's office door. Beneath the black fabric of her cocktail dress, her heart thudded anxiously. Her footseps slowed, then stopped as she paused for a moment to prepare. Smoothing the front of her dress, Kate noticed her glasses seemed smudged.

She'd just finished polishing the lenses, when something caught her eye. A blur, a sudden movement, down at the end of the hall. Kate's heart seemed to liquefy. Two words slammed into her brain: *Chuck Thorpe*. Quickly, she jammed on her glasses. Trembling, she gazed ahead. The scene almost pulsed with stillness. No one, nothing, was there. Leaning against a bank of secretarial stations, Kate waited for her pulse to slow. Then, squaring her shoulders, she proceeded toward Mills's open door.

An open door.

Once more, Kate stopped, her heart beating faster again. Had the door been open earlier? Before she took her glasses off? Not so far as she remembered. But again, she couldn't be sure.

Cautiously, Kate entered the reception area. Nothing unusual here. Clara's desk was cleared for the weekend. A blue cardigan sweater hung over the back of her chair. The door to Mills's private office was closed, but light shone out from beneath. Kate knocked softly three times. Then again with more determination. Still, she got no response.

Maybe he was tied up on the phone. Kate pressed an ear to the door, trying to make out some sound. For an uncertain moment, she considered leaving. But she'd already come so far. And she couldn't keep putting this off. She'd just crack open the door, let him know that she was waiting outside.

She put her hand to the doorknob. The handle turned under her grasp. Then the walls were rushing toward her. Something was terribly wrong. She wasn't sure what she was looking at, but she knew that she couldn't breathe.

Red. Red everywhere.

Blood.

And Carter Mills. Seated at his desk. Slumped to one side in the chair.

She couldn't see his face, only blood.

And clutched in his hand, something small and shiny.

A gun.

Slowly, Kate began to edge back. Time didn't exist anymore. She felt as if she'd stumbled onto a film set. Or into someone else's dream. Her mouth opened wide in a silent cry.

And then, she began to scream.

⚘

KATE stared at Detective Cathy Valencia's vermilion mouth, opening and closing in a rhythmic staccato. It reminded her of folded origami toys she'd played with as a child, inserting thumb and forefinger to make the paper open and shut.

"Ms. Paine?"

"I'm sorry. Could you repeat the question?"

"I just want you to tell me exactly what happened, from the time you left the party until Detective Glaser got here."

They were sitting in Colin Barfield's office. Glaser, the first detective on the scene, was seated at Valencia's left. Kate was dimly aware of a cluster of figures on the other side of the room. Barfield. Martin Drescher. Bruce Stroesser. The power brokers of Samson & Mills.

"I left the party sometime after eight. Around eight-fifteen or eight-thirty. I'd been trying to catch up with Carter for the past couple of days about . . . about a few different things. I thought I'd see him at the cocktail party, but he wasn't there. Then another associate I work with — Peyton Winslow — said Carter was in his office. That's why I went up."

"And then?" Valencia's voice was gently prodding.

"When I got to the outside office, I saw a light under Carter's door. I knocked but no one answered. I thought maybe Carter was on the phone, so I cracked open the door a little. And that's when I saw . . . what had happened. I didn't touch anything. I just sort of backed out of the room. Then I called Building Security."

Kate was surprised by how detached she felt. She could be describing a painting, or a scene in a play. She pulled her cape tight around her. Someone had brought it down from where she'd left it upstairs. The softness was soothing. But the color . . .

Again, she saw the shattered remains of Carter Mills's head, the crimson torrent that had drenched his shirt.

"Ms. Paine? Are you all right? Would you like some more tea?"

Kate realized she was clutching at the arms of her chair. "No," she said, forcing her hands to unclench. "I'm fine now. I just felt a little dizzy."

Valencia went back to asking questions. Kate responded as if by rote, her mind still riveted on what she'd seen.

"Do you . . . have any idea who killed him?" Kate said.

Valencia and Glaser exchanged glances.

"What?" Kate said.

Then she heard a cough. Colin Barfield, standing at the head of the Samson contingent, moved a few steps toward her.

"This wasn't a murder," Barfield said. "It was . . . some kind of accident. We're in the process of piecing it all together." The other partners nodded, as if echoing Barfield's words. Kate stared at the impassive faces. *An accident.* But that was impossible. Why would Mills have had a gun in his office?

"But how . . ." Kate's voice trailed off, as the implication hit home.

Carter Mills, they were saying, had killed himself.

꙳

Music pounded in his ears; water pounded against his skin. Awash in this sea of sound and sensation, he rejoiced in the opera's final chorus. Wer glücklich ist wie wir, dem ziemt nur eins: schweigen und tanzen! *There is only one thing fitting for those happy as we: to be silent and dance!* Jumping out of the shower, he grabbed a clean white towel and vigorously rubbed himself down. Then, still naked, he strode into the loft's main room, the place from where the music came.

Schweigen und tanzen!

Richard Strauss's *Elektra.*

He'd discovered this opera only last week. But he'd instantly known it was perfect.

Except for the flicker of candles, the room was dark. He wanted to scream, to moan, to bellow his news through the streets. But, just as the music said, he had to be silent. To be silent and dance. On a sudden impulse, he flung his arms outward, then collapsed down. The movements felt strange but right. Over and over, he continued the thrashing motions, moving in a large, slow circle around the room. A ritual celebration.

When the CD ended, he pushed Play again. Then he stood in the center of the room, uncertain what to do next. Water still dripped from his hair, running in rivulets down his neck and back. Turning to look behind, he could see a trail of wet footprints leading from the bathroom to where he stood. If he squinted, he could pretend it was marked in blood.

Now that he'd stopped moving, he noticed how cold the loft was. But he didn't feel like getting dressed. He wanted no artificial barriers between himself and this point in time.

Across from his desk, he'd set up a sort of altar. Above a sea of glimmering candles, her eyes followed his every move. He stared at the picture from a distance before moving in for a closer look. So familiar, yet always new. With one finger, he traced her brow. He could tell from her expression she was pleased. Leaning forward, he gently kissed the glossy paper cheek. *Take care of your mother. You're all she's got.* For years, those words had echoed in his mind, an undying reminder of how he'd failed. The guilt had been unbearable. Sometimes he'd managed to drown it out, with cheap gin and later with drugs. But always the voice had come back. They'd told him that he should ignore it. They'd told him it wasn't real. But he'd always known they were wrong. They didn't — couldn't — understand.

She was so beautiful in that picture! One hand pushing back a piece of hair, the other reaching out to embrace him. It was the same picture he'd left for Kate, knowing that she'd understand. A sign that he hadn't forgotten. That it was only a matter of time.

He looked to the metal door, half expecting Kate to appear. As she had earlier that night. What a wondrous turn of events! She'd seen him leave Carter Mills's office. Now she knew that his work was done. But instead of improving his spirits, the thought seemed to pull him down. This was a time of rejoicing, a time that ought to be shared. So why hadn't she rushed to find him? What was she waiting for?

Sunday, January 17

THEY'D managed to keep Carter Mills's death out of the Sunday papers. But whether this was a reflection of Samson's powers or merely a testament to the dictates of daily deadlines, Kate had no idea. Slouched on the sofa, she stared at the Metro page headlines. Beside her Tara was knitting, something in a dark blue wool. Tara had slept on the couch last night after picking up Kate at the office. This morning she looked rumpled but serene, her red-gold curls secured on her head with a heavy tortoise-shell clip. It seemed to Kate that Tara hadn't aged since college. She, on the other hand, felt a thousand years older.

"What are you making?" Kate asked.

"A sweater."

"I didn't even know you could knit. When did you start?"

"About a year ago, I guess."

The words hung between them, another sign of how far their paths had diverged.

"Are you sure you don't want something to eat?" Tara said, glossing over the awkward moment. "I picked up some bagels at H&H."

"Thanks. But I'm not really hungry. Maybe later."

The only sound in the room was the gentle clicking of Tara's knitting needles. Through the window, Kate could see snow drifted up against the window frame. But despite last night's blizzard, Tara hadn't hesitated to come out.

Kate felt grateful, grateful and a little guilty.

"Thanks again for picking me up last night."

"No problem. I'm glad that you called."

"Well, thanks. Really." As she spoke, Kate heard a muffled growling in her stomach. She must be hungry after all. "You know, maybe I will have a bagel."

"Do you want me to —"

"No. That's okay."

The H&H bag on the kitchen counter gave off a yeasty smell. Kate peered inside and pulled out a cinnamon raisin bagel. After slicing the bagel in two, she spread a thick layer of cream cheese over both halves. She tried to keep her mind on what she was doing. But even as she puttered around the kitchen, memories began to seep back.

Dark red blood.

The glint of the gun.

Carter Mills's ravaged body.

Kate put the bagel on a plate and returned to her spot on the couch. Tara was still knitting, her hands skillfully manipulating the skein of yarn. She seemed competent and calm. Kate wished she could be like that.

"D'you think I could learn how to knit?" Kate's voice sounded small, a child's voice.

Tara looked up. "Of course. If you want to."

"Would you teach me?"

"Sure." Tara sounded a little surprised. Kate could imagine why: in all the years they'd known each other, she'd never shown the slightest interest in handicrafts. Except as a consumer, that is. Kate thought back to when she and Tara were roommates at Barnard. They'd been so close then. They used to wear each other's clothes, finish each other's sentences. But after college, they'd grown apart. Perhaps it was only natural. Instead of living together in a two-room apartment, they'd been several hundred miles apart, Kate up at Harvard in law school, Tara still here in New York. Kate had assumed they'd grow closer again once she moved back to the city. But it hadn't worked out that way. If anything, their new proximity only underscored the ways that each had changed.

Suddenly, Kate was determined to bridge the gap. Whatever had happened between them, Tara was still her best friend.

"If I tell you about last night, will you swear not to tell anyone?"

"Of course." Tara looked up from her knitting. She seemed a little confused. After all, she thought she knew what had happened. Just another little murder at Samson & Mills.

"Carter wasn't murdered. He killed himself." *There, she'd spoken the words*. Kate's heart seemed to contract, as if someone had squeezed it tight. She waited for Tara to respond.

"So say something," Kate said. "What are you thinking?"

Tara put down her knitting. "Just that . . . don't you think there must be some connection? With that woman partner who was killed, I mean."

Kate stared at her hands. Leave it to Tara to ask the hard question, to put everything on the table. Tara was right, of course. It was absurd to think that Carter Mills's death was simply a coincidence. But if not a coincidence, then what? What linked the two deaths together? Facts swirled in her head; she didn't know what to say.

Finally, she looked back at Tara. "What sort of connection, exactly?"

"I don't know, Kate. I don't know anything about these people. It just seems like there must be something. I mean, when was the last time a partner at Samson & Mills died of unnatural causes? What are the odds of two unrelated violent deaths?"

"I guess they aren't very high." Kate watched as Tara pushed back a curl. She'd always loved Tara's unruly hair, so different from her own straight tresses. Though she fit right in at Samson & Mills, where all the women had straight hair. Or most of them anyway. Madeleine had once had short, sleek hair, back when she was much younger.

Haven't you ever realized how much you look like Madeleine? The question flickered through her mind. She'd managed to push aside Howell's words; his suspicions had seemed so far-fetched. But what Tara was saying made sense. A suicide and a murder in one law firm where the victims were former lovers. What were the chances of that? Howell claimed that Madeleine had been afraid of Mills. It had seemed a preposterous notion. Still, there must be some reason Mills had killed himself, and she didn't have any other theories. Could Howell possibly be right? Had Mills caused Madeleine's death?

The questions seemed to press in on her, pounding at her brain. Then, with a sudden assertion of will, Kate pushed them away again. This wasn't just any murder, but a brutal and violent slaying. The vicious multiple stab wounds. The candle jammed in Madeleine's vagina. Besides, she'd seen Mills right after Madeleine's death. She'd watched his reactions up close. There'd been nothing manufactured in his response. If there had been, she would have noticed. No, whatever Mills's feelings for Madeleine, she couldn't believe that he'd killed her.

Still, that hardly ended the matter. If not that connection, then what? Madeleine and Carter had once been lovers. The affair hadn't ended well. They'd recently started to work together after a hiatus of many years. It was Mills who'd pushed Madeleine to work for Thorpe. At least that's what Carmen had said. Kate searched for some meaning in these facts, some clue to what might have gone on. Slowly an idea took shape. What if Mills had also suspected Thorpe? Could Mills have blamed himself for Madeleine's death?

"I guess Carter could have felt guilty about what happened to Madeleine." Kate was thinking out loud. "But I still can't see him committing suicide because of it. He just isn't that sort of person."

Tara gave an impatient shrug. "It happens all the time, Kate. The least likely people are the ones to crack."

"Yeah, I guess." Kate hugged her flannel-clad knees.

"You really didn't know this man." Tara's voice was gentle but firm. "You only saw him at work, wearing his public face. You have no idea what went on in his private life. You idealized him. Just like you idealize everyone at that firm. They're just people, Kate. Everyone has demons. Everyone makes mistakes."

Kate felt a tightness in her chest. She had the usual impulse to check Tara's words, but this time she let them pass. It was hard to argue with the facts.

The phone rang.

Kate jumped to her feet. "I'll get it," she said, picking up the receiver as she spoke.

Justin didn't bother to say hello. "Have you heard about Carter?" he asked.

"Yes, I . . . know." Kate nudged her desk chair closer to the phone and lowered herself to the seat.

"What the hell is going on?" Justin demanded. "It's like that Agatha Christie book *And Then There Were None*. One by one everyone gets knocked off. I mean, when is it going to end? I can't believe they haven't found this psycho yet."

It took Kate a few seconds to figure out where Justin was coming from, to realize he still believed that Mills had been murdered. She was about to correct him, when she remembered the instructions she'd been given last night. *Say nothing until further notice.* She was tempted to tell Justin anyway — like Tara, she knew he could be trusted — but something made her hesitate.

"How did you hear?" Kate said.

"They called me."

"Who?"

"Dave Bosch. I guess the partners are calling everyone, trying to prepare for tomorrow. Why? Isn't that how you heard?"

"No." Kate took a deep breath. "Actually, I'm the one who found him last night."

A sharp intake of breath from Justin's end of the line. "You found the *body*?"

"It was during the cocktail party. I went up to his office. I needed to talk to him about something. And . . . there he was." The tightness in Kate's chest grew sharper.

"Christ. Are you okay?"

Kate gave a short dry laugh. "Well, I've been better. So what did Bosch tell you?"

"Just that Mills was found shot to death in his office last night. And they reminded us not to talk to the press." Kate could tell that Justin's shock over Mills's death was fast giving way to concern about her own condition. "You shouldn't be alone now, Kate. I'm coming over."

"No, really, I'm all right," Kate said. "Tara slept over last night. She's still here." It was bad enough deceiving Justin over the phone. It would be worse to do it in person. Maybe by tomorrow morning the news would be public, and she'd be free to drop the subterfuge.

"So what did the cops say?" Justin said. "They must at least have a suspect."

"I don't know," Kate said. "They didn't say much, and I didn't ask. I was pretty out of it, I guess. Basically, they just asked me what I'd seen, and I told them what I remembered. It wasn't much. As soon as I realized what I was looking at, I started to scream. I got out of there and called Security."

"It must be someone with a vendetta against the firm. And it's obviously someone with access. Jesus, the killer must have been in the building last night at the same time we were all there."

Kate was almost swept into Justin's fervor. Until she reminded herself.

Suicide.

Not murder, suicide.

"Justin, you know I'm feeling a little tired. I'm still sort of in shock, I think. Can we talk in the morning?"

Justin was immediately contrite. "Sure. Sorry. This is the last thing you need right now. Are you sure I can't bring you anything?"

"Thanks, but I'm just going to lie low today. I'll call you when I get in tomorrow."

When Kate hung up the phone, she saw that Tara was giving her a dangerous look.

"What?" Kate asked. But she already knew.

"Please don't tell me that you're going to work tomorrow."

"Why not?" As if she didn't know.

"*Why not?*" Tara leaned forward, as if she wanted to take hold of Kate's shoulders and shake her. "Because the partner you worked for just killed himself. Because you found the body. Because this is the second person you work with who's been killed this month. How many more reasons do you need?"

"I'm okay," Kate said. "I'll feel better in the morning."

And the strange thing was, she already did. Even as she spoke, Kate felt herself growing lighter. Tomorrow morning, she'd get on the subway and go to work, just like she always did. She pictured her office at Samson & Mills: the neatly ordered books, the stacks of documents, the Statue of Liberty rising from the Hudson River. With everything that had happened, it was still where she wanted to be. Her work was there. Her life was there. And there were things that she needed to do.

Kate turned to Tara on the couch. "I have to go in tomorrow," she said. "I know you can't understand. But it's where I belong right now."

Monday, January 18

IF the press had been slow on the uptake, they were now making up for lost time. The tabloids carried screaming headlines: SAMSON SLAUGHTERHOUSE. MIDTOWN MAYHEM. Violent death at Samson & Mills was becoming a full-time beat.

Emerging from the subway, Kate saw that crowds had gathered around the Samson building. A security checkpoint had been established at the entrance. Kate took her place in line, scanning the sea of faces, searching for people she knew.

"Name?" The square-jawed guard didn't look at her as he spoke.

"Kate Paine. I'm a lawyer here."

Briefly, the guard's eyes dropped to a list in his hand.

"Picture ID?"

Kate reached into her purse for her billfold. Pulling out her driver's license, she caught sight of her photograph. She was struck by how young she looked. The picture was just a few years old, but she looked like a different person.

It was still early, before nine, and Kate was alone in the elevator. But when she reached her office, Justin was already there. Seated at Jennifer's secretarial station, he was poring over a newspaper. Catching sight of Kate, he began to talk.

"It doesn't sound like they have any idea."

Kate unlocked her office door. Justin followed her inside. Kate went behind her desk to pull up the shades. Justin slid into a chair.

"You look tired," he said, as Kate settled into her chair.

"I didn't sleep too well."

Justin looked back at the paper, now resting on his lap. "I can't believe they don't have any suspects. I mean, it happened right here. Don't they know who was in the building?"

Kate shrugged. If she didn't actually say anything, it didn't feel as much like lying. She glanced down at a firm memo that had been slipped under her door.

The partners of Samson & Mills regret to inform you that J. Carter Mills, the firm's managing partner, was found dead in his office Saturday night. The cause of death was a gunshot wound.

All firm personnel are reminded that contacts with the media on this and all other subjects related to Samson & Mills are strictly prohibited.

All media inquiries should be referred to Martin Drescher, who will serve as the firm's interim managing partner.

The memo continued for several more paragraphs, a brief discourse on Carter Mills's professional achievements, but Kate was too stunned to read on.

"*Martin Drescher?* They're handing over Carter's job to his archrival?"

"I know," Justin said. "It's crazy. Alice in Wonderland."

Kate didn't say anything. She was thinking about what must have happened. Suicide, whatever the provocation, was not the act of a team player. A postmortem punishment was being imposed.

"Kate? Are you okay?"

"Yeah, just a little preoccupied. Listen, would you mind if I catch up with you later? I have to make a phone call now."

Justin jumped to his feet. "Sure. Call me when you're done."

Kate waited until Justin had closed the door. Then, picking up the telephone receiver, she dialed Martin Drescher's extension.

❧

SAM Howell poured another cup of coffee and headed back to the living room. He sank into a chair and retrieved the newspaper he'd left folded open on its arm. Once more, he read the report, prominently featured on the front page of the Metro section. LEGAL STAR SHOT DEAD IN OFFICE. He must have read the article half a dozen times. Now he began again. Nothing could bring Madeleine back to life. But at least Mills had paid for her death.

❧

"AND you're sure that it was Chuck Thorpe speaking?"

"Absolutely," Kate said.

"And the woman?" Drescher persisted. "What makes you think it was the plaintiff?"

"Some of the details were the same. I don't remember exactly. But they were talking about Ron Fogarty. The complaint alleges that Thorpe forced Steph — the plaintiff — to have sex with Fogarty. When I listened to the tape, the pieces seemed to fit together."

Kate eyed Drescher from across his desk. He wasn't looking good this morning. His face was a shiny, mottled red, and he seemed to be short of breath. But at least he was paying attention. He'd listened without interruption as Kate described Thorpe's attack along with her subsequent discovery that the cassette tape was missing from her drawer. With a grunt, Drescher raised a mug to his lips — a little hair of the dog? — and then leaned back in his chair.

"So, Ms. Paine, you're suggesting that Chuck Thorpe took this cassette from your desk? Is that what you're telling me?"

Kate looked at him, surprised. She'd hardly expected to be challenged on this point. If there was one thing she thought she knew, it was that Drescher loathed Thorpe and already considered him a suspect in Madeleine's death. He'd said as much to Carter Mills the night she'd overheard them argue. The night she'd been trapped beneath the very desk at which Martin Drescher now sat.

"It's the only explanation I can think of," she said.

"And how do you think Thorpe knew where to find the tape?"

Because Carter must have told him. Though I'm not sure why. "I have no idea," she said. "But the fact is that he did."

"I see." Drescher continued to study her. His eyes, slightly bloodshot, moved from her face down her body. Kate flushed. Her black knit skirt wasn't short by office standards. But when she sat down, it edged up over her knees. As she tugged at the hem, Martin Drescher smiled.

"Ms. Paine, I'm sure you know these are very serious allegations."

"Yes. I realize that."

"And there aren't any witnesses?"

"No actual witnesses. But Maintenance can confirm that something was wrong with my lights. Maybe even that they'd been tampered with."

"But no witnesses." This time, it was not a question.

"I . . . that's right." Kate was about to say that it had been late, that everyone else had gone home. But that would have been a mistake. *Never try to explain.* It was a cardinal rule for Samson associates, part of the firm's quasi-military ethic. Just answer the question.

"And have you spoken to anyone else about this?"

"No. No one."

Drescher loosened his tie. "Ms. Paine, I'm sure you know that Samson & Mills is at a crisis point. I'm going to be frank. Our resources are stretched to the limit. I can't promise that we'll address this right away. But you have my word that, at the first opportunity, we'll fully investigate your claims. Can you live with that?"

Did she have any choice? "I . . . yes, I guess so."

"In the meantime, I'd suggest that you take some time off. At least a week or two. With full pay, of course."

"Thank you. I . . . I'll think about it."

"If you need any professional assistance, I'm sure we can arrange for that."

Professional assistance. It took Kate a moment to realize that he meant psychiatric help. Again, she flushed. "I don't think so," she said.

"Now, can I count on you to keep this matter to yourself for the time being, until we've had a chance to address it?" Drescher's voice had turned gentle, almost cajoling.

"Yes, of course." The response was automatic. Kate had mentally moved on to the next item on her agenda. Taking a deep breath, she began. "There is one other thing I wanted to mention. It's about Madeleine Waters."

Drescher's head inclined to one side. He was still leaning back in his chair. But Kate sensed a subtle tensing of his muscles. Like a tomcat waiting to spring.

"In light of what happened to me, I think that Chuck Thorpe should be considered a suspect in Madeleine's death. If he isn't already, I mean."

Drescher raised his eyebrows. "Ms. Paine, groping a female lawyer, however inappropriate, is hardly comparable to murder."

Kate felt her skin glow hot. She'd played by the rules. She'd kept their secrets, gone through the proper channels. And where had it gotten her? *Never try to explain.* Well, fuck that. Right now, she was going to explain. And Martin Drescher was going to listen.

"Perhaps I wasn't clear," Kate said. Her heart beat hard in her chest, a caged animal trying to get out. "Chuck Thorpe didn't just grope me, as you put it. He staged an attack. He ambushed me. When I walked into my office Monday night, I was grabbed by a stranger, forced up against the wall, and sexually assaulted. I —" Kate broke off, overwhelmed by a flood of feeling. For a terrible moment, she thought she was going to cry. She sat silently for a moment, her hands curled around the edge of her chair. She wasn't going to break down. Not here. Not in front of Martin Drescher.

Drescher shifted in his seat, a smile playing on his lips. He seemed to be enjoying himself. Kate felt a futile surge of rage.

"Ms. Paine, I might as well relieve you of your concerns about Chuck Thorpe. The things that you allege are, of course, reprehensible and will be investigated. But Chuck Thorpe did not kill Madeleine Waters. What I'm about to tell you will soon be public knowledge. But I'd appreciate it if you'd keep it confidential until then."

Almost imperceptibly, Kate nodded. Something in Drescher's expression told her that she didn't want to hear what he was going to say. She had an irrational desire to stop him. To walk out of the room. To put her fingers in her ears and talk loudly to herself as she had as a very small child, trying to shut out the frightening sounds of her parents arguing. Instead, she sat unmoving in her chair, a prisoner waiting to be sentenced.

"Carter Mills, as you know, killed himself," Drescher said. "What you don't know, what we only just learned this morning, is that the gun he used was the same gun used to kill Madeleine Waters."

Drescher gave Kate a meaningful look. Feeling his eyes on her, she willed herself to stay calm. Her face felt frozen solid, her features carved in ice. But behind the veneer, her brain was screaming. *It can't be true. It can't be.* At the same time, she knew that it was. If Carter's suicide weapon was the gun used to kill Madeleine, then he must have killed Madeleine, too. A Latin phrase leapt into her mind, a rule of evidence she'd learned in school. *Res ipsa loquitur.* The thing speaks for itself. No wonder Drescher seemed so smug.

Unless . . .

A saving question flashed through Kate's mind: *Why should she believe Martin Drescher?* He could be making this up. Or at least exaggerating. Perhaps it was just the same *type* of gun, and Drescher was racing to conclusions. She felt a seed of hope taking root. A subtle easing of tension. The fact was she didn't know anything for sure. Except that she'd heard enough.

"Well, I guess that's everything." Standing up from her chair, Kate carefully smoothed down her skirt. Now that she was on her feet, it came almost to her knees. Then, without saying good-bye, she turned and walked from the room.

Back in her office, Kate still felt rattled, disturbed by her talk with Drescher. Her brief bout of hopefulness had faded, and she could feel depression setting in. While she didn't know that Drescher was telling the truth, she couldn't prove that he wasn't. The mere possibility that what he'd said was true was too upsetting to consider. She felt angry at Drescher, angry at herself, angry at the situation. She decided to do some filing. Maybe the process of ordering her office would help bring order to her mind.

For some time, Kate worked steadily on autopilot. She could feel herself calming down. Then she found herself gazing at a thin stack of papers held together with a binder clip. A set of WideWorld Media's legal bills. What was it doing here? With a start, she realized what she was looking at. The bills from Madeleine's file. These were the photocopies she'd made the night she was trapped under Drescher's desk. She'd meant to tell Carter Mills that Drescher had taken the file. But with everything that had happened, the whole thing had slipped her mind.

Unsure of what to do next, she glanced over the top sheet in the stack. A bill for June 1996. And at the bottom of the page, a signature. J. Carter Mills. She stared at the sheet a minute then flipped to the next page. Another bill. Kate was about to put the stack aside, when she noticed that the page bore the same date as the previous bill. But the amount at the bottom was different. Kate flipped back to the first page, checking to be sure she'd read it right. June 1996. A bill for $87,000. Then back to the next page. June 1996, definitely the same date. But this time the bill was much higher, totaling $108,750.

Strange. She placed the first two sheets side by side. Then she turned to the next page. July 1996. A bill for $94,000. And after that, another bill for the same month. But here the billed amount had jumped to $117,500. Quickly, Kate paged forward, examining the bills one by one. There was a full year's worth of bills in the stack, each one in duplicate. And in each case, the second bill was larger than the first.

Much larger, in fact.

Like an animal sensing a distant storm, Kate felt herself growing uneasy. Again, she looked at the two June bills lying side by side on her desk. Line by line, she compared them. For the most part, the two bills matched. Legal services. Travel. Research. The dollar amounts were the same.

Then she came to a single entry. *Special Services. $21,750.*

Glancing back to the first bill, Kate saw no sign of this category.

She moved ahead to the two July bills. Again, the charges tallied perfectly. Except for a single entry.

Special Services. $23,500.

Kate didn't want to think what she was thinking. But she couldn't help herself. She reached for a calculator and punched in a couple of numbers. Then, flipping to the next set of bills, she repeated the calculation. Over and over, until she'd been through the entire stack. In each case, the result was the same. The amount charged to Special Services was twenty-five percent of the base amount.

When the phone rang, Kate picked it up without thinking, still staring at the papers on her desk.

"Hello. Kate?" The male voice was hesitant.

"Speaking." Kate glanced at caller ID, but the number was unfamiliar.

"It's Douglas. Douglas Macauley."

"Oh. Hi." It seemed like a lifetime since she'd seen him. Vaguely, Kate remembered that she'd promised to call. But the thought barely registered now.

"I feel terrible about what's happened at your firm. About what you must be going through. I know you probably don't want to talk. But if you need anything, please let me know."

"Actually, I'm okay."

A long silence from the other end.

"Look," Douglas finally said. "This may not be the best time, but I was hoping we could have dinner this weekend. It might be good for you to get away."

"Sorry, I really can't." She stared at the bills spread out on her desk. Numbers danced in her head.

"Maybe another night?"

Why? Why had he done it? Why would a man with every advantage — wealth, brilliance, professional regard — risk it all for some two-bit financial scam?

"Yeah. Okay. I'm just really tied up right now."

"Well, what about coffee? We could meet near your office. I could —"

"Listen, I've got another call I need to take. I'll be in touch, okay?"

Before he could answer, she'd hung up.

Special Services. A twenty-five percent add-on. She was surprised at how clear-headed she felt. Almost matter-of-fact. Carter Mills had been a crook. And Madeleine Waters had known. *I think she knew something about him, something that would hurt his career.* That's what Sam Howell had said. And now it was clear what that was. At the time, she'd thought Howell was crazy. But she'd been the one with delusions.

A knock on the door. As Kate shoved the photocopies into a drawer, Dave Bosch entered the room. Kate stared at the young partner dizzily, still reeling from what she'd uncovered. Was Bosch here to give her an assignment? That would be just like Samson & Mills. *Feel free to take some time off, but hey, as long as you're sticking around, might as well bill some hours.*

But that wasn't it after all. "I just spoke with Martin Drescher. He thinks you should take some time off. I agree. We have enough other bodies on the team for now."

Enough other bodies. An unfortunate choice of words. But Bosch didn't seem to notice. He was looking at her expectantly, waiting for a response. Why was he so eager to get rid of her? Was it something Drescher had said? Or something that she had done? Perhaps her impolitic response to the Danbury case. Or was it just the general tendency to confuse proximity with cause, as if her discovery of Mills's body made Kate somehow responsible for his death. Whatever the reason, Bosch clearly wanted her gone.

Kate stood up from her desk. "Actually," she said, "I was just going home."

Bosch seemed relieved. "If there's anything we can do . . ." The words trailed off. "Take as much time as you need. Within reason, of course."

Of course.

After Bosch left the room, Kate quickly collected her coat. On her way out the door, she stopped to check her office mailbox. There was one piece of paper inside, a memorandum from the partners of Samson & Mills.

A private service for J. Carter Mills was scheduled for tomorrow at 10 A.M.

All firm employees were invited.

Tuesday, January 19

THE alarm went off at eight. Kate swung her feet out of bed and
went to the door for the *Times*. Quickly, she flipped through the
pages. LEADING LAWYER'S DEATH CALLED SUICIDE. Bit-
ing her lip, she read the short piece straight through. Martin
Drescher was quoted, along with Detective Mike Glaser. According to both, Mills had ended his life with a .38-caliber revolver.
There had been a note with the body, but its contents were not dis-
closed. Drescher's only comment was a vehement assertion that
Mills's suicide had nothing to do with Samson & Mills. "The note
made clear that Mr. Mills's regrettable decision to end his life was
due to personal concerns. All of us at Samson & Mills are devas-
tated by this tragic event."

❦

SUN glinted through the windows of the Upper East Side church.
The altar was laden with flowers. But the propriety of the setting
only underscored the strangeness of the scene. Eulogists rushed

through their speeches. Mills's family was conspicuously absent. A weird giddiness infused the proceedings, a certain sense of collusion. People knew what their neighbors were thinking, but they weren't discussing it. Yet.

Kate was sitting toward the middle of the church, to the left of the center aisle. She was flanked by Justin on one side, Peyton on the other. Without thinking, she'd taken a seat in approximately the same location she'd selected for Madeleine's service. There was a difference, though. At Madeleine's memorial she'd been with Andrea. Today, Andrea was nowhere in sight. Scanning the room again, Kate could feel her uneasiness building. This was Andrea's second unexplained absence in just a few days. First the firm cocktail party. Now, Mills's memorial service. This wasn't like Andrea at all. Was it possible something was wrong? The thought fluttered briefly in her mind before reason again took hold. After all, Andrea was married. Even when Brent was away on business, he and Andrea talked each night.

A new speaker was taking the pulpit. Kate returned her focus to the front of the church. Charles Harrison was Mills's prep school and college roommate. With his narrow shoulders and spidery form, Harrison looked nothing like his late friend. But Kate could imagine how he must have admired Mills back when they were in school. In the days when beauty and form were the things that mattered most. Of course, the playing field had leveled out since then. Now retired, Harrison had been a partner at Ironson, Baggs, one of the world's premier investment banks. He must have been taking home at least several times what Mills did.

Even taking into account Mills's sideline income . . .

For the first time, it occurred to Kate that the WideWorld bills could be just the tip of the iceberg. What if Mills had been handling every bill this way, and had been doing it for decades? Over time, he could have raked in millions of dollars. Kate thought about the time Martin Drescher had interrupted a meeting to take a broker's cold call. He'd kept several lawyers waiting for close to forty minutes, barking questions into the phone. "So what's the return? *What's the return?*" Kate still recalled Andrea's incredulous face. "*These guys,*" she'd said later, as they'd headed downstairs. "*Their avarice is unbounded.*" Could that be the explanation here as well? Could Carter Mills's downfall have stemmed from common greed?

Harrison was talking about Mills's college years. His career as a champion rower. His academic success. "But it wasn't just these accomplishments that marked Carter Mills for greatness. What really distinguished him was force of character. He had a remarkable ability to draw out the best in all of us privileged to know him. His own high standards raised the bar for what we expected of ourselves."

Which is just how it was with me, Kate thought. But had everyone felt that way? Was it simply a matter of technique? Even now, she didn't want to believe that.

Soon the service was over. After quick good-byes, Peyton disappeared into the crowd. Another mega–networking opportunity.

"Are you going back to work?" Justin asked, as Kate gathered up her wrap and purse. She was wearing a black coat purchased several years back. Her red cape was hanging at home.

"I don't know," Kate said. "I hadn't really decided."

"I could drop you off by your apartment, if you want," Justin said. He'd given her a lift that morning in the aging junker he kept in a lot off Ninth Avenue. It had been a disconcerting trip, Justin still stunned by news of Mills's suicide, Kate pretending she'd had no idea.

"Yeah, okay," Kate said.

Heading toward the door with Justin, Kate caught sight of Charles Harrison, deep in conversation with Clara Hurley. Kate had almost forgotten about Clara. After twenty years as Mills's secretary, what must she be feeling now? Harrison had his arm around her shoulder. Kate could read the raw pain in Clara's face. She'd been in love with Carter, of course. Kate could see how it must have happened. The handsome, brilliant young lawyer. The uneducated but determined young woman, just starting work in the city. She must have been dazzled, Kate thought.

Her eyes still resting on the pair, Kate had a sudden thought. She turned to Justin. "Listen, why don't you go on ahead. I want to talk to a few people."

"Are you sure? I don't mind waiting."

"No, really. It's okay. I know you have a lot to do."

Justin watched her for another moment. Kate could tell he was reluctant to leave her. At the same time, he *did* have work to do. Especially since he was taking time off next week. A long weekend with Laura Lacy. He'd mentioned it this morning. Kate had felt a twist in her heart. She wasn't jealous, at least not exactly. She just didn't want to think about it now.

"You're sure you can get a ride back?"

"Justin, there are hundreds of people here. I'm pretty sure I can manage."

A quick hug and Justin was gone. Kate moved closer to Harrison, waiting for a chance to approach. When Clara turned to walk away, Kate quickly stepped into her place.

"Mr. Harrison, I'm Kate Paine. I was one of Carter's associates."

Harrison clasped her extended hand. "I'm very pleased to meet you. Though I certainly regret the circumstances." His grip was stronger than Kate had expected.

"I was so moved by what you said," Kate said. "All of this has been such a shock. I admired Carter so much. He hired me right out of Harvard Law. I was thinking, well, wondering, if you'd be willing to talk with me sometime. He was such a wonderful man. A legend, really. I'd like to know more about him. From someone who knew him well."

She could see that she'd hit her target. "Yes, it's a tragedy," Harrison said. "All these ridiculous rumors. It's insane. Worse than insane, it's evil. Carter never would have done . . . what they're saying. It's impossible. It just wasn't in him. I'd be happy to talk with you, dear."

Dear. Kate gritted her teeth and smiled.

"Perhaps you could come by the house." Harrison said. "Say, around ten tomorrow morning? Or is that a problem, what with work and all? I've been retired now for so many years, I sometimes forget what it was like."

The *early* early retirement. Another difference between law and investment banking.

"No, no," Kate said hurriedly. "I'll find the time. Tomorrow morning would be fine."

Harrison reached into a pocket for his card and held it out to Kate. "Here's my address. So I'll see you tomorrow, dear."

Wednesday, January 20

KATE took the Seventy-ninth Street bus across Central Park and reached the East Side around nine. After locating Harrison's Fifth Avenue co-op, an impressive Beaux Arts structure near the Met, she cut over to Madison Avenue in search of coffee and a place to think.

Soon she was seated at Eli Zabar's E.A.T, a sort of wildly upscale diner. The coats slung over the backs of chairs were Burberry plaid and fur. The diamonds on female patrons' hands made Angela Taylor's look minuscule. Surveying the menu, Kate could almost think that prices were listed in some foreign currency. Coffee for five dollars. Bread and jam for six.

Welcome to the Upper East Side.

After ordering cappuccino and a sticky bun, Kate pulled out a notepad and pen. She still hadn't decided what to say. What she wanted was to understand. But did Harrison really hold the answers? Could he really explain Carter Mills? Yesterday, she'd felt sure she was on to something, but today she was having doubts. The fact that Harrison had known Mills for decades didn't mean that he understood him. Years of friendship might confer great insight. Or they could simply feed denial. That's what appeared to be happening here. Knowing Mills for as long as he had, Harrison couldn't accept the truth.

Kate took a sip of cappuccino. Should she just forget the whole thing? Tara hadn't minced words when they talked on the phone last night. "I don't know what you expect to get out of this. You're fixated on Samson & Mills." Kate had taken the words with a grain of salt. She'd attributed them to Tara's annoyance that she'd dropped the ball with Douglas. "But you liked him," Tara had said, frustration evident in her voice. "I don't know what you're thinking. Guys like Douglas don't come along every day."

Guys like Douglas don't come along every day. The words had a familiar ring. Now, Kate remembered where she'd heard them before. Andrea had made the same point recently, only she'd been talking about Justin.

Andrea. Now there was another painful subject. Kate had called Andrea's office yesterday afternoon, only to find that she'd left on vacation. Left without a single word. It made no sense, no sense at all. Andrea had been saving up her vacation time for that February rafting trip in Chile. And now, inexplicably, she was gone. Kate couldn't make sense of it. She must have done something to upset Andrea, though she couldn't imagine what it was. But couldn't Andrea have raised the subject, given her a chance to explain? Kate could feel depression setting in, a slow-moving fog across her brain. But this wasn't the time or place. She glanced at her watch, raised her hand for the check.

Right now it was time to get going.

⚜

ACROSS a vast expanse of Oriental carpet, Charles Harrison had been holding forth for the past half hour, almost as if he were talking to himself. Kate balanced a cup and saucer on her knee and tried to look attentive. It occurred to her that this single room was bigger than her whole apartment. Finally, there was a break in the flow of words. Harrison gave Kate a quick glance, as if just remembering her presence.

"More coffee?"

"No thanks, I'm fine." Kate was eager to push ahead, to move beyond the meaningless generalities that were Harrison's preferred mode of discourse.

"It's so hard to picture Carter anywhere other than at Samson & Mills. What was he like in college?" It wasn't much of a question. But she had to move carefully here.

"He was the same," Harrison said. "He was always the same. And that's why I'm quite sure that this whole thing is a terrible mistake. Carter always rejected extremes. He was the essence of stability. The essence of moderation. If he had a passion, that was it. I'll never forget our sophomore year of college. That was 1966, during the Vietnam War."

The word sounded strange to Kate's ears. Vi-*et*-nam, the accent on the second syllable. She'd never thought of Mills as a product of the sixties. Now, counting back in time, she saw that the dates matched up. There was something obscurely upsetting in this, as if it showed yet another failure on her part. A failure to make use of what facts she'd had.

"It was quite a tumultuous time. Protests, that sort of thing. In the middle of it all, the secretary of defense came to speak on campus. Robert McNamara. The SDS crowd was out in full force. I think we all pretty much expected that. But not what came afterward. When the radicals didn't get what they wanted, they stormed McNamara's car. Actually pulled him out of the vehicle, demanding that he answer their questions. It was horrifying. Truly. I'd never seen Carter so angry. Not that he was a strong supporter of the war. Like most of us, he was on the fence. But the idea that students would resort to violence, to personal attacks . . . well, he found that unacceptable."

Kate saw that Harrison was watching her, waiting for a response.

"That must have been very upsetting," she said, trying to match his expression.

"Very upsetting," Harrison said. "Very upsetting indeed. You young people don't know what it's like to live through a time like that."

"No," Kate said. "I guess you're right. And Carter, I mean, was he generally active in campus politics?" Clumsy, but at least she'd pushed the conversation back on track. Back to the subject of Mills.

"Oh, I wouldn't say that." Harrison gave a short laugh. "Despite what you read in history books, a lot more was going on during the sixties than student rebellion. Basically, we just went ahead with our lives. On a day-to-day basis, we were a lot more concerned about other things. Such as whether the Cliffies were going to use our library."

Kate could feel her eyes narrow.

"It didn't bother me so much once it happened," Harrison said quickly. "It was just the change, you know. No one likes change."

Yeah, right. Except those pushy Radcliffe bitches.

Kate smiled sweetly. "I know what you mean."

Harrison looked at her another few moments, as if trying to decide whether he'd misjudged her. Gradually his gaze seemed to soften. "I know how distressing this must be for you, dear. But you have to believe me when I say that James would never do what they're saying he did. Never. He had nothing but contempt for people who took the easy way out."

Kate looked at him, confused. "James?" she said. "You mean Carter?"

Harrison tapped his forehead with a long, thin finger. "Yes, yes, of course. Carter. That's what I meant. Anyway, as I was saying. . . ."

⚜

KATE had just gotten out of the bathtub when she realized that she had yet to check tomorrow's schedule. Wrapped in a terry robe, she sat down at her desk and logged on to Samson's network. A few clicks of the mouse and then her calendar popped up. Thursday, January 21. The space was strangely blank. Just one thing on for the day: her weekly four o'clock with Josie. She'd go into work after lunch.

Water dripped down her neck; she needed to get a towel. But before closing down the computer, she should check America Online. Most e-mail went to her office account, but the occasional message still landed here. *"You've got mail."* She clicked on the icon and scanned the results. Just the usual slew of mass mailings, most from purveyors of porn. She was about to delete them en masse, when one message caught her eye. While sex e-mails usually came with provocative tags, the message line here was blank. The sender was Adam0116. She clicked to open it up.

I have some information that I think would interest you about recent events at your law firm. Contact me if you want to learn more. Staring at the message, Kate felt goosebumps rising on her arms. For a crazy moment, she almost thought that someone was watching her. She whipped her head around, rapidly scanning the room. But, of course, no one was there. Turning back to the screen, she read the message again. *Who was Adam0116?* She clicked on Member Profiles, hoping she'd find some clue. *There is no profile for Adam0116.* The words gleamed back from the screen.

Thursday, January 21

KATE stared at the newspaper spread out on her lap. She'd already fielded phone calls from Justin and Tara, but she still couldn't quite believe it. Again, she read the gigantic tabloid headline. CRIME OF PASSION: SUICIDE GUN LINKED TO LEGAL BEAUTY'S DEATH. Then her eyes moved back to the article's text.

The Press has learned that Samson & Mills legend Carter Mills ended his life with a valuable antique firearm, the same gun used just ten days earlier to kill Madeleine Waters, a partner in the firm who was rumored to be Mills's former lover.

Sources say that the revolver was recovered Saturday night, shortly after Mills's blood-soaked body was discovered in his midtown office. "Ballistics tests leave no doubt that the murder weapon and the suicide gun are one and the same," said an official close to the investigation, who spoke on condition that his identity be withheld.

The reasons for Mills's choice of weapon — which sources describe as a Colt Lightning double-action .38-caliber revolver — remain mysterious. Experts consulted by the Press estimated the gun's value at approximately $2,000 to $4,000, depending on its condition. However, they cautioned that a gun of this age would be of interest primarily as a collector's item, as it could prove unreliable on firing. . . .

Kate gazed at the words. Regret. Confusion. Despair. Pushing the paper away, she rested her head in her hands. How much had changed in the past few days. At first, she'd been so sure that Thorpe was the killer. So convinced of Mills's innocence. She'd wanted so much to believe in Mills, to believe in anything at all. She'd dismissed Sam Howell's suspicions without a second thought. And even when Drescher had told her the truth, she'd managed to write it off. Only with the discovery of the WideWorld bills had doubt begun to creep in. Mills had been cheating the firm, and Madeleine had held the proof. And still, despite everything, she'd continued to wait and hope. Only now did Kate admit to herself how much she'd wanted to be wrong.

If only there was someone to talk to. A name popped into her mind. Chewing on a thumbnail, she thought it over. No doubt he'd be surprised by her call, but at least he would understand.

Sam Howell picked up right away.

"It's Kate," she said. "Kate Paine. So I guess you've probably heard."

"Yes," he said. "I have." His voice was gentle, tinged with regret. He didn't sound smug at all.

From her seat on the couch, Kate could see that snow was starting to fall. "So you were right," she said. "I still can't believe it. What was it? How did you know?"

"It was the letter, I guess. The one I told you about. I knew that something must have happened. For her to write after all those years."

Kate picked at a hangnail. "I think I know why Carter did it.

You said that Madeleine knew something bad about Carter. I think I know what it was. I can't talk about it now. But I wanted you to know."

"And you. How are you?" Howell said, letting the subject drop.

"Oh, I'm fine. Hanging in there." She didn't want to tell him about finding Carter's body. Not in her current state.

"So can I ask you a question?" she inquired.

"Shoot."

"In Sag Harbor, you said you were worried about me. That was why you tracked me down."

"That's right."

"Well, I don't understand. Even if I do look a little like Madeleine, what would that matter? Carter didn't kill Madeleine because of how she *looked*. He killed her to keep her from talking."

When Howell didn't answer, Kate went on. "The thing is, I didn't tell you this before, but right before she died, Madeleine gave me a sort of warning. She told me to be *very careful*. She was going to say more, but the phone rang. I never found out what she meant."

"She saw it, too," Howell said. "She knew what could happen to you."

Tearing at her hangnail again, Kate felt an oddly pleasurable glint of pain. "I don't understand," she said. "Are you saying that Madeleine *knew* she was in danger? That doesn't make any sense. If she'd had any idea —"

"No, no, that's not what I mean." A hint of irritation edged Howell's voice, as if he'd expected Kate to understand. "It wasn't that Madeleine knew she was going to die. Or rather, she knew that she already had. There are many ways to die. There's physical death, the death of the body, and then there's the sort of gradual death that takes place when you give up. Madeleine was murdered on January sixth. But the other death, the death of the soul, if you will, had been a long, long process. It began years ago, when she first gave Carter Mills the right to tell her who she was and what she was worth. It wasn't her own opinion that counted, but his. She may have looked like she was alive, but she wasn't really. Not in the ways that matter. She hadn't been for a very long time."

"I really don't think it's the same," Kate said. "I mean, murder is murder. You're just talking in metaphors."

Ignoring her, Howell went on. "In her letter, Madeline said she'd been thinking about the choices she'd made in her twenties. In the beginning, she'd been flattered by Mills's interest. She went into the affair with her eyes open. At least, that's how she saw it then. It was years later before she started to reassess. By then it was too late. Their careers were completely intertwined. It was terribly painful, she said. On the surface, she'd gotten nothing but benefits from the affair. She got great assignments, became a partner. But there was another side to it as well. The sense of never knowing for sure why she'd done so well. Could she really have done it on her own? Of course, she was an excellent lawyer. This wasn't the case of a bimbo being promoted out of the boss's typing pool. It was much more subtle. But it still had a devastating impact. Certain partners never took her seriously, no matter how many cases she won. There was no room for error. She still had to prove to them — and maybe to herself — that she deserved to be where she was."

Kate twisted the phone cord around her finger. "So what does any of this have to do with me?"

"It's the resemblance. Looking at you, Madeleine must have seen a younger version of herself. She knew what could happen at Samson. And for you the risks were especially high. Since you were working for Carter Mills."

"There was nothing like that between Carter and me." Kate's voice was sharper now. "If anything, he was like a sort of *father*."

Howell laughed out loud. "Did you ever run that by him? I'd love to have heard his response."

"I don't see how you can —"

Howell cut in. "Look, all I'm saying is that he must have been attracted to you. You look so much like Madeleine. He had to have noticed that."

"Not our eyes," Kate said.

"Excuse me?"

"Our eyes," Kate repeated. "They're different colors." She didn't know why she had to make this point, but something urged her on.

"I have blue eyes. Madeleine's eyes were green."

A pause and then Howell continued.

"Anyway, you were certainly his physical type. And I can tell that you idolized him. Honestly, what would you have done if he'd approached you?"

What would she have done? She wanted to jump right in with a defiant contradiction. But the fact was, she couldn't say. Not for sure. Carter Mills had represented safety, security, protection. And if he'd offered to take her in? To give her a special place in his life?

"There's something else Madeleine said in her letter. That her feelings for Mills had been so powerful at first, she'd assumed she had to be in love. But thinking about it years later, she saw she'd made a mistake. She'd been right about the strength of her feelings. On that she was perfectly clear. Her mistake was in thinking the feelings were love when they were really closer to hate. It was surprisingly easy, she said, misjudging emotions that way."

Kate realized she'd been clutching the receiver so hard that her hand was hurting. "Listen, Sam, I've got another call. I'll have to get back to you later."

⁓

As the elevator rose through the air, Josie stared straight ahead. She tried to look relaxed, to pretend she belonged, but she sure didn't feel that way. The men and women standing around her looked like people on TV. No one said hello to her. No one seemed to notice her at all.

She was already feeling nervous. She'd hardly slept at all last night for thinking about what to do. Mama hadn't been back for two nights now. They were out of money and almost out of food.

She just couldn't do it anymore. Since November, her grades had tanked. She knew her teachers were worried, though they didn't know what was wrong. Her English teacher, Ms. Gardner, had even asked if she was doing drugs. She'd almost started to cry right there. How could anyone think that about her? Especially her favorite teacher.

Josie knocked on Kate's door. Kate called out to come in. Heart swimming in her chest, Josie walked in and sat down. She'd gone back and forth about who to tell, before finally fixing on Kate. More than anyone she knew, Kate could get things done. You could tell that from watching her. Kate looked beautiful today, just like she always did. She was wearing a black-and-white checked dress along with a stiff silk scarf. Where did you buy clothes like that?

"So did you bring those essays we were working on?"

"Uh, yeah." Josie was caught off guard. Usually, they talked before starting to work. But Kate was all business today.

Reaching into her backpack, Josie pulled out several sheets of notebook paper, slightly crumpled at the edges. She put them down on Kate's desk and tried to smooth them out with her hands.

"Josie, you can't just stuff papers into your bag." Kate's eyebrows arched in irritation. "You need to get some sort of a folder. When you turn in an assignment like this, it looks like you just don't care."

Josie stared at Kate, at the straight line of her mouth. *But she did care! She cared so much. Couldn't Kate see that at all?* Josie felt something slide shut inside her, a door closing down on her heart. On her way to the law firm today, she'd felt okay, even a little hopeful. She'd believed that Kate cared what happened to her, that Kate would be able to help. Now she saw that she'd been fooling herself. Kate didn't care, not really.

Friday, January 22

It was almost seven by the time Kate got home, after a full day of shopping. She dumped her bags on the sofa and headed to the kitchen for food. After tossing together a quick dinner — frozen pasta with red sauce from a jar — she carried her plate to the living room and sat on the sofa to eat. She was glad she hadn't gone to work. The day off had done wonders for her mood. She'd marveled at the lights, the colors, so different from Samson & Mills. Peering in the windows on Madison Avenue, she'd felt an almost giddy excitement. Like a child on Christmas morning. Like Dorothy plopped down in Oz.

After another bite of pasta, Kate picked up her plate and carried it to her desk. She sat down and turned on her computer. Still chewing, she clicked on the icon for America Online. As she waited for the modem to connect, Kate's eyes fell on a black-and-white picture of Mills, clipped from yesterday's *Times*. She studied the familiar, trusted face. For years, decades even, he must have kept up the act. He must have known the risks he was taking. Must have suspected that his luck could run out. And yet, he'd never given any indication. The thought gave her an uneasy feeling, and it wasn't hard to figure out why: if she could be so wrong about Carter Mills, who else might she be wrong about? She wanted to believe that there'd been clues. That if she'd been more skeptical, looked more closely, she could have figured out the truth.

"You've got mail." Nervously, Kate clicked on the e-mail icon and scanned the incoming messages. Just a few pieces of junk mail. She felt let down but also relieved to find no follow-up to last night's message.

Again, her eyes drifted to the photo, to the distinguished, handsome face. Who was this man she'd so admired? Had she really known him at all? Thoughtfully, she turned back to the computer. She clicked on the mouse a couple of times to pull up the search engine Infoseek. She stared at the screen for several long seconds. Then she typed in the words "Carter Mills."

A list of twelve responsive documents flashed on the screen. Kate quickly scanned the results. The first few hits were legal records, pleadings from cases Mills had handled. Next came several articles about Mills's pro bono work for the Lawyers Civil Rights Forum. None of these was what she was looking for. But the next document piqued her interest: a news account of Madeleine Waters's contentious partnership election. Justin had mentioned a piece like this, something in *American Law.* He'd promised to send her a copy, but it must have slipped his mind. This was a shorter wire-service piece. Still, it was worth checking out.

The phone rang, but Kate didn't answer. She was busy reading the report. No new information to speak of, but it whetted her interest all the same. Frustrating to be stuck with the Internet, with better resources so readily available. She'd have come up with many more hits if she'd signed on to Lexis-Nexis, a database used at the firm. But unlike the Internet, Nexis cost a bundle. Before you could perform a search, you had to type in a client billing code. She could try billing the search to Office General, but then she'd have to cook up a story, a way to explain the charges. Another challenge that she didn't feel up to.

Kate forked up another bite of pasta, already unpleasantly cold. Pushing aside the remains of her meal, she glanced at the now-silent phone. The message light was still dark. Briefly, she wondered who the caller had been. Then, picking up her plate, she headed for the kitchen to wash up.

⤥

BENEATH the lofty ceilings of the Metropolitan Museum's Greek galleries, he was one among hundreds of people, blending into the polite cacophony of a Friday evening. Strains of baroque — the Muzak of the bourgeoisie — wafted in from the museum's cafe. If only he could make an announcement, tell everyone what he'd done. He imagined their stunned faces, horror blended with a grudging awe. For how could they not admire him?

Moving down the wide gallery, he stopped at a set of plaques dating from 450 B.C. Scenes from Odysseus's return. The first piece was broken, the terra-cotta fragments pieced together, but through the cracks he could still see the image. Odysseus's nurse washing the hero's feet, still unaware of his true identity. Only after slaying the interlopers and resuming his rightful place would Odysseus cast off his beggar's disguise.

And then: *He wept at last, his dear wife faithful in his arms. . . .*

Odysseus's triumphant return made him think of his own success. He, too, had come disguised to the scene of battle. He, too, had enjoyed an unqualified victory. What cause for celebration these past weeks had been! He'd not only slain Carter Mills, deprived him of life itself. He'd also deprived Mills of his legacy. Madeleine's murder would be blamed on Mills. Mills's disgrace would be complete.

Yes, he had every reason to be happy tonight. Yet something, or rather someone, was destroying his peace of mind.

Kate Paine.

The thought caused his muscles to clench. He'd called her earlier tonight, but she hadn't answered the phone. Not that he would have spoken. He'd planned to hang up when she answered. But he'd needed to hear her voice. It had never occurred to him that she wouldn't be home. He'd checked her schedule, of course. Kate always kept her calendar up to date. Just like Madeleine had. Something must have come up, some last-minute invitation. Still, that was no excuse.

If she was going to be out tonight, she ought to have been with him.

Which raised another disturbing question.

It had been almost a week now. And still she hadn't mentioned their encounter. What could be stopping her? He had no doubt that she'd seen him. She had to know what he'd done. So why was she holding back? Why hadn't she come forward yet?

The questions burning in his brain, he moved on to another display. A small bronze statue of a discus thrower. The coiled power of the statue blended with the tension in his own arms and legs until he couldn't quite tell the difference. He *was* the statue; the statue was him. It was speaking to him, whispering with the wisdom of the ancients. It was telling him what to do.

Carpe diem.

Once again, it was time to act.

Saturday, January 23

STONE lions stood guard at the entrance to the New York Public Library. Kate walked past them, through a revolving door, and into a cavernous entry hall with soaring ceilings and a marble floor. Prominently displayed on the walls were plaques setting forth the library's benefactors. The older plaques listed names familiar from history books: John Jacob Astor. Alexander Hamilton. Andrew Carnegie. Plaques of more recent vintage recorded names of corporate donors. RJR Nabisco. Chemical Bank. A visible testament to economic change.

She'd come here to continue the research she'd begun last night. After getting directions from the information desk, Kate headed down a long hallway toward the DeWitt Wallace Periodical Room. She felt the weight of the building around her, the thick marble walls and floors. It occurred to her that she'd spent much of her life in such massive structures — at Barnard, Harvard, and

now at Samson & Mills — buildings that might seem either op-
pressive or comforting, depending on your perspective.

The periodical room was an airy space, built on a more intimate
scale. Winter light spilled in through tall windows. Patrons sat quietly reading.

"Excuse me." Kate tried to get the attention of a woman at a
computer terminal, seated behind a low counter.

The woman did not look up. "I don't work here," she said, her
eyes still glued to the screen. "They're down that way." The words
came with an indeterminate flick of the head.

"Oh." Kate was about to ask her where exactly "that way" was,
when her eyes fell on a booklet beside the computer. *Lexis-Nexis.
Directory of Online Services.* Was it possible?

"May I help you?"

Behind the typing woman, a librarian had appeared.

"Yes, please," Kate said. "I just noticed that you have Nexis here.
Can anyone use it? I mean, is it available to the public?"

The librarian nodded. "You can sign up for a half-hour slot."

"Is there a charge?"

"No charge. You can't print or download, though."

Free Nexis. Who cared about downloading or printing? She
could always jot down citations and look them up later off-line.
Kate signed up for the next available spot, then sat down to for-
mulate her searches.

When her turn arrived, Kate plopped herself down at the computer and immediately signed on to the U.S. News database. Then
she typed in the first search: Carter w/2 Mills. A few seconds later,
she had her results. A total of 587 articles that mentioned Mills's
name. The first piece was a wire-service report of Mills's suicide.
The next hit was the same piece, reprinted in a Connecticut paper.
The third was yet another copy of the same article.

Kate sat back in her chair to think. Obviously, this wasn't going
to work. The search she'd framed was too broad, picking up too much
useless junk. What she really wanted was in-depth pieces, reports
from *American Law* and other similar publications. Maybe she'd

have more luck if she changed the database to Legal News. She typed in the change and waited. Twenty-seven results. Much better.

Quickly, she scanned the list. Carter Mills's comments on an antitrust case. His thoughts on a Supreme Court decision. Farther down, he was quoted in an article concerning associate dissatisfaction with life at large firms. "This is an extreme environment," Mills said. "It's not for everyone."

Finally, Kate found what she was looking for. The *American Law* piece about Madeleine Waters's partnership election. Kate scanned the first few paragraphs and then copied down the citation. After moving through a few more pieces, she found an *American Law* profile of Mills written just after his elevation to managing partner. Now that was definitely worth a look.

It took Kate about fifteen minutes to skim through everything of interest. Picking up her notebooks and coat, Kate approached the reference librarian. "Where do I find back issues of *American Law?*"

"Syble." Or that's what it sounded like. Kate pictured an ancient prophetess in flowing robes, clutching a *Federal Reporter*. But she must have misunderstood.

"Excuse me?"

"Syble," the librarian said again. "S-I-B-L. The Science, Industry, and Business Library. On Madison at Thirty-fourth."

Entering the Science, Industry, and Business Library, Kate felt as if she'd stumbled into some alternate world. Could this ultramodern facility, replete with chrome, glass, and polished wood, really be a public library?

Kate found her way downstairs, past a bank of televisions broadcasting business news, to the McGraw Information Services Desk, where she was given a call number and dispatched to the B. Altman Delivery Desk across the room. Where the main library building had broadcast its donors' largesse by way of discreet plaques, SIBL shouted its corporate benefactors' names from every available surface. It took only a few minutes for Kate's call number to flash on the marquee. She picked up a small square box containing a microfilm roll.

There were just a few people in the Henry and Henrietta Quade Microform Center. Kate had no trouble finding an empty microfilm reader. She managed to thread the film and then, after a little more fiddling, managed to bring it into focus. The first issue on her screen had a January date. The issue she needed was April. Turning the knob to the right, she let the images fly by. Then she adjusted the knob, slowing the film's progression so she'd be able to see when to stop. Only half paying attention, she watched the pages drift past. Listings of big deals, with the names of lawyers set out in boldface type. A gossipy article about morale at a Chicago firm. A profile of a Silicon Valley deal maker.

And then, there it was.

The microfilm photo of Carter Mills looked weird and hyperexposed. The whole report was only six pages, and Kate decided to print it out. She stuck her new copy card into the appropriate slot, centered the screen image, and pressed Copy. Five minutes later, she was done. She rewound and boxed the microfilm, gathered up her effects, and went back to the central room, where she dropped off the box at the delivery desk and settled into a black mesh chair.

As she'd expected, the piece about Mills was filled with the predictable accolades. From his ascent at the firm, the article moved on to explore his family roots. A firm historian had compared Mills favorably to his grandfather Silas, one of the firm's two founding partners. Martin Drescher had no comment for the record. The one jarring note was a cryptic comment from Mills's father. "I'm sure he'll make a success of this as he has of everything else," James Mills had told the reporter. "My son has never let anything, or anyone, get in his way." Perhaps the senior Mills hadn't intended the acid tone; maybe he'd only meant to say that Carter accomplished what he set out to do. But something in the tenor of the words told Kate that the two men had had their struggles.

It suddenly occurred to Kate that she'd heard the name James recently. At Charles Harrison's apartment. He'd referred to Carter by that name. At the time, she'd barely noticed, considered it a slip of the tongue. Now she saw it was something more. J. Carter Mills. It wasn't too much of a leap to see that the J had to stand for James. Carter must have been named for his father. He must have used that name when he was younger, and Harrison had fallen back on habit. But why had he made this change? Was it just to avoid confusion? Or had other factors come into play? It wasn't a lot to go on. But for the moment, it was all she had.

Half an hour later, Kate was seated at a computer terminal in the Elizabeth and Felix Rohatyn Electronic Information Center, signing on to Nexis again. She went first to the Legal News database and typed in a search: James w/2 Mills. Seven documents came up. But, quickly browsing the files, she saw there was nothing of interest. Two of the articles quoted a James R. Mills, a partner in a Florida firm. The other five were equally inapposite, referring to lawyers in Tennessee, California, and Michigan. Kate decided to try a broader search. Broad but not too broad. She switched to New York News.

She was almost through the results when a headline flashed before her eyes. *Unsolved Murders: Ten Crimes That Have Stumped the NYPD.* Kate stared at the screen for a moment before scrolling down, past the headless body found in the East River, past the execution-style slaying of a school teacher, to the item she was looking for.

January 16, 1973.

A cold winter evening.

Maria Bernini, an attractive twenty-five-year-old with dreams of becoming an actress, was returning to her Eleventh Avenue walk-up shortly after 2 A.M. After completing a double shift at the Echo Diner, where she'd worked as a waitress for the past three years, Bernini stopped by a friend's to pick up her sleeping four-year-old son.

It was the last time she was seen alive.

The next day, Bernini was discovered dead in her apartment, the victim of a brutal slaying. She'd been sexually assaulted and stabbed before being shot through the head. Her son, also bound and gagged, was discovered unharmed, propped up in a chair across from his mother's mutilated body.

The Bernini case took a surprising twist when the gun used in the killing, discovered at the scene of the crime, was traced to James Mills, an independent historian from a prominent Boston family and a collector of historic firearms. Mr. Mills, who was never charged in the case, said he had not noticed the disappearance of the gun, an 1877 Colt Lightning. . . .

Colt Lightning. Kate stared at the words, heart pounding. *It was the same gun.* It had to be. The same gun used to kill Madeleine. The gun Mills had used to kill himself. Even the modus operandi was the same. Maria Bernini had been brutally stabbed and shot in the head. Just like Madeleine Waters.

Kate closed her eyes, trying to stop her head from spinning. 1973. That's when Maria Bernini had died. Carter Mills would have been in his early twenties. Roughly the same age as the murdered young woman. The woman he must have killed.

"Miss? Are you almost finished?"

Kate looked up with a start. A bespectacled man was anxiously waiting his turn.

"I'm finished now," she said. "Just let me get my papers together."

By the time she got home from the library, Kate had already made up her mind. What she'd suspected about Carter Mills she couldn't just keep to herself. She would have liked to go directly to Detective Valencia, but that wasn't a viable option. She was still an employee of Samson & Mills. And firm policy was crystal clear: first, she had to go to Martin Drescher.

At loose ends, uncertain what to do next, Kate decided to type up her notes. She sat down at her desk and turned on her computer. As the screen flashed on, Kate felt her stomach drop. *I have some information that I think would interest you about recent events at your law firm.* She signed on to America Online. But there was nothing unusual in her AOL mailbox. Just several more pieces of junk mail. She deleted the entries and moved on.

From AOL, Kate switched over to the Samson network. She felt a little uncomfortable putting her notes on the firm's computer system, but Samson's was the only word processing program she had access to at home. She'd never had much faith in the firm's computer security. How hard could it be to figure out that everyone's password was PASSWORD? But she was just being paranoid. After all, who was she? A lowly second-year associate. Anyone sniffing out Samson secrets could surely find more interesting targets.

Sunday, January 24

HE couldn't believe his eyes. By now, he'd read the sentences so many times he'd lost count. He'd hoped to find another interpretation. Some sign that he'd misunderstood. But instead, it was just growing worse. The ridiculous conjectures and speculations. Why was she doing this? None of it made any sense.

He could feel a coldness deep in his core, gradually spreading outward. From his stomach it had moved to his heart and liver, and still it was edging on. Down toward his testicles. Up toward his shoulders. From there it would flow through his arms to his hands, now locked on the computer keyboard. But he was grateful for the cold, grateful for the creeping numbness. It allowed him to think clearly. Clearly and without emotion.

Again, the questions circled his mind, like vultures come in for a kill. Could she really believe what she'd written? That Carter Mills had killed Madeleine? That Carter had killed himself? But she'd seen him leaving Carter's office! What did she make of that?

She was ruining everything, destroying his faith in her. Why hadn't she just asked? Didn't she know he was waiting? Instead, she'd gone off on her own. As if he played no role in her life. As if he *didn't exist*.

Something was terribly wrong. He gazed across the room, at the photograph pinned to the wall. *What should I do?* he silently pleaded. *Where do I go from here?* He stared at the picture, waiting. *The most beautiful woman in the world.* And then the answer came clear. Just as he'd hoped it would.

Kate Paine belonged to him.

It was time she acted that way.

Monday, January 25

KATE awoke to the sound of sirens blasting just inches from her head. Her mind demanded that she get up, but her body refused to move. She lay for a time in stunned dismay, the noise assaulting her ears. Then, as her mind engaged, she realized that she was in bed. The screeching was just her alarm clock. She reached over and turned it off.

Even after she'd gotten up, the grogginess seemed to linger. Maybe breakfast would help. Why not take advantage of her flexible schedule and make herself something to eat? There was nothing in the house, of course. So she put on her coat and went out.

There had been a light dusting of snow during the night, and the short walk to Zabar's refreshed her. Crowds already clogged the aisles of the legendary food emporium. Carts and strollers vied for position as shoppers grimly forged ahead. By the cheese counter, a mother grabbed her small son by the arm. *"If you don't change your attitude, I'm going to knock you down."* Nearby, a sleek male executive type turned to his lookalike partner and said, "*I want to be just like him, stupid and a nymphomaniac.*"

Kate was still mulling over this last remark — could nymphomaniacs be male as well as female? — when she reached the smoked-fish counter. After a brief wait in line, she acquired a packet of smoked salmon before heading to the dairy case. She was moving toward the cash register when she had another thought. She'd been meaning to buy a toaster. Why not take care of that now? She made her way to the stairs that led to the second-floor housewares department.

Upstairs, Kate was about to ask where the toasters were when her eyes lit on a set of cookware enameled in a deep, rich blue. She lingered in front of the display, studying a five-quart Dutch oven. There was something both comforting and seductive about the piece. It brought to mind dinners in front of a fireplace. Wine-rich beef stews. Spaghetti Bolognese. Beneath the display, she found a carton containing an identical item and heaved it into her arms.

Still carrying the Dutch oven, Kate proceeded to the toaster aisle, where she picked out a white Braun model. She was tempted to browse a little more, but she had about all she could carry. Besides, who knew what she'd end up with if she stuck around. A bread-making machine? A waffle iron? She headed for the checkout line.

She didn't have to go to work today. She didn't have to do *anything*. But the thought of spending the day at home left her feeling restless and bleak. If she went in to the office, at least she'd be around people.

"You are a *most unhelpful man*. I bought this yesterday, and it's broken. *Broken*. I demand to see the manager. Do you hear me? *Immediately*."

The middle-aged man in front of her clutched a plastic blender to his chest. The clerk at whom the anger was aimed stood there looking frankly bored. *It's just a blender*, Kate thought, annoyed. *It probably cost thirty bucks*. Still, ten minutes later as she left the store, the scene lingered in her mind. Her sense of condescension was gone, and she felt unaccountably sad. In her mind, she saw the irate customer, shrieking at the bland-faced clerk. It was then that she understood. *It's not just him. It's what he represents. We're all scared at some level, afraid we can't protect ourselves.*

And who can blame us, really? Just think about Madeleine. . . .

The subway platform was almost empty. She must have just missed a train. Peering down the tunnel for a sign of light, Kate noticed that her glasses were fogged. She stepped well back on the platform — out of reach of any lurking psycho who might push her onto the tracks — and reached in her purse for a tissue.

As she pulled off her glasses, the subway platform dissolved in a gloomy blur. Hazy dark forms and gray-blue light. She'd almost finished with her lenses when a shadow crossed her line of vision. Instantly, Kate's heart began to race. She couldn't breathe, couldn't think. What was happening? What was wrong? Was she having a panic attack?

Hurriedly, Kate restored her glasses, looking wildly back and forth. But there was only a woman's retreating back. A woman in a black wool coat. Kate stared after her for several moments, trying to calm herself. Slowly, the fear subsided.

Just a woman in a black wool coat.

Still she felt anxious, on edge. Dizzy. Frightened. Confused. How to explain this response? The woman's figure had triggered something. Brought back a memory.

Then, in a flash, it came back.

Saturday night. The corridor outside Mills's office. Then, too, she'd stopped to polish her glasses. And then, too, she'd seen something. Just like today. Some shadowy form had appeared, then vanished. Disappeared down the hall . . .

Kate stood frozen on the subway platform. An announcement blared from the loudspeaker, but she barely noticed the sound. Her whole being was focused on the memory, the thought that had just broken through. If she was right — and she was sure that she was — then Mills hadn't been alone that night. It was possible, just possible, that Mills hadn't killed himself.

Impatiently, Kate stepped forward, willing the train to arrive. But as she stared down the looming tunnel, the logic of her thoughts struck home. *If Carter Mills hadn't killed himself, then a murderer was still at large.*

⁕

MARTIN Drescher fidgeted with a paper clip, unbending it, then pushing it back. The skin on his face hung in loose gray folds. His eyes were cloudy and inert. Kate wasn't even sure if he'd been listening. But when she stopped, he finally looked up.

"But you didn't have on your glasses," he said. "And without them you're virtually blind. That's what you said yourself." Drescher's eyes wandered back to the paper clip. He'd flattened it out on his desk. Now he began to restore its shape.

"That's true," Kate said. "But I know that someone was there. I just couldn't see who it was."

"And why didn't you mention this Saturday night?"

"Like I said, I didn't remember. I was still in shock, I guess."

"So right after it happened, you didn't remember. Then two days later, you suddenly do. Is that what you're telling me?" Drescher had adopted the sort of tone that might be used on cross-examination.

"That's right," Kate said stubbornly. "Saturday night I was in shock. I wasn't thinking clearly."

"And during this time that you weren't thinking clearly, you *think* that you saw something, some sort of blurry figure outside of Carter Mills's office?"

"I was still thinking clearly at that point," Kate said. "And I know that I saw something." She refused to let Drescher throw her. What he wanted, Kate knew, was for her to change her story, to admit that she might have been mistaken. But as long as she stood her ground, he couldn't do anything to touch her.

Drescher shifted heavily in his chair. Absently, he edged the paper clip under his left thumbnail. He fiddled with the clip for a moment or two, then moved to his index finger. Kate watched him, fascinated. Could he really be cleaning his nails? For some time the room was silent. Then, putting down the paper clip, Drescher was speaking again.

"Ms. Paine, I understand your reluctance to believe the truth about Carter Mills. You worked for him. I'm sure you admired him. But you have to accept the facts. Carter Mills killed himself. Before that, he killed Madeleine.

"Now, I'm going to give you the benefit of the doubt. I'm going to assume you believe what you're telling me. But you're absolutely wrong. And I have no intention of letting you or anyone put this firm through further disruption. Do I make myself clear?"

By the time Drescher finished his speech, Kate was so angry she could barely speak. It was one thing for Drescher to be skeptical. Another for him to stop her from going to the police with what might be evidence of murder. But she wouldn't lose control again. Biting her lip, she met his eyes.

"Perfectly clear," she said.

Still seething five minutes later, Kate appeared at Justin's open door. Justin was on the phone. Still talking, he flashed a smile and gestured for her to wait. Kate slouched into the room and flung herself down on a chair. As she stared blankly out the window, random phrases caught her ear: "stockholder class action," "fraud on the court," "10b-5 liability." Simply hearing Justin's voice seemed to soothe her. She was almost sorry when he hung up.

"What's going on?" he said, giving her a closer look.

Kate raised a dismissive hand. "Oh, just the usual," she said. "Nothing worth discussing." How many times had she deceived Justin in the past few weeks? By now, she'd almost lost count. But it wouldn't be fair to involve him. She had to deal with this herself.

"So what's up with you?" she said. "You look pretty busy."

"Just trying to wind up a few things before Wednesday."

"Wednesday?"

"Laura and I are leaving that night. I want to get out of here early."

"Oh. Right." In the press of events, Kate had forgotten about Justin's out-of-town tryst. A dull weight settled in her heart. Justin would go off with Laura. And she'd be alone again.

"So where are you going?" Kate said, hoping her feelings didn't show.

If he noticed anything amiss, Justin didn't let on. "Connecticut. Some bed-and-breakfast. I don't remember where, exactly. Laura made the reservations."

The weight on Kate's heart increased. She pictured Justin and Laura conferring, making plans for the trip. Justin had a whole life now, a life she knew nothing about. And this was just the beginning. Moodily, she gazed at a family photograph on the bookshelf next to her chair. Justin sat on a love seat, with one arm around his sister. Behind them stood their parents. Sarah Daniels's flaxen hair was piled on top of her head. She wore a lavender silk dress and pearls. Next to her was Justin's professor father, tall and self-possessed.

Staring at the picture, Kate felt utterly alone. She thought of the lonely little match girl in Hans Christian Andersen's fairy tale. That was how she felt right now. Normal people had families, people who stood by them and loved them no matter what. But she had no one. She could feel the self-pity seeping in. What had life brought but an unending succession of losses? Sometimes it seemed like she was being punished. Of course, she knew this wasn't true. The bad things that had happened in her life — her parents' divorce, her mother's death, Michael's betrayal — they really weren't her fault. But maybe she wanted to believe that they *were*. To believe that events took place for a reason.

"Kate?" Looking up, she met Justin's eyes.

"Sorry. I'm a little distracted." With one finger, Kate traced the wooden arm of her chair. "Remember in law school when we learned about the rule of reliance? How, even if you don't have a contract, you can still force someone to perform? Like if someone mows your lawn by mistake and you know what they're doing but let them finish. You know that they expect to be paid. You can't get out of it by saying you didn't ask them to do the work."

"Yeah, I remember." She couldn't be sure Justin was really listening. But, warming to the subject, she didn't much care. "Well, I think that relationships should be like that, too. Like if you tell someone you love them, you shouldn't be able just to change your mind. Not if there's detrimental reliance. Not if the other party — the other person, I mean — has already done something not in their best interest because they believed what you said."

Justin laughed. "Gee, Kate. As a legal matter, I don't quite see how that would work."

"I'm not saying it would *work*," Kate said, a slight petulance creeping into her voice. "I'm just saying that it's how things should be. In an ideal world. If life were fair."

"So I guess you're not a big fan of no-fault divorce?"

Kate shrugged. "I don't know. Maybe in the real world it has to be that way. But that doesn't mean it's right. People should do what they say they'll do. They shouldn't just be able to change their minds. To pretend that the past never happened."

Justin was covertly eyeing the stack of documents on his desk.

"I should go," Kate said. But she really didn't feel like moving. Instead, she remained in her chair, her eyes fixed on Justin's face. He looked tired today; he probably hadn't gotten much sleep. But he was willing to indulge her, to be there if she needed to talk.

For a moment, Kate felt like crying. A swell of emotions stirred in her chest: Gratitude, sadness, yearning, and another feeling she couldn't quite name. It was an old feeling, a sensation almost forgotten. Pleasurable but also frightening. A feeling that seemed equally equipped to save or destroy her. And then, with a start, she knew what it was.

Love.

Kate looked at Justin, stunned. The familiar curve of his cheek. The faint lines around his eyes. Warmth flooded through her body.

It was like something was melting or breaking in her chest, something she hadn't even known was there. Kate felt her lips curve into a smile. She almost laughed out loud. Why hadn't she realized? Why hadn't she seen it before? The world seemed to resolve into a single thought, a single realization. *She was in love with Justin.*

"You know, I should really get back to work. Laura's going to kill me if I have to stay late on Wednesday."

Like a punctured balloon, Kate felt herself spiraling down back to earth. What had she been thinking? Justin was happy now. Happy with someone else. Looking down at her lap, Kate thought of another fairy tale, the little mermaid who'd loved the prince. In exchange for a human form, she gave up her tongue and the power of speech. She also accepted unending pain: every time she took a step it felt as though knives were piercing her feet. And still she didn't get the prince. He married another mortal.

Abruptly, Kate rose from her chair. "So I should get going," she said.

Tuesday, January 26

DETECTIVE Cathy Valencia squinted at the fluorescent numbers on the radio alarm clock: 3:12 A.M. She was usually a heavy sleeper, but lately her nights had been fitful. Now she felt wide awake. Slipping out from under her sleeping husband's arm, Valencia climbed out of bed.

Downstairs, the kitchen was warm and quiet. Valencia put on a kettle of water, then sat down at the dining table. She fished a copy of *Glamour* from under a pile of newspapers and began to flip through its pages. She never thought much about her appearance, as long as she was neat and clean. She'd loved those early days on the force when she hadn't had to think what to wear. Half asleep, she'd pull on her uniform. In minutes, she'd be on her way. Still, it was strangely soothing to look through fashion magazines. To study the too-thin models, with their vacant eyes. Perhaps she envied their apparent ability not to care about anything at all. She had always cared too much.

The kettle had begun to whistle. Valencia turned off the burner. She dumped a packet of fat-free instant cocoa into a mug imprinted with the words "Save the Humans." Then she filled the mug with hot water, stirred, and went back to her chair to sit down. Sipping the hot drink, she felt a heavy softness press against her leg. "Why, hello there, Mr. P." Valencia reached down and stroked the cat's silky back before pulling him up to her lap. He was a fine fat tom with an orange-brown coat. His name — short for Mr. Potatohead — came courtesy of her three-year-old niece. For a long moment, the cat's yellow eyes gazed up at her face. Then he circled once around, plunked down on her thighs, and was instantly fast asleep. If only she could learn his secret!

After another sip of cocoa, Valencia leaned back in the chair and closed her eyes, willing her mind to be silent. But her brain just wouldn't shut up. Once again, her thoughts moved back to Samson & Mills. For days now, she'd tried to forget. After all, the cases were closed; they'd received exceptional clearance. Still, Valencia couldn't get over the feeling that facts had been overlooked.

In the clutter of papers before her, Valencia came up with a notepad and pen. She opened the notepad to the first blank page and drew a straight line down the middle. She labeled the two columns "Pro" and "Con." Then, frowning, she tore out the sheet of paper, balled it up in her hand, and tossed it toward the trash can in the corner. On the next blank sheet of paper, she drew two lines, this time creating three equal columns. The first two she again labeled "Pro" and "Con." The third she labeled "Inconclusive."

Still holding the pen, Valencia thought through what she knew about Carter Mills's death. First, there was the issue of motive. If Mills had, in fact, killed Madeleine Waters, that certainly might explain why he'd killed himself, whether due to remorse or fear of discovery. And if those weren't sufficient motives, there were the billing improprieties that Drescher had brought to their attention. Valencia briefly noted these facts under "Pro" and then sat back in her chair.

What else did she know about Mills's last days? He'd certainly seemed preoccupied. But that could have been a normal reaction to a colleague's death. Especially when that colleague was a former lover. Under the column labeled "Inconclusive," Valencia wrote "Demeanor/Mood." Then there was the typed suicide note, with its vague allusions to failure and despair. The typed note had been a red flag. Was it possible that someone else had typed the note, that the words had been the work of Mills's killer? She couldn't dismiss that thought. Still, she didn't have any proof. Another point under "Inconclusive."

The physical evidence, what there was of it, also provided little guidance. While Mills's fingerprints were all over the gun, gunshot residue tests on his hands had all come up negative. Still, this was far from uncommon. While the presence of residue would have been proof that Mills fired the gun, its absence didn't mean that he hadn't. It simply left open the *possibility* that someone other than Mills had pulled the trigger. The fact that the gun had been found on Mills's desk was similarly unhelpful. If the gun had been found clutched tightly in Mills's hand, this "cadaveric spasm" would have proved his wound was self-inflicted. But this was a rare phenomenon; some cops even claimed that it didn't exist. Again, she couldn't draw any conclusions.

Absorbed in the problem before her, Valencia had almost forgotten her cocoa. She raised the mug to her lips, but now it was only lukewarm. Lifting the sleeping Mr. P. from her lap, she stood up and returned him to the chair. The cat raised his head from a haze of sleep and blinked a few times before again curling up in a ball. Valencia stuck her mug in the microwave and punched in two minutes.

Waiting for the cocoa to reheat, Valencia had an idea. She walked to the living room and headed for the bookcase under the stairs. Its shelves held a motley assortment of volumes. Paperback bestsellers and criminology texts crammed in with books on cooking and home improvement. It took a little time to find what she was looking for. *Practical Homicide Investigation: Tactics, Procedures, and Forensic Techniques.* She pulled down the stout blue book and carried it back to the kitchen.

After retrieving her now-hot cocoa, Valencia gave Mr. P a gentle nudge. He opened a languorous eye and then, with a reproachful look, hopped down from the chair and slunk from the room, bound for more peaceful environs. Back in the chair, still warm from Mr. P., Valencia turned to the index and looked for "Suicide." Beneath this entry was a column of type, investigative checklist . . . investigative considerations . . . background information . . . equivocal death.

Equivocal death. That was what she was looking for. Valencia took down a few more page numbers and then turned to the first of the references. The words, highlighted in yellow during some past perusal, jumped out at her from the page. "Equivocal death investigations are those inquiries that are open to interpretation. . . ." For some time she continued to read. Then, looking up, she thought back in time. Carter Mills's blood-drenched office, the shattered remains of his body. The Samson partners, circling their wagons, tight-lipped as the members of a street gang. The shell-shocked young lawyer who'd discovered the scene.

And, Valencia realized, it wasn't just Carter Mills's death that had her unnerved. Her uneasiness extended beyond that, back to the Waters murder. There, too, the facts didn't add up. There were loose ends, missing pieces. And Carter Mills's supposed suicide had done nothing to clear them up. First, there was the fact that Waters's body had been moved from the actual crime scene, dumped where it was sure to be discovered. Someone had taken the trouble — and risk — of leaving the body in plain view. Why? What possible reason would Mills have had for wanting Madeleine's body found?

The fact that the body was left in plain view; it had to be by design. The expert-for-hire quoted in the local paper knew the value of a sound bite. But in labeling Madeleine's killer disorganized, he'd jumped to conclusions far too quickly. Whoever killed Madeleine Waters had managed to escape undetected. Had managed to transport and dump the body, all without arousing suspicion. Even the spread-eagled display of the body reflected an effort to control. And most telling of all, perhaps, the killer had concocted the telephone scheme that lured Madeleine to her death. He'd known of her scheduled dinner with Thorpe and called to reschedule it. In essence, he'd set a trap. Such actions required planning, a patient attention to detail. They were hardly the work of a disorganized killer, someone veering toward insanity.

True, there had been some basis for the expert's comments. The lack of semen at the scene. The random postmortem stab wounds to the face and breast. The candle in the victim's vagina. Such acts were generally committed by disorganized types. By a perp unable to complete the sexual act, filled with uncontrollable rage. But these elements could have been designed to mislead; it had certainly happened before. An organized offender could stage a crime scene, mimic a disorganized perp. While detectives searched for a psychotic loner, someone barely functional, the real killer got on with his life. He might be a model citizen, a family man. No one would ever guess.

Carter Mills's alibi was solid, but not until after eight. It would have been tight, but not impossible. At least, that's what she'd been telling herself. Possible and yet . . . was it likely? She couldn't seem to get a grip. As a rule, homicide detectives relied on the theory of transfer and exchange, the notion that a perp leaves traces at the scene. And that the scene, in turn, leaves it marks on him. But here they'd come up dry. No fingerprints. No foreign hairs. No semen. And lab reports indicated that the only blood was the victim's. Perhaps these dead ends partly explained why she and Glaser had given in. That and pressure from the mayor. Mills's suicide had come as a stroke of luck, letting them both off the hook.

But the fact was, before Mills died, she'd thought they were getting somewhere. They'd finally gotten their hands on a copy of Waters's will. A document that bequeathed all earthly possessions to her former husband, Sam Howell. Not a little surprising in light of Howell's claim that he hadn't seen his ex-wife in years. They'd been on the verge of asking Howell to take a polygraph test. Of course, that plan had gone out the window with news of Carter Mills's death.

But thoughts she'd banished from consciousness still haunted her sleep each night. Now, wide awake at 4 A.M., the questions rang in her mind.

What was the story with Howell?

Had they written him off too soon?

♰

IN the morning, Kate again washed her kitchen floor, now cleaner than it had been since she'd moved in. Her apartment and her life seemed to bear an inverse relation, the former becoming ever more orderly as the latter veered out of control. She'd just squeezed out the mop when she heard the phone ring. Once, twice, three times, before the answering machine engaged. From the next room, she could hear a male voice, vaguely familiar from the distance. Was it Douglas Macauley, perhaps? She didn't much care right now.

She was still reeling from yesterday's meeting with Drescher, still didn't understand what had happened. Even with his hatred of Mills, how could Drescher be so cavalier? How could he ignore the fact that a killer might still be at large? It didn't make any sense.

Unless . . .

Kate froze in her tracks. What if Drescher himself was involved? He'd certainly had access to Madeleine's schedule. And who had more to gain than Martin Drescher from Carter Mills's untimely death? As for Madeleine, there was no shortage of possible motives. Perhaps a love affair gone wrong, if she believed what Jennifer had said. Or something to do with the WideWorld bills that had been stored in Madeleine's desk. It was even possible that Drescher had planned the whole thing, killed Madeleine to set up Mills.

Kate thought back to the night of Mills's death, trying to remember when she'd last seen Drescher. He'd definitely been at the cocktail party, but she couldn't be quite sure when. It would have been easy enough for him to slip away. Could Drescher have killed his rival and then returned unnoticed?

On the heels of this disturbing question came another chilling thought. Her meeting yesterday with Drescher. She'd told him everything. And if he'd been the lone blurred figure, the shadow she'd seen in the hall? How could she not be a threat? Kate leaned the mop against the kitchen wall, her mouth gone dry as paper. After quickly wiping off her hands, she went to find her purse. Stuffed in her billfold was Valencia's number, copied down from the card she'd been given. Ignoring the flashing message light, Kate picked up the phone and dialed.

Wednesday, January 27

2 P.M. Cathy Valencia chewed on the end of a ballpoint pen and thought about what to do next. She'd been trading calls with Kate Paine since yesterday afternoon and still hadn't been able to reach her. It was almost as if Kate was avoiding her. But that didn't make any sense. Kate, after all, had called her.

Kate had asked to be called at home. Normally, Valencia would have respected the request. But something in the young lawyer's voice made Valencia eager to reach her. She'd waited long enough. Besides, if she used her private cell phone, only Kate would know who had called.

"Kate Paine's office." The woman who answered the phone had a soft, ebullient voice with a hint of Brooklyn at the edges.

"Is she in?" Valencia tried to sound casual, as if she were a personal friend.

"No, I don't expect her today."

"D'you have any idea when I could reach her?"

"I couldn't really say. But I'd be happy to take a message. She'll definitely be checking in with me today."

"That's okay. I'll try back later." Valencia was about to hang up, when the young woman spoke again.

"If you don't reach her today, I'm pretty sure she'll be in by four tomorrow. She has an appointment then."

⁂

ARRIVING home that night, Kate felt like she was floating. She'd finally taken Tara's suggestion and spent the day at the Peninsula Spa, where she'd been rubbed, wrapped, and pounded into a grateful torpor. But one look at the phone was enough to douse her good spirits. The message light was flashing. While she was out, five calls had come in.

In the end, it wasn't so bad. Three calls were from Cathy Valencia, who seemed pretty anxious to reach her. A message from Tara. Another from Sam Howell. "I've been thinking about you, Kate. Just wondering how you're doing. I don't know what your schedule's like, but I'll be in the city this weekend. If you have time, I'd like to see you."

Howell's call came as a surprise. Their encounters had been so strange. Her frantic flight from his home in Sag Harbor. The abrupt conclusion of their recent talk. She hadn't gotten back to him even though she'd said she would. Tomorrow she'd call both Sam and Tara. Valencia, however, she should try right now.

But even as she reached for the phone, a part of her seemed to pull back. Her day at the spa had relaxed her, done wonders for her mood. Would it be so wrong to prolong it? All the things that had seemed so pressing now seemed as if they could wait. That shadow outside Mills's office. Could she really be sure what she'd seen? What had her so convinced that the movement was a human being?

Slowly, Kate lowered her hand. She'd put off the call to Valencia, return it tomorrow as well. For now, she'd just check her e-mail. And then, she'd climb into bed.

"You've got mail." Glancing through her new e-mail messages,

Kate pressed a hand to her mouth. There it was. Another commu-
nication from Adam0116. Her spa-induced calm was instantly
gone, replaced by a sense of foreboding. Her heart lurched against
her sternum, a cold fist lodged in her chest. She clicked on the
message line.

*I have important information about a subject that interests you. I'm
sure you know what I mean. If you'd like to know more, meet me tomorrow at the Royalton Hotel at 9 P.M.*

Kate stared at the lines as if hypnotized. The Royalton Hotel. A
popular watering hole for glitterati types, it was just down from the
Harvard Club.

I have important information about a subject that interests you.

Of course, she shouldn't agree to the meeting. It was absurd,
maybe dangerous.

Still, she stared at the screen.

Kate thought about the Royalton Hotel. She'd been there for
drinks a few times. No place could be more public. No place could
be more safe. She moved her hands to the keyboard. *I'll see you
there,* she typed.

Thursday, January 28

IT was a little after three when Kate arrived at her office. At the sound of her approach, Jennifer's head bobbed up from behind a magazine. "Hi!" she said. "I was wondering if you'd get here today."

"Yeah. Well." Kate didn't feel up to chatting. All day, she'd been fighting off a dull headache. If it weren't for her appointment with Josie, she'd have spent the day at home in bed.

"Some woman's been trying to reach you. She's called three or four times today."

"Thanks. She'll probably try again." Kate rummaged in her purse for the keys to her office door.

"It's already unlocked," Jennifer said. "I was about to tell you. Justin's waiting inside."

"Justin?" Kate looked at Jennifer in surprise. Justin was supposed to be out of town by now, off to Connecticut with Laura.

As she cracked open the door, Kate's heart beat faster. It was Justin, all right. Right there in her chair, studying something on the computer screen. He looked up. Their eyes met. In an instant, Kate's headache was gone, and she was flooded with a sense of well-being. She didn't know why Justin hadn't left. She didn't care. It was enough just to see him there, a bemused smile on his face.

"Why are you still here?" Kate said. She knew she was grinning like an idiot, hardly an appropriate reaction. But she couldn't seem to help herself. And the funny thing was that Justin was smiling, too.

"Close the door, Kate."

"What?"

"Close the door. There's something I want to show you."

Her heart beating pleasantly fast, Kate complied. "So what is it?" she asked, trying to keep her voice light. "Don't keep me in suspense."

"Come over here." Justin gestured toward the computer screen. "I want you to see something."

Kate walked toward her desk. "What are you —" She broke off in midsentence. There, on the screen, were her notes about Carter Mills, the notes she'd culled from her library research. Uncertain, she stared at Justin.

"What is this, Kate?" The words carried a hint of reproach.

"Honestly, Justin, I would have told you, but I didn't want to get you involved. Anyway, I don't even know what it means. Maybe it's nothing."

"But you don't *think* it's nothing, do you?"

Kate was about to answer when it struck her that there was something very strange about this whole encounter. Why was Justin here? Why was he reading her computer files?

"What are you *doing?*" Kate asked.

Justin didn't respond. He'd gotten out of his chair. Now, they were standing quite close, with not more than two or three feet between them. Kate could see the dark stubble on Justin's cheeks, the thin layer of perspiration on his upper lip. Then he seemed to be moving toward her. For a confused moment, she thought he was going to embrace her. Which is what she'd wanted all along, and yet for some reason she felt differently now, and she didn't want him to touch her. Almost involuntarily, she took a quick step back.

"Is something wrong, Kate?" The smile had returned to Justin's lips. "I knew you'd be in today. I waited for you. Aren't you glad to see me?"

"I . . . I . . ." What was going on? Maybe she was really going crazy. Maybe everything that had happened was finally pulling her under. This was Justin, after all. *Justin.* How could she possibly feel frightened?

Kate shook her head and laughed weakly. "I don't know what's wrong with me," she said. "I just had the weirdest feeling —" Again, she broke off in midsentence. There was something that didn't make sense, and she wanted to figure it out. Distracted, her eyes followed Justin's hand as he reached into his jacket.

It was then that she saw the gun.

⁓⁓

Josie dragged her feet down the hallway leading to Kate's office. Fifteen minutes late today. Kate was going to be mad. It was all because of the subway. But why should Kate believe her this time?

Kate's secretary looked up and smiled. "Hi, Josie," she said. "How've you been?"

Josie dug a Nike-clad toe into the floor. "I've been okay," she said. "The subway broke down at Forty-second Street. That's the reason I'm late."

"It's all right," Jennifer said, tossing the girl a reassuring smile. "Kate went out a while ago, and she still hasn't gotten back. She's the one who's late this time."

"She *is?*" Josie stared at Jennifer, eyes wide.

"Yup. Guess you can give *her* a hard time today, huh?"

Josie grinned. *Kate was late!* For once, she'd really lucked out. Not that she planned to press her luck. This was the very last time she'd be late. *Ever.*

Jennifer gestured toward an empty chair. "Why don't you sit down and wait? I'm sure she'll be back soon."

⁓⁓

THEY moved down Fifth Avenue, edging through the rush-hour crowds. Justin pressed close against her, his left arm clamped around her waist. In his right hand, shielded by her cape, he jammed the gun into Kate's side. Her cheek rubbed against Justin's shoulder. The wool of his coat scratched her skin. Frantically, Kate tried to catch someone's eye, to signal her distress. But the multitudes swept by unseeing. No one seemed to look her way.

Kate's feet moved mechanically forward, mirroring Justin's stride. She had no idea what was happening, no idea at all. She went over the facts in her mind, searching for some sort of clue. Justin hadn't gone away with his girlfriend. Instead, he'd been waiting for her. He'd been reading her notes about Carter Mills. And then he'd pulled out a gun. But the more she thought, the more confusing it seemed until she thought that this must be a dream.

A left turn on Forty-fourth Street. Kate had a moment of hope. They were actually headed toward the Harvard Club. The very place Justin had said they were going when Jennifer asked for a number! Approaching the club, Justin's footsteps slowed, and Kate felt her heart grow lighter. How ridiculous to be scared. Of course, this must be some kind of joke. That was the explanation. Smiling, she glanced up at Justin's face, looking for confirmation. But Justin's mouth was a rigid line. The smile faded from Kate's lips.

Justin steered her into the club. Kate glimpsed the club's entry hall. A man with a very red face and no hair. A woman in a snug brown coat. Quickly they moved past the doorman, toward the wide crimson-carpeted stairs. Words floated up from below. *"You know, the last time that I was in Cambridge. . . ."* Then the voices were fading, as they proceeded up the stairs. Kate felt as if she were playing a part. Could this really be happening? As if in answer, she felt the gun, boring into her ribcage. "Justin," she whispered. "Shut up," he hissed. The metal bit into her side.

Stunned, Kate lapsed into silence, her eyes focused on her shoes. The stairs seemed to go on forever, each landing leading to another set, an endless crimson ascent. Past the club library and reading room, past various meeting rooms. She'd never known there were so many floors. Her eyes were alert, but her mind was blank. And still she kept climbing stairs.

They walked down a corridor lined with numbered doors. Lodgings for club members and guests. These rooms were in great demand, almost always booked. *So where was everyone today?* One more flight of stairs and then Justin unlocked a door. Kate caught sight of the number 512 before Justin shoved her inside. She stumbled forward into the room. The door clicked shut behind them.

Kate struggled to get her bearings. A spacious if blandly furnished room. Two armchairs. An armoire. A two-poster double bed. The windows were shrouded in draperies, and Kate couldn't see outside. But the absence of street noise told her that they couldn't be facing the street.

"What are we doing here?" Kate asked. "Justin, what's going on?" Now that they'd stopped moving, her fear had abated somewhat. Some core part of her had burrowed deep inside, where outer events couldn't reach it.

"Sit down, Kate." Justin was standing with his back to the door, the gun pointed straight at her. He was smiling again, but his eyes were cold.

Kate sat down on the side of the bed. The mattress was hard beneath her thighs. A few feet away was a small round table, set for a lovers' feast. A bottle of champagne. Cheese and fruit. A cutglass vase of red roses. In back of this display, the wall was covered with a dozen or so photographs. Among the hoary likenesses of Harvard alums, a single image jumped out. A beautiful dark-haired woman, one hand outstretched toward the camera. Heart pounding, Kate stared at the picture. She knew that image, had seen it before. The photo from the red-sealed envelope. The photo she'd given Carter Mills.

"That picture. Who is it?" Kate realized she was trembling.

Justin's smile faded. When he spoke, his voice was petulant, the voice of a thwarted child. "You know who that is, Kate. She brought you to me in the first place."

She brought you to me in the first place. What was he talking about? Kate leaned forward uncertainly, her eyes searching Justin's face.

"Justin. It's me, Kate. Listen. Whatever you think is happening, it's not like that. You're imagining things. Please. We can talk about this." She realized she was pleading, begging Justin to come back. Memories flashed through her mind. Justin bringing her soup the night that Michael walked out. Justin insisting that she interview at Samson & Mills. He'd always been there when she needed him. He'd always believed in her. Now he was sick. He needed her help. She couldn't give up on him.

Justin was smiling again. "Okay, Kate. What do you want to talk about?"

Kate swallowed hard. "Why are you doing this?" she asked. "Did something go wrong with Laura?"

Justin gave her an impatient look. Roughly, he rubbed his neck, as if he were trying to clean it. "Nothing went wrong with Laura, Kate. Laura doesn't exist."

"What do you mean, she doesn't exist?" Kate's heart struggled in her chest.

"Exactly what I said. She doesn't exist. I made her up. I needed to know if you loved me. You see, after I killed Madeleine, I wanted to —"

Kate stared at Justin. The passage of time seemed to stop.

"I didn't really care about her, you know." Justin's tone was conversational, as if what he was saying didn't much matter. "It was really all about Carter."

"About Carter," Kate repeated. A hollow place was growing inside her.

"Yes, Kate. I killed Carter. Don't pretend that you didn't know. You saw me that night. You looked straight at me as I was leaving."

I killed Carter. Kate's breath locked in her throat. Her mind was spinning. She tried to think but the thoughts wouldn't come.

I killed Carter.

Again, she tried to pull him back. "Justin, I have to get back to work. I have a meeting with Josie. They'll be looking for me. Remember? You told Jennifer exactly where we'd be. This doesn't make any sense."

"Oh, I'm not worried about that," Justin said coolly. "D'you think they're going to search all the guest rooms? Come on, Kate. You're smarter than that. Don't you see? That's the fun of it all. You've got to go right up to the edge, and then stop. That's what makes it exciting. I'm not a criminal, Kate, I'm an *artist*."

Justin's eyes were bright. He was smiling. As if he thought that she'd understand.

Suddenly, she had to get away. Her muscles tensed. She poised to spring. Then, just in time, she remembered. The door was chained and locked. She'd never make it out in time. Slowly, she sank back on the mattress. Head down, she took several deep breaths, trying to steady herself. Still the words pounded in her mind. *I killed Carter. I killed Carter.* It couldn't be true; it couldn't.

"Why are you saying these things?" Kate's voice was barely a whisper.

Justin bit down on his lower lip, the smile giving way to a scowl. "I had to do it. You know that. I had to do it for *her*. I had to do it for *us*."

Kate could feel her body shaking. Again, the impulse to escape, but this time she couldn't control it. In an instant, she was on her feet, a scream curled at the base of her throat. But before the sound could emerge, Justin tackled her from above. One hand smashed down on her mouth, the other coiled around her waist. She tried to wrench away, to bite Justin's hand, to kick, but she couldn't seem to shake him loose. In one powerful movement, he hurled her down on the bed, and threw himself on top of her. With his right hand, he clapped a piece of cloth down on her face, heavy and damp with some awful smell. And then she was feeling light-headed. She made one last effort to escape, but her limbs fell back on the bed. The last thing she saw was Justin's face, bearing down from above.

❧

ALMOST five, and still Kate hadn't shown up. Josie fidgeted in her seat. Kate an hour late? No way. Not unless something was wrong.

"Jennifer?"

Jennifer looked up from her fat paperback.

"You think something coulda happened to Kate?"

Jennifer looked at her kindly. "No, kiddo. But I'm starting to think she forgot you were coming."

"Kate never forgets things like that."

Putting down her book, Jennifer leaned toward Josie. "Things have been really strange around here lately. I don't know how much you've heard about what's happened. But there were two people killed here. Kate knew both of them pretty well. She's had a lot on her mind lately. It's my fault. I should have reminded her you were coming."

Josie didn't say anything. She was thinking about the people who were killed. "You know where she went?" she said.

"They said they were going to the Harvard Club."

Harvard. That was the fancy place Kate went to school. A school for people who were very smart. The kind of people who got jobs here.

"The Harvard Club," Josie said, testing the words in her mouth. "Where's that?"

"I'm not sure. Somewhere around here, I think."

"Oh."

"Listen, Josie. Why don't you just go home? I'll tell Kate you were here."

Josie stared at the carpet, thinking. When she looked up, her mouth was set.

"I think I'll just stay here and wait," she said.

❧

HER eyes fluttered open. Too groggy to turn her head, Kate stared at the printed bedspread. Fuzzy patches of mauve and green swam against a cream-colored background. The room was hot. Music played in the background. Something weird and dissonant and modern. She was conscious of a pounding headache and a punishing thirst. Everything was hazy. She needed to find her glasses. Confused, she tried to sit up. But something stopped her from moving. She tried to speak, to cry out, but her mouth seemed to be stuffed with cotton.

"How are you feeling, Kate?" Justin's voice sounded far away. "You know, I didn't want to tie you up like this, but you didn't leave me much choice."

Kate tried to remember what had happened. She'd been so glad that Justin had canceled his trip. He'd been in her office, waiting. But at that point something went wrong. She'd tried to escape, that was it, tried to get away from Justin. But no, that couldn't be right . . .

"I've been doing some thinking." Justin was speaking again. Kate felt the mattress dip as he sat down on the bed beside her. She could smell his familiar scent, wool mixed with some woodsy soap. "Maybe I've been unfair. I thought that you'd understand. I didn't think I'd have to explain. But maybe that was asking too much. What do you think, Kate? Have I expected too much of you?"

The bedside lamp sent out a pool of light. She must have been asleep for hours. Now Justin was stroking her hair. He gave her an appraising glance. The sort of look a parent might give a disobedient but beloved child.

"I'd like us to be able to talk," he said. "But you have to promise to be quiet. There's no reason to be frightened. You have to let me explain, okay?"

Kate nodded, her face hot against the stiff bedspread. Memories had begun to drift back. She was at the Harvard Club. Justin had brought her here. He'd pulled out a gun, forced her to come to this room. She knew she should be afraid, and maybe she was a little, but not nearly as much as she should be. A fog swirled through her mind. Nothing was clear anymore.

Justin stood up from the bed. A few feet away, Kate heard him open a closet door. There was a rustling of fabric, as if he were looking for something. Then he was back beside her. Kate saw that he was holding a knife in one hand. In the other, he still held the gun. Kate watched Justin, mesmerized. The fog seemed to waver, to dissipate, as a shot of adrenaline raced through her.

Justin leaned down from above. "Be still, Kate. I don't want to hurt you." The knife's cold tip edged under the fabric strip wrapped around her mouth. With one quick movement, Justin sliced through the cloth. Then, putting down the knife, he reached into her mouth and removed the soft mass stuffed inside. The gun still pointed at her head.

Kate's body sagged in relief. "Thank you," she whispered. Her throat was raw. "May I have something to drink?"

"Of course." Justin was sitting in a chair beside the bed. He picked up a glass and tilted it toward her lips. Kate took a long sip, then started to choke. Instead of the water she'd expected, she got what tasted like a mouthful of acid. She clamped her eyes shut, as if willing herself back to sleep. Hot tears sprang up beneath her eyelids.

"Darling, what's wrong?" Justin was touching her face, tracing a tear's wet trail. "Don't you like champagne?"

Champagne. A dark chasm was opening inside her. She felt herself teetering on the brink. "Could I just have some water, please?" she said. "I'm awfully thirsty right now."

Justin looked at her quizzically. But he got up and walked over to the table. Then he was back at her side, handing her a tumbler of water. He watched as she quickly drained it.

"More?"

Kate shook her head. "No. I'm fine now." But of course she wasn't; she wasn't fine at all. Now that the fog had burned off her mind, she was conscious of a growing terror. *What was she going to do?* She had to come up with a plan. She had to calm down, to think. If she could just keep Justin talking. At least that would buy her some time. Desperately, Kate pored over Justin's words, searching for something to take hold of. *I needed to do it for her. I needed to do it for us.*

Kate took a long, ragged breath. "I know you did it for us," she began. "But I want to understand more. Can you tell me about what happened?"

Right away, Justin's face relaxed. She could see she was on the right track. "I thought that you knew," he said. "I was sure that you knew."

Kate shook her head from side to side. "No, really I don't," she said. "Please. You'll have to explain."

❧

"I don't know where she is. She should have been back by four."

Cathy Valencia bit her lip. She'd been running late all day, had cut short another meeting to rush over here. But there was no point in taking out her frustration on Kate's secretary, a pretty young woman with spectacular hair.

"Well, thanks for your help, Ms. —"

"Torricelli. Jennifer Torricelli. Would you like to leave her a note?"

Looking down at her watch, Valencia saw it was after five. "Yeah, maybe that's the best option," she said. "She's been pretty hard to catch up with."

Valencia was gazing at a blank sheet of paper, when she sensed someone standing behind her. Turning, she saw a teenaged girl, staring at her intently. The girl's brown eyes were enormous. She clearly had something to say.

"I think we should look for her," the teenager said. "I'm pretty sure something's happened."

❧

Justin was singing along with the opera. Something in German, she thought. Then he stopped and met her eyes.

"It didn't have to be like this," he said.

They were sitting up now, Kate on the bed, Justin on a nearby chair. Kate held a glass of champagne. She'd eaten three strawberries and a water biscuit spread with some kind of cheese. Everything tasted like chalk.

"I gave him chances along the way." Justin's voice was heavy with resentment. "I tried to talk to him. But he just wouldn't listen."

Kate nodded gravely, as if she understood.

"She's beautiful, isn't she?" Justin said. Slack-jawed, he stared at the photograph, the dark-haired woman on the wall. The phrase *fugue state* fluttered in Kate's mind, the relic of a college psych course. Furtively, she checked Justin's right hand. But his grip on the gun held fast.

"You left her picture for me, didn't you? On my desk. You wanted me to see her."

Still gazing at the picture, Justin nodded. "I didn't want you to think that I'd forgotten."

"No," Kate said. "Of course not." Her eyes shifted to the woman's picture, then back to Justin again.

"It's a wonderful photograph," Kate said. "Why don't you tell me about her?"

Justin shrugged. "What do you say about your mother? Where do you want me to start?"

"Your mother?" Kate tried to conceal her shock. "But that woman isn't your mother. I've met your mother, remember? At our law school graduation. Her name is Sarah. She's tall and blond, and she doesn't look anything like that photograph."

"Sarah isn't my mother, Kate." Justin seemed almost amused. "She's just the woman who adopted me. My real mother died. Sarah was my counselor. In the group home where I lived. Sarah Llewellyn. That was her name when I first met her, before she got married I mean. I used to call her *Screw-ellen*. Then she became Sarah Daniels, old Screw-ellen did. But why am I telling you that? You already know that, Kate." Justin laughed, an odd gulping sound. "She thought I had *potential*. That's why she adopted me. And she was right, too. Just not the kind she was talking about."

Kate opened her mouth to protest, then clamped it shut again. The room seemed suddenly hotter, filled with a shimmering haze. Of course, she'd known that Sarah Daniels was a child psychologist, that she was working on a book about adoption. This part of

Justin's story had the ring of truth. And if this part were true . . . But she wouldn't think about that, not now.

"They made me go talk to Sarah 'cause I was a *bad kid*." Justin seemed to relish the words. "I was heading nowhere fast, that's what they said. At first, I didn't want to talk to her. She was just another asshole social worker. Another do-gooder who didn't know shit."

Even the cadence of Justin's voice had changed. Kate thought crazily of *The Exorcist*. Linda Blair. Split pea soup. Justin's head turning round and round.

"I don't know why I was even listening that day, the day that everything started," Justin said. "Maybe I was just too hung over to do anything else besides listen. But she said this thing. She said that I had to have *goals*. I remember when she said that, something clicked. It was like my mother — my *real* mother — was there, helping me to get on with my life. The plan didn't come all at once. But that's when it started. That's when *everything* started."

"Your mother. The woman in the picture." Kate tried to sound detached, but her voice was shaking. "What happened to her?"

If Justin heard what she said, he didn't acknowledge it. "She was just nineteen when she moved to New York. *Nineteen*. Do you know how young that is?" His head snapped around to Kate. He glared at her, as if expecting an answer.

"It's very young," Kate faltered.

Again, Justin didn't seem to hear her. "She worked as a waitress. To pay the bills, I mean. Really, she was an actress. That's why she'd moved to the city. And she was good, too. I've talked to the people who knew her then. She could have been a real success. She could have done anything. You can tell that from looking at her picture. But then he had to ruin everything. He told her he loved her, and she believed him. That was her only mistake. She thought he was telling the truth."

At that instant, she knew. "You're talking about Carter Mills."

Justin smiled at Kate, the old lopsided grin. "Of course I am, Kate," he said. "I'm talking about my father."

My father.

The words thundered in her mind. Kate tried to turn away, but she couldn't stop staring at Justin's face. Slowly, like some sort of trick drawing, the similarities began to emerge. The strong eyebrows, the perfect teeth, the square-cut jaw. She couldn't believe it. *Wouldn't* believe it. At the same time, she knew it was true.

Justin was Carter Mills's son.

A fire was burning in her brain. Still, she pressed ahead. She needed to know everything. She needed to know the truth.

"Your mother," she said. The words came out in a whisper. "Her name was Maria, wasn't it? Maria Bernini. The M on that red wax seal. The letter stood for her name."

"Very good, Kate. I was sure you'd figure it out."

Fragments of what she'd read at the library flooded back through Kate's mind. The single mother. The antique gun. The child found bound and gagged.

"And you . . . you saw Carter kill her?" Her mouth was so dry she could barely speak.

"I don't *remember*," Justin said. His voice had taken on a slightly petulant tone. "I was only four years old. You know that. You read about it in the papers. I don't remember. I only know what they told me."

Kate pressed on. "What?" she said. "What did they tell you?"

Justin sighed, an elaborate, manufactured sound, a child putting on a show. "My mother's friend told me what happened. Her name's Elizabeth. She took me in after Mama died. But then I got to be too much for her" — here he gave a strange, cold smile — "and she had to give me away. The thing is, it's not like he exactly killed her. I mean, if he had, I could just have turned him in, right? That would have done the trick. He *should have* killed her himself. That would have been more honest. Instead, he let someone else do it for him. That's how he operates."

"You mean he hired someone to kill Maria? To kill your mother, I mean."

Justin was starting to pout. "No, Kate. That's not what I'm saying." Again, he sighed. "Okay, I'll tell you. This is how it happened. Mama had to work to support us. She was very proud. My father never knew that she was pregnant. She didn't want him to know. That's what Elizabeth said. Anyway, after I was born, Mama worked all the time. She stopped trying for acting jobs. She was going to school, to be a nurse. And she was working in the diner. Then, one night, she was coming home late. She'd just picked me up down the street. Someone followed us in. He did things to her, you know?"

"Yes," Kate said, her mind moving sickeningly to Madeleine Waters, on whom similar horrors had been visited.

"Then he found this gun that she'd had. It was an old gun, something my father had given her years earlier to use for protection. She'd been followed a lot, you know. It was a pretty rough neighborhood, where we lived. And she was so pretty. Beautiful, really. That night, she must have managed to pull out the gun. She was trying to protect herself. And me."

Justin leaned toward Kate. She could feel his breath, warm and faintly sweet, on her face. "Funny, isn't it? The gun was supposed to protect her. But instead, she ended up dead."

Kate felt as if she'd stepped inside Justin's mind. She could see exactly what had happened. In some insane way, it had all started to make sense. "You blamed Carter for her death," she said. "And that's why you killed him."

"That's right," Justin said, pleased. "That's exactly why I did it. To make up to her for what happened. If it weren't for him, she'd still be alive. Remember, Kate? How we talked about that in law school. The problem of causation. Where can you fix legal blame? Well, sometimes the law doesn't go far enough. So someone else has to step in to make things right. This time, that someone was me. My father gave my mother the gun. It was because of him that she lived in that crappy walk-up. Everything that happened to her was because of him. He was the 'but for' cause of my mother's death, isn't that what we called it in school? If it weren't for him, she'd be alive today. That's why I had to destroy him."

Fleetingly, Kate wondered at Justin's collapse, how every-thing — law and death and family ties — had been woven into one delusion. How Justin's breakdown was not without its own weird logic.

"And Madeleine," Kate said. "Why did you have to kill her?"

"That came later. After I got to Samson & Mills. When I saw her, I knew right away. She looked like my mother, you know. I knew that he'd tried to replace her. I could hardly stand to look at her. But I forced myself. Even asked to work for her, remember? Then it came to me, how she could be part of my plan. How I could kill Madeleine and make it look like he had done it."

"And the . . . the things you did to her? Why? Is it because that's what they did to your mother?"

Justin gave Kate an angry look. "Not exactly," he said. "I didn't make Madeleine suffer. I killed her right off. Shot her through the head while she was still unconscious. That's not how it happened with my mother. She was awake for all of it. She was awake and she felt everything. *Everything.*" A sheen of perspiration covered Justin's face. Veins bulged out from his neck. Fear bubbled up in-side, but Kate forced herself to keep going. At least if she kept Justin talking, he couldn't do anything else.

"The gun," she said. "It was the same one used to kill your mother. How did you manage to get hold of it?"

Justin seemed pleased by the question. He gave a modest shrug, his mouth turned up in a small, tight smile. "It wasn't really that hard. I did some detective work, made some phone calls. The gun was a valuable one, some sort of family heirloom. After the police were done with it, my granddaddy James made sure he got it back. Disgusting, isn't it? That's all he cared about. Getting back his stu-pid antique. By this time, though, old James had kicked the bucket. So I called my father, pretended to be a collector. Turns out he'd donated it to some historical museum. A small outfit near Boston. Almost no security at all. During our last year of law school, I made a little field trip. That's when I got it back."

Justin paused for a moment, reflective. "I was worried about taking on Madeleine. Thought I might be going too far. But now I'm glad I did it. The other things, too."

"Other things?" Kate said faintly.

"Oh, nothing to speak of. Though I did have a lot of fun." Justin laughed. "This one thing I did. You'll get a kick out of this. You know how the firm compensates partners, the lockstep draw? Well, there was this secret move to do away with it, to give bigger shares to the rainmakers. I found this memo in Carter's computer, explaining everything. I forwarded the memo to McCarty. Made it look like Drescher had sent it. Too bad I couldn't see their reactions."

The lockstep system. That, too, was Justin's doing. He'd gotten access to Carter's files. Just as he had to her own. And probably Madeleine's as well. It explained so much. His vast store of knowledge about Samson & Mills. His knowledge of Madeleine. . . .

In the background, Justin gave another laugh. The sound snapped Kate from her thoughts. The fear that had been weirdly dormant now blasted through with new force. *My God!* She had to do something, she had to get away. But what could she do? She tested the bonds around her wrists and feet, but they were wound tight. If she screamed, Justin would be on her instantly. Her only hope was to make contact, to break through his fantasy world.

"Justin, you have to stop this. Please. Untie me. Let me go." As she spoke, Kate realized she was crying, hot tears pouring down her cheeks. The irony crashed in on her. For years now, she'd tried to control her own life. Every decision she'd made, every step she'd taken, had all been with that end in mind. And where had it led? To this moment, where she lay bound and powerless, completely at Justin's mercy.

Justin's eyes had gone back to the picture. "The moment I saw you, I knew," he said dreamily. "Do you remember, Kate? In the law school commons? You were having lunch. A tuna sandwich on rye and a Diet Coke. You looked just like her. I came over to your table. You asked me to sit down. After that, I knew we'd be together."

Desperately, Kate searched his face, seeking some spark of recognition. "But we were friends, Justin. Just friends. Always good friends. Remember? I was going out with Michael. Michael and I were going to be married."

Justin had gone back to stroking her hair. "I had to put a stop to that," he said. "I'm sorry you had to suffer. But I had no choice."

Kate felt a prickling beneath her clothes. "But Michael broke up with me," she said. Her voice was no more than a whisper.

Justin's hand stopped moving. "Come on, Kate. Think," he said impatiently. "Who told you about Ingrid and Michael?"

All air seemed to drain from the room. *No, it couldn't be, it couldn't be.* But her mind was already traveling back, back to the day Justin told her he'd seen Michael kissing Ingrid. She hadn't believed it at first. Michael and Ingrid were simply friends, colleagues on *Law Review*. There had to be some mistake. But Justin knew what he'd seen. When she'd confronted Michael, he'd denied it outright. But she'd kept at him day after day. Until, finally, a week or so later, he'd simply walked away. And that had been the end.

"It was all so easy," Justin mused. "After I'd gotten rid of Michael, I just had to get you to Samson & Mills. And that almost took care of itself."

❦

VALENCIA had already checked the dining rooms, the second-floor library and reading room. Overstuffed chairs and stuffed shirts. The Harvard Club was just what she'd expected. Except for one thing: no sign of Kate Paine. She returned to the registration desk.

"I'm sorry, but no one by that name is staying here."

Valencia sighed. "Okay, then. Thanks anyway."

She headed for the cloakroom to collect her coat. She told herself that she'd done everything she could, gone well beyond the call of duty. Anyway, there was probably some explanation. Kate had only been gone a couple of hours. Hardly a lengthy absence.

But somehow, the thought didn't reassure her.

❦

THE minutes flowed into hours; the words poured out endlessly. Now Justin was talking about his childhood: the foster parents who beat him, the years of addiction, the escalating petty thefts. And then the new life he'd embarked on as Justin Daniels. The perfect son of perfect parents.

"I was such an ideal candidate for the Ivy League," he said, nostalgically. "Just think of the obstacles I'd overcome!"

Kate gazed at him without speaking. She'd tried everything now. Nothing had worked. A childhood prayer floated up from the past, the prayer she'd said before sleep. *Keep me safe all through the night, and wake me with the sunshine bright.*

And then she had an idea. A long shot, but worth a try.

"Justin," Kate said. "I really need to use the bathroom." Her heart was pounding so hard, she imagined that Justin must hear it. "It's been a long time," she said. "And after all that water and champagne . . ."

Frowning, Justin studied her face. She could read the suspicion in his eyes. She'd almost given up hope when he abruptly stood up from the bed. "All right, then," he said. "But don't try anything. I'll be right here waiting." With the gun still pointing at her chest, Justin cut through the bonds on her feet. Kate hoisted her legs over the side of the bed and sat up. She slid awkwardly to the edge of the mattress, her wrists still bound together. The blood coursed down through her ankles and into her tingling feet. Just inches away, she saw her glasses lying on the bedside table.

Well, at least this was a start. Standing on shaky legs, Kate glanced toward a closed door across the room.

"Is that —"

"Yes," said Justin. "It's right through there."

Kate took a couple more steps before turning back toward Justin. "Uh, this is a little embarrassing." She tried to sound girlish and shy. "But do you think you could . . ." She raised her bound hands a few inches. "I can't . . . you know."

Justin hesitated a moment, as if making up his mind. Then, with a shrug, he stepped forward and cut through the tightly wound bindings.

She was free!

It was all she could do not to rush for the door. But she managed to control the impulse. Slowly she crossed the room. Turning to close the door, she caught sight of Justin's face.

A moment of frozen silence.

Then everything happened at once.

With a roar, Justin lunged forward. Kate slammed shut the door. "Open up, Kate." Justin's voice shook with rage. The door shuddered under his fists. But all of it came too late.

She'd already turned the lock.

᳙

As she emerged from the Harvard Club, Cathy Valencia almost stumbled over the girl waiting on the sidewalk.

"Did you find her? Is she okay?"

The teenager from Kate Paine's office. Josie, that was her name.

Valencia touched the girl's shoulder. "She's not in there. But I'm sure she's fine."

Josie looked at her hard. "Something happened," she said stubbornly. "Otherwise, Kate would have been there today."

Valencia was about to demur when she saw Josie's fixed expression. She decided to change her tactics. Maybe she could reassure both Josie *and* herself. Intuition was one thing. Cops relied on it all the time. But it had to have some basis in fact.

Reaching into her purse, Valencia pulled out her cell phone. "For all we know, she's already back at the office."

By now, she knew the Samson number by heart. She dialed and asked for Kate Paine's office. *Hello, this is the phone mail system. The party you have reached* — midway through the recording Valencia ended the call.

Josie looked at her inquiringly. "Maybe she just went home," Valencia said, trying to convey a calm she didn't feel.

She had Kate's home number on speed dial. But the answering machine picked up.

Josie stared at the facade of the Harvard Club. "Maybe you should check there again. Maybe you just didn't see her."

Someone tapped Valencia's shoulder. A worried middle-aged

man. Then she realized who he was, the registration clerk from inside. "I just got a call from upstairs," he said. "Someone walking by Room 512 — they just heard a woman scream. The guest's name is Robert Bernini. I think there's a young lady with him."

But Valencia was already gone, bounding toward the stairs inside.

❧

"HELP! Help!" Kate screamed as loud as she could. But the walls were thick. There were no windows. Her voice seemed to bounce off the tiles.

A crashing thud and then a grunt.

The entire room seemed to shake. She realized that it must be Justin, hurling his weight against the door. A short silence and then another crash. But this time, Kate also heard a splintering of wood, as if the door had started to give way. Trembling, she shrank back toward the shower stall. But there was really nowhere to go.

Wildly, Kate searched for some way out, for something to protect herself. Without her glasses she had to squint. But in the blurry confines of the bathroom, she saw nothing that would serve as a weapon. A sink. A mirror. A wastebasket imprinted with the Harvard Club crest. Reaching over the sink, Kate took hold of the mirror, strained to hoist it off the wall, But the frame wouldn't budge. It was firmly affixed on all sides.

Another immense blow to the door.

Kate renewed her cries. "Help!" *Why wasn't anyone coming?*

At the top of the door, it seemed as if the hinges had started to pull loose. But the door was solid, how could this be? Adrenaline flooded Kate's body.

Then her eyes lit on a small glass shelf, suspended over the sink. In an instant, she'd swept off its contents. With both hands, she grabbed and yanked.

With the next blow, Kate heard a cracking sound, and then fragments of wood flew by. Through a jagged break in the door, Kate saw Justin's hand, reaching, grasping the lock. Raising the glass shelf high overhead, Kate pressed herself into the sink. As Justin charged through the open door, Kate smashed the shelf down on his head.

Blood gushed down Justin's face; he let out a piercing cry. He briefly staggered back before lunging toward her again. Then his hands were around Kate's neck, and he was squeezing tighter and tighter. Kate made a futile jab at Justin with the glass fragment still in her hand. *He must have put down the gun. If she could only . . .* But her thoughts were growing dimmer. The glass fell to the floor. As if from a very great distance, she heard it shatter below. Colors exploded behind Kate's eyes. Then everything started to fade.

A banging sound. Very close by. The pressure around her neck slackened. Gasping for breath, Kate collapsed toward the sink, desperately clawing for support. But before she could regain her balance, Justin was on her again. As he wrestled her into a headlock, cold metal bored into her scalp.

"Put down the gun. Now." Through her own harsh breathing, Kate heard the woman's voice, just yards from where they stood. Pleadingly, Kate looked at Justin. His pupils were twin black holes. For a long moment, his eyes bored into hers. Kate felt as if she were falling. Then something flickered in Justin's eyes, some brief spark of recognition. Wrenching his gaze from Kate, he took an unsteady step back. Before Kate knew what was happening, he'd jammed the gun in his mouth. An instant of total stillness.

Then the whole world seemed to explode.

Friday, January 29

THE phone message light was blinking as Kate walked into her office. One week ago, in another lifetime, she would have immediately responded to its call. Today, she let it go. It was a little before one. She'd come by to pack up, to collect what she needed of her personal effects. The rest would be sent home later. Tara had urged her to put it off. After all, she was still reeling from the shock of last night. Her arms and face were bruised, her body sore. She hadn't slept at all. Still, she had to come in today. She wanted to get it over.

Expertly, Kate folded together a cardboard box, a task she'd done hundreds of times before while preparing for hearings and depositions. This time, however, she was packing up her own belongings. She started in with books. Farnsworth on *Contracts*. Tribe on *Constitutional Law*. Miller on *Civil Procedure*. These were volumes from her personal library, acquired during her years in law school. As she began to fill the box, Kate felt a wrenching nostalgia. How hopeful she'd been when she bought these texts. They'd seemed to hold the keys to a new life. She'd made it through Harvard Law School. Made it to Samson & Mills. She'd fought so hard every step of the way. Was this part of her life really over? It still just wouldn't sink in.

There was a sound at the door. Turning to look behind her, Kate met Andrea's eyes. For a moment they looked at each other. Then Andrea broke the silence.

"I'm so sorry," she said. "If I'd had any idea . . ."

Kate didn't say anything. She was vaguely surprised to see Andrea, but that was all. Her emotions had been used up.

Andrea lingered in the doorway. "Can I come in?" she said. "I really need to explain."

Kate stood up and brushed off the legs of her blue jeans. "Yeah, sure." she said. "Have a seat if you can find one."

Andrea moved a stack of dusty papers from a chair to the bookcase and sat down. She was wearing a stylish brown pantsuit that Kate had never seen before.

"I thought you were in Chile," Kate said.

Andrea shook her head.

"So where were you?" Kate asked finally, curiosity kicking in.

Andrea studied her freshly manicured hands, as if they might hold the answer. Then she looked back at Kate. "Madeleine's death really spooked me. At first, I thought I'd get over it. That it would take me a week or so. But after the memorial service, I realized that wouldn't happen. I needed to get away, to figure cut what was going on. That's why I took time off."

Kate looked at her, disbelieving. "Why didn't you just tell me that?"

"I don't know." Andrea looked up. "Now I can see how strange it seems. But at the time . . . I didn't want to talk about it. I just needed to clear my head. Brent and I started talking about the future. Where we are now and where we want to be. I realized that I wasn't sure anymore that this was the place for me. And then I started to get paranoid. I kept thinking about Marcia Weygand.

How, once they found out she was job hunting, they had her working around the clock on all these crappy assignments. Then when the holidays came, she didn't even get her bonus. I just didn't want to risk something like that. Please. Try to understand."

Kate looked at Andrea, a sense of sadness welling up inside her. The fact was, she did sort of understand. She didn't want to, but she did. For all their late-night camaraderie, she and Andrea had never really been close friends, not in the way she and Tara were. What they'd been was allies, comrades in a hard-fought campaign. Members of the same battalion. But intimate friends? What did she really know about Andrea? A few biographical facts. Her tastes in sushi and Chinese food. The fact that she liked to travel.

Andrea's voice interrupted her thoughts. "Your glasses," she said. "I've never seen you without them."

Kate shrugged. "They're somewhere at the Harvard Club, I guess. I'm wearing contacts today."

Andrea was still staring at her, a quizzical expression on her face. "You remind me of someone," she said.

Kate quickly changed the subject. "So, did you go away at all?" she asked.

Andrea shook her head. "We just stayed put. I needed some time to think. Brent and I both did, really. We did some research, made some calls. We figured we have enough savings to travel for six months or so. Maybe a year if we find work along the way."

"So you're actually doing it? You're leaving Samson & Mills?"

"I gave notice today, actually. Next Friday's my last day. Normally, I'd have given more notice, but with everything going on . . . , well, I figured they'd let it pass."

"I would think so," Kate said dryly.

Outside, the sky was a rich, deep blue. The Statue of Liberty floated in the distant harbor.

"So how are you feeling?" Andrea said hesitantly. "I understand if you don't want to talk about it. I mean, Justin. God. You and he were . . ."

"Yes," Kate said quickly. She didn't want to hear what Andrea would say next. She felt as if she might start to cry. "We were. But I'm doing okay. I think it's just going to take time. I still can't really believe what happened."

"No," Andrea said. "Neither can I."

"It's like things are never what you think they are. Here's another weird thing. I'd been getting these e-mails. Someone claiming to have information about the firm. I'd actually made plans to meet the sender. Last night at the Royalton. But you know who it turned out to be? *Douglas Macauley.* This practical joker guy I'd gone out with once. I'd stopped returning his calls. Well, he talked to my friend Tara — she'd fixed me up with him in the first place — and figured out I was obsessed with what was happening here. He came up with an invitation he thought I couldn't refuse."

Andrea's eyes widened. "That seems a little extreme," she said.

Kate gave a faint smile. "Yeah, well. That's just the sort of guy he is."

Another long pause.

"So what will you do?" Andrea finally asked. "Have you had time to make any plans?"

Kate twisted the ruby ring on her right forefinger. It had been with her through everything. "I'm leaving as well," she said. "They're giving me a leave of absence. But I can't imagine coming back."

"Will you be okay for money?"

"Yeah, I don't really have much student loan debt. Before my mother died, she set up this trust. It pretty much covered my education. Living expenses, too. After school, I sort of forgot about it. I get these statements from my mother's brokerage house. But I haven't really paid much attention. Maybe it was a way of pretending she wasn't really dead." Again, Kate studied the ruby ring. She remembered how excited she'd been when she unwrapped it on her sixteenth birthday, how pleased her mother had been.

"Anyway, last night, I opened the most recent statement. And there's . . . there's a lot of money there now. Enough to take care of me for a couple of years, at least."

Kate looked up. Andrea was staring at her, incredulous.

"What?" Kate said.

Andrea shook her head. "I'm sorry, but I just can't . . . You mean you were working here, and you didn't have to? I mean, I just assumed you were here like I was, to pay off loans, to get a little cash together. But if that wasn't it, then *why?*"

Kate gave her a rueful smile. "That's one of the things I'll have to think about," she said. The past seemed to swim through her mind. Her campus interview with Carter Mills. The day she arrived at Samson. Late nights in the conference room with Andrea, giggling over Chinese food and endless mountains of work. Michael. Justin. The hopes and fears of a lifetime, all now to be reexamined.

Again, Kate looked out the window, at the blue of the water and sky. This really was the end. She felt another surge of sadness.

"There's an amazing view from this office," she said.

From behind, she heard Andrea rise from her chair, come around to stand behind her. "I'll tell you a secret, Kate," she said. "It looks just the same from outside."

Two hours later, the boxes packed, Kate waited for a porter to collect them. In the meantime, she checked her messages. Just two calls. The first was from someone in personnel, calling to arrange her exit interview. The second was from Peyton. "Hi, Kate. I wanted to let you know that the Thorpe case settled today. Thanks for all your good work. Oh, and sorry we'll be losing you. Good luck."

Slowly, Kate hung up the phone. *Thanks for all your good work.* So the Thorpe case was over. There was sure to be a story there. Briefly, she wondered what had happened. Then she realized she didn't really care.

Only one thing left to be done. Kate stared at a thin white envelope, the sole object left on her desk. Without looking, she knew what was inside. The single gold cuff link from beneath her desk.

A cuff link once worn by Chuck Thorpe. It wasn't much in the way of evidence. Still, it was a beginning. Again, she picked up the phone.

"District attorney's office."

Kate took a deep breath. "I want to report a sexual assault, something that happened to me. Can you tell me who I should talk to?"

Saturday, January 30

KATE examined herself in the mirror. First the front, then the back of her head. She turned to Hercules, beaming.

"I *love* it!" she said.

Hercules studied her appraisingly. "You said you wanted a change," he said. "I know I cut off more than you asked for, but it's exactly what I had in mind. I always thought short hair would suit you."

Again, Kate looked in the mirror. Her hair, wispy around her face, was short as a boy's. And yet it didn't look unfeminine. She thought of the French word *gamine*. Of Audrey Hepburn. Winona Ryder. Not that she looked like them. Or anyone for that matter. The person she looked like was *herself*. For the first time that she could remember.

"You're a genius," she said to Hercules.

He lowered his head. "I know."

She was pulling on her coat, preparing to leave, when Hercules edged up from the side.

"I read in the papers about what happened," he said. "I hope you're doing okay."

"Yeah. Well. I guess it'll take a while."

"You know the last time you were here, I was worried. That was right after —"

"I know," Kate said.

"It's just that you looked so much like her. I couldn't figure it out."

Kate looked at him sadly. "Did everyone see it but me?"

Hercules shrugged. He seemed a little embarrassed. "Listen," he said. "I have a show that's starting next Thursday. In a gallery a few blocks from here. I've got some passes for the opening. If you're interested." She could tell he was trying to sound casual. But it obviously meant a lot. With a shudder Kate thought of the mutilated dolls, the banged-up Lincoln Log cabins. But who was she to judge? Whatever she thought of his creations, Hercules had followed his heart.

"Sure," she said brightly. "I'll take two. I might want to bring a date."

Sunday, January 31

AN unseasonably warm day. Boats dipped and bobbed in the harbor. White jetties cut a bright swath through deep blue water. Unzipping her parka, Kate turned to Sam Howell.

"I'm glad I came out," she said. "You were right. I needed to get away."

"Hungry yet?"

"Not really. I'd just as soon walk for a while."

They were strolling down the wharf at the foot of Sag Harbor's Main Street. For the moment, Kate was at peace. Back in the city, her old life still lay in tatters. But she didn't have to think about that now. Kate inhaled deeply, taking in the fresh sea air. It seemed like the smell of new beginnings.

"I really do like the hair," Howell said.

"Thanks," she said. "Me too."

Reaching the end of the dock, they stopped and looked out across the shimmering water, at the cottages nestled in the distance. Kate thought of the view from her Samson office. But what Andrea had said was right. It *did* look just the same from outside. Better, even. With nothing to separate you from the endless blue. She looked back at Sam Howell.

"I got sort of a shock this morning," she said. "My boyfriend — ex-boyfriend, I should say — just got married. The wedding announcement was in the *Times*."

"Someone important?"

"Yeah." Kate stared down at the water. The sea that looked so blue at a distance was a thick bottle green from above. "I thought we were going to get married."

"What happened?"

"What happened?" Kate kicked a pebble off the dock, watched it hurtle down, then disappear. "I didn't trust him enough. Someone told me he was cheating on me. I believed them. I guess you could say I drove him away."

"Regrets?"

"At first. For a long time, I guess. But when I looked at the paper this morning, I realized something. It wasn't just that I didn't trust Michael. I didn't really trust myself. I was looking to him to change that. To protect me, to keep me safe. I gave him an impossible task. No wonder he finally gave up."

"It doesn't mean he didn't love you."

"No," Kate said. "I guess not." She gave Howell a sideways glance. She had some idea what he was thinking.

"Madeleine still cared about you, you know," she said. "A photo you took — a picture of the Maine coast — was hanging in her office. I asked her about it once. She obviously loved it, said that she'd always had it with her."

A smile flickered across Howell's face. "Thanks for telling me that," he said. "I know she cared. It's just that —" He didn't finish the sentence.

"I know," Kate said. "I know."

For a short time, they walked in silence.

"The thing is," Kate continued, "even if Michael really loved

me, I'm not sure I really loved him. I don't think I really *knew* him.
I was so focused on what I hoped he'd give me. On the bus out here
this morning, I was thinking it through. How after Michael and I
broke up, I headed straight for Samson & Mills. But it was really all
the same thing. I was afraid of taking charge of my own experience,
afraid that I'd mess it up. I wanted guarantees. I thought I could get
them from being Michael's wife. Or being a Samson lawyer. It's like
I thought I could bypass *life*."

"I think you're being a little hard on yourself," Howell said.
"There's nothing wrong with wanting someone to love. Or work
that you care about."

"No, of course not. But that's not exactly what I mean."

Kate paused for a moment. Absently, she fingered her ruby ring,
then looked down to adjust it. She sensed Howell watching her.
"My mother gave me this," she said. "It's my birthstone. I'm a Cancer. Cancer the crab. You know what they say about Cancers? That
we develop hard shells to protect ourselves. I never really saw that
in myself before. But actually, I think it's true."

Howell touched her shoulder. Without speaking, they turned
around and began walking back toward town.

Kate continued on a different tack. "I was talking to one of the
detectives. About how she knew that Carter Mills hadn't killed
himself. There was this term she used. Equivocal death. It's a term
of art used in homicide investigations. When they can't tell from
the crime scene whether a murder occurred. Anyway, when I heard
those words, it made me think of something you said. You told me
that there are lots of ways to die. That physical death isn't the only
kind. I didn't understand then what you were getting at. I guess I
didn't really want to. But now I see how it applies to me. In the
ways that are really important, I've only been partly alive."

"Well, there's plenty of time to change that. Years and years,"
Howell said. They'd turned onto Main Street and were heading
back toward town. "Any thoughts about what you'll do now?"

"I'm not sure, really. I've got a lot to sort out. I've promised to
help Josie with some family problems. Her mother's a crack addict.

That's why she was having trouble making it to our meetings. When I found that out . . . I mean, my God. You realize how little you really know about anything. And there I was, assuming she just didn't care. I could kick myself. Anyway, for now, she's staying with a great-aunt. But we have to come up with some long-term plan. I told her I'd help with that. She has a brother and sister, and she's desperate to keep the family together."

"She's lucky to have you."

"Not as lucky as I am to have her. She actually saved my life. How's that for irony? The fact that I was a jerk to Josie about being on time. That's how she knew that something was wrong. Cathy Valencia — the detective — told me that it was Josie who insisted she go looking for me."

"But what about you? Any thoughts on that score?"

Kate felt suddenly self-conscious. "I still have some loose ends to tie up," she said. "There's this thing that happened at work. Aggravated sexual abuse, that's what they call it. It's a felony. I've talked to the D.A.'s office, but I'm not sure how strong the case is. I don't have much evidence."

Howell stared at her. "You mean, something that happened to you?"

Kate cut her eyes away. "Yeah," she said uncomfortably.

"When?"

"A couple of weeks ago, I guess." She found the warmth of Howell's voice unsettling; as if it was thawing some part of her that she'd just as soon stayed frozen solid.

"I had no idea." Kate could see the wheels turning in Howell's mind, as he thought back over the time since they'd met.

"Yeah, well . . . , you know I used to look at people who'd had bad things happen to them, and find reasons they were to blame. There was this woman — her name was Linda Morris — she was a witness in this sexual harassment case I was working on. She sort of slouched around like some sexed-up ghoul in dark nail polish and really tight clothes. She worked for this men's magazine. I always had a strong reaction to her, like I just had to get away. I saw her in the gym one day and practically ran out the door. At the time, I didn't know why. But I think I've figured it out. It's like I knew that she and I were really in the same position. I might have a Harvard degree and work at Samson & Mills, but those things couldn't protect me. I didn't want to admit that."

A wind had come up from the water, and Kate pulled her parka closer. On Main Street, people were hurrying by, preparing for the evening to come. Down the street, Kate caught sight of the Paradise. Suddenly, she was very hungry.

"You know what?" Kate said. "I could use some food."

Howell didn't answer right away. When she looked up, she saw that he was watching her, compassion mingled with sadness.

"What?" she said. "Why are you looking at me like that?"

Howell turned away. For several moments, he gazed into the distance, toward the rippling blue of the sea. As if he were looking for answers. As if all that had happened might still be redeemed. Then, turning back to Kate, he smiled. "I just wish you could have known her," he said.

ACKNOWLEDGMENTS

THE fact that you now hold this book in your hands is a testament to the unswerving support, encouragement, and commitment of one person. Nicholas Ellison is a remarkable agent and an even more remarkable friend. Our serendipitous introduction, just days before I was slated to quit practicing law, is the closest thing to a fairy tale that's ever happened to me. Words can't express my gratitude.

My publisher, Little, Brown & Company, has been a writer's dream. Profound thanks to my brilliant editor, Judy Clain, who did so much to help shape and improve the manuscript. Her incisive comments are felt throughout. Also at Little, Brown, I'd like to acknowledge Sandy Bontemps, for editorial suggestions and help with everything else; Michael Ian Kaye, for coming up with a cover that so marvelously captures the spirit of the book; and Betty Power, copyeditor extraordinaire. I'm sure this list will rapidly grow. Thanks in advance to everyone who is working so hard to make this book a success.

At Nicholas Ellison, Inc., a big thank-you to Alička Pistek for her enthusiasm and skill in finding homes abroad for this book. Thanks also to Jennifer Edwards and Whitney Lee for all their good work on my behalf.

When a former white-shoe lawyer sets out to write a thriller, you can be pretty sure she'll need to do some research. On the subject of homicide investigation, I turned to Vernon J. Geberth, retired Lieutenant Commander with the New York Police Department and author of *Practical Homicide Investigation: Tactics, Procedures, and Forensic Techniques*, and Raymond M. Pierce, founder of the Criminal Assessment and Profiling Unit of the New York Police Department's Detective Bureau. Both men generously gave of their time, talent, and vast stores of expertise to keep me from looking stupid. (Of course, any errors are entirely my own doing.) I owe Vernon Geberth a special debt since he introduced me to the term "equivocal death."

On the subject of antique guns, I found a terrific source of information in Dominick Cervone of Martin Lane Historical Americana in Manhattan. Thanks, Dominick.

I am grateful to Linda Fairstein, chief of Manhattan's Sex Crimes Prosecution Unit, for responding to questions about sexual assault.

Thanks to Don MacLeod for quick answers to computer-related queries.

Throughout the writing of this book, I relied shamelessly on many extraordinary friends. I'm immensely indebted to Kirstin Peterson, who helped with every aspect of this book, from untangling plot twists to excising extra commas. Huge thanks to all those who took time from phenomenally busy schedules to read and comment on the manuscript: Adam Cohen, E. W. Count, Ruth Diem, Barbara Feinman, Daniel Kornstein, Brad Kurkowski, Lisa Lang Olsson, Marissa Piesman, Polly Saltonstall and John Hanson, Peter Shimamoto and Louisa Smith. Thanks to Mark Epstein, Tom Firestone, Jessie Krause, Denise Lanctot, Ruth Lautt, Christine Martin, Linda Olle, Priscilla Rodgers, Leah Ruth Robinson, Lillian and Erik Ross, Ron Rosenbaum, Nita Sembrowich, and Emily West, for all sorts of advice and support.

Many thanks to Nicholas Delbanco and Nahid Rachlin, two wonderful writers who are also inspiring and supportive teachers. I'm also grateful to members of the various writing classes and groups that workshopped early drafts; sorry I can't mention all of you by name.

Extra special thanks to Mikel Travisano, who did so much to sustain me during the final months of work on this book.

Finally, I'd like to acknowledge the late Jonathan Larson, author of the Pulitzer Prize–winning musical *Rent*. During my last year practicing law, I spent many months on litigation related to *Rent*, a member of the team representing Jonathan's family. While I never met Jonathan, I was privileged to read many of the papers he left behind. His unshakable determination to pursue his dream, his willingness to take risks, fed my own nascent desire to break away from the life I was leading. For that, I'd like to thank him.

This book is dedicated to my family. Much love and thanks to my mother, Janet Franz, who has always believed in me and encouraged me to follow my heart; to my brother, Peter, who took time from the whirlwind of investment banking to give the manuscript a careful and perceptive reading and who staunchly championed my choice of title; to my father, Froncie, who has maintained a steady interest in my progress; and to my sister, Karin, also a writer, whose warmth and good spirits help keep me on an even keel.